# Also in This Series

*A Death Most Cold*

# Other Books by Jaroslav (Jerry) Petryshyn

**Fiction**

*The Man with the Notable Face*

*The Fenian Season: A Canadian Historical Thriller*

**Non-fiction**

*Peasants in the Promised Land: Canada and the Ukrainians
1891–1914*

*"Made Up To A Standard" Thomas Alexander Russell and The
Russell Motor Car Company*

*Butterfly Farmer (poetry)*

# BURDENS
# TO
# BURY

A Tarasyn/Osprey Alberta North Mystery

Jaroslav (Jerry) Petryshyn

**IGUANA**

Publisher: Cheryl Hawley
Editor: Allister Thompson
Proofreader: Amanda Feeney
Front cover design: Jonathan Relph
Front cover illustration: Melissa Novak

ISBN 978-1-77180-611-4 (paperback)
ISBN 978-1-77180-610-7 (epub)

This is an original print edition of *Burdens to Bury*.

*For my friend Don*

*And, as always, Diane, Alisha and Halyna*

# Prologue

He did it with a ferocity he barely recognized. It was surprisingly easy — a quick twist and a faint snap.

He didn't mean to do it, not really, he told himself, but he had been provoked. An uncontrollable urge lunged out from the darkness and had its way; a compulsion he couldn't quell.

Quite bewildering was the sudden shot of energy that coursed through him. He felt power — power emboldened by the terror in her eyes. Suddenly, he felt in control. It was a moment of high dizziness — *heavenly lightness,* he thought with a sardonic snort. Intuitively, he knew it wouldn't last.

What followed was an intruding paralysis and panic. He resisted his own fear, his own inner screams and rising bile. These were not the result of what he had done but rather what he needed to do next. There were consequences if he didn't, if he were found out.

He fought off the mounting anxiety, letting the massive amount of adrenaline steadily drain from his veins. He settled into a calm. He was, after all, special … and smart. The question was how to hide her so that she could never be found. No body — no consequences! He knew just the place.

# Chapter One

Billy Bob Boyd was an unflattering example of manhood, at least as far as Alex Croft was concerned. Aside from his stupidly alliterated name, he was a slob, grossly out of shape, with loose, flabby flesh dangling everywhere beneath his misshapen and wrinkled seersucker suit. *Yeah, slob is the word.* Croft saw it and heard it when Boyd ate, shovelling heaps of food into his mouth that stayed open during the chewing and drooling, all the while making annoying chomping and clacking noises that turned whatever went in into lumpy gruel before being flushed.

Moreover, Billy Bob was a drunk, guzzling whiskey like it was draft on tap, and not the good stuff, but the kind of malt that went down like forty-grade sandpaper. No wonder at times he reeked like a bootlegger's still when he came to the office!

Nevertheless, Croft could live with all of that. In fact, he had for five years. And why not? They were making money; Atop Realty and Land Development Company had been a successful venture indeed — until now. Billy Bob was skimming — no, worse! As far as Croft could tell Boyd, and by implication Croft himself, was guilty of investment fraud and gross misrepresentation. Croft couldn't be sure of the actual amount, but it had to be at least $800,000 from fifteen investors who thought they were getting in on the ground floor of a subdivision on the outskirts of Great Plains that supposedly included commercial development. An investment opportunity entitled "Legacy Community Inc.," according to Boyd.

Atop, Boyd proclaimed confidentially to his clients, had acquired a choice couple of quarters of prime real estate and was in a position to offer a ground-level investment opportunity. The problem was that

Boyd took the investment capital but did not invest it as intended; Atop's acquisition of said land was grossly exaggerated, with only a tiny parcel actually belonging to their company. How Boyd pulled that off, Croft was not quite sure, but it was a massive criminal fraud. The investors' money, as far as Croft could determine, did not go into a trust account as required, but, it seemed, into Boyd's, with some spillage into his expenditures and the firm's business account. Although his name was on the documents as Boyd's business partner, Croft had known nothing of the slimy bastard's activities until a chance meeting with one of Atop's investors who wondered how the project was going and if it was still on its projected five-year timeline. Quite clueless, Croft mumbled some reassuring generalities and set about investigating. A very late clandestine trip to the Atop Realty building, an uninvited foray into Boyd's office, and jimmying of his filing cabinet enabled Croft to acquire sufficient documentation (but by no means all of it) to discover the extent of the fraud. Enough, if convicted, to send Boyd and, by association, Croft to prison, not to mention paying the restitution costs. How Boyd made it all look legitimate and respectable was hard to fathom. Boyd was not that clever a con man. But there it was!

Tonight, Croft would confront his business partner, who had not only defrauded the firm's clients, but had also put him in legal and financial jeopardy, as well as ruining his reputation in the community. He'd make Boyd confess, admit his crimes, absolve his partner, and agree to the subsequent ramifications: restitution of funds (faint hope given that the clients' money was gone or stashed in offshore bank accounts) and what other penalties the court and justice system required. Otherwise, Atop Realty and Land Development would go belly-up, and they both would end up in prison.

*How did he think he could get away with this?* wondered Croft as he parked his Jeep Cherokee in an alcove behind the Atop Realty building. Dousing the motor and lights, he unfolded his tall, wiry frame from the vehicle. He had asked Billy Bob to meet him at the office at 9:00 p.m. He apologized for the lateness of the hour, but he had come from a lengthy drive up north where he had done a farm appraisal, and he really needed to talk to him. While inconvenient, the late hour was not unheard of, especially during the summer months when daylight remained well into the evening. Of course, it was early August, and night shrouded the city; the darkness would come progressively earlier now with each passing day.

Boyd grumbled, sounding somewhat slurry over the telephone, but agreed to meet. *Good!* Croft thought. He was going to have it out with Billy Bob, make him not only admit that he was solely responsible for the duped investors, but also put his John Hancock on the two-page confession Croft had prepared. *How in the world did Billy Bob think he could get away with this? Only in his wildest dreams,* thought Croft. Both the provincial realty board and, more importantly, the attorney general would investigate and, in the end, find gross criminality, financial fraud, and no doubt other irregularities.

Croft arrived early; he needed time to set up and arrange an unanticipated situation for Billy Bob to encourage the sleazy jerk to tell all. He had brought a roll of gaffer tape, along with the document he had carefully prepared for Boyd to sign. He'd give him an opportunity to sign it more or less voluntarily, but if he didn't, Croft, a much fitter man with a black belt in karate, would persuade him to do the right thing. He switched office chairs, putting Boyd's inside the door of his office and shoving his own into a corner. He rehearsed the scenario in his mind. Secure Boyd firmly into his chair with the tape, arms and mouth initially, and then terrify the man into signing. He even had his lines: *I'm not taking the fall for you or going down with you.* Croft had realized a week and a half ago that if he did nothing, Boyd might not only implicate him, but also frame him as the culprit! That wasn't going to happen.

Croft wheeled the purloined chair farther into the middle of his small office. He then made sure that the heavy, broad cloth curtain was totally shut over the diminutive window overlooking the rear alcove and lane. Boyd would be pulling in to his regular slot in back beside the Cherokee. While he waited, Croft switched off the room lights and clicked on a small desk lamp. He then, for the hundredth time it seemed, read the self-indictment that Boyd was to sign. Croft couldn't think of anything that was left out. *I did it all — conceived, planned, and executed the fraud(s), and my business partner, Alexander James Croft, knew nothing of this and in no way was party to it or a participant...* Croft's perusal was cut short by the sounds of Boyd's Lincoln Town Car easing into the designated parking spot beside the Cherokee.

Through a slit in the curtain, Croft saw Boyd get out of the car, his bulky frame silhouetted in the weak dome light as he took a final drag of his cigarette before flicking it to the pavement.

"Show time," Croft muttered to himself, feeling a rising level of anxiety. He noticed that his hands had suddenly become sweaty. Croft had left the back door opened; still, he heard the jangle of keys — force of habit, he supposed.

"Hello, Alex." Boyd stepped in, the door partially open.

"I'm here," Croft said, moving from the side and behind, giving the door a gentle push to close it. Boyd was searching for the light switch.

"Ooph." Boyd let a gust of air out. "You scared me there for a sec," he exclaimed, laying the palm of his right hand over his heart and stepping back. "Sort of snuck up on me in the dark.... So, why do we have to talk now and not tomorrow morning? What's so urgent?" He finally located and clicked the overhead lights. "There, that's better."

"We don't need those," Croft said, turning the light switch off and gesturing toward his office. "This couldn't wait," he added in a neutral voice.

"Oh?" Boyd followed him in, noticing the lit desk lamp with a document beside it.

"You need to explain and then confess..."

***

It did not go well. Whatever Croft had expected, it wasn't a belligerent man who, rather than feeling beleaguered and remorseful, actually threatened his partner with reprisals.

"I've got you by the balls," Billy Bob spat, his eyes bulging in the dim light of Croft's desk lamp. "So don't threaten me; I've arranged it so you'll go down with me at the very least. So fuckin' well keep your mouth shut." Then he gave his patented thin smile. "How did you figure it out? I've been particularly careful."

"The point is I did," Croft stated, teeth clenched, anger rising. He could feel his muscles tensing. It was a little like his sparring matches in the Shorinryu Karatedo dojo. *Remember the golden rule that over the years earned you a black belt,* he thought. *Be relaxed, outer calm, inner strength — eyes first, feet with measured movement, the distance breached — strike!* Croft had no intention of striking just yet, but Boyd seemed impervious to any verbal assault. Croft had believed, foolishly as it was turning out, that Billy Bob would break down, confess, and sign the document — admit that he was the sole perpetrator of the hundreds of thousands of dollars he had milked from his clients.

"Congratulations!" Boyd sneered. Croft could smell the cheap whiskey on his breath. "Now, I suppose you'll want a cut — be part of the action?"

"What?" Croft presented a shocked expression.

"Blackmail, is it?" Boyd continued, almost chuckling.

"No! I want you to confess here and now — a signed confession. I've got to live in this community ... how could you swindle people, your neighbours, forge my name and implicate the company in ... in this stupid, impossible scheme?"

Croft hoped that Boyd would appreciate the gravitas of what he had done, perhaps try to explain why he did what he did — maybe say it was a mistake. *I'm sorry, I can still fix this... Where do I sign?*

Instead, Boyd shrugged. "Gambling debts, you know. They have to be paid." He then waved a hand in dismissal. "I've had enough of this." He shoved his way past Croft toward the office door.

Croft's inner calm lost its hold. He grabbed the smaller, stouter man forcibly from the back by the arms and muscled his lump toward the swivel chair strategically placed in the middle of the room. Scenario two, which Croft hoped to avoid, came into play.

"Hey!" squealed Boyd, caught off balance. "Let go. I'll—"

"You'll what?" Croft demanded, anger reddening his cheeks. "Call the police?"

Boyd's right arm broke free from Croft's grip, and he took a swing, a wild, looping right fist that failed to connect. Croft reacted with a quick open hand thrust to the throat that staggered Boyd. He stumbled backward and collapsed into Croft's solid oak desk. His head hit with a thump against a corner. Boyd moaned and tried to get up "You bast — ugh."

Croft seized and hauled Boyd up like a rag doll by his jacket lapels and without much resistance deposited him into the chair with a pronounced swoosh from the cushion. In two quick steps he snatched the piece of tape he had set aside on the desk and stuck it across Boyd's mouth before he could utter another sound. The gagged man's eyes widened into full alarm. Croft then produced a roll of tape and quickly wound Boyd's arms to the arms of the chair just above the wrist. First the right and then across to the left, efficiently done before Boyd could marshal much resistance.

Satisfied with his handiwork, Croft leaned in and in a surprisingly even voice said, "Now you're going to sign your confession." He stepped back, took hold of the back of the chair, and wheeled it to the front of his desk. He took the document lying beside the lamp and waved it in front of Boyd's face. "This outlines what you and only you did." He fished out a ballpoint pen with *Atop Realty* printed in gold along the shaft. "Here, I'll make this easy." He placed the pen and the typed letter on the desk. "There, I believe that you've got enough flexibly to write your signature — at the bottom of page two, please."

Billy Bob tried to get up from his confinement, emitting an annoying sequence of muffled grunts. Croft noticed that there was blood on the back of the chair. Boyd had banged his head when he fell. Now he shook his head and refused to accept the pen Croft was attempting to place in his right hand.

"Sign or I'll start getting really nasty," he threatened, not knowing exactly what he would do. He grabbed Boyd's head and jerked it back "Do you understand me?"

Boyd's eyes opened even wider in unadulterated fear. "Nod if you do," Croft said as he released the head. Boyd complied. Once again, Croft thrust the pen forward, this time between the thumb and forefinger. Boyd awkwardly, with his strained and constrained movements, signed where Croft indicated.

Croft had a sudden realization. Why hadn't he thought of this before? Tape Boyd, get him to unequivocally state in his own words how he perpetrated the swindle, and have him absolve his partner. It would be an insurance policy when the shit hit the inevitable fan.

Croft took the document, folded it, and put it into his coat pocket. Next, he opened the desk drawer and brought out a recording machine before rummaging around for a blank cassette tape. *Should have thought of this sooner,* he berated himself again.

"Okay, now you're going to record who you cheated, how much, and how you managed it. Each item — in your own words."

Boyd shook his head violently and pulled against his restrains. Croft thrust his hand under Boyd's quivering chin and pushed up. "Listen, Billy Bob, I'm going to rip this tape off your mouth, and you're going to talk. That is your most pleasant option."

Croft didn't know why he said that, but it seemed the right tone to set as incentive — he probably heard it during a movie at some time.

When Croft with one steady motion removed the tape, Boyd's mouth expelled a rush of foul air, formed a ragged O, then slackened while his eyes rolled back. A moment later, he shuddered into a massive convulsion that lasted an eternity, or so it seemed to Croft, before he suddenly gurgled one last breath and went limp, his head flopping to the right in a most unnatural way.

Croft stood there, riveted in shock with the sticky tape still attached to his fingers.

"What the fuck!"

\*\*\*

For the second time in the evening, events hadn't gone the way Croft planned. *This wasn't supposed to happen,* he desperately mused. *Totally insane...* He started to pace the room. *Got to get it together, think logically...*

First thing — just to make sure — he put two fingers along Boyd's neck, feeling for a pulse. There wasn't any. "Okay ... no vitals, but don't panic," he whispered to himself. *The man is dead; you didn't kill him. He was out of shape, drank too much, and had high blood pressure.* The cops wouldn't see it that way, though — he was put under duress, stressed, forcibly restrained, and did hit his head on the desk during an altercation. Assuredly, Croft would be charged, and ultimately the court would take a dim view of his actions, even if Boyd was a crook. No, calling the RCMP was not an option. This had to be treated as a problem to be solved. "What I really need to do," he concluded, muttering under his breath, "is to clean up the place, remove any evidence of what occurred, and get rid of the body permanently."

It took some time to think it through, but Croft believed he had a workable plan. He carefully parted the curtains to see if anyone was about in the back alley. Sometimes the odd homeless person took a short cut through it, but there was no activity in the dark laneway.

*Good,* thought Croft. Now he could proceed with his first step: how to get Boyd's body into a vehicle. What he had, Croft realized, was dead weight that would be extremely difficult to move and manipulate into the desired space. He was fit and quite strong, but dead weight was dead weight.

Before tackling the moving issue, there was the matter of transport. Croft thought about depositing Boyd's corpse into the Town Car's trunk but discarded the idea: not only would there be the awkwardness of stuffing it into the trunk, but it would be risky as well. Boyd had to disappear, which would mean that Croft would have to drive it to a particular destination, get rid of the car as well as the body, and find his way back. He didn't see how the logistics could work. The Lincoln would have to stay parked; he'd let the RCMP try to figure it out.

Turning off the desk lamp, Croft gave one more peek through the limp brown curtains before exiting the office and opening the rear door. He quickly got into his Jeep and turned the key. The big V8 roared to life a bit too boisterously for him, but no curious individual appeared to take note. Calming himself, he backed out into the laneway, moved ahead, stopped, put the vehicle in reverse, and aimed for the door. He got as close as possible while still leaving himself enough room to lift the tailgate. He got out and popped it open but restrained its rise, gently letting it rest in place until he was ready with his load. Luckily, the old canvas tarpaulin rested against the back seat; he had meant to take it out and air it. Thank God he hadn't.

Inside, Croft carefully, and as expeditiously as he could, wheeled the office chair with Boyd in it to the door. He was worried that if the body slipped off, he wouldn't be able to get it back into the chair or carry or pull it to the rear exit. The dead man's shoes dragging on the tiled floor threatened to arrest Croft's progress, but he managed. Once in position, he opened the back door, again surveyed his surroundings, and lifted the tailgate. Manoeuvring the laden office chair through the door's threshold and out was tricky, but he got there. The real hard work was lifting over 200 pounds of jelly into the Cherokee. Croft found himself sweating profusely, despite it having cooled to a frosty zero degrees Celsius. Finally, his load was inside. He quickly spread the tarpaulin over it, exited, and closed the tailgate. Next, he needed to clean up the place.

Fortunately, he found bleach, Lysol spray, and lots of paper towels in the janitor's closet beside the washroom. As best and as efficiently as he could, Croft sprayed and wiped down the area of the desk where Boyd had fallen and the chair (he thought briefly about taking the chair with the body, but people might have wondered about Boyd's missing chair; besides, he wasn't sure if he could get it into the Jeep's cargo bay, given what occupied it). Half an hour or so later, he gave the room one last look over. Nothing seemed amiss — he hoped. He thought about leaving Boyd's signed confession on the desk as a way to point the finger in the right direction. The man had stolen from his clients and his partner — or at least the business — and was about to disappear; his parting shot and/or only concession to doing the "right thing" was to leave the confession letter. *I'm gone. Here's why… Sorry, Alex… Catch me if you can!* At least that was the scenario that went through Croft's head. In the end, he decided against it. Forensic audits would find whatever discrepancies were to be found. Boyd would be gone, and his distraught business partner would be left wondering. Besides, his fingerprints on the document would have been tough to explain. Having Boyd suddenly disappear with no explanation was best.

Which begot the next problem: where and how was Boyd to disappear? Croft thought about that as he was cleaning up, and a locale kept regurgitating into his mind, probably because he had just been in the area doing a property appraisal. God's Light Commune — or so the hand-painted, weathered sign indicated — was a quarter section of rugged terrain consisting mainly of spruce and aspen and populated mostly by moose, bears, and other smaller creatures. Its proprietor was one Hans Trovotka, who had founded a Tolstoyan colony of sorts — or so Croft heard. *A Christian fundamentalist by any other name*, he thought, who was at odds with just about everybody — oil and gas companies and their fracking practices resulting in sour gas well leaks; the provincial government that allowed it; his neighbours who didn't appreciate Trovotka's belligerently patriarchal preaching; and anyone else, for that matter, who ventured too near. Croft knew well the oil company roads that bordered Trovotka's property and focused on a particular location that would serve his needs nicely.

Before trekking out, however, Croft had to make an unavoidable stop at his home and pick up a few things: stronger flashlight, boots, work gloves, warmer clothes, and a shovel. He was going to have a busy night. Thank God, he was living alone with the wife gone to her mother's apartment in Kelowna — *possibly for good*, he reflected bitterly. They hadn't been on good terms for a long time, and he knew she desired a divorce. *If I survive tonight, I might just oblige*, he half mused, half cursed.

Besides his general state of dread and anxiety, there was also a looming time pressure. He had to do his business with Boyd's remains and get home to shower, shave, finish packing his bags, and be off for the five-hour or so drive to the Edmonton International. Some months ago, he had registered for a realtor convention in Las Vegas. He needed to stick to his normal schedule. Fewer questions would be asked. Boyd would normally have gone too; he loved playing the casinos and some of the other attractions of the desert city, but he had suddenly begged off. *Probably too busy fleecing our clients,* Croft surmised in retrospect. *Good thing,* he thought, *might have complicated things.*

\*\*\*

The God's Light Commune was approximately fifty kilometres northwest of Great Plains. For a good thirty-five kilometres of that, Croft stayed on the main highway, making sure to adhere to the speed limit. Traffic was light at that time of night, and his greatest fear was not the RCMP but an animal suddenly appearing on the road. He saw the shining button eyes of more than one creature piercing through the straggling underbrush and trees as he motored. Moose were the most dangerous and most assuredly nocturnal, although he remembered a nature show on which that was actually debated!

Just under an hour later, before entering High Lights, a quiet village on the main highway about forty kilometres from Great Plains, Croft found the turnoff he was looking for. He was a little worried that he might miss it at night, although he was pretty familiar with the area. A small sign in the headlight beams indicated that at the end of this undulating gravel road was the Jones Lake Hutterite Colony. He turned off before that eventuality onto to a smaller, rougher road that took him to a T — the left lane ended at the commune; the right led to a landmark of sorts adjacent to the commune. In fact, it was provincial land where a settlement had been established after World War One. It lasted until the mid-thirties and then disappeared. Croft didn't know why, exactly, but could guess, given the depressing times. What remained were a couple of dilapidated buildings, the ruin of a Catholic church with remnants of a cemetery, or at least a number of headstones nearby. However, what made the place unusual was the grotto constructed to Our Lady of Fatima by the pioneering community before all was abandoned. The parabolic stone enclave housed a well-worn yet undisturbed statue of the Virgin Mary.

It was to this landmark that Croft drove his Jeep. Loose stone chips that beat his rocker panels unmercifully gave way to soft dirt with a pothole here and there. Croft slowed to a crawl. He was tempted simply to stop, haul Boyd's body out, dump it, and depart. But, of course, he couldn't do that, he reminded himself; the whole plan depended on Boyd disappearing after defrauding his clients and partner at Atop Realty.

Croft had been to the grotto earlier in the summer with a surveyor who took him to see a number of property owners eager to sell. The land was a harsh mistress and the ruin of many potential sod busters in the area. Farmers did not have subsurface rights on their lands, but they could lease their property to gas and oil companies. The extra income, however, often exacted a price. The gas wells dotting the landscape produced hydrogen sulphide that not only smelled bad but was also harmful both to animals and humans. It only took a very small quotient (about 500 parts per million) to inflame the eyes, scorch the throat, impair lung capacity, induce debilitating headaches, and interfere with the reproduction cycle. At 600 parts per million, or .06 of 1%, Croft had read somewhere, death was imminent. For many, that provided more than enough reason to sell out, particularly if the oil company was buying just above the market price. In this area, however, there was an added incentive for selling; while some of Trovotka's neighbours agreed with his fight against what he labelled "Big Oil," they simply did not care for his antagonistic philosophy of life, his holier than thou preaching, and his hints of retribution for those who "did not see the light." Many concluded that he was certifiable and wanted no part of his brand of Christian fundamentalism mixed with select environmental concerns. They were more than willing to leave.

Croft didn't blame them, although he'd had no direct dealings with Trovotka. He spotted him once at a Tim Hortons in Great Plains: a big, dishevelled man whose thick, bushy, greying beard and coal-black eyes made a strong impression, reminding Croft of an image he had once seen in an old Russian history book. *Rasputin, as I live and breathe ... weird guy by any measure,* Croft remembered thinking.

Croft shook away his wandering thoughts for the pressing matters at hand. He needed to bury Boyd somewhere close to the grotto, perhaps near the two or three standing sheds, and do an efficient enough job that animals couldn't dig up the carcass. It would have been ideal to stick Boyd on commune property, since there wouldn't be that many visitors, but Croft deemed it too risky. Trovotka had erected *No Trespassing* signs everywhere, and as luck would have it, he would be spotted, even in the dead of night. Maybe he was just paranoid, but he wouldn't put it past Trovotka and his followers to have cameras strategically placed along his fence line.

After driving over grass and twigs, Croft finally rolled to a stop and killed the lights. The ground was soft enough to dig a sizable hole without Herculean effort. In fact, it was the vestiges of a garden now engulfed with dying weeds. According to the surveyor, a homesteader with his wife and child had tried to make a go of it where the village had been. That had been a couple of years ago, and apparently, after their modest dwelling had burned down and the wife became ill, he gave up. They either moved to parts unknown or joined Trovotka's commune, the surveyor wasn't sure. Regardless, Croft could plainly see the outline of what once was a garden, and with a flashlight in one hand and the shovel in the other, he searched for a suitable "to bury" site.

As Croft sank his shovel into the damp soil, a thought flitted into and then ignited in his brain. Why bury Boyd in an open field where he could be more readily discovered when there was a cemetery with old, forgotten graves scattered about? Surely it was more prudent to bury Boyd in front of a crumbling headstone. Hide him undercover among the dead! *A bit macabre perhaps, but a stroke of genius nevertheless,* he thought, his lips curling into a thin smile.

After repositioning and backing the Jeep onto the graveyard, Croft chose what he deemed was an inconspicuous and neglected headstone. *Theodore Polanski (1896–1931),* faintly etched into the weathered grey stone, was about to receive company.

Croft was a strong man in good shape; nonetheless, digging a substantive hole was tasking work and drained most of his strength. He wasn't exactly sure how deep a hole he'd need so that the animals wouldn't resurrect Billy Bob, but he figured at least four feet. On the other hand, for some undefined reason, he didn't want to disturb the resting

Polish settler. Then there was the body to remove from the Cherokee and drag to the gravesite. He dare not drive the Jeep too far in for fear of getting bogged down in the soft soil. Once he moved and repositioned the vehicle as close to the hole as he felt safe, Croft removed the tarpaulin, spread it out on the cold, frost moistened ground, and with the flashlight strategically perched to one side of the tailgate, he pulled and then rolled the body off onto the tarpaulin. He dragged the load, hands gripping the covering's corners, laboriously working his way to the hole. Boyd was finally deposited into the abyss, landing with a soft thud, face up. Croft folded up the tarpaulin and laid it on his former partner.

As quickly as he could, Croft shovelled the dirt back into the grave and patted the area down. Alas, not surprisingly, it looked like a fresh burial plot, but, he decided, that couldn't be helped. Hopefully, no one would take notice and the weeds and grass would re-emerge soon enough. Ditto for the drag marks through the vegetation. Besides, the weather forecast suggested rain mixed with possible snow in the next couple of days, which would help eradicate the fresh topographical features — he hoped.

After a final cast about with the flashlight to make sure he hadn't forgotten anything and that all was as tidy as it could be, he placed the shovel into the cargo bay, closed the tailgate, got in, fumbled, and then fished out car keys from his coat, took a couple of minutes to calm himself, started the Jeep, and with great deliberation drove off.

Timing was everything, and that included literally getting away with murder. Dawn was well established by the time Croft hit city limits. *Still, not to worry*, he thought. Clean the cargo area and after that shower, shave, grab a couple of hours sleep — *don't want to be a zombie behind the wheel*, he mused — and off to Edmonton midmorning. Fortunately, the flight didn't depart until the evening. Once underway, Croft relaxed; only one panicked thought came to mind. What did Helen, Boyd's wife, know? Probably nothing of her husband's shady dealings, but had he told her he was meeting his partner late that evening? Did he leave a calendar … write a note? After a few kilometres on the highway, he decided that it really didn't matter. Whatever her knowledge, he had covered his bases. Viva Las Vegas.

# Chapter Two

Raglan Bullock was a resilient, energetic individual who was keen on trying most activities life had to offer. At that moment, though, the nineteen-year-old college student was having a regrettable experience. Never mind that she had gone along with this (Kyle would have been more than happy having a couple of beers and making out in his pickup in some secluded spot). Never mind that she had voted with their other friends to go out of town into a boreal forest of snarled black spruce and muskeg and have a bush party! It was still his fault; he should have talked her out of it. They had gone to the spot, Kyle's buddy, George, knew about — basically a camping ground with a few fire pits, a shed of cut wood, and a portable outhouse. "It's a little rough, but it'll be fun, and we can drink and smoke up with no bother. No one out there…"

*True enough,* thought Raglan, *there is no one out here except nasty wildlife lurking about!* And that was the problem; there was *nobody,* and in short order the "back-to-school bush party" simply fizzled. They drank too much, ingested an inordinate amount of dope, and now had to hunker down for the night. Luckily, the wood in the firepit was burning, and they had sleeping bags to keep them warm from the increasingly chilly air. It didn't exactly make for a good time, particularly since Kyle had more or less zonked out beside her atop their conjoined sleeping bags.

Her bladder woke her; she needed to go. Alas, the outhouses were locked — for the season, she presumed. Thus, arising rather stiffly with a mounting headache, Raglan decided to sleep in the truck when she came back from her business — let Kyle weather the night or what was left of it (she noted the lightening predawn sky) on his own. Grabbing the flashlight he had liberated earlier from the truck's tool kit, she sought to pick a direction. She was feeling woozier than she thought — overindulgence in booze and hash, no doubt.

Raglan was a tallish 5'7" with well-proportioned features. She had a rugged beauty with a strong, square face crowned by thick chestnut hair, pellucid brown eyes, a freckled straight nose, and a wide, friendly mouth. She straightened her wrinkled jeans and pulled down on her brown, Great Plains College–embossed sweatshirt and none-too-warm denim jacket. She'd just wander behind a couple of trees and hope that nothing bit her.

*Now, where in the hell am I?* Raglan thought, trying to shake off a persistent, buzzing mental haze amid a ground fog that seemed to have come from nowhere and settled like a curtain on the surrounding shrubbery. "My bathroom break couldn't have taken me that far from camp," she muttered to herself, squinting into the bush. She tried to sharpen her focus, establish her bearings, but it was difficult. It was as if she had somehow sleepwalked into an impenetrable forest.

"Hey!" she yelled (which seemed to come out more as a croak). She heard nothing — no response. "Kyle!" she tried again. *Silence.* Kyle, George, and Mona were probably out of it, asleep or both, she deduced. *I can't be that far away,* she reassured herself as she cast the feeble illumination of the flashlight around. *Can I? The battery is going to give out any moment,* she thought. *Thank goodness it's getting lighter.*

Stumbling forward, not sure of her direction, Raglan was about to succumb to full-blown panic when she emerged on the edge of a narrow road with some sort of clearing beyond. Her dimming flashlight cast a host of gargoyle shadows in the distance. She recognized the place — the old grotto to the Virgin Mary. Although she had never actually been here, she had heard stories when she was growing up that it was a shrine built by those religious hillbillies. She couldn't remember what their settlement was called. All she knew was that they were strange, that they kept to themselves, and that it was best to stay clear of them. She was fairly certain that the road would lead to their settlement. And whatever stories she heard, notwithstanding, surely they would help her out.

Technically, she wasn't lost now; however, she was cold, nauseous, and not feeling too well. Kyle and the others were most likely still passed out and wouldn't be in a position to know where she'd gone, let alone go looking for her. Daylight wasn't that far off, thank goodness, and she'd just follow the road. *Yeah, time to get real, get out of the here,* she thought. She wished she had one of those new cell phones coming on the market. Maybe she'd look into picking one up when she got back to Great Plains. *Probably couldn't get reception here anyway,* she realized. *Surely, there'll be a phone at the colony or settlement or whatever it is.* Raglan would phone her best friend, Amanda, first and her parents — at least her mother — only as a last resort, given her predicament. She'd catch up with Kyle and friends later in the day and give *him* hell.

As Raglan made her way onto the road, she saw the taillights of a car speeding away. *Damn, damn, damn.* She could have gotten a ride. She started to yell and wave her hands, but the vehicle was too far down the road. She looked about for other vehicles or signs of human activity. She didn't know what the car had been doing here in such an isolated spot, but there was no one else around. *Weird place for a couple making out, if that's what it was,* she surmised. It dawned on her that she must have wandered in a stupor for some distance to arrive at this road. *Is it parallel to or does it criss-cross the road to the campsite?* she wondered.

With a more determined gait, Raglan made her way past the dilapidated sheds and the grotto. *Just follow the yellow brick road,* she mused grimly. She doubted she would find any more traffic on what was really an expanded trail. Her best bet was to look for Trovotka's place; she was sure it wasn't far.

\*\*\*

Isaac Trovotka was not completely whole, and for a long time he had an imprecise recognition of this fact. He knew that he was "damaged" because his father had said so. However, his father also said that this was not necessarily a bad thing, perhaps it was even a good omen. Indeed, it made him one of God's special souls. Isaac had learned this one evening listening to his parents talking when he was supposed to have gone to his room. He had quietly lingered on the other side of the partition that separated the kitchen from the living area and absorbed large swaths of their conversation.

"Don't worry," he heard Hans Trovotka proclaim to his nodding wife, "he'll be fine here, God willing, provided for, given home schooling, and be able to contribute to the household."

It took years to figure out what his father meant — and the old man got it at least half right, but not quite in the way he perceived. Perhaps, in a fit of pique at the Trovotka clan, God had added a little wrinkle into his makeup. Whether it was a good or bad thing was not for Isaac to judge.

As was his wont, Isaac rose well before the crack of dawn and slipped out from the house. He liked the stillness and the dark, although he couldn't explain why. The only one who would see him was Hans, who too often got up that early. Isaac sat down on the wooden bench inside the porch door and methodically put on his work boots, carefully lacing them up. This was followed by a thick sweatshirt, the lighter puffer jacket, and a toque. Too early in the season for winter apparel, and he found that even with a cold wind sweeping down from the B.C. mountains, he quickly became warm hiking through the woods. Lastly, he grabbed his hunting knife from the shelf above the coat rack and clipped the sheath onto his belt.

"Not taking your bow?" Hans peered around the corner and made his way to the kitchen. He plugged in the kettle — step one in his coffee-making ritual.

"Not hunting today — just a walk."

"Well, check the eastern fence. I saw some oil-worker types sniffing about the other day. Never can tell when they'll decide to wander over and cause trouble. And don't be too long about getting back — livestock to feed, you know."

"Yeah."

With that, Hans heard the heavy wooden door close with a thud.

Greta Trovotka came into the kitchen, tightening the frail cord around her threadbare housecoat. She was a sparrow of a woman, always in the background fidgeting, on edge while her husband pontificated on whatever struck him as worthy of his thoughts at that moment. A worrier by nature, Greta's inclination toward anxiety was reinforced by her husband's Old Testament views on women. They were either harlots to be scorned and stoned or homebodies producing and looking after broods of children, submitting to the male in the household and in general, knowing their place when it came to thought and action.

Like Gideon, Trovotka obeyed a rather mean-spirited God, and she felt inadequate in that she had given Hans only three sons. Two were now long gone into the secular world to earn their crust of bread. Only Isaac remained, different but gifted, she hoped. What that meant remained achingly undefined. There were also two beloved daughters gone as well. The first was stillborn, quickly taken into God's bosom, the other died in an accident that Greta couldn't quite comprehend. The girl was only five years old when the tragedy occurred.

***

Isaac invariably ended up at the grotto. He didn't know why exactly — a compulsion with no rationale, it seemed. Unlike his father, he was not religious, at least not in the way a true believer would be. In fact, he thought the old man a fanatic and a fool who fomented much ado over nothing. Still, he recognized unshakeable belief as a useful tool to muddy the waters, to hang his toque on if needed. His father had made it work from the conviction that he was somehow ordained to lead his struggling tribe, composed of two other couples and their offspring on the property, to virtuous lives on the "promised land." What this translated into was a war against "Big Oil" and "Godless" neighbours. In regard to the former, Isaac knew that his father would settle for a reasonable buyout, which would not only enable his flock an exodus to a warmer, more fertile "promised land," but also eliminate the need to deal with the latter. Isaac knew this because he had heard Hans expound on his grand plans to his mostly silent mother.

Isaac felt decidedly indifferent to his father's machinations or his otherworldly motivations. Still, he was attracted to the grotto and ended up there almost every morning. He didn't know why — maybe it was a sanctuary of sorts, a place where he found affinity with himself, his thoughts. He knew that it was only a construct built by the pious; nevertheless, it was there, an obelisk in the form of Madonna on real estate that God, in a less than pleasant mood, gave to Canaan. Isaac smirked at his clever reference, even as he knew he could never leave this piece of Earth. *A special place for a special person.* He smiled at the thought.

Any further rumination was cut short when he spotted lights spearing through the darkness. They came from the derelict Catholic graveyard. As he cautiously made his way from the grotto across the road, he spied a lone figure with a shovel filling in a grave. Mesmerized, Isaac stopped, crouched behind a gravestone, and watched from the shadows. *He's not supposed to dig there. That's my spot!* A momentary panic engulfed Isaac, but then he realized it was the wrong grave. *But what or whom did he bury?* Isaac wondered as the man completed his task, giving his handiwork a final pat down before placing the shovel in the back of his vehicle.

The sun was just beginning to peek over the horizon when Isaac heard the motor start and the Jeep ease its way onto Grotto Road, quickly speeding away. *Must be one those survey crews the old man mentioned,* he thought, *out and about real early.* The Jeep headed back toward the turnoff to what Hans called the "company road," built to allow Big Oil access to the area. Well, he had something to report! But what the hell had the man buried? He'd have to investigate further later that night.

Then, he heard the shout — muted and at the same time distinct. "Hey..." He saw her running along the road, waving her hands frantically before abruptly stopping and giving up.

***

Raglan took a moment to recover, hands on knees, head down, breathing hard. When she finally looked up, she saw the figure emerging from the graveyard. He was tall, with a posture that seemed to tilt to the right, as if there was an extra well of gravity pull there. From a distance, he appeared dishevelled, his jacket and jeans hanging loosely on his frame. As he walked closer, she noted that he was a little older than she had initially thought, maybe even thirtyish. His face was pale, lacking the rosy tinge that normally would result when exposed to fresh morning air. On his head rested a yellow toque with a brown bob at the end. She recognized it as the kind sold in Great Plains last February as part of a "cabin fever beatdown" campaign. Brown, wavy strands of shaggy, unkempt hair stuck out from beneath. What really caught Raglan's attention was the grey-blue eyes, one of which was intently focused on her and the other staring lethargically, not quite on point.

She knew him — Trovotka's kid (maybe not a kid anymore, on second glance, but it was hard to tell, she decided) — she couldn't remember his name. She had seen him driving a battered Chevy pickup; he'd stopped at the Tim Hortons for coffee and a box of doughnuts, and Amanda had pointed him out. She thought him and his family strange, and certainly his mannerisms in the coffee shop hadn't suggested otherwise. He had stared straight ahead with that same slightly slanted posture, suggesting a lone, wind-bent pine. Amanda had whispered that she'd heard from an undetermined source that he had a screw or two loose. And here he was.

"Hi, I'm lost," she said, somewhat petulantly, trying to keep the strain from her voice. "I need to get to a phone. Can you help me?"

There was no immediate response. *The guy seems to be in a trance*, she thought.

"I need to get out of here," she tried again, "get to a phone. Can you help?"

His lazy eye quivered. He turned his head slightly and smiled.

"Sure," he said in a low, calm voice.

\*\*\*

After finishing his coffee, Hans Trovotka went out for his own walk, usually down to the company road turnoff and back, a distance of just over two kilometres. Today, he was especially contemplative, his thoughts sombre and askew. He had not been feeling well for quite some time, experiencing abdominal pains, and lately, blood in the stools. Greta suggested that he get checked out at the hospital, since they didn't have a family doctor. He wouldn't hear of it. "God will see me through," he said. *If He so chooses,* he silently added.

There were, however, two other pressing issues. Regardless of how self-sufficient they were, finances remained a mounting problem. He could no longer endure long hours in the construction trade, while his "off the books" carpentry skills could only bring in so much. It was all getting to be a tougher row to hoe. Fortunately, his followers contributed: one had a janitorial job in High Lights, while the other, ironically enough, worked in the oil patch. It galled Hans to turn the other cheek. But he prayed with his tenant and family. It was agreed the situation was a temporary aberration and that other, more righteous employment would be sought. In the meanwhile, they would continue to homestead on his property and receive the blessings of his God's Light Church. Hans considered this a reasonable compromise. After all, God applauded those who managed their money wisely and more so if they made a profit!

The same held true with Trovotka's fight with Big Oil. Annoy, disrupt, even sabotage on the one hand while extending an olive branch on the other, letting it be known that if the right amount of cash was offered for his section, he would accept. He was more than willing to vacate, move, and start over again, perhaps in the interior of B.C. or South America, where the climate was less harsh and the land more fertile. God, he knew, would approve.

Everyone carried their weight in his domain, with the exception of Isaac, who constituted his third concern. Hans had to be honest; Isaac was becoming a challenge. At times, it seemed that Isaac was lost, that his faith had faltered and that evil secular thoughts had clouded his judgement. But then, allowances had to be made; perhaps this was God's test of Hans and his resolve. Isaac had stood apart from his other siblings, and not always in a good way. It wasn't that he could accuse him of any sacrilegious act or some sort of betrayal. Nevertheless, just beneath the surface Hans felt his son's smouldering resentment that he couldn't quite put his finger on. Then there was the accident.

Isaac had taken Hannah to pick Saskatoon berries on the property. Somehow, they got separated. It was Hans who found his son traumatized (he presumed), staring vacantly at his sister, floating face down in the bracken-filled slough.

He really couldn't fathom how it happened. Over the years, he and Greta had tried to make sense of it. "She must have slipped and couldn't get out ... swallowed too much water and mud," he explained to his wife, who nodded fatefully, grieved, and pronounced, "God does what He will." They both had waves of unrelenting guilt: they should have been more careful, watched their daughter more closely, and not assigned responsibility on this occasion to Hannah's twelve-year-old brother.

The image of Isaac staring enigmatically at his sister in the sluggish water stayed imprinted in Hans's mind. He knew that it was unfair to blame his son. Still, he couldn't shake the unsettling thought, the fleeting suspicion that Isaac, if not responsible, could have done more to save his sibling. In his solitary moments of reflection and atonement, Hans prayed that it was nothing more than a tragic accident. God, however, remained eerily silent, almost as if he reserved judgement.

That Isaac was "wired" differently, Hans had no doubt, but it was not entirely an environmental or natural affliction. Hans liked to believe that a divine hand made him "special." One question remained elusive, with no clear resolution: would Isaac be able to take over as God's instrument to the true path of the virtuous life, which he tried to practice in God's Light ministry?

As Hans came closer to his turnaround point, deep in troubled thoughts, he saw in the early-morning light a red Jeep coming toward him from the grotto before turning onto the company road. It appeared that there was only one person in the vehicle and that he seemed familiar from somewhere, but he couldn't be sure.

*Now what was he doing out here so early?* Hans thought.

# Chapter Three

"Crap! Here we go," exclaimed Corporal Rob Rainy as he put the phone down. He was seated at his desk next to a thin panel wall, on the other side of which Corporal Freta Osprey had just settled in. It was 7:10 a.m., and they were in what was called the bullpen, a large room with scattered desks, separated by ubiquitous grey partitions. While many members of the force considered their police vehicles their true office, these desks were the anchors of any detachment office, almost as necessary as the basement lockers. There were twenty-eight officers in the Great Plains Detachment, statistically constituting approximately 158 cops per 100,000 of the area's population. Of those only three were female, including Freta. Ever since she got there, she had noticed the place exuded an abundance of testosterone, accompanied by the faint odour of tobacco and jockstraps.

"What's up?" Freta asked, placing her Tim Hortons takeout on her desk.

"Got a missing persons report. Apparently, a teenager wandered off into the woods during a bush party. Hasn't been seen since Saturday morning. Parents are beyond worried — just got off the phone."

"Where was this?"

"Secluded campground close to Beaver Valley — Forbes, I think it's called. Not much used."

"Right, I know the place," said Freta, popping her head above the partition. "Near that commune — God's Light, is it?"

"Oh yeah, I remember, Hans Trovotka and his group of religious weirdos. Like to avoid encountering them again."

Both Rainy and Osprey had been involved in executing a search warrant for Trovotka's property a few months back. They were looking for evidence of ecoterrorism after a number of local gas wells had mysterious fires and other forms of sabotage. Nothing incriminating was found.

"Hopefully it won't come to that and she'll be found," said Freta.

"Well, she may not be the only missing person." Freta and Rob turned their heads to see Matthew Reuben, the superintendent of the Great Plains Detachment, emerge from his office. A tall man with a sprawling belly, round face, and balding scalp, he was a no-nonsense administrator who soldiered on in the knowledge that he'd soon retire to warmer climes on Vancouver Island.

"Apparently one of our fair city's more notable real estate moguls is also missing — at least according to his wife. William Boyd went to his office late last night to meet his partner, she said, and he hasn't come home."

"Kinda early to declare him a missing person?" asked Rainy, getting up from his chair and stretching.

"Probably it's just a miscommunication and there's a logical explanation." Reuben shrugged, turning toward Freta. "But better to check it out, though. Make some enquiries. Rob, you continue with the missing party camper or whatever she is."

Freta nodded. "Yes, sir. So, what do we know?"

"Not much," said Reuben, looking down at the piece of paper in his hand. "Just what the wife said. Went to the office and never came back. Go talk to Mrs. Boyd, drop by the Atop Realty office, and see his partner, a Mr. Croft. There's got to be a simple explanation."

*** 

Helen Boyd was a small woman who fidgeted nervously as they sat on the sofa. "Are you sure you wouldn't have some tea?" she asked Freta for the third time, clasping and unclasping her hands. *Full anxiety mode,* thought Freta.

"No, thank you… So, to recap," she said, "your husband got a telephone call late at night from his partner, Mr. Croft."

"Alex, yes."

"And you know that for certain?"

"Yes, William told me that he was going to the office because Alex said it was urgent, and he sounded like he was in a bit of a snit."

"About what?"

"I have no idea. Something to do with business, I would think."

"And that was it? He didn't say anything else, and you haven't heard from him since?"

"Yes, that's right. It isn't like William to just … disappear without phoning."

"Well, thank you, Mrs. Boyd. I'll let you know as soon as we have any news." And with that Freta gently extricated herself from the Boyd home.

Backing out of the Boyds' wide executive home driveway, Freta took stock of the neighbourhood, a newly built estates community, which, she bet, Atop Realty had a hand in developing. Her pet peeve about such developments was that all the trees were cut and the land stripped. The seemingly automatic clear-cutting in these new developments was immoral somehow, although, of course, the area would be landscaped. Still, a sporadic sprinkling of saplings was a poor substitute for the mature woods removed. She was happy to leave the sterile suburb for the older south side section of the city where the Atop Realty building was located — just off the main street, in fact.

There was only one compact car in the little lot of the squat two-storey edifice. Like other, older structures in the city, it was a little drab-looking and could have done with a little sprucing up of the brick and clapboard façade. The element that didn't look a bit tired was the Atop sign, a bright red and blue affair that averred *For all real estate needs, Atop succeeds.*

Freta walked in and saw a young woman sitting behind an enormous desk, which seemed to overwhelm the reception area. To Freta it felt more like she had entered a seedy used car sales office than a posh retail space.

"May I help you?" squeaked the petite person behind the desk, smiling. She had a number of files scattered on the desk, ready to stick in the filing cabinet behind her, Freta surmised.

"I'm looking for Mr. William Boyd," Freta announced. "Would he be in?"

The young lady's smile faded, and she frowned. "No, actually … and he is supposed to be here. I had to postpone a meeting scheduled with a client."

"Sorry, and your name is—"

"Marcy, Marcy Bergh. I work for Mr. Boyd and Mr. Croft, part-time, Monday to Thursday."

Sounding a touch frustrated, Marcy seemed to belatedly notice Freta's uniform; her eyes widened, and she straightened up in her seat, giving the Mountie her full attention.

"You don't know where he went or when he'll be back?" Freta asked in a matter-of-fact manner.

Marcy brushed her hand through her brown, frizzled hair. "No. That's just it. He was supposed to be here for his ten o'clock appointment." She threw her hand up, annoyance added to her frustration. "He's usually very punctual when it comes to clients. And his car is parked out back!"

"What about Mr. Croft? Is he in?"

"Oh, no. Actually, I know where he is. Left for Edmonton yesterday to catch a flight to Las Vegas — a realtors' convention. I made the arrangements over two months ago."

"Okay." Freta had her pen and notebook out. "You say Mr. Boyd's car is out back?"

"Yup. You can see the corner of it from the window behind me — that fancy Lincoln. He always parks it in back. He thinks it's safer than the front lot, you know."

Freta walked over to the window, and sure enough, there was a maroon Town Car sitting there forlornly. She'd check it out, but first she wanted to have a look in Boyd's office.

"Is Mr. Boyd's office open?"

"Y–yes," Marcy said, shoving her thin-rimmed, oval glasses farther up the bridge of her nose and fiddling some more with her hair.

"I'd like to take a look."

Marcy's frown deepened as she thought about the request. "I suppose it's all right."

She got up from her seat, nervously straightened her short, brightly coloured print skirt, and walked into the little hallway that led to two offices, one on either side with a washroom adjacent to the office on the left and a janitorial closet to the right beside Boyd's office, as it turned out.

"Is–is Mr. Boyd all right?" Marcy asked, cluing in that perhaps something was amiss.

"We don't know that yet," said Freta. "Do you know him well?"

"Not really," Marcy said as they approached Boyd's office door.

"What is he like to work for?"

"Okay, I guess. Not as finicky as Mr. Croft. He is more hard-assed, if you know what I mean," she added.

Freta nodded and filed that away for further follow-up, if needed.

Freta didn't have a search warrant, but she had permission, and she figured there was enough probable cause to have a quick canvass of Boyd's office. His wife had reported him missing, after all.

With Marcy standing in the doorway, not sure whether she should stay or go back to her desk, Freta quickly surveyed the room, which consisted of a desk similar in dimensions to the one Marcy occupied (bought as a package deal perhaps), a brown leather sofa in the corner, two matching armchairs, and a black high-back swivelling chair shoved against the desk. A well-worn beige carpet lay underfoot, and a low, perforated tile ceiling hung from above, complete with an array of pod lights. There was a small window — blinds drawn — to the right of the desk and a wall bookcase with no books but a variety of beer mugs along with other bric-a-brac.

As she moved around the desk, what brought Freta up short and instantly riveted her attention was what appeared to be relatively recent bloodstains on the chrome legs of the swivel chair. She also noticed a tiny piece of duct tape stuck to the arm of the chair. *What the hell?* She motioned to Marcy to stay where she was while she inspected the area more closely. No other tell-tale stains appeared either on the chair, desk, or surrounding carpet.

"This area is now out of bounds," she declared to Marcy, indicating the whole hallway and inner sanctums — not just Boyd's office. "Please make sure no one enters." She steered the stunned receptionist back out to the lobby area.

As they made their way down the hall, on impulse, Freta tried the knob on Croft's office door and was surprised that it was unlocked. The forensic unit would have to go through it, but a quick peek wouldn't hurt, she decided.

The office appeared identical to Boyd's both in space and furnishings. Nothing seemed out of place until she spotted dark crimson droplets on the right corner of the desk, along with tiny stains embedded in the carpet around the desk leg.

"I don't understand," Marcy protested.

"I'm afraid that Atop Realty is closed for now," Freta replied in her most officious voice as she emerged from Croft's office, quietly closing the door. "Mr. Boyd's office and the surrounding area — this building — may be a crime scene."

After settling Marcy down, she told her that she would be spoken to later, but for now she needed to cancel whatever appointments were on the calendar.

"What about Mr. Croft?"

"I'll take his contact information. We'll get a hold of him. He's in Las Vegas, you mentioned?"

"Yes... He'll be most disturbed."

After recording Marcy's home phone number and address, Freta told her to provide a key to the front door and go home. Then she phoned the superintendent to arrange for a forensic identification team. This time, she was not going to play detective — strictly by the book. Once burned, twice shy. She informed Reuben that some sort of confrontation appeared to have occurred in Boyd's and/or Croft's office, that his car was parked around back, but that she had not yet checked out the vehicle.

Reuben ordered her to stay inside and secure the scene, and he'd arrange for more uniforms and the Ident unit to inspect the car and back alley.

***

Late in the day, as Freta was writing up her notes, Reuben motioned her to his office. "Have a seat," he said, gesturing to the sturdy but hard oak chair in front of his paper-strewn desk. Certainly, no one was going to get too comfortable while talking to the detachment head. "No luck with Boyd's car — at least no evidence of foul play there — and no body in the dumpster beside it. Forensic guys are certain that its human blood in Boyd's and Croft's offices, although it'll take quite some time to determine if it's his. Now, there could still be a simple explanation, but given that Boyd's missing…"

"And the duct tape?" Freta asked.

"Yes, that too, a small piece, but more strips were found in the storage room and evidence of a clean-up. I'd say that there was some sort of altercation in Croft's and possibly Boyd's offices. So…" He paused, furrowed his eyebrows, and put his hand to his chin, giving it a couple of rubs. "I've officially deemed this case as suspicious with potential foul play involved and have notified Major Crimes. They will detain and interview Mr. Croft on his return to Canada and examine his car. However, the investigation centre is here, so … a detective from the K Division will be assigned to our detachment and arrive in the next couple of days. Since you are on the case and have had previous experience," Reuben said this with a guarded chuckle, "I'm assigning you as our liaison officer to help out in whatever capacity required."

"Yes, sir," Freta said, taken by surprise at her sudden new assignment.

"But remember, you're not a detective, so don't overstep your bounds. Understood?"

"Yes, sir, and thank you for the opportunity." And indeed, she understood most clearly after taking the flak in the "suspicious" death of the college president.

"And I trust you'll keep your amateur sleuth/college professor friend at arm's length?"

"Yes, sir."

"Good…" It appeared that the superintendent wanted to say more but decided to drop it. "Carry on then."

"Yes, sir."

"Oh — 'til the detective arrives, give Rob a hand with the missing camper case."

# Chapter Four

Myron Tarasyn had just finished his second class of the fall semester, feeling both apprehensive and excited. But then he felt that way at the beginning of every year: new students, a new course (The Soviet Union) and, inevitably, new colleagues. This academic year also featured a new president and administrative team.

*Heady stuff,* he thought, particularly since he had been, quite inadvertently, involved in solving the murder of the previous president, which resulted in a wholesale removal of the administrative team. A tumultuous set of circumstances for all in the institution, since, as it turned out, the duly selected acting president was charged with the murder of his predecessor while he was recuperating from being poisoned apparently by a competing Dean — although that was never proven. Considering that the president had fired her dean of finance and administration just before her own demise, and the dean accused of poisoning the dean who actually perpetrated the homicide resigned, the depletion of the administrative team was complete, except for one inconspicuous registrar who became acting president for a few months until a new one was selected.

How Myron got involved in the police investigation was both happenstance and serendipitous. While in the throes of a marital breakup, he was conscripted by Corporal Freta Osprey of the RCMP to be her "inside man" at the college.

"Ask around," she said. "Give me some real dope on who's who doing what."

Somewhat reluctantly, he had agreed. He found Corporal Osprey had a certain alluring charm despite his uncertain marital status —

recently resolved by divorce proceedings. Nadia, his former wife, was happier, and it showed. She was much friendlier to him on the couple of occasions that their paths crossed. And why not? She could afford to be; he heard that she and her new man were leaving town — the province, in fact, back to Ontario. *No doubt a new and exciting start for her,* surmised Myron. No wonder she was so cheerful when he last encountered her on Main Street, coming out of a coffee shop. One chapter closed; a new chapter opened.

A new chapter opened for him as well, revolving around Corporal Osprey and her unusual request. In true amateur sleuth fashion (albeit not quite the way Miss Marple would have done it), he had bumbled along into ascertaining who did what to whom — although some details still remained vague in his mind. Nevertheless, charges were made, and the case was resolved — mostly.

What wasn't resolved was his relationship with Freta. It seemed that they were still in the process of figuring it out. They continued to fraternize on a regular basis, especially since they lived in the same apartment building, with Freta's two-bedroom abode a floor directly below his. He didn't know why there remained an element of ambivalence on the part of both parties to fully commit. Maybe it was too soon for him, and Freta certainly wasn't rushing things along. It seemed that they were well satisfied with their current living arrangements. To be sure, he didn't mind popping in on Freta when she was available; they enjoyed each other's company, not to mention great sex!

Freta was on his mind when he entered his office and noticed that the answering machine was flashing. *Speaking of karma,* he smiled. Freta had phoned and suggested a coffee at the Tim Hortons around three, if he could manage it. Since his class, World History 101, ended by two thirty, the timing was perfect. "Great! I'll be there," he said cheerfully into her answering machine. He wondered what was up, since as a rule they didn't get together for lunch "dates" or coffee, in part, he presumed, due to her unpredictable schedule as a police officer.

Myron proceeded to extract his lecture notes from the filing cabinet for quick review, count the students on the class list, and double-check the pile of course outlines on the shelf behind him to make sure he had enough copied. All was in order: *bring 'em on,* he silently averred as Ted, his next-door colleague and incorrigible friend, came into the office and dropped heavily into an empty chair.

"Sheesh! Here we go again," Ted exclaimed, looking a bit askew despite being nattily dressed in a rustic suit jacket with a matching vest, a rose-tinted shirt, and red bow tie.

Myron was suddenly self-conscious, realizing that he, in contrast, was not making a particularly striking impression in the first days to his students with a very wrinkled Zellers-sourced shirt (minus a tie — not only because it was the worst form of careerism but also because he was hopeless at tying knots) and a rather limp grey tweed sports jacket that didn't have the prerequisite leather elbow patches.

Ted Mack, MBA, CA, was a large man, with a long torso, generous belly, and short legs. Undoubtedly, he had just finished his first class and was already showing signs of frustration.

"I think it'll take a whole frigging month for them just to get the basic concepts, if this group is any indication!" he fumed, running his hand through a thick patch of red hair.

"Canadian tax law, right?"

"Hardly that difficult," he retorted.

"If you say so," Myron said. He would beg to differ. To him, the subject was byzantine and quite incomprehensible, and that was why he paid Ted to do his taxes every year.

"Did you want to go for a walk?" Ted asked. "I need some fresh air before my next go-around."

Myron and Ted had hit it off from the first day, when they simultaneously arrived at the college, and over the years they had taken to extended caffeine breaks, walking to the local Robin's Coffee shop. Dubbed "Mutt and Jeff" by a cynical colleague who snickered that they were underworked and thus had too much time on their hands, they defiantly continued their routine when they were free and weather permitted. Sometimes it proved the highlight of the day, not only because it was good exercise but also because they engaged in a wide gambit of conversation, covering a variety of topics from global affairs to office politics. For his part, Myron looked forward to what Ted had to say, since he had an unusually incisive mind with interesting perspectives. Besides, with Ted there was an added bonus: he was a walking sponge who absorbed, digested, stored, and, when needed, regurgitated all manner of communication, including nefarious rumours and scandalous gossip. Surprisingly enough, Myron discovered that where there was smoke, there was a smouldering fire at the very least, and Ted's information was surprisingly accurate most of the time.

"Wish I could. Got a class in about twenty minutes."

"Okay." Ted sounded disappointed. "Is it your new course on the Soviet Union?"

"No, that's Thursday night. Haven't checked out the latest enrolment numbers, but it looks like there's a lot of interest."

For some inexplicable reason, Ted was fascinated by the Soviet Union — or the idea of it. He couldn't quite understand how it could work, especially the economics. That it survived and, moreover, become a superpower was quite beyond comprehension for him. He had raised the subject on numerous occasions with Myron when pertinent news stories surfaced.

"I would have liked to sit in," he said.

"Sure, you're welcome to."

"Can't. I have a night course on Thursday as well."

"Oh ... too bad."

"Pretty crappy timing... But answer me one question?"

"If I can."

"The Reagan shooting — when was that?"

"Four or five years ago," replied Myron, puzzled by Ted's unexpected segue into a seemingly unrelated topic.

"Right. That was before the new guy, Gorbachev?"

"Yeah, Brezhnev was still in power—"

"Right. So, what the hell is wrong with the Russians?"

"I don't follow. What d'you mean?" Indeed, Myron had lost Ted's train of thought.

"Well, the U.S. president goes down — Bush and that general..." Ted waved his hand dismissively, "Haig are arguing over who was really in charge... Why didn't the Russians invade Poland?"

"Oh, you mean take advantage while the Americans were preoccupied."

"Exactly!" Ted emphasized in his booming voice. "Strike while your nemesis and free world superpower is distracted. Normally, the Russkis would do just that — bring in the tanks lickety-split. Am I right?"

"The chances were high," Myron said, "given the looming showdown with the Solidarity movement at the time… But unlike in '56 and Czechoslovakia in '68, it didn't happen. If it's any consolation, though, Moscow did replace the Polish Communist Party leader, and martial law was declared for a couple of years… Why?"

Ted shrugged. "Just wondered if the Russians had gotten soft and the seat of ruthlessness moved to Albania."

"Where are you getting all of this from?"

"A thriller I'm reading that involves Kremlin plans to invade Poland while Reagan was down and out. Wondered if it was a real plan…"

"Didn't happen."

"Yeah, but it's not total fiction — they thought about it?"

"I'm sure they did. Probably had it high on the list as a possible scenario."

"Well, there you go." Ted visibly brightened. "And Reagan and Gorbachev are good buddies now." Ted, it seemed, was about to go off into another segue, albeit somewhat related.

"I wouldn't say that exactly, but Reagan did visit the 'Evil Empire' and didn't think it that bad…" Myron's chair squeaked as he reached back for a stack of course outlines. It was almost time for his second class.

Ted sighed and got up from the chair. "So, Darth isn't so bad after all." He chuckled. "I better let you go. Catch you later. You can tell me more about the Evil Empire and what you know about *our* new president."

How the two related, Myron didn't have clue. Ted could turn his thoughts on a dime, from the shooting of Reagan to Soviet machinations to the college's new CEO.

"I'll catch up with you tomorrow," Myron said. "We'll find time to go for a walk."

\*\*\*

The first week of a new semester was bound to be a nervous and anticipatory time for both students and faculty. Certainly, Myron felt that underlining excited buzz in the hallways, and it was all good. However, he faced what he considered a rather embarrassing handicap. While he never forgot a face, he rarely remembered a name, and there would be many returning faces with blank names in his classes. Moreover, at some point during the semester he'd have to memorize new faces and assign their proper appellations — no small feat for him when there were over thirty students per class.

World History 101 was packed with close to forty students, to be expected since it was a mandatory course for arts/education students moving on to the University of Edmonton. After handing out the course outlines, he went through the roster of registered students, reading each name from the list (hopefully not butchering their names too badly), and after receiving acknowledgement, trying to burn their shining faces into his brain. Invariably, as in past years, he lost "match the face to name game" by mid-roster, and unless there was something truly unusual about the individual, Myron had to admit that they would become a blur forthwith. He thought of assigning particular seats as a form of identification and/or taking Polaroids of each pupil, but that seemed rather extreme and perhaps would not be accepted by the young adults before him. So, as with every other year, he'd just have to muddle through and be apologetic when necessary. *A politician I'm not cut out to be,* he concluded as he glanced down at his notes on the mini podium sitting on a table before him.

As in his previous class, he was going to deliver a full lecture rather than just handing out the syllabus, going through it, and making a few introductory remarks. He considered it a statement of serious intent: getting down to business from day one. Some of his colleagues, he knew, preferred to be less formal, satisfied with deliverance of a course outline, student roll call, a chat, and dismissal. To be sure, students were still shuffling in and out, dropping and adding courses, not finding the correct classrooms and, in some cases, not yet arrived at the institution, but for Myron, getting off the mark running was important.

Thus, he gave his patented "What Is History" lecture, musing on concepts and perspectives, from Lord Acton's optimistic opinion that the historical process was the inevitable progress toward "liberty" (defined in terms of European Civilization) to Henry Ford's observation that it was bunk! After some discussion of collective memory and continuity of events, Myron talked about the inherent assumptions and other numerous variables that came into play in historical research and writing. It made a difference, he solemnly affirmed, if events in nineteenth-century Europe, for example, were seen and thus interpreted through the lens of a revolutionary nationalist fighting to establish a new nation state or a Marxist who believed in the inevitability of historical forces. Finally, warming to his subject, he pointed to biographical and psychological studies that emphasized the complexities of personality, the rise of charismatic leaders who became heroes and/or villains.

He smiled from his podium forty-five minutes later, informing his class that they had come to the end of his preamble to the first lecture proper, entitled "Toward Civilized Man." He could also hear the internal groans of *what a wind bag* or, more pointedly, *asshole* and *how much longer do I have to sit here.*

*I'm setting the tone,* he reassured himself. These classes were scheduled for eighty minutes, and they had to know what to expect. For the next thirty or so minutes, he gave a quick verbal romp through Homo sapiens' life on earth from the Palaeolithic era (circa 50,000 BCE) to the Neolithic dawn (circa 3,000 BCE) and the rise of Egypt and Mesopotamia — all good stuff, Myron thought, to get them started on the right foot...

The lecture went well and right on time, from Myron's perspective, with most of the students attentive enough and seemingly interested, but then it was always like that for the first couple of weeks before interest and attendance started to drop off.

At the end of class, one particular student lingered as the others filed out. Myron, not surprisingly, couldn't remember her name from the roll call but did note that unlike the majority of eighteen-to-twenty-year-olds who sat before him, she was what the institution officially designated a "mature student," which, in this case, Myron judged to be anywhere from the late twenties to early forties. He was notoriously poor at ascertaining the ages of attractive "mature" women, which undoubtedly this one was.

"I've enrolled in your night class as well," she announced, giving her blond locks a backward shake.

"Great! Are you a history major?"

"Education," she announced brightly. "Change of career and all of that."

Myron nodded, taking in the full measure of the petite person before him. An elfin face, hazel eyes accented by a hint of bluish eye shadow, a small, pert nose, and a wide mouth with a touch of rouge on the lips adorned in stylish, tight-fitting jeans and a simple white T-shirt sticking out from beneath a denim jacket.

"I'm Alexandra Enfield. It must be hard to remember the sea of faces in front of you."

*Oh you don't know the half of it, but you're going out of your way to make sure I remember you!* Myron pondered as he gathered up his lecture notes from the podium. Was she a naturally friendly person chatting up the prof (he wasn't particularly good at chit-chat), or was there something specific she wanted to ask or inform him of? He had seen her before (or thought he did) but couldn't place where or the circumstances. His mind searched furiously as he smiled, maintaining what he hoped was a cool demeanour.

Whatever else Alexandra had on her mind, she was interrupted by a group of noisy students bustling into the room. Myron glanced at the clock on the wall; the next class was scheduled to commence in three minutes.

"Well, I'll see you next time," Myron said cheerfully, getting ready to exit the room.

"Thursday night, actually," she said, smiling, stuffing her notebook into a large handbag.

"Right! See you then."

# Chapter Five

The Great Plains RCMP detachment building was a square three-storey edifice located just off the city's main drag and, more importantly, only a block and half from Tim Hortons. *How apropos, not to mention convenient,* he snickered silently as he wheeled his distinctive lime green Audi Fox into the parking lot. Cops and doughnut shop images were hard to shake off.

The customer line was short, and he managed to order almost right away, his usual one cream, two sugars, small, and a medium black for Freta who, it seemed, had a stronger bladder. He couldn't resist adding two sourdough unglazed (to cut down on the calories) doughnuts. He had just set his purchases down on a small corner table when Freta strolled in, spotted him, and made her way to where he sat.

Corporal Osprey was a striking woman, especially in uniform, a fact Myron appreciated from the moment he first saw her a few fate-filled months ago. Freta was tall (which translated into not quite 5'10", which was his height), trim without resembling Twiggy, and she possessed admirable features, from the luxurious dark strands of hair peeking out from her regulation cap to those midnight eyes, full lips, slight upturned nose, and nicely rounded chin. Not exactly Wonder Woman, but not far off, Myron concluded.

Strangely enough, he had never got to sorting through the nitty-gritty of her life and career, just as she had never gotten totally to his, except for their immediate circumstances. All that he really knew was that she had been adopted; that her adoptive father was deceased, but her mother was still living in Saskatoon, where she spent her youth; that she had an estranged half sister a couple of years younger; and that she'd had at least one relationship, which did not end well. There were many blanks to fill in on either side, but neither he nor she was overly eager to do that. Letting sleeping dogs lie suited Myron fine. Although eventually, as their relationship blossomed (he hoped), he'd want to know more. Of course, it took two to tango, so he'd have to be more talkative and become more of a sensitive new-age guy.

Freta sat down opposite him as he moved the coffee and doughnut across the tabletop.

"Thanks," she said. "What's the occasion?" She eyed the doughnut.

"Myron smiled. "Thought you might like one. Trying to stay on your good side."

"Really? And it's not a statement about cops and doughnuts? Never mind, if you're offering, I'll take one. It's been one of those days."

"Oh?"

"Count them — not one but two missing person reports came in from over the weekend!"

"Connected?"

"Don't think so. One is a real estate developer. Wife phoned after he failed to come back home after supposedly going to a meeting with his partner. We're trying to get a hold of said partner, but according to the office secretary, he's gone to a conference in Las Vegas."

"That's nice," Myron said, taking a large bite from the doughnut and sipping his coffee. "You sure he didn't dump his wife and go to Las Vegas as well?"

"At this point I'm not sure of anything, but Mrs. Boyd insists that it was way out of character for her husband not to phone if he was delayed or stranded somewhere. Atop Realty — heard of it? Run by the aforementioned William Boyd and Alex Croft."

"I know Alex, in passing," Myron said, finishing his doughnut.

"You're looking to buy real estate?" Freta asked, taking her first bite. "I'm surprised you didn't get me a Boston cream."

"Actually, thought about it for both of us. Messy and calories… And no, I wasn't looking to buy any real estate. I joined one of the local karate clubs — Shorinryu. He's a black belt — third-degree, I think — helping the sensei with the instruction."

"I didn't know you were into martial arts." Freta raised an eyebrow.

"Hardly. It was a diversion for a couple of months, and I let it slide. I was like that guy in a Far Side cartoon — I think it was Far Side — where the guy comes out of the dojo with a couple of bandages on his face and an arm in a sling, and the smiling sensei informs him that his first lesson was free."

"Okay, so Bruce Lee you aren't. What is Croft like?"

"A good instructor, from the little I saw. I know him well enough to say hi, and that's about it."

Freta nodded with a somewhat bemused smile.

"So … what about your second missing person?"

"Well, here you might be able to help, or at least provide info. A college student has disappeared after a weekend 'back-to-school' bush party. It seems — reading between the lines — that she was drinking and possibly had a toke or snort or both, and wandered off. Volunteers are being summoned and a search organized as I speak."

"What's her name?"

"Raglan Bullock. Know her?"

Myron's ears perked up. "Yep." He remembered her, to his surprise. "Had Raglan last year in Canadian history classes. Did okay, I think." His brow creased into a frown. "Hope nothing's happened to her."

"So do we."

"Not exactly a budding scholar, but likeable enough — took the course with exuberance. Where was this bush party?"

"Out in the middle of nowhere," Freta answered with a grim expression. "Not that far from the Jones Lake Hutterite Colony and near Hans Trovotka's place. Heard of him?"

Myron nodded. He had heard some uncomplimentary comments about a wild Bible-thumping nut who had a commune of sorts and a few followers somewhere northwest of the city.

"Well, it could be problematic; the RCMP and Trovotka don't get along. He had a run-in with us a while back — suspected of sabotaging some gas wells and destruction of company property, including at least one explosion and fire. That was before my time, but I did serve him a warrant last year, searched his place for evidence and stolen property. I just hope that Raglan hasn't wandered onto Trovotka's land ... that creates all sorts of issues. Not sure whether we'd need a warrant again. Probably..." Freta trailed off.

"What can I do?" Myron asked. He appreciated that Freta continued to confide in him, even though it no doubt broke RCMP protocols, if not worse. He had become her unofficial police consultant.

"Not sure what you can do at the moment. Maybe volunteer for a search party if you can spare the time. Rob has talked to Raglan's parents and is coordinating with the search-and-rescue team as I speak.

Myron remembered Corporal Rob Rainy, Freta's partner, who had looked into the demise of the college president or the "affair," as he called it in retrospect. Rainy was a no-nonsense fellow who kept a low profile during the investigation and later got reprimanded along with Freta for overreaching their authority by not calling in the Major Crimes unit sooner.

"I'm really, really hoping that she's just lost and will eventually wander out of the bush on to a road and find help. It's the best-case scenario," Freta said in a lower, serious tone.

Myron nodded. "If she drank too much and was on drugs to boot, it might take a while for her to sleep it off and get her bearings. What about her friends?"

"Useless. It appears that they all fell asleep or passed out and didn't know that she was missing until hours had passed. At any rate, there is something that can be done." She drank the last of her coffee and placed the lid over the paper cup, seemingly having made up her mind about something. "You know what? I'm going to make a courtesy call on Hans Trovotka. Just a friendly visit to enquire if by any chance Raglan ventured onto their property." She paused and gave him a conspiratorial look. "You're welcome to ride along — if you're free."

"A ride-along? More than happy to. So happens I don't have any more classes today."

"Great."

"Shall I drive, since my car is here?"

"No," Freta replied thoughtfully. "Drive back to the apartment, and I'll swing by and pick you up. A show of authority like an RCMP Crown Vic is probably not a bad thing when dealing with Hans Trovotka."

***

Freta drove about ten kilometres over the posted speed limit. "Everyone does it, so why wouldn't law enforcement?" she informed Myron. She did so for almost forty-five kilometres before turning off on dusty Concession Road 39 on the outskirts of High Lights. "Otherwise known as the Jones Lake Road — takes us straight to the Hutterite Colony," Freta said, her eyes straight ahead. "But that's not where we're going."

A few kilometres later, she turned left again onto a less travelled road and within a short time came to a T-junction. Another left turn. "Trovotka's place straight ahead," she informed him.

"You certainly know these parts," Myron said, shifting around a little more to face her. The middle console was fully packed with all manner of bulky police equipment, including a computer.

"As I said, Hans is well known to us, and I did execute a search warrant."

"What was he accused of again?"

"Basically, everything from vandalism and destruction of property to sabotage and terrorism, but nothing was found to make any charges stick. What happened was — and a lot of this was before my transfer to the Great Plains Detachment — a number of gas wells were sabotaged by cement poured down drilling shafts to a couple of explosions and fires, one of which ruptured a pipeline."

"So, what were you looking for with your warrant?"

"Dynamite, for one thing, and other tools of ecoterrorism. Of course, it was like looking for needles in multiple haystacks, and despite twenty of us searching, no incriminating evidence was found.

In retrospect, it doesn't surprise me given that on a quarter section they could have hidden anything with pretty good odds we would never find it."

"So … why did he do it?"

"He had grievances — many valid. The drilling and construction of gas wells was hazardous to his family's health. Case in point, his youngest son, Isaac. A bit strange, that one, and maybe it's true that too much sour gas was inhaled and the DNA got a little scrambled. Trovotka certainly blames the companies that have leases in the area. Still, I can't begin to fathom his reasons for his actions or the way his mind works. Here we are!" she exclaimed in a voice somewhere between a sigh and determination.

The cruiser came to a rolling stop in front of a fenced gate, beyond which lay a sprawling two-storey house. It looked like various rather haphazard extensions of wood and stucco had been added over the years.

"So, what role do I play?" Myron asked, undoing his seat belt.

"Bodyguard," Freta answered with a smirk. "I'll do the talking. You use your keen powers of observation, dear Dr. Watson."

"Righty-O, Ms. Holmes…"

\*\*\*

As Freta and Myron got out of the Crown Vic, a stilted, solitary figure approached the chain-locked gate. He moved with a leisurely but purposeful gait toward them, his right hand squeezing what Myron presumed to be a red, rubbery object of some sort.

As they move closer to the gate, he stopped a few feet away, blinked rapidly as if to adjust to the sight of these potential trespassers, then narrowed his eyes.

"Suspicious fellow," muttered Myron as Freta took a step forward.

"Runs in the family. No one around here takes too kindly to the law," she answered in a whisper. "Smile… Hi," she said. "Is Mr. Hans Trovotka in?"

"Yeah, he's in the house," the young man answered, eyeing her closely, as if trying to get a measure of her intent.

"We'd like to talk to him."

There was a long pause. "He's in the house," he repeated. His lazy eye shifted and refocused completely on Freta.

"Could you tell him we're here?" Freta said, still smiling,

"Sure."

"But while we've got you here, perhaps you can help us as well."

"About what?" he asked tersely.

Myron noted the young man's eyes wandered from Freta to him, maybe because of his stare at the man's white knuckles repeatedly squeezing in and out what looked like a red ball cupped in his hand. The look they exchanged was one of curiosity, balanced by intrinsic dislike. *A dislike at first sight,* thought Myron. *Was there such a thing?*

"We're looking for a missing person. Your name is?"

"Isaac."

"And you're Hans's son."

"Yeah."

Freta nodded as if to confirm. "As I said, we're searching for a camper who has wandered off from a site, the old Forbes campsite not far east of here. Evidently she lost her way... You haven't seen anyone who seems lost or possibly confused?"

"Only seismic crews and a man with a shovel." Isaac smiled for the first time. A private joke, it seemed to Myron, that only the joker got.

Before the conversation carried any further, Hans Trovotka came striding toward them.

"Isaac," he said in a strong, forceful voice, "you're needed in the shed." Myron's gaze shifted to a number of rough structures behind the main dwelling, one of which he presumed was "the shed."

"Yeah." And without another word, Isaac abruptly turned and walked away, furiously working the ball in his hand.

Hans Trovotka was archetypical of what Myron imagined a cult leader to be. He had the presence of a grizzled Moses who had just descended from the mountain: solid in form and no doubt unshakable in his beliefs and the instructions the Almighty had bequeathed to him. He almost expected Trovotka to raise his arms and declare "Deliverance is at hand."

Physically, Hans was big — at least 6′1″, Myron reckoned — with plenty of girth and a massive head. In his younger days, Myron could envision quite a handsome lad: a flowing mop of blondish hair under a wide, increasingly furrowed forehead, piercing grey-blue eyes, a slightly angled nose (probably broken at least once), a wide mouth, and perhaps a trimmed beard or fashionable stubble. He'd be attractive to women. The older Hans before him, pushing sixty, Myron judged, was more untamed in appearance, and if the stories were correct, unruly in his behaviour. At any rate, the hair was greasy and long, and covering his jowly cheeks was a dishevelled beard bursting with prominent patches of grey. His eyes were wary, the expression stern and without humour. *A po-face if ever there was one,* thought Myron.

The package presented was deceiving, however, because it didn't take long to realize that he and Freta, in particular, were dealing with an intelligent, shrewd individual who was also most articulate.

"Officers," Trovotka acknowledged politely, especially focussing on Myron, assuming perhaps that he was a plainclothes detective in charge.

Freta took the lead. "Mr. Trovotka… You might remember me — Corporal Osprey. I have visited before."

"Ah, yes." He gave a knowing nod, shifting his gaze from Myron to her. "Some time ago. You and an army of officers, as I recall, executed a search warrant."

"That's right."

"Well, I'm surprised that you're still here. I heard that the RCMP frequently transferred their people from detachment to detachment."

Freta did not take the bait, if indeed that was Trovotka's intent. "I'm here on another matter."

"Well then, what can I help you with today?"

Myron noted that other individuals had emerged from the house to witness the encounter with authorities, including a couple of youngsters and a small but erect, spritely-looking woman who he assumed was Trovotka's wife. They all kept their distance.

Freta got to the point. "A teenage female has gone missing over the weekend from a campsite in the vicinity of your property."

"Ah, yes… I heard. Youth these days … no discipline, no moral code — drinking and carrying on — and where are the parents?" He shook his head as if bewildered.

Ignoring the short diatribe, Freta said, "If you or others on your property have seen her or happen to see her, please notify us."

"Of course. No one has, or I would know, and we would never leave any soul in distress without providing aid. But we'll keep a watchful eye."

Freta reached into her inside jacket pocket and produced a card. "Thank you. I would appreciate a call if you come across anything that might be even remotely related to our missing person."

"I will. I understand that a search party is being formed. We're ready to help."

"Thank you," Freta said officiously. "We'll let you know."

"Glad to help…" Trovotka shifted his gaze to Myron then back to her. "Does he talk?"

Myron gritted his teeth and retorted, "I do when I need to."

\*\*\*

"Well, that was less than helpful," Freta said as they drove away.

"And he obviously doesn't appreciate the strong, silent type," Myron added in a somewhat chagrined tone. "You didn't ask if he'd give permission for searchers to access his property?"

"A bit too soon for that. I don't want to force the issue yet. Hopefully, Raglan went nowhere near Trovotka's domain and will be found soon."

"Strange man, though, in charge of what looks like a strange family, including Isaac."

"Hans's youngest can be very off-putting. I remember him from executing the warrant — belligerent and more than a bit creepy.

Wasn't too obnoxious today, actually. I have a feeling he's a bit socially challenged. Probably doesn't get out much, certainly not to Great Plains."

"So he's not known to the local constabulary? Doesn't terrorize the bars and chase women?"

"Hardly. I don't think we have him on file at all. Clean-living country boy! Hans, on the other hand..."

"Yeah, I'm trying get a read on what he's really about."

Freta gave Myron a sideways glance as she turned right, retracing their route to the "main" Jones Lake Road. "Definitely sees himself as some sort of prophet-saviour."

"You mean he has a Messiah complex — saving his flock from the evils of the modern world," said Myron.

"If by modern world you mean the oil and gas companies and their activities around here, then yes. But for him it's also about getting back to fundamentals. And he does have a following. At least two other families reside on his property. By the way, you don't mind if I make a stop at the bush party campsite? Just want to see how Rob's doing with the search-and-rescue operation."

"I'm good..."

They rode in silence for a couple kilometres, Myron mulling over their encounter with Trovotka and his son.

"Out of curiosity, where did Trovotka come from?" Myron asked after a while. "Northern Alberta doesn't seem to be an ideal spot to begin a messianic movement."

"Maybe not, but out in the bush there's less chance of being ridiculed or rejected than, say, an urban area. Lots of nonconformist types around here. I don't really know — just a guess. If I remember his file correctly, the Trovotka clan is from the U.S. ... well, somewhere from Europe originally, then Pennsylvania. Don't know the history there except that Hans got into trouble with his Pennsylvania Dutch brethren. Apparently, he was a bit too radical even for them. Not sure exactly what precipitated it, except that he lost his pastor position and was kicked out and ostracized from church and community. Moved up here with a small entourage of loyal followers sometime in the sixties, presumably because the land was cheap and there was plenty of it for homesteading. Some of his followers have drifted away over the years, but he's got two families living on his land now, although neither originally came with him."

"Must have been difficult to survive, never mind earning a living," Myron commented.

"Lots of fortitude for sure, and becoming quite self-sustaining, and he worked building houses. I heard he was a skilled carpenter. Don't know much more about him than that," Freta concluded.

"Well, he can be irritating."

"Oh, you mean his comment about your talking — or lack thereof?"

"That too."

"So … back to getting a 'read on him.' Hardcore fundamentalists are also misogynists who believe that women have a certain prescribed role and place in life, and it isn't in uniform or asking questions while the man in this case remains mute."

"So he was put off that I *was* your strong, silent subordinate."

"Bodyguard," she corrected with a smirk.

***

There were numerous dusty pickup trucks, quads, and police cruisers parked along the dirt road that led into the campsite. More vehicles had spilled to the camp proper, including Rob's Crown Vic. In reality, it was little more than a clearing with a couple of fire pits, a small shed half-filled with cut wood, and a couple of bear-proof garbage receptacles, apparently little used since paper and plastic packaging along with aluminum beer cans were strewn about. Only one "Johnny on the spot" portable sat with a hanging lock dangling from door. It was a pretty basic set-up.

"Nothing yet," declared Corporal Rob Rainy as Freta and Myron approached. He was leaned over, studying a terrain map of the area spread on the hood of his cruiser, each corner weighted down by a fist-sized rock.

Corporal Rainy was a handsome man in his early to mid-thirties. He was, Myron judged, almost six feet, with a broad, pleasant face, focused grey-green eyes, and under that regulation cap of his, Myron knew, was a fine growth of closely cropped brown hair, no doubt RCMP-approved. Myron had the sense that Rob was a bit too straight-laced and officious for Freta, although in their last case together he did go along with Freta's suggestion (despite his better judgement, he later related) of delaying for a couple of days the suspicious nature of the college president's death. Freta wanted to "poke around" before calling in the Major Crimes detectives from the K Division. Thus, standard protocol was not observed, even though Rob, having the same rank as Freta, could have forced the issue. The power of Freta's forceful persuasion had ruled the day, Myron surmised at the time.

Rob and Freta escaped severe reprimands because, in essence, the case was satisfactorily solved with the homicide detectives belatedly called in and taking the credit. Still, Freta wasn't sure that Rob was completely mollified. Myron too was probably in Rob's doghouse, even though he played a crucial role (if he did say so himself!) in cracking the case and saving their collective asses. From Rob's point of view, Myron was a civilian who, like in those silly TV cop shows, became a special consultant or some insightful "Sherlockian" guru who was smarter than the police. It was as if coppers couldn't figure things out for themselves or put two and three together! And here he was again with Freta…

"You squared away with Rob?" he asked Freta shortly after the repercussions of the fallout from the case had settled.

"Yeah, he was a bit out of sorts with me. Don't blame him. We pushed the envelope a bit too far, but we survived and are none the worse for it."

Now, "How many showed up?" asked Freta, taking a good look at the map.

"About thirty or so. Organized them into teams and sent them off. God, I hope they find her alive and well, hopefully emerging onto some seismic cut-line or oil/logging road none the worse for wear. It's bear and cougar country, never mind wolves. Wouldn't be the first time someone's gotten lost, though…" He shook his head. "Thankfully, it's not too cold yet."

Freta nodded while Myron, feeling a bit like a fifth wheel, gazed pensively into the woods.

"I've called the K9 unit," Rob continued, "but it will take a while to get here, and the forecast calls for rain later today. That may screw up not only the dogs but the searchers as well."

"Speaking of which… How many have experience?"

"Some, but most know this neck of the woods, and we've divided the area into grids with small teams spaced out. If they don't find anything initially, then they'll double back. Trouble is we don't know what direction she may have wandered off or how far she may have gone, really. We're spreading out every which way from here."

"Just to let you know we've—" Freta nodded toward Myron, "—been out to Trovotka's place, a friendly somewhat unofficial visit."

"And? Was he friendly?" Rob straightened up from the map, giving Myron an inscrutable look and begrudging acknowledgement.

"Friendly enough. Said he and his flock haven't seen any missing persons, although he was well aware that we were looking."

"He's slick and sleazy," Rob said with a trace of venom. "It's against his nature to help or accommodate the RCMP. We're the enemy. It wouldn't be easy getting on to his property if our initial search turns up no sign of Raglan."

"Yeah, I know. Trovotka is touchy about things like that — his civil rights and all that."

"We'll probably need a bloody warrant if it comes to that."

"Then we'll get one," Freta said emphatically.

"Well, let's hope that it doesn't come to that," Rob said. "Still got a lot of ground to cover before we officially bang on his door."

# Chapter Six

Hans Trovotka was uneasy; the visit of the RCMP female and her companion, whom, oddly enough, she failed to identify, could potentially prove problematic. He couldn't risk another massive incursion on his property by the RCMP, even if they were searching for a person rather than incriminating materials. They might quite inadvertently find his stash of bomb-making paraphernalia and/or traces of dynamite, particularly if dogs were involved. He was fortunate the last time — no dogs and the sticks of dynamite hidden in a pit under a storage shed had been missed. Dogs wouldn't have missed that, he believed.

Even if their purpose was entirely different, the risk remained, and if they got lucky, he would be incarcerated and God's Light Church finished. Surely, God wouldn't allow that to happen; all he could do was pray and hope that that wandering harlot was found before the police and search parties reached his gate. He doubted he could prevent them from trespassing.

The other object of his unease was Isaac. What was he really up to? It niggled at him that he had grown estranged from his son and that he truly didn't know him. Increasingly, Isaac had kept to himself, especially the last few months, and had frequently gone off into the bush where, Hans suspected, he had built some sort of cabin or hut. He had been surreptitiously taking building materials, tools, nails, and such, over the spring and summer and disappeared for long periods. Hunting, he said. Certainly, he had the skills to build a personal shelter; as a teen he had helped his dad on many construction jobs and developed into a worthy carpenter's apprentice.

This unease concerning Isaac was nothing Hans could directly put his finger on. But Isaac had changed in dark and unhealthy ways over the last three or so years, he reckoned — more removed, more capricious about church activity, and more unsettling in his behaviour toward Hans's followers, and indeed Greta and himself. He exhibited coldness, even meanness to those around him in general. God's special lamb was evolving into a lone wolf...

Hans wished that Isaac hadn't spoken to that RCMP female. Osprey, it read on her card. But it seemed innocent enough — no harm was done. What harm was there to be done? Still, without being too obvious, he'd see what his son was doing in the bush and check his lair — if that's what he had erected. What was Isaac up to in general? He needed to know.

*** 

*Maybe I should've stayed out of sight,* thought Isaac as he walked away from the policewoman on the other side of the gate, his shoulders slumped, his mood sour. Somehow, he felt inadequate even as he stood his ground like he belonged there. And that man with her... He couldn't decide whether he was a cop or just along for the ride. Instinctively, he felt defensive about him and his silent, reproachful gaze, at his hand squeezing the "fuzz" ball. That might turn out a mistake — on both their parts...

That was the least of his preoccupations, however; his mind played over and over the events of early Sunday morning, from the "man with the shovel" to Raglan.

It started well enough with her — until he led her into the bush. Her tone changed from chatty to concern to something else: judgement. Meanwhile, his head was spinning with thoughts... She shouldn't have given him nasty, provocative stares or ordered him about.

"Stop!" she'd commanded, her voice climbing in pitch. "We're way too far off the road."

"Short cut through the woods. We're almost there."

Then, as they suddenly came upon a small structure nestled in a grove between two spruce trees, she abruptly did stop. "This doesn't look right. No one is here. I need to go back to the road."

"Sure," he replied in a mechanical tone. "But I wanted to show you something…" He gestured to his private place.

"I don't think so," she responded, backing away.

"All right," he said reassuringly. He didn't want her to run away while, at the same time, knowing he couldn't let her escape — not now. A momentary desperation and panic had nipped at him like the time in Great Plains when he tried to convince an underdressed vixen to get into his battered Chevy pickup. She showed interest, then, as she got closer, she told him to fuck off before hurrying away into the night. He overcame it and calmed himself. He was in full possession of his faculties, with no tell-tale shakes in his hands. He was prepared this time and in control. Still, he had made a mistake.

Raglan began to run, and he overreacted. He caught her and restrained her — not violently but so that she would not continue to flee. Fright and revulsion flashed in her eyes at his touch. "Stay away from me," she screamed. Then she kneed him in the groin, turned, and ran again.

Dark, tormenting thoughts stirred within him, followed by a sudden serene reflection. He was special, and she shouldn't be running away. He lunged after her and in a kind of oblivious haze gave her neck a twist, and she dropped like a sack, her eyes open but empty. It was like he had caught up with the chickens he chased as a child and one by one twisted their necks … or Lucy…

He didn't mean to do it. "I'm sorry," he whispered, at a loss to say or react in any other way but stare at the crumpled corpse in a paralyzed stupor.

It took some time before he retrieved his wits and put what had occurred into perspective. Yes, he was sorry that she died, but he also had to acknowledge that her death wasn't the issue, only that she died prematurely. He had other plans… Now, the question was *What am I going to do*? His head was pounding. Leave her? Bury her? Just run… No. He needed to think. He was smart and could figure this out!

First, he had to check that she was really dead. He knelt and right away, from the distorted angle of her head and the blank eyes, he knew. Second, he couldn't leave her there exposed to the animals or to be found by the RCMP. With a cascade of sweat rolling down his back and neck, he dragged her to a tree, propped her up as best he could, and let the body flop over his right shoulder. Then he resolutely walked down into the grove to his primitive cabin, undid the latch, opened the door, and deposited Raglan against a corner wall.

The cabin was no more than 6 x 5 feet, containing little of note, some hanging pelts — trophies from his hunts — assorted equipment and supplies for that purpose, dried food in a plastic bin, a sleeping bag, extra clothing on a couple of hooks, another pair of boots, and a stool. He hadn't yet figured out exactly how he was going to utilize this, his private space, but it did provide shelter and sanctuary. Alas, hiding a body was not what he had in mind.

*I made a mistake, true,* he thought as he sat down heavily on the tiny stool. *But she shouldn't have tried to run away... I need to fix this. The RCMP will come looking for her; they'll search the property, find my place, and here she is...* Even if he buried her, the dogs could sniff her out. He'd read that some dogs were particularly good at locating buried bodies. So, again, what to do?

He had an idea that grew as his urgency to act escalated. He was smart, and it would work. The question was did he need his dad to help him? He debated this for quite some time. The old man was gullible enough... Isaac could almost envision the scenario. First thing, he'd blurt out what was on his mind: "Isaac, what have you done!" And here Isaac would play God's special lamb: "Nothing. I came across her in the grove. She must have fallen and broke her neck. I–I didn't know what to do, so I got you..." Of course, his father would strain to believe him. However, in the end, he would accept his version and pray for his son's soul and divine guidance.

After that, though, Isaac couldn't be sure whether his father would help him get rid of the body and not report the "accident" or decide that he had no choice but to inform the RCMP of the unfortunate discovery on their land. In all probability, the cops wouldn't believe his story that he just happened to come across the deceased. Moreover, there was always a chance that they could prove it wasn't an accident after examining her and conclude that he killed her. He had read that too. And he definitely didn't wish to go to prison. No, he decided; he had to forget about his dad and do what needed to be done and soon — tonight.

The how wouldn't be much of a problem, Isaac figured; the body could be transported off the property without too much difficulty. He'd park his truck down the road away from the house after putting the necessary tools in back. After dark, he'd simply slip away, drive the Chevy to the most advantageous spot off the road, hike in to his hut, and carry her out to the vehicle. The question was where from there?

The answer jolted him like a divine bolt from Heaven. It had unfolded before him in the predawn light Sunday morning. He was smart, and now to his smarts he could add very clever…

*** 

Isaac wandered off to his private place after his brief encounter with the RCMP woman. He hadn't been there more than an hour when he was startled by a knock on the rough wooden door. Evidently, his place wasn't private any more…

He peeked through a large crack, silently cursed, and opened the door.

"So … this is where you hide yourself," said Hans with forced cheerfulness.

"Dad! What are you doing here?" Isaac tried to keep his annoyance at bay. *Play this cool,* he told himself.

Hans smiled and peered into his son's mostly dark and foreboding sanctuary. "I wondered if you had built yourself a cabin."

"It's a hunting hut."

"Right — a sort of hideaway."

There was an awkward pause. Isaac was not giving anything away, and Hans, a man of many biblical words, struggled to find the right ones to engage his son. "Well… After our guests left, I decided to go for a walk and … and here I am."

*You mean you came looking for me,* Isaac corrected but kept his peace.

"We need to sit down and have a discussion about a number of matters," Hans said.

*You mean about why I'm weird — as if you knew what weird wasn't. Why I am not doing anything? Have I lost my way to God's temple? Pray with me to help you. And let's plan the next attack on Big Oil — encourage them to buy us out!* "Sure, sometime soon."

"Good … that's good, son…" Hans hesitated as if he wanted to say more but decided that it wasn't the right time.

"The two cops at the gate—"

"Looking for a lost camper — not to worry. Has nothing to do with us. Hopefully she will be found and disciplined before they come over snooping our way."

"Yeah."

Hans changed the topic. "This … project — shows initiative. So… What do you do here?"

Isaac shrugged. "It's a shelter. I have some supplies and stuff…" He trailed off. He really couldn't say why he built the hut — not in a logical way. It was important that he had built it and that it be private. The old man had complicated things by suddenly showing up.

A long silence ensued as Hans took one more look around as if to make sense of it. "Well, I better get back," he finally said. "The sky is starting to spit and growing darker. A downpour is forecast."

"I'll be here a while longer," Isaac said amicably, "sort out some of my hunting stuff. Be home later."

As Hans made his way up the grove and disappeared into the bush, Isaac was relieved on two counts. The old man thankfully had not found his place a couple of days earlier, and after holding off, the rain would now come at a most fortuitous time.

# Chapter Seven

"So, what do you think of our new president?" asked Ted as they walked out of Myron's small office, down the two-tiered staircase onto the main concourse and out the south door of the building, headed for Robin's Coffee shop. It had rained for most of the night but had cleared nicely with the sun peeking out midmorning. A bit cool, thought Myron, but perfect for a brisk stroll and brew before his two o'clock class.

Their route usually took them through what was dubbed "college park," a mature section of the city with older, modest homes along with scattered newer duplexes onto a paved pedestrian path that led to their destination. They'd often buy their coffees and take a more circuitous route back, which, if time permitted, they could extend farther to include a trek around the small reservoir on the western side of the college. Today, however, that would have been an indulgent detour for Myron. He needed to get back, so they decided on the more direct return.

"I really have no meaningful opinion other than our new prez checked off most of the boxes the selection committee and board had on its list."

"But you're on the board."

"Was on the board," Myron corrected. "My last official duty was to go through the process of meeting and greeting the shortlisted candidates of the respective selection committees — potential presidents and deans — then voting."

In truth, Myron had no particular insight into the institution's new president, Anthony Botenworth, other than he presented himself well, smiled a lot, exuded charm, and had a sense of humour. If pressed, Myron would have guessed that the selection committee and board hung its collective hat on these favourable impressions and the fact that he had been vice president of a much larger community college in British Columbia and had all the prerequisite qualifications and experience. Certainly, Botenworth cut an imposing figure: tall and fit-looking, without the obvious tummy bulge, he had an unusually long face accented by an aquiline nose, under which was a manicured moustache somewhere between that of Errol Flynn and Adolf Hitler. On top he sported a mop of tightly curled black hair with the appropriate streak of distinguishing grey flexing through it.

However, all that was superficial to the job. What lay hidden was a mystery. Myron and the rest of his colleagues at the institution would discover in due course the true nature of the CEO they had selected.

"Still," Ted persisted as they rounded the corner of the main building and onto the laneway that led them toward the student residences and beyond into the quiet streets of the neighbourhood, "you must have some thoughts and impressions."

"Ask me at the end of the academic year when he settles in and the new deans are on board."

"About the deans…" Ted refocused, scratching his nose. "Haven't seen hide nor hair of them since their introductions at the board barbecue."

"That's because they're probably extremely busy, and like the prez, they too will come out in the wash."

There was no question that the so-called "Deans' War" had created an unheard-of situation in the institution — an almost complete turnover in senior administration from the president on down, including the dean of finance and administration, fired by the preceding president just before getting killed herself. The dean of career studies and dean of arts (yet to be filled) were necessitated by the former resigning over allegedly poisoning the latter, who fortunately survived the attempt but himself was about to stand trial for manslaughter in the death of the previous president. The only senior administrator who survived the "Deans' War" was the college registrar.

"I heard a rumour that the new president was involved in hand-picking the new deans."

"Well, he had a role," Myron said. He couldn't deny that. After his selection, Botenworth was indeed consulted in the selection process — and, as it turned out, the two deans hired had either worked for him or knew him well. But it only made sense and was why the board chose the president first. He had to build a team with personnel with whom he could work — at least that was the rationale presented. "And it makes sense," Myron continued, trying not to sound defensive. "Look what happened the last time: a dysfunctional group turned deadly, quite literally."

In the end, though, the question hit a nerve; he wasn't completely comfortable with the logic because it had too much of the "I scratch your back and you scratch mine" philosophy. Nevertheless, the members of the board, not without justification, saw it differently, and the new president had rather decisive input into two of the three positions to be filled (the dean of arts was still outstanding, but a decision was close). In this last selection, Myron wasn't included, since his term as faculty representative on the board had expired with the beginning of the new academic year.

"Well…" Ted lowered his booming voice, although there was no one within screaming distance on the street. "I heard a rumour that the new president is thinking of adding a VP — doesn't like the college's flat administrative model and wants a number two."

Myron nodded. "He did mention that in his interview."

"We'll be top-heavy with administration," Ted remarked with a tinge of disdain.

Myron smiled, knowing where Ted was going with this; more administrative positions equalled fewer teaching positions. "May not be such a bad idea, though — having a second-in-command in case the new prez gets bumped off again. Besides, faculty shouldn't complain too much. It just evens things out a bit. After all, for most of the year senior administrators were a rare, endangered species."

"Very funny, and not the faculty's fault. Who knew that the species were such carnivorous beasts and would do each other in... We carried on."

"Yes, we did!" Myron agreed. "Hopefully, the 'Deans' War' is over and, for now, all that we will add is a dean of arts."

"Will Botenworth have a say in who it will be as well?"

"Probably he will, if he hasn't already. The good news in this scenario is that it likely precludes the possibility of anybody internal getting the job."

"Who would be silly enough to apply?" Ted said and stopped himself. "Oh, you mean our friend, Dr. Sidney Sage." He ruefully emphasized the "doctor" in a sarcastic tone.

"Always a possibility. He might aim a little lower this time — a dean instead of prez — although I think he's learned his lesson." Myron thought back to the ambitious political science instructor who had applied for the acting president position, going so far as attempting to influence the board decision via the student representative by offering various forms of inducements and rhetorical pressure — at least that's all he tried, Myron hoped. Sage failed and was called out on it by Myron, who felt he needed to as the board's faculty representative. Although Myron did this discreetly in Sage's office to save him further embarrassment (and possibly unethical behaviour charges) they were now barely on speaking terms. This came after the matter of Sage's dubious PhD obtained from a dubious university in California came to light.

For the last few months, Sidney seemed to have made a strategic withdrawal from any potential limelight, lying low (which Myron knew was not his usual style) and diligently tending to his courses. Nevertheless, Myron reminded himself it was just the beginning of the semester...

\*\*\*

Myron could have called it coincidence, happenstance, or karma, but the instant he and Ted entered the coffee shop, he spotted Hans

Trovotka huddled in a corner table with a small, fidgety woman he recognized from the homestead and presumed was his wife. They appeared engaged in a whispered but tense conversation, leaning toward each other from across the table. Notably, the woman's dark eyes stared at the wild beard — not quite meeting his eyes. *Wonder what that's about?* Myron asked himself.

Ted followed his gaze as they lined up in a small queue. "Ah," he said, "the Trovotkas, Hans and Greta."

"You know them?" Myron asked, quite impressed.

"I know of them," Ted corrected. "And the names are easy to remember, like in the Hans and Greta fairy tale."

"It's Hansel and Gretel."

"Close enough. Consider Hans and Greta the more unsavoury version. Anyway, they usually take a weekly excursion to Great Plains — buy groceries and whatnot. Before they go back home, they usually stop for a coffee. Not here, though. Usually it's Timmy's at the north end."

"And you know this how?" Myron asked, surprised (although he knew he shouldn't have been) at Mack's uncanny ability to relate nuggets of poignant, if not immediately useful, information.

"They're a bit of a celebrity couple — not in a good way," Ted added, noting Myron's raised eyebrow. "Anyway, I forget who told me, but it was said to be their routine, maybe ritual. I don't suppose there's anything in Trovotka's version of the scriptures that precludes a coffee shop stop and even a doughnut!"

After securing their java (Ted's turn to pay), Myron led his colleague to a table where they had a direct view of the Trovotkas.

"Odd pair," Ted remarked, noting Myron's surreptitious glances their way. "You spying on them or something?"

"No ... no ... just curious."

"Yeah, well, they do look like sixties hippies ... turned religious nuts living off the land — complete with their own set of followers."

"Like in a Tolstoy commune," Myron mused.

"If you say so — don't they work better in California, where you can wear flower-printed pastel shirts all year 'round?"

"Touché, Ted, touché…" Myron took a swig of coffee. "What do you know about them?" A rumour-monger extraordinaire like Ted, Myron thought, was as good a person to ask as any. The problem was one of evaluation, how to separate the kernels from the chaff. Sometimes Ted's info was suspect. On the other hand, more often than not it was spot-on.

Ted's eyes narrowed, and he produced a mischievous smile. "You investigating or something? Is it about the missing student? Heard that's where she went missing."

"Shh," Myron whispered, "lower your voice. No, I'm not investigating. I just wanted to know. Indulge me."

Myron could tell that Ted wasn't convinced but went on. "They'd been around fifteen or twenty years — not exactly sure. Doing their thing in the bush and blowing up gas wells — so everyone thinks. There's two or three families with the Trovotkas, his followers, I guess, all with numerous kids. They belong to his church. Not true homesteaders, though; I think at least one is gainfully employed off the res, so to speak. Then, so was Trovotka himself, a woodworker, I think. Strange bunch, though — probably not all there, if you get my meaning."

Myron nodded, taking another sip of coffee while his eyes involuntarily wandered over to the Trovotka table.

"Anyway," Ted continued, "no one's sure how they support themselves — off the land, I guess. They're anti-government of any kind or form and, of course, Hans has had run-ins with just about everyone, from his neighbours, oil and gas companies, to the RCMP. Nothing has stuck legally. He was suspected of bombing a gas well and rupturing a natural gas pipeline, and the cops did raid his place, but nothing was found and no charges were laid. You were around, you know."

"I didn't pay much attention at the time," Myron said. He honestly had little recollection even if it undoubtedly made news locally and provincially. In fact, he was only vaguely aware of Trovotka and his God's Light Church — not until the student's disappearance and Freta asking him to accompany her out to Trovotka's home. He couldn't tell his friend about his sojourn with

Freta to talk to Trovotka without inviting many questions, and Ted, for all his brilliant attributes, could not list discretion as one.

"Don't know about his background," Ted continued. "Has an Eastern European name but came from the U.S. Heard that he might have been one of those Navy Seals, but don't quote me on that. Don't think the Seals would let a fellow like that into their ranks." He chuckled. "If he's the gas-well bomber, though. He would have acquired the know-how from somewhere."

"Don't worry, Ted, I wouldn't quote you."

"You *are* investigating, aren't you?" Ted leaned in conspiratorially. "And it *is* about the student who's gone missing. Right?"

"No, I'm not. Just putting a few things together, that's all," said Myron, not sounding that convincing.

"Okay, okay. I guess I'd be suspicious too. Someone goes missing near the loony bin commune where Mr. and Mrs. Weird Cult live."

"No. Not at all, Ted, and they have as much right to have a coffee as anyone else without being gawked at."

"So why are you gawking?"

*Touché again!* "All right." Myron sighed. "I was out to the campsite where Raglan went missing. It isn't *that* close to the Trovotka place, by the way—"

"You were out there — when?" Ted almost had his coffee go down the wrong way.

"Yesterday afternoon. Went out to see if more volunteers were needed for the search." A rather larger lie than Myron wanted to tell. He couldn't afford to let Ted know that he and Freta had gone out there together and spoke (however, briefly in his case) with Trovotka. He'd rather not have a rumour flying about that he was involved in yet another police investigation. "At any rate, my services weren't needed. There's a large community of knowledgeable search-and-rescue types who know the area. I would have been ... redundant in the circumstances."

Myron hated to risk raising Ted's rumour antenna further, but he did want to know more about Isaac Trovotka. "Have you ever met him?" he asked after broaching the subject.

"No," Ted said, obviously not totally mollified and wondering what was with all the questions. "All I know, as I said, is there are two or three families or fragments of families living out there, and some of the offspring are a bit off, including Isaac."

"Off?"

"You know — a bit psycho, mentally challenged. Isaac hears voices and sees spirits, or both." Ted shrugged and set his empty mug aside. "Ol' Clem Barnard told me that once. He has a farm not too far from the Trovotkas. He thought that Isaac might be a bastard from one of Trovotka's long-gone followers. Don't know about that. Also heard that woe to anyone who crosses Mrs. Trovotka… Who knows? Clem might be as batty as Hans over there." Ted gave a slight nod in Trovotka's direction. "So who knows?"

"Interesting family dynamics," Myron said, quietly thinking about Isaac's odd, stilted posture and mannerism. A man of few words. "Did — does Isaac go to school, I wonder?"

"Not to the college… Never seen him anyway. And he's a bit old for high school, I'd imagine," Ted theorized. "Probably home-schooled — I don't know. Clem thought him strange when he was trying to be neighbourly and paid a visit. Kept his distance since … because they turned out to be all strange, he said. Don't know what about now. Haven't spoken to Clem in a long, long time. We're losing our prime attraction, by the way…" Ted broke off his commentary as Hans and Greta got up and made their way to the door.

En route, Myron made eye contact with Hans, despite his efforts not to. The leader of God's Light Commune gave him a nod and smile in recognition.

A couple of minutes later, Myron and Ted followed suit. The sun lay hidden behind the clouds. The air seemed heavy with rain again, and Myron needed to go back and read over his notes for the two o'clock class. As they turned toward the street, Myron spotted Trovotka's muddy Ford van with Greta in the passenger seat. Hans materialized before him from behind the vehicle, moving toward him, maintaining eye contact.

*Okay,* thought Myron, *he wants to say something to me!*

He turned to Ted. "I'll catch up with you in a moment."

Ted noted the interaction. "Right."

"You're not a policeman, are you?" Trovotka asked without preliminaries.

"No … I'm not."

"I thought so when the RCMP lady did not identify you."

"No … I came along for the ride, to see if any more volunteers were needed … for the search," Myron said lamely.

"Sad business." Trovotka shook his head. "That's what happens when kids are allowed to grow up undisciplined … with no rules. They get lost. Well, I hope she is found."

With that, he nodded and walked back to the van.

*What was that all about?* wondered Myron.

"You *are* investigating," Ted stated emphatically as they made their way back to the college.

\*\*\*

"Any news on the missing persons?" Myron asked as he settled into one of Freta's Scandinavian-style chairs.

Myron's Wednesday-night routine was to drop in for a nightcap, which quite often turned into an all-nighter, so much so that he had an extra toothbrush and toothpaste in Freta's bathroom, along with other toiletries. He'd invite Freta to his apartment a floor above, but it wasn't nearly as comfortable. When Nadia left, she took most of the notable pieces of furniture they had accumulated. Although Myron had gone on a buying spree, everything from a fancy Sanyo stereo system to a couple of sad-looking (in retrospect) love seats, it just wasn't as inviting and comfortable as Freta's abode. Myron had to admit that he was not a particularly tasteful home decorator and that his apartment lacked a certain ambience, had an odious (only to some individuals) pipe tobacco smell — despite liberal applications of fresheners, and, it seemed, had important items missing, like an extra bowl for the salad or, more critically, a corkscrew. Thus, Freta's place was the logical choice, almost by default. The only downside was that he couldn't light up his Brigham pipe, a sacrifice he was prepared to make.

Myron's relationship with Freta was hard to define. A work in progress, he supposed. They were comfortable with each other during the last number of months and had, more or less, fallen into a routine. Neither wanted attachments; Freta had her reasons buried deep in her psyche, and while fresh from a divorce, he was not quite ready for a serious commitment, even if he was getting over his state of semi-denial about his failed marriage to Nadia.

Fate had thrown them together in the case of the "frozen president," and now there were two missing persons to deal with, or at least for Freta to deal with. Although he knew, however tenuously, the individuals involved and accompanied Freta to the God's Light Commune, he was definitely on the outside looking in. And he knew that he was never going to be considered as one of those "gifted" police consultants one saw on TV shows helping to solve particularly clever crimes because the cops were too dense to figure out the clues. He didn't see himself as a Jessica Fletcher or, God forbid, Miss Marple, amateur sleuths with uncanny instincts and an eye for detail who inserted themselves into investigations. Why did female sleuths come to mind, he wondered? Because, Myron realized, the male counterparts left something to be desired. Hercule Poirot, who even Agatha Christie couldn't stand, he found an insufferable, obnoxious character, and those unflattering thoughts extended to other detectives including Nero Wolfe and, yes, even Sherlock Holmes, all too full of themselves. Before he could muster more detectives, his thoughts were punctured and then dissipated.

"Yes and no," replied Freta, taking a sip of her Merlot and stretching out on the sofa while pulling one leg beneath her. She was wearing faded blue jeans and a revealing white T-shirt. "There's still no word from search-and-rescue on Raglan, which is becoming more and more worrisome as the hours pass, but there are developments in the case of Mr. Boyd's disappearance. Still, it's the vanishing of Raglan that is surprising to me. Normally, with such resources committed, she should have been located. The rain didn't help, making the dog tracking option iffy at best."

"But the search will continue?"

"Oh yeah, as long as it makes sense. They'll push out the grid that will include Trovotka's land while having another look at areas already covered."

"What do you think happened to her?" Myron was trying to wrap his head around the lengthening ordeal for everyone involved.

"That's the question. Certainly, there is no shortage of possible scenarios. One," Freta started counting them on her fingers, "she's still out there in the bush, dazed or injured, maybe immobile, and the search parties simply haven't located her yet. Seems more and more unlikely to me, given the passage of time. Second, it's rugged country, inhospitable, with wild animals, from bears to wolves and cougars. As much as I might hope it's unlikely, attacks have been reported, probably more than I think. Third, she may have family/friends/school issues and decided to disappear."

"I didn't get that impression last year," said Myron, setting down his wine glass on the coffee table before him. "She seemed well adjusted. As I said before, she did well in class and had lots of evident friends."

"I totally agree. According to Rob, her parents gave no indication of an unhappy, disgruntled daughter," Freta said. "This is a highly unlikely scenario, but if we're covering all the possibilities, it has to be included. Which leads me to a fourth more likely and much more troubling scenario: she met with foul play — kidnapping or worse."

"What about her friends at the campgrounds? They didn't see, hear, notice anything?"

"Not only were they apparently too intoxicated, but they diddled most of Sunday away getting them selves sorted out, then calling for her and then discovering that Kyle's truck keys were missing. He thinks she has them — only his supposition — and that she may have wanted some item in the truck. Who knows?"

"Saw Hans and Greta Trovotka at the Robin's Coffee shop today," Myron said, not sure of the relevance to their discussion. A conscious link to their visit on Tuesday, he supposed.

"Oh? Did you speak to them?" Freta readjusted her sitting position and shoved her other leg beneath her.

"More like he spoke to me. As Ted and I came out, he approached me and asked if I was a policeman." Myron shrugged. "I said no, a volunteer in the search — had to say something plausible — and after a snarky comment about lack of discipline in this generation of young people, he hoped that she was found soon. Then he turned around and went to his van. That's it."

"Well, if Raglan isn't found in the next three or four days, guarantee there'll be searchers and police personnel on his property."

"I got the feeling that he was well aware of that... Ah, you were saying there were developments in the other case?"

"This is on the QT, but this one's shaping up as foul play. I don't think Mr. Boyd disappeared voluntarily."

"Does that mean you suspect Alex Croft?"

"I'm not supposed to say anything on an active case. If my boss knew..."

"I wouldn't breathe a word. I'm Dr. Watson, remember?"

Freta sighed. "Let's just say Mr. Croft is a person of interest at this point. But that's not the exciting news."

"Oh?" Myron noted Freta's sudden perked-up inflection.

"The superintendent of the detachment — I think you might have met him once — assigned me to a detective from Major Crimes on this case. I guess after solving the last one — with your help, of course — Reuben believes that I have some detective squad potential. Anyway, this detective is flying in from Edmonton to interview Mr. Croft at the detachment on Friday. Apparently, he's cut his Vegas trip short."

"That's great! What are you to do for this homicide detective?"

"Haven't got a clue." Freta shrugged. "Probably sit in on the interview, take notes, and what other grunt work he wants me to do. I just think it's a great opportunity. I'll learn a few things, get some experience. I do eventually want to move up the ranks to Major Crimes."

"That's good and bad at the same time," Myron said cryptically.

"Why bad?" Freta frowned.

"'Cause unlike the last time, now that you're solving a crime above-board and with a real, live detective, I'm out of a job! I doubt that I'll be allowed to, quote unquote—" he made air quotes "—be the police consultant, officially or unofficially."

"Uh, no … no more Dr. Watson for you. I don't think either Superintendent Reuben or Detective LeBlanc would be thrilled."

"But you'll keep me informed, particularly where Raglan is concerned?"

"I will, although technically it's Rob's at this point, and in all probability, I'll be yanked off it as long as it remains a missing persons case. But enough cop shop talk…"

Freta sprang up from the sofa and helped herself to another splash of Merlot. "Are you staying tonight or going back to your apartment for a smoke?"

"As much as a good smoke is a good smoke, your company is much better."

"Right answer. You can tell me all about your day — in bed!"

# Chapter Eight

Isaac Trovotka was pleased with himself. He *was* smart, and he had come up with a clever plan. Now he needed to make sure it succeeded. He didn't know the identity of the man with the shovel, but apparently his dad did! That very day, Hans had asked if by any chance he'd seen a red Jeep barrelling down the road from the grotto in the small hours of the morning. Isaac said he had, from a distance. He made no mention of what he saw the man doing at the cemetery.

Hans nodded as if to confirm his own sighting. "I recognized him," he said, "but can't quite place him. It will come to me. Such things always do."

"Why?' Isaac asked cautiously. "Is it important?"

"No," his dad replied. "Curious is all… What was he doing out so early in the middle of the land that God gave to Cain?" He chuckled. Isaac gave a small smile; he had heard it before.

Then, just before turning in to bed that night, Hans remembered, seemingly a eureka moment. He blurted out the name and the company in Great Plains. "Met him once … property hunter, probably scouting for 'Big Oil,'" he snorted disdainfully.

Isaac said nothing but was cheered inwardly. This was a critical piece of information and would ensure that his clever plan succeeded. It would be easy enough to check the telephone directory and get an address. Then, a drive into town; an evening visit was in order.

\*\*\*

Alex Croft was not enjoying his sojourn to Vegas. Understandable, he supposed. He was too distracted — traumatized, actually — to do anything but go through the motions. It had gone wrong, after all, but it wasn't his fault! He took care of it as best he could and was reasonably certain that he was in the clear.

Still, niggling doubts plagued him. What had he forgotten or overlooked? What did he not see? What bases had he not covered? Surely, once the audits were completed the most likely assumption would be arrived at: Boyd disappeared with the money. They'd wonder where had he stashed it? Over $800,000 was missing — gone. That should be enough, he reasoned, to send the cops down a long, tedious rabbit hole — he hoped.

In retrospect, he realized that perhaps his timing was a little off. Forcing the issue with Boyd the night before heading out of the country didn't look good. But he didn't want to change his plans, and it was all supposed to be so simple: a confession, contrition, and perhaps, if possible, some restitution. He had been a little naïve and certainly misjudged Billy Bob Boyd's character, thinking that he'd start snivelling and cave.

Now his stay at the Bourbon Street Hotel and Casino was cut short by a telephone call from the RCMP. Could he please come back to Canada; it was about the whereabouts of his business partner. "Oh, yes of course ... and what about Billy Bob?" he asked. *To be continued when you are back in Canada was the answer.*

Croft hadn't expected the alarm to be sounded so soon. Didn't they wait at least forty-eight hours for missing persons? Someone got on the case in a hurry. Did Boyd's wife say something? Did they find something? How could they? Regardless, he had little choice but play it cool and be cooperative.

He had bought a ticket to see Wayne Newton, which he managed to pawn off to a fellow conference goer, from Calgary as it turned out. Just as well; it wasn't that he was particularly a fan of the "Danke Schoen" crooner, as one tabloid labelled him, but the guy had staying power and was one of the longest running acts in Vegas — over twenty-five years! For Croft that alone was worth taking in his performance and getting his mind off things. God knew he'd be stressed when he returned home.

Determination and keeping it together, Croft decided, would see him through. It was the key to his financial success, although it didn't prevent him from making bad choices, like his spouse and business partner, as it turned out.

It took a bit of time and extra expense, but he managed to rebook on a Western Airlines flight leaving four days earlier than he originally scheduled. *There, I'm cooperating. Hope the authorities appreciate this,* he thought after he paid his hotel bill and grabbed a cab to the airport. He knew that the moment he entered the Edmonton International terminal and identified himself at customs, he'd be greeted by the RCMP. What he didn't expect was his vehicle examined by the forensic unit and that he would be subject to a series of lengthy questions. "Nature of your trip — conference, was it? And Mr. Boyd didn't go? Did you know him well? And you got along? When did you see him last? Did he say anything about going away? Did he seem upset or agitated when you last talked? What did you talk about?" In the end, questions boiled down to: "Do you know anything about Mr. Boyd's disappearance?"

When the two rather expressionless and humourless plainclothes detectives finished, they made it clear that he would be summoned to the RCMP detachment office in Great Plains for a further interview — Friday afternoon, in fact. For now, he was free to go; his Jeep was parked where he had left it. "Remember your appointment, and have a nice day."

\*\*\*

Isaac thought carefully about what he was going to do. He arrived in Great Plains just after 4:00 p.m., driving directly to the Atop Realty office. He wanted to know if a certain Alex Croft was there. However, the lot was empty, and when he tried the door, it was locked. *Okay ... that's unusual for a business,* he concluded. He found a phone booth up the street and called the office. It rang four times before a female voice announced that they were temporarily closed and would reopen soon. "Well then ... not going to find out anything here," he muttered to himself, replacing the receiver. "On to step two then."

Isaac looked at the piece of paper beside him on the front seat with the address he had scribbled from the phone directory and made his way from downtown to the north side. He wasn't overly familiar with Great Plains but knew the general area. His destination took him out to the city bypass and just past the main college entry, where he turned right, followed by a left and a right again into a wide cul-de-sac with big, fancy homes. Croft lived at the apex of the curve. *Ritzy for sure,* he thought. *The guy's got money.*

It was a quiet neighbourhood with few cars about and evidently no one in at Croft's split-level brick-and-stucco house. No lights were on, and the curtains were closed. He thought about risking a move, but there was still daylight and thought better of it. In this area, his old truck stuck out, and he couldn't afford to be noticed. *Best come back after dark...*

Meanwhile, he'd drive around a bit, grab a burger and fries at McDonald's, then come back, stake out the house, and see if anybody came home. He'd park in a dark area on the avenue, some distance from the house and streetlights. What he was going to do was the insurance part of his plan. He'd leave nothing to chance, and that made him smart.

\*\*\*

For someone who had just made a four-and-a-half-hour flight from Vegas to Edmonton (short stop in Salt Lake City included) and had been subjected to a tense interview by the RCMP's Crime Division, the five-hour drive to Great Plains was exhausting. But he pushed on, running on adrenaline. He wanted to arrive in Great Plains in good time, get plenty of rest, and be prepared for the interview tomorrow. He made only one stop for a piss, fuel, and coffee at Fox Spirit, roughly midway between Edmonton and Great Plains. Fox Spirit was yet another emerging town based on natural resource exploitation; in this case, a pulp-and-paper mill was added to gas and oil exploration and service industries. He gassed up at a Husky station that, alas, served terrible coffee, making him wish there was a Tim Hortons. The town was almost big enough to get a franchise by some ambitious local entrepreneur.

Croft made excellent time — really pushed it. It was not quite eight when he wheeled the Jeep onto his driveway. He was so tired that he decided to leave his travel suitcase in the vehicle and just took out his smaller duffel bag that had his toiletries. Sleep tonight; tomorrow bring the stuff in, phone Marcy, visit the office to establish a routine, or at least convey the appearance that it was business as usual. And, of course, there was that interview at two o'clock.

He sighed, got out of the car, and started to climb up the front porch stairs. In his peripheral vision he noticed that the garage side door was slightly ajar, like it had been forced. "What the hell…" he cursed. That would be the topper. His home vandalized while he was gone.

Setting the duffel bag on the porch, he slowly approached the side door. *Jimmied? Hard to tell without a flashlight handy. Doesn't look like anyone's inside — no stray beams of light or noise. Probably gone.* Or maybe the would-be home burglar had heard his car.

Croft consoled himself that there was nothing of importance in the garage to steal: his tools, camping gear, and the usual junk collected over the years, including a fridge with Labatt's pilsner, which the thief or thieves were welcome to…

He opened the door, slowly cringing at the prolonged creaking it emitted. He stepped forward and half turned to the right, his hand searching for the light switch. As he began to grope around, he sensed a presence coming at him from his left.

Martial arts instincts kicked in, and he swung up his left arm in an upper block. It proved an effective parry, and his forearm connected solidly with another forearm, nullifying the blow to come. He heard a yelp and the clang of an object hitting the cement floor. *Weapon dislodged!* He then delivered a forceful punch with his right hand to a surprised torso. It landed just below the ribcage. That bent his assailant forward, and with his open palm, Croft thrust a quick jab into the man's face. It wasn't as direct a hit in the dark as he had hoped, so he heard no crunch of bone or cartilage. Certainly, he did not completely flatten the nose, but it felt like substantial damage was inflicted.

Unfortunately, as Croft thrust, he had to readjust his footing to a wider stance and lost his balance in the process. He wasn't quite sure what he subsequently tripped over, but it gave the assailant the opportunity to flee, particularly as he dropped to one knee and had a shelf of half-empty paint and aerosol cans land on top of him.

"Shit," he spat, attempting to extradite himself from the shelving and other debris that pinned him down. He caught a glimpse of the intruder in the doorframe, a large male sporting a hooded sweatshirt, as he fled into the darkness. The good news was that he was hunched over in decided pain!

*Good! Some damage was inflicted,* Croft thought, the adrenaline still coursing through his body and all tiredness dissipated.

Getting up stiffly, he turned the light on and took stock of the damage and what might be missing. He quickly ascertained that the home invader never actually made it into the house, since the inside door was locked and intact. Nor, it seemed, was anything taken. Nothing substantive anyway. He tried to visualize if the robber ran off empty-handed — and couldn't.

As he stood the metal shelf back against the wall — one end had a distinct yaw — he thought how bizarre. He decided to clean up in the morning.

Later, as he was getting into bed, he experienced an annoying stab of pain in his right knee. *Must have tweaked it in the fall.* He smiled, though, consoling himself that it was not nearly as uncomfortable as what the other man was feeling.

Before finally dropping into a deep sleep, he briefly debated whether he should call the police, quickly dismissing the notion. Why give them the opportunity to come tripping through his garage? Why draw further attention to himself and the neighbourhood? No harm done, at least to himself, and nothing seemed to have been stolen. Besides, he was absolutely too tired to answer any more questions.

\*\*\*

Isaac's left side hurt and his nose felt smashed, blood flowing freely, and he had trouble breathing through it. He reached his truck weak-kneed and barely able to straighten up. When he got into the cab, he fumbled with the keys and with a shaky hand managed to finally insert the right one into the ignition. A twist, and the engine roared to life much too loudly, but it couldn't be helped. Jamming the column shift into drive, he sped away, tires squealing in the still night while he anxiously stared with watery eyes into his side mirror, terrified that Croft might be charging.

Everything hurt; he could hardly see, and as he made his way out of the mini labyrinth of streets and onto the bypass, he inadvertently turned onto the main entrance of Great Plains College. He didn't mean to, but his sight was blurred, and he was slightly confused. He noted that the parking lot was far from empty as he swung in and stopped the truck in the darkest, most remote corner he could find. He needed to regroup and think.

Having been taken to the college once to hear a well-known fundamentalist preacher, one of the few his dad admired, Isaac realized that just inside the Lot A entrance doors were washrooms. With a bit of luck, he could make his way in unnoticed, assess the damage, especially to his face, which felt like a heavy boot had stepped on it, and perhaps clean himself up. He still had a bit of a jaunt to get home.

*Scratch that,* he thought, *not home directly...* He had one more stop to make at the old cemetery. This was part of his cleverness. Admittedly, the plan had gone sideways for him, but it was a minor upset — the mission was accomplished. Through his latex gloves, the kind the old man had used in his workshop when he wanted to leave no prints, he felt the pocket of his sweatshirt. *Yup, still there!*

\*\*\*

Myron looked forward to his Thursday night class because, although it was three hours in length, it was a new course for him: the Soviet Union. He had lobbied for it as a second/third-year level offering, and it was finally approved by the University of Edmonton (as well as other provincial institutions) and put in the provincial transfer guide. Late nineteenth-century Russia/twentieth-century USSR history had been his third field of comprehension in his PhD studies and gave college students a more exotic senior course to complement the pre- and post-Canadian and world history survey courses he was obligated to give. He looked forward to sinking his teeth into the sinewy meat of twentieth-century Russia, beginning with Lenin and his Bolsheviks.

Thus, it seemed somewhat anticlimactic to read the title of his first lecture: "Introduction and Perspective." *Just sounds boring.* Still, it set the stage for the excitement to come. He therefore carefully outlined why that part of the world was worthy of study. He discussed obvious reasons, such as it being the first country to succeed in establishing a Marxist state and becoming the centre (indeed directing) worldwide communist movements, with profound influence not only in a number of Western democracies but in emerging Third World countries too. Moreover, although economically a Second World state, with the acquisition of nuclear technology (most of it stolen — he couldn't resist that insertion), it rose to its status as the second superpower.

Once he established the USSR's place in the international setting, Myron delineated more of the nuts and bolts: ethnic composition, population, territorial boundaries and influences, strategic neighbours, and the level of economic and technical resources. An overview was a necessary foundation from which he could delve into the Soviet society and political system, starting the next class.

Of the nineteen individuals in the classroom, none was more attentive than Alexandra Enfield. This was now the third class of his she was taking: pre-Confederation Canadian history on Mondays and Wednesdays, world history (apparently switched over from another course) on Tuesdays and Thursdays, and this night course. It seemed a little history intake overkill — particularly from one instructor — but who was he to discourage her?

During the mid-class break, he made his way to the Starbucks kiosk. The brew it served guaranteed to get him revved up for part two of the class. Alexandra was off to the side initially, chatting with a couple of students in the concourse. Before long, she disengaged from her fellow students and moved his way. He ambled over, not really intending to, but it would be rude not to. Her eyes beckoned, drawing him in. *Siren call? Don't be silly*, he thought.

"So ... how are you enjoying the class so far compared to the others?" Myron added a bit self-consciously.

Alexandra pushed up her slim steel-rimmed glasses with her right hand and smiled. It was a cheerful smile, lighting up her elfin face. She was very pretty in a perky Sally Field as the Flying Nun sort of way, Myron thought, with a small, tight body that belied her mature thirty-something years.

"They're all interesting," she enthused. "And so diverse! I can hardly decide."

"What program are you in?" Myron asked lamely, feeling a bit tongue-tied.

"Education. Came back to school — decided to change up my life." The smile seemed to widen.

Myron nodded. "Well then, Canadian and world history certainly fit the program. In fact, Canadian history is a prerequisite for social science teachers — if that's your goal."

"Haven't quite decided on the primary or secondary route yet."

"Umm ... the course on the Soviet Union is an extra to either program."

"It fit well into the schedule, and night outings are not a problem. I do live in town now — Lady Elizabeth Apartments on 100th Street," she added as an unabashed afterthought.

"You're not from Great Plains then?" *But then very few people are...*

"Edmonton until a couple of months ago."

"What did you do before coming back to college?"

"Stewardess for Time Air."

Myron nodded again. Time Air was a regional carrier affiliated with Air Canada, he believed. He had taken one of the airline's turboprop Dash 8s on numerous occasions to Edmonton and other parts of the province. She might have been a flight attendant on one of the flights, but he didn't think so. He'd probably remember. "Well…" He took a quick glance at his watch; the ten stretched to fifteen-minute break was coming to an end. The coffee crowd was dispersing. "Once more unto the breach!"

Alexandra's smile never wavered. "Absolutely."

\*\*\*

It wasn't that Myron couldn't stand the pressure, but an hour plus lecture and discussion followed by a healthy dose of Starbucks java, like booze, seemed to course right through him. He had need of a urinal stop before the resumption of class.

Excusing and extraditing himself from accompanying Alexandra back to the classroom, he hurried to the closest washroom near the east entrance of the concourse. It was with great surprise, followed by horror, that upon entry Myron saw Isaac Trovotka raise his head from a blood-streaked sink. Isaac's eyes, too, widened like shiny saucers.

Myron spoke first. "Isaac … huh, what happened to you?"

"Nothing — slipped in the parking lot … face-plant on the pavement." He looked like a deer caught in the headlights of an oncoming truck.

"Are you all right? Should I call emergency?"

"No! No…" Isaac's voice hedged between panic and alarm. "I'm okay — just a bloody nose."

He didn't seem okay to Myron, but there didn't seem any point in pressing.

"You taking a night course?" Myron steadied his voice, getting over the initial shock but was now curious. Isaac didn't seem the college type.

Isaac hesitated. "I'm not sure."

Not sure? What kind of answer was that? Myron frowned. Perhaps he was trying one out — auditing maybe…

"I've got to go," Isaac said, turning and squaring himself to Myron. It wasn't a particularly belligerent tone, but neither was it friendly.

*Big lad,* Myron thought for no obvious reason. "Yeah, right, so do I, actually… You've still got a dribble of blood oozing from your nose." He lifted his hand and pointed.

Isaac reached into his sweatshirt pocket and nervously pulled out a wad of toilet tissue, pressing it to the indicated spot. In the process of yanking out this wad, Myron noticed more tissue had tumbled out, including a small item that rolled under a toilet stall.

Totally flabbergasted, it appeared, by his unexpected encounter with the policeman who had visited the homestead, Myron later surmised, Isaac was unaware that he had lost an artefact. Myron was about to say "you dropped something" but let it go. Isaac was moving forward, obviously anxious to leave. If important, it could always be returned later. Could prove a point of connection, he reasoned. Besides, he really had to get back to class. Students had undoubtedly returned from the break and were awaiting him. "Well … take care then."

"Sure," Isaac said, exiting quickly as Myron stepped aside. *Certainly, my commanding presence won't stop you.*

*That was strange,* he thought, walking out of the bathroom before abruptly turning right back. There were two bits of unfinished business. First and foremost, he needed to relieve the pressure, followed by a retrieval of whatever fell out of Isaac's pocket.

# Chapter Nine

**Friday, August 16**

"Well, now it's really official: Boyd's disappearance is suspicious," declared Superintendent Reuben to Freta as she tried to get comfortably settled on his oak chair. "Based on what you found and a search of Croft's vehicle — more traces of blood, albeit minuscule — it appears that Boyd's disappearance was not voluntary. Still waiting for a match to Boyd's blood, but the betting is that it will match."

"That's quick work locating and impounding Croft's car." Freta knew from experience, although limited, that investigations were often stalled by the bureaucracy getting its ducks in a row. In this case, K Division acted promptly.

"Yes," Reuben agreed, "and the moment he got off the plane in Edmonton, Croft was detained and interviewed. But the centre of the investigation is here, and, as I mentioned, a detective has been assigned, an R. B. LeBlanc. He'll be arriving tomorrow morning to take charge. As I mentioned the other day, you'll be the liaison. So … first thing, meet him at the airport; welcome him to our fair city; provide whatever support he needs; and keep *me* informed of developments as the investigation proceeds."

"Yes, sir."

***

R. B. LeBlanc turned out to be Roberta Beverly LeBlanc, a large woman of average height with short, thick, salt-and-pepper hair and dark eyes, complete with emerging pouches underneath. She had deep sad lines at the corners of her mouth that were accentuated when she frowned and loose wattle from under the chin to the throat. Now, she sat beside Freta on one side of the table with Alex Croft on the other in the detachment's interrogation room, a drab 17′ by 14′ with faded off-white walls, a nondescript brownish ceiling (no doubt made so by cigarette smoke over the years) and a single pod light fixture. On entry, it smelled of Lysol and body odour.

The furniture consisted of a small table and three not particularly comfortable chairs. There was a small shelf on the one wall with recording equipment and a video camera. A microphone hovered over the table, extending down from the tiles above. The other wall had what looked like an opaque window but in fact was a two-way mirror.

Upon his arrival in Edmonton, it was decided that Croft should be allowed to continue on his own reconnaissance (and vehicle) to Great Plains, where an interview would be arranged. So here he was, passively sitting across the table from the older female detective as she opened a file and pursed her lips.

After the formalities of recording the day, date, time, and names of those present, Detective LeBlanc noted for the record that Mr. Croft had not been formally charged with any crime but had voluntarily come in to assist the police in their inquiries. *But definitely a person of interest,* thought Freta, sitting beside LeBlanc with notebook in hand. Her job was to take notes, despite the fact all was to be recorded.

First impressions? Croft appeared somewhat haggard, like he hadn't slept well lately, but was remarkably composed. He wore a frumpy blue jacket with a black polo-neck shirt underneath and grey slacks. It was casual dress, suggesting that he was relaxed and unruffled by what was to transpire. He straightened his posture as LeBlanc began to speak and focused his attention on the detective, his body language giving nothing away.

"Mr. Croft, on the night of August 10, you went to meet Mr. Boyd, co-owner and your partner at Atop Realty."

"Correct."

"And you have been partners for how long?"

"Over five years now. We established our property development company jointly."

LeBlanc nodded. "You were on good terms?"

"Yes."

"Okay… So in this particular meeting, what happened?"

"I–I'm not exactly sure what you mean?" he replied, tensing up slightly.

"It was an unusually late meeting, was it not?"

"Not necessarily, but there was some urgent business that Billy — Mr. Boyd — and I needed to discuss that had just been brought to my attention."

"Which was?" LeBlanc pressed.

Croft hesitated. "It is of a rather delicate nature that I'm reluctant to discuss for confidentiality reasons — at least not without my solicitor present."

LeBlanc pursed her lips again. "I see…" Freta could almost read LeBlanc's train of thought. *No lawyers — don't go there if it can be helped — not at this stage!* "Okay… I'll skip that for a moment. What happened at this meeting in general terms and thereafter?"

"Nothing — nothing unusual. We discussed what we needed to discuss, and I left."

"You left," LeBlanc raised an eyebrow, "leaving Mr. Boyd alone at the office."

"That's right." Croft kept his gaze even on the older detective, giving her a half smile.

"And he was fine and well?"

"Most certainly."

"And you didn't see Mr. Boyd leave?"

"No, I had to go because I was driving to Edmonton early in the morning to catch a plane and needed to finish packing and get some shut-eye."

"Right. So you have no idea what happened to Mr. Boyd?"

"None. I didn't know he was missing until I arrived in Edmonton and was greeted by you folk — and my Jeep was examined," he added petulantly.

LeBlanc tried a different tack. "Is there any reason why Mr. Boyd would want to disappear voluntarily?"

Croft let the question hang suspended for a few seconds. "There might be."

Both of LeBlanc's eyebrows shot up; Freta shifted in her seat. This was becoming interesting.

"Mr. Croft, please answer. Why would Mr. Boyd wish to disappear?"

Croft sighed and leaned forward slightly, his aquiline nose seeming to inhale extra air, a stray lock of hair edging onto his forehead. "I was hoping to avoid this discussion earlier or have my solicitor present at the very least. I have no proof as of yet, you see."

LeBlanc waited patiently, willing him to continue.

"All right, if I must." Croft sighed again. "I have just recently come to suspect that Billy — Mr. Boyd — was cheating clients and stealing from the firm, or, more precisely, from me. And I don't mean a small amount! That's what the meeting was about. Of course, I can't prove it at the moment — a complete audit will need to be done."

"So you had a confrontation — had it out with your partner?"

"Correct. You can call it that," Croft agreed.

"And how did he react?"

"Not well. He was offended about my accusation and raved about how dare I. But he didn't actually deny it. So, when I learned that he disappeared and that the police wanted to talk to me, I thought … maybe that he decided that the jig was up and departed for parts unknown, leaving me holding the bag as far as the company's clients are concerned." He shrugged nervously. "Just my speculation at this point."

"So you left and had no further confrontation with Mr. Boyd, either verbal or physical?"

"Correct. I told him I'd file a complaint with the appropriate regulatory authorities and let my solicitors and the auditors sort out what he had been up to."

"And his immediate response?" LeBlanc pressed.

"As I said, he became agitated, and I simply walked out his office, got into my Jeep, and drove home."

"To go to a conference in Las Vegas, despite what you found out?"

"The trip had been scheduled for months, and there wasn't much I could do except get my solicitor and auditors on the case."

"So you left Mr. Boyd sitting in his office?"

"Correct. He was actually pacing, waving his arms around, telling me I didn't know what I was talking about."

"Okay…" LeBlanc paused and flipped a couple of pages in the file before her. Freta knew where she was going and that she was about to spring a surprise on Croft. "How then," LeBlanc continued, "can you explain the traces of blood stains found in Mr. Boyd's office, along with pieces of duct tape and residue stuck to his chair? Moreover, there were more traces of blood found in your office and the back of your Jeep. Forensics, I can only assume, will find these samples a match to Mr. Boyd's blood."

"I see," Croft said coolly, leaning back in his chair. "You have me at a disadvantage there. I can't answer that because I have no idea. For all I know it may have been Billy setting me up while leaving town. However, at this point, I do insist on having my solicitor present."

\*\*\*

"Well, that was interesting," LeBlanc remarked cryptically afterward.

"So we wait?" They were seated at Freta's desk, the interview suspended while awaiting Croft's lawyer.

"We wait," Roberta replied with a hint of deflation. "He's a cool customer, and with a lawyer who knows the ropes, I doubt we'll get far."

"Croft's lawyer is Jack Hoar, and he's experienced," said Freta. She had heard Croft ask for him while allowed to make his phone call; she was actually surprised he hadn't come in with a lawyer for the interview, but he obviously had Hoar on speed dial.

Freta had met Hoar during the "college case"; he was the board of governor's vice-chair and gave a brief statement to her in the course of her enquiries. Although not a criminal lawyer — she discovered that he was the city's quintessential corporate lawyer, with his firm having most of the big government contracts — he evidently took on criminal cases, or more accurately, in all probability, had one or more of his associates with the appropriate specialization do it. Indeed, if Freta was to make an educated guess, Hoar's firm, in all likelihood, was Atop Realty's solicitor, and Croft and Hoar were friends who travelled in the same circles.

"So what we've got is," Roberta recapped, "circumstantial evidence that an altercation of some sort occurred. Croft's explanation — or should I say speculation — as to how the blood came about both in Boyd's office and the back of his vehicle is hardly convincing. But Boyd is missing, and there is no body... On the other hand, the distance between Great Plains and Edmonton is over five hundred kilometres without much in between. But then bodies are generally found after a while, no matter how cleverly disposed off. Still," LeBlanc sighed, "without a confession or a body, we'll have to let him go for now. We need more evidence — forensic or otherwise."

Freta's phone buzzed; it was the detachment receptionist. "Mr. Croft's lawyer has arrived."

"Okay, thanks, send him through."

"Well," said LeBlanc, getting up from her seat, "shall we take another crack at him?"

As it turned out, Croft, after consulting with Hoar, had little more to say. As to the blood samples found in the Boyd's office and Croft's Jeep, first it hadn't been established that it was, in fact, Boyd's, and even if it was, Croft's theory that Boyd planted the evidence to frame him while disappearing with embezzled funds could not be dismissed as "unreasonable." Indeed, it was quite possible, Hoar averred, tilting his silver-haired head toward his client and accenting a trace of flabbiness around his jaw. "Diabolically leaving my client to carry the can, so to speak."

"Really?" LeBlanc replied in a benign but incredulous tone while Freta furiously made notes.

Hoar cleared is throat. "My client has provided a reasonable explanation for the inexplicable presence of blood in both instances. And you don't know if it even matches that of Mr. Boyd."

"True. That will be ascertained by forensics shortly. And we will go through Atop Realty financial records to verify Mr. Croft's claims of financial impropriety on Mr. Boyd's part—"

"In the meantime," Hoar cut in, "are you holding my client? Is he being charged?"

LeBlanc paused and pretended to ponder the question. "Not at this time," she finally said and then turned to Croft and delivered one of the oldest lines in law enforcement, "But don't leave town."

Croft nodded to her and his lawyer.

"You're free to go — for now," LeBlanc declared. "But make yourself available."

# Chapter Ten

At last, Isaac was safe in his room. He had driven in very late and parked his Chevy some distance from the house. He didn't want to meet and have to explain himself to anyone. Thankfully, all was dark; the household was asleep. He'd explain in the morning how he slipped and hit his head on a log. Now, he was just glad to close the door, strip off his clothes, and crawl into bed.

Sleep eluded him, however, not only because every part of him hurt, but his thoughts also wouldn't let him be. *Croft, Croft, Croft,* he festered like a dull toothache. What emerged wasn't that the man had beaten him but where he lived: a ritzy neighbourhood, which meant the guy was rich.

The synapse was finally bridged. That flowing spark that made him smart allowed for another clever idea. Why not make Croft pay to keep his secret? Financial payback for what happened in the garage, Isaac reasoned, and it still wouldn't upset his original plan — in fact, it could quite possibly strengthen it. How much, though — $5,000? Seemed a bit on the cheap side; $10,000 seemed like a just right sum that a wealthy guy like Croft could quickly raise.

The next question was how to make the demand. Mail a letter? No … too long and complicated. He'd have to write or type his demands and send it out. He'd read somewhere that letters could be traced back to the sender. He could personally drop off his letter in Croft's mailbox. No, that, too, was very risky. It would require that he physically appear, stop his truck, walk up the front steps, and deposit it into the slot. He'd already been there and may have been seen by someone, and if not him, his truck — or more precisely his licence plate number, particularly if Croft reported it to the police. Besides, it was the old man who knew how to write letters; he wrote enough of them to oil companies and the government.

A solution did present itself before sleep overcame him. Why not telephone? Phone from the booth he had used already. He had the office number; maybe it opened on Monday, and Croft would be in. Disguise his voice, make the demand, and tell him to deliver the money to ... where? He'd need to think about that. Fortunately, he had a couple of days. For now, it was best to recover. Already his nose was better, although the cheek was puffy on the left side and the eye exhibited a bluish-yellowish tinge underneath. It was the ribs or something around there that were most painful, making it hard to draw large breaths. A bruise was forming there as well.

Aside from the harrowing confrontation with Croft, two other events bothered Isaac. The first was his unexpected encounter with that RCMP at the college. That was just plain weird. Maybe the cop was taking a course or giving one?

After some thought, Isaac decided that no harm was done. Certainly annoying and a bit unnerving, given his night, but he didn't think problematic. How could it be?

The other event of passing concern entailed the loss of one of two items he had snatched from Croft's garage. He could have lost it in his struggle and getaway, or perhaps it was still rolling around somewhere in the truck; he'd look tomorrow. Fortunately, he still had the second item, now deposited where it did the most damage to Croft. Two objects would have been preferable just in case, as insurance, he reasoned. On the other hand, and he debated this, it might be overkill to the point of suspicious. So, one it was, and he was satisfied.

It was much later, morning in fact, as his eyes popped open — the left remained semi-shut — when he realized that another item had been lost. His flashlight went flying when Croft put up his hand. It skittered away somewhere and hopefully would stay there. Even if it was found, there was nothing incriminating about it. He had, after all, used gloves. The old man had always insisted on such precautions when they made their forays into the gas and oil patch!

It was almost noon before Isaac got up from his bed, got dressed, did his toilette, and came downstairs into the kitchen area. The only one there to explain his battered face to was his mother. She took a closer look and told him to be more careful in the bush. He said he would and after a quick breakfast hurried outside. Feed and check on the chickens and the pigs, then it was off to his private place. He needed to think about what to say to Croft — make sure he knew that his secret was no longer a secret and would pay up. He also had an emerging idea of where Croft should deliver the money.

***

Hans Trovotka knew in his marrow that Isaac was hiding something, if not being downright deceitful. It was more than not receiving honest answers or avoiding topics or even looking him straight in the eye. It was as if a hovering menace was swirling about, a malevolent force trying to lay claim to his lost lamb. Isaac had become sullen, moody, disdainful, no longer interested in participating in church activities, including the post-sermon bible reflections. He either wandered off into the bush or drove off in that worn Chevy of his.

When Isaac didn't make it home for supper that Thursday, Hans thought it was time for him to seek some guidance. As a result, he strolled over to the special extended part of the house and entered the God's Light Church proper, which doubled as a rectory and meeting room. The space could accommodate about twenty individuals in a pinch. The Trovotka clan and the two families who homesteaded on his land came to fourteen. Since there were no followers outside his immediate circle — try as he might, they didn't materialize — the space was more than sufficient. In fact, no expansion had been necessary from the day he finished the building extension as God's holy place.

It was not extravagant in design or furnishing. No icons or relics (that, he joked, was for the Catholics and other idolaters). A large but simple wooden cross that he had fashioned and secured to the back wall dominated the small, raised platform in front. The only other thing he'd erected was a rough pulpit that he rarely used now. He simply walked up, bible in hand, and delivered God's word. The congregation sat a couple of steps below him on three wooden benches.

Every Sunday (and when the spirit moved him at other times), Hans extolled the virtues of living the simple life as God demanded, one that fought against the Godless new infidels, including those that promoted elements of modernity that enticed women away from their proper place; the state that encouraged all sorts of hedonism at the expense of thrift and hard work; and the greedy Big Oil executives who despoiled the land and made his family sick, along with the livestock on the property. For Hans, the simple life as God prescribed was under attack in general by those who had the morals of Babylonian whores and the rapaciousness of capitalists in search of the almighty buck. And he needed to fight back!

At the moment, his worry was Isaac. Thus, Hans sat on the first wooden bench and prayed for guidance, whatever God in his wisdom advised to prevent a total falling out with his son and, moreover, that God's blessings penetrate Isaac's soul so that he could truly see. Hans feared that Isaac was on the verge of going down the wrong path.

No inner voice spoke back to him, but Hans wasn't discouraged. Sometimes it took a while for God to answer, but invariably He always did. Meanwhile, Hans decided that he should revisit Isaac's hut — alone. He needed to look around inside. Not that he distrusted him, Hans reasoned, but Isaac could get confused. He had in the past. And a girl was missing, not that it in any way related to him. Still, the RCMP would extend the search to his doorstep if she were not found. It was best to double-check and make sure that there was nothing untoward to be found.

Since apparently Isaac had a long night and was sleeping late, Hans decided that he would take a detour from his usual walk to the hut and see what was what. A father's curiosity, he rationalized. Now that he knew it was there, he couldn't understand why. Its purpose and Isaac's need to build it eluded his grasp.

While pondering this conundrum, he retraced his steps, turning north from the Grotto Road over a ridge with a thin stand of spruce and entangled bush into a gully on the other side. Although well hidden, it wasn't that far from the main house and Grotto Road. Nevertheless, not a particularly good spot, thought Hans. Higher ground would have been preferable, both strategically as an observational post (if that was its purpose) and in terms of drainage. But it was what it was.

It had rained steadily on and off, and his boots sank deep into the sodden leaves and mould. *Definitely not a great location!* As he approached the structure, Hans discovered another disappointing, if not disturbing, sign. A huge padlock was attached to the door through the tongue of a metal latch. There was no way to get in without busting the lock.

"What is that boy up to, truly?" he muttered, not knowing whether to be angry or alarmed. He could, of course, break the lock and have a look inside. But that wouldn't be right; moreover, Isaac would know. Why that was important, Hans couldn't quite sort out in his mind, but the hairs on his neck stiffened at the thought and he began to sweat heavily, even though it was not a warm morning. He had to admit, if only subconsciously, that there was something about Isaac that frightened him — a little, at least. Somewhat like himself, who put the fear of God in others while at the same time leaving them uneasy, so did his son extract unease, God not included.

Hans believed that Isaac had nothing to hide in that shack of his, but he wished he could look. There was a missing teenager, and the RCMP was going to forcefully knock on his door, he reminded himself. He needed to talk to Isaac at length and seriously.

Taking a quick look around the perimeter of the sad construction and finding nothing of interest, Hans sighed and started back up the incline. His foot slipped on the sloped ground, and as he put his hand down into the mixture of rotting leaves, spruce debris, and soft loam, he spotted a small ring with a set of car keys — from a Ford 150, to be more precise.

*Where did these come from?* he wondered, reaching forward and picking the item up. After a cursory glance, he stuffed the key ring into his jacket pocket. He couldn't very well ask Isaac about it, considering where it lay — not without saying he found it elsewhere on the property.

In the end, there was nothing of note to discover around Isaac's place. And with no particular enlightenment to be had, he might as well go home, make another coffee, and see if Isaac was up yet.

# Chapter Eleven

Alexandra Enfield knew straight away that she would be beguiling. It was just in her nature. The question became why him? There was an undeniable surge of excitement the moment she entered the first class, and she wanted him to notice her. Subtlety was not her strong suit.

Her reaction still begged the question: why pursue him? Handsome: sort of, but a bit scrawny. Intellect: not a major selling point — could be snobbish — but still better than a dullard who spewed vulgarities in monosyllables. Position: a history instructor hardly made the grade for prestige and/or wealth. Yet from the moment she saw him nervously shuffling his notes about at the podium — no wedding ring on the finger — she recognized an ephemeral quality: earnest, with a friendly disposition and an endearing touch of naïveté. She appreciated that and could play the glassy-eyed "mature" student.

Would he take up the scent? She believed so. She would entice him, and he, like the proverbial fly, would get entangled. She trusted her instincts, even if it hadn't worked out for her the last time.

Admittedly, after her experience in Edmonton, perhaps she was both impulsive and aiming too low. But then the big one had gotten away, and not without nasty repercussions for her. A good reason, then, for moving back to Great Plains and luring a more modest target.

Was that an unfair assessment? Probably, but an understandable one: a small-town college prof, complete with a rumpled tweed jacket and a somewhat befuddled demeanour was not a great prospect. But not a disaster either.

Above all, though, there was his aura, a nimbus surrounding him, drawing her into its corona. The aura was unmistakable, strong, and the attraction was inescapable, just like the last time, which, alas, was subverted by interference from an unworthy other. She quickly shuttered the image. That episode was over — an unfortunate aberration, and she refused to be haunted by it. The re-emergence of the aura — blue shades on the periphery, pulsing white toward the centre, blending into definitive form — was a sign that she could not ignore. This time she'd be more resolved!

She spied him in the college parking lot on his way to the car and decided to discreetly take her game up a notch. It wasn't hard to follow a distinct lime-green sedan in her less than distinct Nissan Sentra. He made a stop at a burger place, getting out of his car and hurrying in. She was tempted to follow and "accidentally" bump into him but decided that it might be awkward if he was meeting someone. Instead, she parked and waited. About ten minutes later, he came out with a takeout bag. He was off again soon enough, and five minutes later she watched him pull into the Mackenzie Towers apartment's parking lot. She drove on with a smile.

***

Friday night, and the world unfolded as it should, Myron reckoned. The A&W Papa Burger and order of fries smelled good. Lately, it had become his meal of choice. Sure beat making a bowl of Kraft dinner or a grilled cheese sandwich — his cooking skills didn't progress much further than that up the gourmet ladder. Burgers worked fine, and rarely did he vary the menu with, say, Kentucky Fried Chicken or a fried baloney on a bun.

Admittedly, his cuisine had become considerably restricted since Nadia departed. He ate more often in restaurants, but they tended to be the fast-food variety, since he was a bit self-conscious about dining alone at a higher-end establishment. Only more recently had he and Freta gone dining out on a regular basis. But tonight Freta was working late with, he presumed, the homicide detective, and he was on his own.

Actually, his altered life wasn't too bad — or was he lying to himself? He had developed a routine, albeit rather sedentary, in the evenings. Being sedentary wasn't an issue, though, since he took time during the school day to exercise in the gym or go for a jog. He preferred to work out and shower at the college, given the convenience and state-of-the-art athletic facilities. Nevertheless, his nights were perhaps overly relaxed if he wasn't going out.

He quickly disposed of his burger and fries, made drip coffee (having weaned himself off instant), and indulged his sweet tooth with a serving of McCain's chocolate cake. (At other times it'd be ice cream, preferably pecan or butterscotch.). Thereafter, it was clean-up of utensils and other accompanying chattels, followed by a long, leisurely smoke — Sail or Amphora tobacco stuffed into one of his numerous Brigham pipes.

Sometimes he would read, especially if hooked on a good mystery. Lately, however, since the purchase of a new Sanyo stereo system, he listened to music, everything from classical orchestral pieces to Manfred Mann. He was particularly partial to the accordion, being a player himself, although abandoned since becoming an apartment dweller. Recordings by accordion artists were hard to come by, but his collection was growing beyond the usual myriad of "polka kings" and Myron Floren's arrangements on *The Lawrence Welk Show*. About the only music that he couldn't quite wrap his head around was the emerging hard rock (give him The Beatles, Dave Clark Five, and Gerry and the Pacemakers any time) and jazz. The former sounded like loud noise, and he just could not understand the latter's free flow motif — too purist, perhaps, with no musical roadmap that he could discern. A rendering of "Summer Time" — yes, a little Moe Koffman, even Dave Brubeck, maybe — otherwise, a decided no.

He was also beginning to watch a lot of television, getting hooked on cops shows like *T. J. Hooker, Hunter,* and *Miami Vice,* all to varying degrees featuring renegade officers and their engaging partners outwitting dastardly villains. It provided comic relief from all the Westerns he had endured as a kid.

He was especially fond of what was dubbed *NBC Sunday Mystery* — movie-length episodes of *Columbo, McCloud,* and

*McMillan & Wife* presented on a rotating basis. There was a fourth, but he couldn't remember. His favourite was *Columbo*, a.k.a. Peter Falk as the understated, rumpled L.A. homicide detective who was always asking "just one more thing." He also liked Dennis Weaver as Sam McCloud, the local yokel from some town in New Mexico on loan to NYPD as a sort of "special investigator." What bothered Myron most about *McCloud* (aside from the absurd premise) was McCloud's prop — not the horse but the Plymouth Horizon (Chrysler no doubt was a sponsor) — that the lanky Weaver had to fold himself into. No self-respecting westerner who came from "big country" with "wide horizons" landscaped with pickup trucks would stoop (literally) into a motorized shoebox. Finally, *McMillan & Wife* was palatable, but barely; Rock Hudson was full of himself as the police commissioner with a wife too impetuous (or flaky) by half.

Alas, Myron was disappointed that the series simply disappeared. He read somewhere that NBC had cancelled it, and thus his channel search for suitable replacements. None of William Shatner as *T. J. Hooker*, Fred Dryer as *Hunter*, or Don Johnson as James "Sonny" Crockett quite filled the void, but they would have to do.

Myron was just setting in to see what Friday night TV offered when the phone rang.

It was his mother.

\*\*\*

Marta Tarasyn finally had her suspicions confirmed: Myron and Nadia were no longer together. The information leaked out in drips and drabs. Tell-tale signs inevitably appeared, despite Myron's best efforts to be obtuse. The jig was up when he went home alone in the latter part of June for a three-week stay. After a couple of days of his moping around the house, she bluntly asked: "So ... you and Nadia no longer together?"

"No, we've separated."

There was a long pause, then in a softened voice, she said, "Oh ... too bad."

No further inquisition followed: no questions about why, who did what to whom, and could he fix it. It was more along the lines of "I'm sorry that it didn't work out" and "you can tell me as much or as little as you want."

Myron was surprised at how well his mother took the news. She liked Nadia, and they had gotten along well. But maybe it wasn't that surprising; mothers are a protective lot, and after a while of digesting the news more fully, she typically made the best of a sad situation, blandly telling him that there were "many feesh in the sea."

However, she started to call more frequently, wanting to know how he was doing and what he was up to. The "feesh in the sea" discussion always had the preamble of "no hurry — you have lottsa time." For his part, he let the discussion hang there. She knew nothing of Freta other than he had met a female RCMP officer because of an "incident" at the college.

Most of the time they talked about what was happening at home. Usually, the same old, same old, which translated into "not much." His younger brother was always mentioned. Andrew had become the tech guy of the family, graduating with a computer technology diploma from a college in Scarborough. Now he was gainfully employed by an insurance company and living and working in Toronto. Their father, Bohdan, on the other hand, was barely brought up. He rarely came to the phone. Myron suspected he was getting happily corked in the garage while Mother talked and that the timing of her calls was quite deliberate.

These days his mother was fairly upbeat, even when she mentioned her husband. To her, Bohdan had become a deadbeat over the years. It troubled and strained family relations. As she once said, "Alcohol has peekled his brain." Then with a shrug, "But vhat can you do."

Marta did what she had to do, as it turned out. First, she got a job at a furniture factory, then she obtained a driver's licence and bought a car. Thus, over time she became independent, and now, thirty-seven years after arriving in the country as a displaced person, she was in control. Life might not always be tranquil, but for her it became much better.

Underlining her phone calls were two questions: "Are you all right?" and "When do you vant me to veesit?" Myron appreciated her concerns and had a stock answer. All was well and she could come to Alberta sometime in the spring, but for now ... he'd be home for Christmas. That seemed to satisfy her.

\*\*\*

Myron often felt at loose ends on weekends. This one was no exception. Once the semester got into full swing, he would firm up his routine: morning coffee and big breakfast in a proper diner with the weekend edition of the *Globe and Mail* to peruse if he had time or a coffee and muffin at Robin's if not. Then he'd make his way to the college, work out at the gym, and mark papers.

This Saturday morning, he settled for a coffee and toast at home, a grocery shopping trip to IGA, and some pipe tobacco at Sam's Place, a downtown magazine and smoke shop that carried a wide assortment of brands and accessories like cherry wood filters for his Brigham pipes.

Meanwhile, he still had half the morning and the rest of the afternoon to kill. He needed to keep himself occupied until the CBS Saturday Night Movie could distract him in the evening.

Although cool, the day was shaping up to be pleasant enough and would only get warmer as the sun rose higher. Thus, he decided to go down to Saskatoon Berry Park, one of Great Plains's more attractive recreational areas, and take a long walk along the Creek Bottom Trail that practically wound its way around the city. There, a stream that cut through the park enlarged (man-made) into a sizable pond beside the newly built chateau-style pavilion and administrative centre. In the winter, the pond was cleared of snow and became of hub of activity as a public skating area. The stream funnelled from the large reservoir just to the east of the college grounds. The amount of water flow depended on the small dam/walking bridge at the southern end of the reservoir. Today, Myron noted, that the foamy flow, mostly because of the runoff from farmers' fields, was moderate.

He could have driven home and parked his car, followed the trampled path into the valley, and intersected the trail near the pavilion. However, if he did, he'd want to take the groceries out and put them away and, in the process, decide that he didn't feel like a constitutional. Instead, he drove directly to the pavilion, angle-parked his car, got out, zipped up his jacket, breathed in the cool, fresh air, and started walking. The groceries would keep in the car just fine.

On his return from a brisk one-hour jaunt that took him to the south side of the city, he experienced his third coincidence of the week, or so it seemed to him: Hans at the coffee shop, Isaac in the washroom, and now Alexandra at the pavilion. He wasn't sure why he connected her with the first two. All were happenstance, he presumed. He literally almost ran into his student as he was going into the pavilion to use the facilities.

"Oh!" she exclaimed. "So nice to see you."

She was wearing a tight-fitting red plaid jacket and a matching tartan cap with red bob on top. Her jeans were even tighter, ending in ankle hiking shoes. She could have been a poster child for fashionable outdoor ladies' attire as far as Myron was concerned. Not disagreeable at all.

"Hello, Alexandra." Suddenly he had little else to say, as if his tongue was out of sync with thoughts that he could not quite capture.

She took up the slack. "I see you've come out for some fresh air as well."

"Just finished, in fact," he said quickly. "Very pleasant — making my last pit stop." He didn't know why he added that last part.

"I was about to start, but if you were getting a coffee," she gestured to the coffee kiosk inside the pavilion.

"I'd love to, but I'm running late. I said I would meet a friend downtown," he lied. The only activity on the schedule was a sketchy promise to himself to clean his apartment.

On the other hand, he didn't want to be standoffish and rebuff her. It wasn't like he was going to unduly fraternize with his student. Common courtesy dictated a more positive response!

After a brief hesitation, he said, "What the heck! I've got time for a quick coffee."

He bought two coffees, and they sat at a small table overlooking the pond. There were a few parents and kids about, as well as dogs and presumably their owners. A number of cyclists were gathering around a picnic table.

For a few moments they chatted about how great the park and pathways were and what a family-friendly place the community was before moving on to more personal space.

"You mentioned that you were new in town?" Myron asked.

"Well, yes and no," she answered. "I'm actually from here, grew up, went to school in town but have been living in Edmonton for most of my working life. This is a homecoming of sorts."

"You mentioned that you were a stewardess for Time Air."

"True, I was. Enjoyed most of it, but after a little while…" She shrugged. "I needed something else, a change or more a challenge perhaps, and so…" She smiled and gave him a reflective gaze.

"You decided to come back to the college and enrol in the education program." *As opposed to a university or a larger institution in Edmonton?* "You didn't want to stay in Edmonton?"

"I wasn't homesick, if that's what you mean. There were extenuating circumstances," she added with what sounded to Myron a tinge of regret.

Having dropped that morsel of information, Alexandra changed the subject. "What about you? How long have you been at the college?"

"Not that long — four … almost five years thereabouts." Myron had lost count, and the last couple of years had been a whirlwind for him.

"Obviously you're not from this area?"

"No, in fact, very few instructors are. We come from all across the country and abroad, even Ontario, in my case. Nature of the profession."

"And you came here because?"

"Like most, for the job. I did a two-year stint as a sessional lecturer at the University of Edmonton. My time ran out. There was an opening here. I applied, and the rest is history, as they say."

She tilted her head forward and moved closer across the table as if to have a more confidential conservation, but he, perhaps subconsciously, with a touch of apprehension glanced down at his watch. She drew back. He didn't mean it as a hint, but she took it as such.

"Oh sorry, I'm keeping you from your appointment."

"No … no. It wasn't an appointment really."

"Actually, I better get a move on as well if I'm going to hike. It's a lovely day after all that rain, and I should make the most of it. Thanks for the coffee."

During his drive home, Myron felt some unease but couldn't quite put his finger on it. Certainly, Alexandra was putting out vibes, and he didn't want to step on any mushy madness from which to extricate himself. He wouldn't allow that to occur — simple as that. Besides, it was only his paranoid mind at work, still heavily invested in a post-mortem of a failed marriage, that made him … uneasy. His immediate happy place centred on Freta, and he was not about to let Alexandra become a distraction.

***

Sunday brought some measure of relief from Myron's growing restlessness, verging on boredom. Freta called him around 9:00 a.m., suggesting that he take her out for a Sunday brunch. "The Great Plains Inn would do nicely," she informed him.

"I'd be delighted," he said. "Swing by your door around eleven?"

"Great!"

The Great Plains Inn served a pretty swank brunch buffet that allowed for everything from eggs Benedict to exotic waffles. Myron stuck closely to basics: bacon, eggs, and toast with the eggs done so hard, they had to bounce! He hated runny eggs; it made for such a messy plate. Freta was slightly more extravagant in her choices but was satisfied with eggs Benedict, a croissant, and a fruit plate. The hotel restaurant was not very busy when they arrived, and they were directed to a cozy table in a corner with a ledge where rested a large palm plant of some sort.

It wasn't until their second cup of coffee that they talked shop.

"So, there's no news on any front?" Myron asked, finishing up the last of his toast and marmalade.

"Nothing significant. Rob and the search team are still out there. It's getting bleak, though; they should have found Raglan by now or some evidence of where she has gone. But nothing, nada… The rain has let up, so maybe that'll help with the dogs. Everyone is in a foul mood and getting impatient. If nothing comes up by the end of Tuesday, Rob is ready to take Trovotka's place apart — no matter how irrational that sounds."

"Speaking of which," Myron interjected, "odd thing during the break at my Thursday night class. I ran into Isaac Trovotka."

"Really? I didn't know he went to college?"

"I'm not sure he does. When I asked, he became nervous and noncommittal, if not evasive. But that's not the interesting part. He looked like a Mack truck had run into him — bloody nose, cut lip … was trying to clean himself up in the men's can."

Freta frowned. "Did he say what happened?"

"Said he tripped in the parking lot."

"And?"

"That's it! To paraphrase: he planted his face into the pavement. Seemed a bit rattled when he saw me."

"Hmm… Probably thinks you're a cop," Freta said, popping a sliced melon into her mouth.

"Well, I didn't dissuade him from that notion … neither did you at the homestead, commune, whatever they call it — neither the son or the father, although Hans knows better now. He ferreted that out quickly at the coffee shop."

"Yeah. He would have gotten suspicious and wondered who you were from our visit."

"At any rate, Isaac didn't stick around very long after meeting me. Made his escape *tout de suite*. And I had to go back to class."

"I wonder if he had an altercation with someone?"

"If he did, he certainly wasn't saying who … speaking of which, tell me about the Major Crimes detective. What's he like?"

"For one thing, he turns out to be a she, Roberta LeBlanc, and I like her. She's good. Enjoyed working with her."

"Did you crack the case?"

"Hardly." Freta lowered her voice, although no one was within earshot. "One realtor is still missing, and the other has lawyered up — no less than Jack Hoar, who sits on the college board of boards, if I remember correctly."

Myron nodded. "So what does this mean?"

"Well, we don't have enough to hold Croft at this point, so we're waiting for more from forensics, and starting Tuesday we'll be conducting interviews — Mrs. Boyd again, the office secretary again, and a list of close associates of both Boyd and Croft. Then we'll take another run at Croft, hopefully with more forensics on our side. We'll need it without a body, especially since, according to Croft, Boyd embezzled sizable client and company funds. He intimated that his partner may have flown the coop, leaving him holding the bag."

"Do you believe him?"

"Don't know… Need an audit of company books to verify, which, of course, will take a little time. Meanwhile, it's a plausible defence."

"Well, good luck."

"Yeah, we'll need it."

# Chapter Twelve

**Monday, August 19**

"Mr. Croft?" The voice sounded muted.

"Yes."

There was a hesitation, then, "Mr. Croft."

"Yes, yes, speaking."

"I know what you did." The voice became more confident, assertive.

"Pardon?"

"I know what you did at the Grotto Road cemetery — I saw you."

"What!" Croft rose from his chair and took a peek into the hallway of his open office door. "I don't know what you're talking about."

"Oh yes, you do, and I will tell." The muffled tone rose slightly. It was as if someone was talking with a stocking pulled over his head. Croft had the absurd image of a bank robber.

"Hang on a sec…"

He laid the receiver down, walked across the room, and closed his door.

Back at his desk, he lifted the receiver and expelled enough air to inflate a balloon. "I don't know what you saw or think you saw—"

"Yes, you do, and you have a choice."

"Choice?"

"Bring a duffel bag with $10,000 cash to the grotto. Place it in the trash can nearest to the statue. Six. Wednesday evening. Come alone. Don't hang around. You'll be watched. If you don't come, the police will know."

"I don't—"

"Six p.m. Wednesday."

The phone clicked and reverted to a dial tone as Croft stared at the receiver.

Croft sat down in shock. *What the fuck. How can this be? He saw me? There was barely any light. There was no one out there. And yet he knew where — the old cemetery at the end of Grotto Road. This is insane. Call his bluff! No, stop … get a grip … think. What to do?*

Croft started to pace. Certainly, he could get the money, but that would be an invitation to blackmail ad nauseam. Go to the police? Admit what he had done? *I'm being blackmailed because someone saw me bury a body.* If he did that, even if he had a very good lawyer, it was still manslaughter and undoubtedly serious jail time. Get out of Dodge. And go where? He could try to find the blackmailer. Then, do what?

Ten thousand big ones; he sighed, resigned. Easily obtained on short notice, but it would only be the beginning. Of that, he was sure.

*\*\*\**

Isaac was pleased with himself. He laid it out, short and sweet, not giving Croft a chance to protest too much or make excuses. He even gave him a couple of days to get the money — smart. And Croft would comply. What choice did he have?

It was a cool but pleasant day, with a few wispy clouds in a high Alberta sky. Winter, though, was not that far off; he could feel it in the air as he emerged from the telephone booth, stretched, and put away the oily rag he used to cover the mouthpiece of the receiver. He smiled; truly he had done good.

He knew that he should now go back to the homestead, lay low, let events play out. Not yet, he decided. Besides, lately each passing day became more and more stifling, what with the old man hovering nearby all the time waiting for him to what — bare his soul?

Hans was a suspicious sort. "And so he should be." Isaac chuckled, climbing into the truck. If he knew what his son was really up to or what he had done… *Well, me and the Man Upstairs will have a real reckoning,* mused Isaac as he twisted the key in the ignition. The motor roared to life.

He would have appreciated his status of the "special one" if his father and his mother, who always seemed to be wringing her hands somewhere in the wake of her husband's shadow, just realize that he *was* special, not because he was slow or a retard but because he was smart! And now with unexpected income!

To celebrate, he decided to grab a bite to eat and cruise around town for a while. Later, when darkness settled in, maybe he'd find someone to celebrate with. He had to be careful, though; the last pickup turned out badly. If only she had stayed quiet…

Raglan didn't count because that was more or less an accident, or at least he didn't mean it to happen quite that way. She ran; he overreacted. No matter…

The old man was right about one thing: women were temptresses who needed to know their place.

✳✳✳

Hans was anxious and frustrated. His son had become uncommunicative, and dare he say it, deceitful. Certainly, Isaac didn't simply fall over a log and sustain that kind of damage to his face — and elsewhere, for all he knew. (He did seem to walk rather gingerly, as if in pain.) He was too familiar with the woods to be so careless or inept. His explanation just didn't ring true. Nor did a number of others, including his frequent trips to Great Plains. What did he find so alluring there?

More to the point, the girl was still missing. Hans didn't know why he juxtaposed Isaac's behaviour with her disappearance, but he couldn't seem to shake it from his thoughts. The question kept re-emerging: Did Isaac know anything, or was he hiding something? That shack: its purpose? Why build it? Most importantly, Hans realized, what was inside? *I need to do a thorough search in there before the police do,* Hans told himself. It wasn't that he thought Isaac did something bad; he couldn't allow himself to conclude that simply because, at the moment, the lad didn't want to talk to him. Still, better be safe; better be sure, he decided. After all, he did find the keychain with keys to a Ford 150. Who did those belong to? Were there other items scattered about for cops to find?

His thoughts went back to his encounter with Isaac earlier in the day. When he tried to approach his son, Isaac jumped into his truck and said they'd talk later. "Got to go to town." And with that he closed the cab door and sped away, leaving Hans shaking his head.

This was no way for a son to treat his dad, disregarding basic teachings of the scriptures. Honour thy father — or at least obey him. He needed to put a firm hand down and set his son straight, but first he had to protect him, and that meant getting into his shack.

The lock was easy to pick. Darkness spilled out as he pried open the door. Taking the flashlight from his coat pocket, he brought it to bear, a wide sweep of light in a confined space. It was as he saw it, however briefly, the week before. Of course, back then he hadn't gotten past the doorway. A couple of hanging pelts (he wasn't sure what that was about); old work clothes attached to a hook on the far wall with a pair of well-worn boots underneath and a rolled up sleeping bag in the corner. In the centre was a wooden stool. There was a strong smell of rancid meat and something fainter — paraffin wax, maybe, mixed with stinky feet? Hans shook his head. Not only was the structure ill conceived, shoddily constructed, and in a bad location, but it appeared to serve no real function.

"Might as well get on with it," he muttered grimly. *Make a careful inspection and close it up.* Isaac would never know he'd been there.

It didn't take long after Hans spotted a slight depression radiating out from the western corner of the wall. It looked like some sizable animal had lain there for some time — or a body. Hans winced as the thought slipped out. On his haunches, he carefully inspected the indentation, and there in the mud, under some matted vegetation, he spied it, and his heart sank.

# Chapter Thirteen

Myron liked to use maps in his classes as a "show and tell," particularly if those maps were large and colourful and could easily be hung over the blackboard or on an adjacent wall. So he came prepared for his Monday morning pre-Confederation Canadian history class with Map F7: "Original Inhabitants and the Routes of Explorers to 1650." It was the perfect segue prop after his Canadian history and geography lectures the week before. Time to identify and give a sense of locale to the Indigenous peoples before the arrival of the Europeans.

Map F7 was especially helpful, since it divided the original peoples into eleven linguistic families (those with similar language roots), six of which, he noted, inhabited, oddly enough, the coast and interior of B.C.: Tsimshian, Wakashan, Haida, Kootenay, Tlinkit, and Salish. He said the names quickly (or he'd stumble over the pronunciations) as he pointed out their colour-coded territorial boundaries on the map.

The lecture proper, however, began on the east coast — Newfoundland, to be exact — with the Beothuk nation, the first northern peoples to come into contact with the Europeans. Briefly, he related their sad story of essentially being driven into the interior and disappearing completely in the nineteenth century, with the last Beothuk dying (as far as could be gleaned from the records) in 1829!

Myron chronicled the Beothuk demise because it riveted students' attention. Most them had no idea that a whole distinctive linguistic and cultural population had basically been annihilated.

Next, Myron moved on to the Inuit and Algonkians, covering a huge number of tribes that extended from the Mi'kmaq in the east to the Plains Cree and Ojibwas on the prairies. This was followed by the Huron–Iroquois, consisting of a number of Huron tribes and the five members of the Iroquois Confederacy. They may have been old trading enemies and fought fiercely with each other, but they had come from the same linguistic stock, understood each other, and, unlike the nomadic Algonkian hunters, set up semipermanent residences, cultivating corn, pumpkin, and tobacco.

Finally, and closer to home, a large brown splash across the map from Hudson Bay across the Mackenzie River valley and into the Rockies, were the Athabaskan language group of tribes, who spoke what some scholars concluded was a language similar to Tibetan-Chinese. Myron was skeptical of the claim, but it was quoted in the literature, and he mentioned it because it piqued interest, especially since Great Plains and environs was in the heart of Athabaskan ancestral lands. Students tended to be impressed by poignant facts that hit close to home.

After making his cursory survey across the continent, Myron returned to the Huron–Iroquois since, as he explained, from the date of Jacques Cartier's first voyage up the St. Lawrence in 1534, the histories of the Huron–Iroquois and Europeans would be inextricably connected.

Myron noted with satisfaction that he had managed to retain everybody's attention, although Alexandra seemed to be focused on him rather than the subject matter. She kept giving him coy looks — nothing particularly untoward but distracting and a bit uncomfortable. Hopefully, it wouldn't escalate into a problem. But why should it?

Under different circumstances, he might even reciprocate! After all, she was a pleasant, mature woman showing an interest, he guessed. However, there were at least two mitigating factors in play. First, he already had a beautiful, mature, pleasant lady with whom he was exploring a relationship. And second, it would create an ethical issue in terms of instructor-student involvement. Alexandra needed either to drop her courses with him or wait until the semester was over.

Alexandra, Myron decided, was a prime example of why a number of male profs followed an unofficial protocol: keep your office door open when you're with a female student.

***

No sooner had Myron gotten to his third-floor office when Ted appeared, striding toward him from the opposite direction.

"I'm boring. My students are boring," he lamented as Myron opened his door.

"What are you trying to say?" Myron asked, sticking his rolled-up map in the corner and setting his lecture notes on the desk.

"Maybe I should have a prop, like that map of yours. I don't know. I had a pretty anaemic group of pupils today. You'd think they didn't appreciate Canadian tax law!"

"Uh-huh." Myron dropped into his chair. Ted followed suit into the visitor's. "Wonders never cease."

"Even college politics is boring," continued Ted, ignoring his colleague's snide remark.

"It's only our second week into the semester. Give it time."

"Meanwhile, let me in on your investigation."

"What investigation?"

"The case of the missing student."

"Ted, I'm not involved."

"Unofficially."

"Officially or unofficially. I'm Myron Q Citizen who happens to know an RCMP officer — that's it!"

"A little better than know," Ted interjected.

"Okay… Know well a policewoman. That doesn't mean I'm privy to any cases."

"I was there, remember? When you had a hushed tête-à-tête with old Hans in the parking lot. What was that really about?"

*Got me there,* thought Myron, wincing at the thought.

"He saw me staring at him and thought he recognized me from somewhere. That's all."

"I stared at him too!"

"Ted…"

"You and I would make a good team," he said abruptly, "like Starsky and Hutch. We've already had some adventures together."

*More like Mutt and Jeff,* but Myron didn't say it.

The only adventure that came readily to mind had occurred at least a couple of years before when Ted asked him to come along for a scenic ride to the Banff School of Fine Arts. There was a commerce conference, and Ted registered as part of a PD opportunity.

"It's a quickie," he explained. "Saturday to mid-Sunday. In and out. On the road by 4:00 p.m. Stay in my room, enjoy the great outdoors while I listen to bean counters."

Ted was persistent, Myron said yes, and off they drove in Ted's little red Honda Civic.

It was autumn, Myron remembered, and a layer of snow salted the ground. Sessions finished in good time that Saturday, and Ted felt cramped and restless. Myron suggested, perhaps too ambitiously, that they ascend Sulphur Mountain along a well used, not too steep path that would take them to the cosmic ray station at the top.

"And no, it's not the home of the Fantastic Four," Myron mused, "but a national historic site park with plaques and interpretative displays commemorating Canada's contribution to high-altitude studies in the late fifties. We'll walk around and take the gondola down."

"Sounds good to me," Ted said. "Cosmic rays, eh — from outer space. Didn't they give those comic book characters their superpowers?"

"Actually, Stan Lee did," Myron replied.

The subject was left there, and they made good progress until about halfway up. Suddenly, compelled by some primal force, Myron vigorously whirled around 180 degrees — the proverbial sixth sense violently kicking in — only to be confronted by an elk, which abruptly halted her charge about a metre from where they stood. Myron's unexpected action had broken her run.

"What the h–elk," Myron exclaimed with unabashed alarm.

There was no doubt that the wapiti facing them was malevolent and could inflict harm. The animal's head was raised high, ears pinned back, nostrils flared. Rivers of jagged red ran through her wide, angry eyes. What really got their attention, though, was the tight, crooked mouth foaming froth between the hisses.

"What do we do?" Myron whispered to his friend.

"I dunno," he replied, exhibiting a calm that belied prospects for a happy resolution.

Fortunately, it seemed that the copper-coloured elk with dark intentions was as stupefied as they were.

Awkward seconds passed — a forever tick of time. All parties remained motionless, caught in a stare down.

Finally, by some innate telepathic ingestion, Myron figured, they choreographed themselves toward a giant pine, doing their best Charlie Chaplin shuffle, hoping not to ruffle the agitated beast. Once behind the tree, they grew measurably bolder, threw snowballs in her direction, and yelled a warning to other trail users.

After a further contemplative pause, the elk appeared satisfied that they posed no overt threat. With a final percussive snort, she turned and hoofed it back up the mountain.

"I don't know why that elk was so belligerent," said Ted as they resumed their trek. "Protecting her offspring? Bad day at the rut? Or maybe she just didn't like our looks!"

"Or," Myron said, some levity coming back, "it was those cosmic rays that made her crazy, and she thought we were aliens invading her domain. But with no field guide on the effects of cosmic rays on elk, we'll never know."

Myron supposed that that counted as an adventure, and indeed it was, but he couldn't envision Ted being an investigative partner — informant yes, amateur sleuth, no.

The phone rang, monetarily jarring them both. It was Freta.

Ted heaved himself out of the chair. "Got to go, prepare for boring students part *deux*."

"I'll catch you later," Myron said as he picked up the receiver. "Maybe go for a walk."

"Myron, I caught you." Freta sounded breathless.

"You sure did."

"Well, that's good… Want to go out tonight to a fine, upscale eatery? And I don't mean a club house at Zellers."

"Wow. Two days in a row."

"Like you to meet Roberta. I'm showing her around town later and thought we'd have dinner — say seven. What's a good spot?"

"Let me think, since the Zellers restaurant has been ruled out. How about The Province — fairly high-end, judging from their prices. I presume the force is paying?"

"The Province will do nicely."

"Great!"

"So, we'll meet you at the front doors, seven sharp, and oh … no, I repeat, no police shop talk."

"Got it."

\*\*\*

Myron had just parked and was making his way around the corner to the front of the restaurant when he literally ran into Alexandra.

"Oh," she exclaimed.

"Sorry," he said, gathering himself. *This is getting really weird.*

"Gracious. We seem to be bumping into each other constantly."

"It does seem that way, doesn't it?" He laughed nervously. *And why is that?* he wondered. The coincidences were piling up.

Before any further awkward pleasantries ensued, he spotted Freta and, presumably, Roberta walking toward them. The older woman had a smartly tailored suit and low black pumps. Freta, too, had freshened up and looked good in a similar combination of jacket, shirt, trousers, and shiny shoes. They could have been mistaken for mother and daughter. *Well, not quite. An unfair comparison to Freta!* Myron cleared his head and refocused.

"Hello!" He waved.

Alexandra turned in the direction of his gaze, her eyes turning cold, her smile frozen.

Freta waved back, giving him a cheery grin.

"Myron, this is De — Roberta LeBlanc."

"Pleased to meet you." He shook Roberta's hand, noting that her fingers were short, with no adornments of any kind. She had a no-nonsense grip.

"Likewise."

"Oh ... sorry. I'd like you to meet Alexandra; she takes a number of courses from me at the college. Freta and Roberta," Myron added redundantly.

Freta nodded. Alexandra looked at her blankly, the smile frozen in place.

"Pleasure," said Roberta, regarding her rather intently. "Have we met before? Your face does look familiar."

"No, I don't think so," responded Alexandra, her voice stiffening to a sharp staccato. Then, abruptly, she said, "I've got to go. See you in class, Dr. Tarasyn."

With that she turned and walked away.

Roberta frowned, distracted, her eyes singeing the back of Alexandra's head.

"Small world and all that," she remarked, "but I'm pretty sure I have seen Alexandra before. It'll come to me... However, right now, I'm famished. Shall we proceed?"

"By all means." Myron opened the door and allowed the ladies through.

"Remember," Freta whispered as she passed by. "Absolutely no shop talk!"

"Right."

# Chapter Fourteen

**Tuesday, August 20**

The next day in the detachment office, Detective LeBlanc and Freta were sorting their respective paperwork. LeBlanc formulated her questions for Croft's interview that afternoon while poring over the latest forensics while Freta read her original notes and the notes from re-interviews she conducted with Helen Boyd and Marcy Bergh, Atop Realty's secretary. Croft's office door was closed while she was there, but she saw his parked Jeep. No doubt he was in there taking care of business or hiding. She wouldn't have questioned him anyway. Whole different ball game with lawyers involved. She wondered briefly if Croft would be accompanied by Jack Hoar or whether there'd be a specialist from the Hoar, Michet, Barsky & Partners law firm. Meanwhile, she was putting together a list of other close associates of Boyd's who might shed some light on his disappearance.

Once they had gotten their coffees, settled into their respective chairs, and finished chit-chatting about the pleasant dinner they had enjoyed — good food, good wine, and good company was Roberta's assessment, remarking that Myron seemed a "good sort" — the RCMP detective turned to another subject. "The person we met last night. I thought I recognized her."

Freta looked up, puzzled. "You mean in front of the restaurant?"

"Yes. What was her name again?"

"Alexandra, I believe Myron said."

"And she is in Myron's class at the college?"

"At least a couple of them, he mentioned."

"Alexandra…" She rolled the name out. "Yes. That was Alexandra. I do know her, or more precisely of her." Roberta leaned back in the chair.

"Oh?"

"She was a stewardess for a regional carrier working out of the downtown airport in Edmonton. Got herself into a real jam, as I recall."

"Okay … now I'm interested," Freta said, putting her pen down and leaning forward onto her desk. The two were facing each other.

"Well, the incident made a brief but spectacular splash in the dailies: then it went away — hushed up, I suppose — lucky for her."

"What'd she do?"

"I don't have all the details. No doubt they're buried in the files somewhere, but she, quote unquote, violently attacked a rather prominent major league sports figure. A hockey player, I think. I don't do sports myself."

"What?" Freta was still processing the "violent attack" part.

"I wasn't the lead investigator. Came in at the tail end to finish the paperwork. Didn't matter. As sometimes happens, the Crown attorney decided to drop the case. No charges were laid."

"So why were no charges laid if this was some sort of violent assault?"

"As I say, she was fortunate — extremely fortunate."

"Still begs the question. Why was she not charged if it was a serious incident?"

"Not due to a lack of evidence!" LeBlanc stated emphatically. "The hockey player, I'm pretty sure he was well known, although I can't remember his name…" The detective paused. "At any rate, he decided not to press charges. I suspect their affair was messy, and the publicity wasn't doing much for his career — or his marriage," she wryly added with a whiff of a smile.

Freta managed to keep her mouth from completely dropping. "The case was just closed?"

"Crown's prerogative," LeBlanc confirmed. "I think the lady has some serious psychological issues to resolve, not that the guy she attacked was a stable genius himself, I suspect. I only had a cursory glance at the file before the case was shut down, so..."

"Was he badly hurt?"

"Fortunately not. A few wild slashes across the arms with a kitchen knife. Again, a bit of luck. Saw her coming just in time to defend himself as best he could."

"That's unbelievable. Was there any assessment done of her mental state?"

"A preliminary one with inconclusive results but no follow-up. I can only hope that's behind her now, a one-off episode. Surprised she's here and going to college."

"Her behaviour and resulting publicity probably didn't do her career prospects much good. Maybe that's why she's here and at the college."

LeBlanc took a gulp of her coffee and wrinkled her nose. "You could be right. Fresh start and all that. She may have been fired or quit or just took a sabbatical. Can only wish her well in her studies and getting her life in order. Maybe she already has."

"Maybe..." Freta answered doubtfully. In her experience, rarely were such incidents one-offs. She suspected Roberta knew that all too well but chose to be optimistic.

Before Freta could press the matter any further, Superintendent Matthew Reuben came striding in. "Just got off the phone with Corporal Rainy. There's been a development. A body has been found."

"What?" Roberta and Freta exclaimed, almost in unison.

"Where?" asked Freta.

"At the old cemetery, end of Grotto Road."

"Oh, no..." Freta had a bad feeling, given the location.

"No identification yet, but it is female. K9 unit came upon it. Remains were buried in a shallow grave dug over an existing grave."

"A homicide then?" LeBlanc asked.

"At the very least foul play."

"So potentially we have two major crime cases here," LeBlanc confirmed.

Reuben nodded. "Could be. You may be investigating two separate cases. But now there's a body — at least for one."

"We better get out there then."

"Keep me posted," Reuben said, turning toward his office.

"Oh…" LeBlanc pursed her lips. "We're probably in for a long day. We had an interview scheduled with Mr. Croft—"

"Say no more. I'll reschedule it," Reuben said over his shoulder.

"Thanks."

\*\*\*

When Freta and Roberta arrived, the crime scene was still in the throes of organized chaos. A forensic tent had been erected, and individuals in white hazmat suits flitted about. Corporal Rainy met them on the periphery on the other side of the taped-off zone. He handed them latex gloves and blue shoe coverings.

"So…" said LeBlanc, taking the lead. "What do we have?"

"Still need positive ID, but it looks like Raglan Bullock, the missing college student."

"Any indication of what happened to her?"

"Not at this point. They're just completing the excavation around her. Coroner hasn't had a good look yet. We were lucky to have found her. The downpour stifled the dogs but also partially exposed the body. Very shallow grave. Thank God the wildlife had not gotten to her."

"Well, let's have a look."

Rob Rainy nodded and led LeBlanc and Freta inside the tent. Two forensic Ident officials were working carefully around the body. One was on his haunches, scraping away mud and debris, collecting and bagging potential evidence. The other was taking photographs from every conceivable position.

There wasn't much to see: a prostrate human form, clothing spattered and caked with mud, her hair plastered in long strands across her blackened face, the head resting at an odd angle. Freta turned away, thankful that at least the eyes were closed.

"We found this." The man huddled beside the body handed a plastic bag to Rainy, who gave it to LeBlanc. Freta swivelled to face them and cleared her throat. "This is Detective LeBlanc of Major Crimes. She is now in charge of this investigation."

The small man looked up and nodded, then went back to his grim business.

"Looks like a piece of torn clothing with a button still attached," LeBlanc observed, raising the bag up to better lighting.

"It was found clutched in her right hand," the man offered.

"Possibly the victim ripped it from her assailant," Freta ventured.

"Possibly," said LeBlanc, still studying it. "Looks like it's from an old work jacket. We need to get this checked out for prints ASAP." She then gave the bag back to Rainy, who was in charge of establishing a chain of custody. "Do we have an idea of how long she has been dead?"

"Not precisely, but the coroner, who was here a few moments ago," Rainy took a quick glance around, "believes almost a week."

"About the time Raglan went missing then," said Freta.

"Yeah, about that," agreed Rainy.

LeBlanc focused on the weathered tombstone for a moment: *Theodore Polanski 1896–1931.* "Buried on top of an existing grave." She pondered that. "What made him/her/them think of that?"

"Convenience," theorized Rainy. "Ground is softer here with less vegetation, of course, and it would have been made so by the act of digging…" The logic, even as he said it, Rainy realized, crumbled onto itself. He pushed on. "Good place to hide a body — who would look for a body at a gravesite?"

A twisted smile appeared on LeBlanc's face. "It's a Catholic cemetery, right?"

"Old Polish settlement — Catholic to the core," affirmed Rainy.

"Well, I wouldn't read too much into this. You're no doubt right. It was a convenient spot and quite clever. Poor soul underneath is probably spinning in his portion of the consecrated ground."

"So we started with two missing persons," LeBlanc said, taking one last glance at the corpse before moving toward the tent opening.

There really wasn't much to do until the coroner and the forensic team finished processing. "One has definitely been found — certainly no accident — people don't go burying themselves. And the other, my actual case, where there's a potential suspect but no body! Right ... we have to give this one priority — for now. Agreed?"

"Yes," said Freta. Rainy nodded.

"Okay... Who lives around here?"

"Hans Trovotka and his commune members," said Rainy. "His property is adjacent to this area. And Mr. Trovotka has had run-ins with the law before, although nothing like this," he added.

"I've heard of Trovotka. Ecoterrorist, is he?" said LeBlanc.

"Nothing was proven," said Freta. "We executed a search warrant a while back, looking for dynamite and bomb-making materials on his property. Found nothing."

"Well, this is a totally different matter. Tomorrow you and I will be knocking on Mr. Trovotka's door. Hopefully by tomorrow morning we'll have a clearer picture of how Raglan died."

"Still need a positive identification," Rainy reminded the detective.

"Right ... contact the parents ... sad business." LeBlanc sighed. "Sad business indeed."

\*\*\*

Freta hadn't phoned Myron all day. She thought she'd get a hold of him when she got home, but she was exhausted and didn't really have the energy to talk. All she wanted was a hot shower and sleep. She'd catch up with him Wednesday night as usual.

Never mind that she had much to tell. Not only the tragic news regarding Raglan, which, no doubt, he would learn soon enough — the media would be all over it, if it wasn't already — but also the disturbing backstory about his student. Maybe Roberta was right and Alexandra was rehabilitated and getting on with her life. Nevertheless, being forewarned is forearmed... *I'm being a bit melodramatic,* she decided, running her shower.

Tomorrow she'd be in especially early. LeBlanc had a list of items for her to cover. Here was her opportunity to work a major crime case officially, and she looked forward to it despite some unease and trepidation that she might not be up to the task and/or somehow screw it up.

An old anxiety and part of her baggage growing up, she supposed. Not knowing her real parents or why she was abandoned, and initially being bounced around the social services system in Saskatchewan did little to instil confidence. Finding her way into a stable, loving home brought comfort and security, but occasionally she faltered and had doubts.

Successfully completing her RCMP training and the subsequent upward mobility through the ranks toughened her mentally and bolstered her resolve. *I can do this* had been her mantra. There were obstacles, particularly for females, but she ignored the sexual innuendoes and avoided the more nefarious attempts to compromise or be compromised in a chauvinist male-dominated environment. She emerged mostly intact.

There had been some hiccups along the way, including a bad relationship with a fellow RCMP graduate who, thankfully was now stationed somewhere out in the Maritimes, about as far away as he could be. He was not one of her better choices.

She had survived that, too, and in some respects thrived to the point where Reuben thought she had been overconfident and presumptive in handling what he called "the college case." "You got to play it by the book. Major Crimes should have been brought in immediately," he'd admonished her.

Ironically, her "overconfidence" was now being rewarded with this assignment, and she didn't want to blow it. In fact, she saw it as the beginning of a potential move into the ranks of detective. Despite an undeniable curmudgeonly streak in LeBlanc's makeup, Freta liked her, and their rapport was relaxed, as if they had been partners for years. She needed to acquit herself well.

Freta sighed, staring at the ceiling. She thought she'd fall asleep as soon as her head hit the pillow. No such luck. Her brain was overstimulated, and she tossed and turned into the morning hours with the last image that of the grave and body indelibly caught like the forensic photographer's snap shots in her mind's eye. She hoped that Roberta was sleeping better, ensconced at the Great Plains Inn, one of the city's finer hotels.

# Chapter Fifteen

**Wednesday, August 21**

Roberta and Freta were in the detachment office early; Freta had much to do, including sifting through numerous preliminary reports while the detective met behind closed doors with Reuben. As a consequence, it was after eleven before they could head out of town to Trovotka's property.

Roberta filled Freta in on her meeting with Reuben. "I requested additional help. It's official; as of this morning, Corporal Rainy has been assigned to our team."

"Good," said Freta. She liked the sound of "our team." "He deserves to be."

"The superintendent thought so too. And it's appropriate, since technically it's his case and he took the lead with the search operations. Anyway, the coroner — sorry what's his name? He mumbled it quickly over the phone, but I didn't quite catch it…"

"Backie, Dr. Roman Backie."

"Right. According to him, Raglan died of a broken neck. And he thought it unlikely that it was the result of some sort of fall, although he couldn't rule it out. A clear snap. So … suspicious to say the least. That means we start at the beginning."

"Which is?" Freta asked as she wheeled the Crown Vic onto the main highway that took them northwest into the hinterland and the God's Light Commune.

"Already got Corporal Rainy on it. Going over the original statements of Ms. Bullock's companions who were out in the bush, and doing so in excruciating detail. Corporal Rainy might not believe it, but they cannot be discounted as suspects. Who's to say? Any one of them, or collectively they could be responsible. You know a party that got out of hand; a fight with her boyfriend, Kyle Burnam, perhaps. Corporal Rainy told me that he either lost or Raglan took his truck keys. There's no mention of keys in the forensic reports. I know it's early days, but still, a loose detail. Could be he had an extra key and took her to the cemetery. Or maybe his buddy, George, used his truck. Kyle could have got his friends to help him."

"You mean everyone was in on it?" A group cover-up for whatever went down?" Freta asked incredulously, taking a glance over at Roberta, who stifled a yawn. Apparently, she hadn't slept that well either.

"I know, I know … wild speculation. But we need to think out of the box, and while Corporal Rainy is highly skeptical, it just can't be ruled out! That's why at this moment he's preparing the necessary paperwork to impound the vehicles. If either was used to transfer Raglan to that gravesite, there might be fibre and/or soil samples. A long shot, but part of due diligence."

"I suppose that's true," said Freta. It seemed a somewhat jaded view; however, she really couldn't argue. Maybe developing a healthy cynical streak was part and parcel of becoming a detective.

"Now … tell me about this Hans Trovotka. I've glanced at the file you have on him. So I know he's a religious fanatic and an ecoterrorist and bomb maker. Besides that, is he a killer?"

"You mean is he psychologically capable of murder?"

"Let's back up a bit and do a profile — a reading of his character, if you will."

"I don't know that much about his character."

"More than me. You've spoken to him, interacted with him, saw his body language. I bet you know more than you think! For example, he is a true zealot. When he gets up in the morning and looks in the mirror, does he think 'yes, I'm the man'? Maybe not exactly Moses, but climbing up there! You'd be surprised at how many of these holier-than-thou types are phoney; in their heart of hearts, they are fraudsters, don't believe what they preach, but it gives them notoriety, power, and in a lot of instances buckets of money."

"I don't think he's a phoney," said Freta. "He believes what he says, misguided as it is."

"So tell me, when you served the warrant to search his property," Roberta shifted around toward Freta, "how did he react to you personally?"

"I rubbed him the wrong way."

"Because you are a woman and in authority, right?"

"Can't argue with that. Took it as an affront."

"Contemptuous of you?"

"Not only of me but of authority in general. Doesn't trust the police, who he sees as in place to prop up the state. Has no use for rules that don't square with his beliefs. Professes to live by the rules given from a higher power."

"Yes, but it still boils down to you and what you represent," insisted Roberta. "I've run across his ilk before. Selected Old Testament views that are not very charitable or empathic of the opposite sex, especially those who are not compliant or otherwise present a challenge. Man is superior, woman not so much is the general message."

"Well, with a search warrant in hand and half a dozen officers around, he had no choice but to comply."

"You questioned him the other day, you said."

"Briefly, it was just a 'letting you know I'm here visit' looking for a missing person — for Raglan."

"Did he have any useful information?"

"Nope, only that he was willing to help search, which I interpreted as a rather glib offer. But that's par for the course. Hans can be civil, even exhibit superficial charm when it suits him, or he can leverage it somehow — probably more so with his followers. That's my experience anyway."

"I can assume that he has a big ego that needs occasional stroking. That and a high opinion of himself... Many shallow people do," Roberta added as an afterthought.

"I can't say he's shallow," Freta amended. "As I said earlier, misguided, yes, but well-read, articulate, and knows what he's doing."

"There," remarked Roberta with a smile. "You do know a lot about him and what makes him tick. And that gets me to my final point. Given what you said, would he strike out — kill if provoked? The Old Testament is a pretty violent read."

"You mean is he capable of killing Raglan?"

"Yeah. The broken neck doesn't sound premeditated, but a quick brute-force reaction."

"To be honest, I really can't say."

"What about the other members of the commune, church, whatever it is he runs?"

"There are two other families, both with young kids. Pretty much keep to themselves. I'm not sure what the arrangements they have with Trovotka are, but they're homesteading on his land. The wives stay home while the husbands have regular employment off the commune. They constitute, I presume, the bulk of Trovotka's congregation."

"Well, we'll need to talk to them."

"And then there's Isaac, Hans's son. He's hard to get a read on. A bit challenged in the social graces and perhaps in other ways as well."

"Oh?" Roberta perked up.

"Doesn't say much and by all accounts behaves oddly. In some ways a chip off the old block, but less refined, more difficult to gauge. Still, he hasn't run afoul of the law — at least not that the local RCMP know about."

"All good to know," Roberta said.

"We'll be there soon," announced Freta, turning onto Jones Lake Road. "Another fifteen minutes or so..."

As it turned out, the trip proved a bust, leaving Roberta in a bad mood. Neither Hans, his wife, or Isaac were home. Indeed, all the adult males were gone, leaving their wives with a mess of kids to interview. They neither saw, heard, or even knew about a missing person until their respective husbands told them.

"Well, fuck a rubber duck," muttered LeBlanc as they got back into the cruiser. "Let's have a quick look at the grave."

"Any particular reason?"

"No, other than we're close, we've wasted our time, and it hardly matters if we waste a little more at this moment."

The area remained blocked off with yellow police tape. The tent, however, was in the process of being dismantled. The Ident team was almost done their work without anything new uncovered.

*** 

"They will be coming, and it is only the beginning. There will be no peace," said Hans in a low, steady voice. He was sitting across from his wife at a secluded table in Robin's Coffee shop.

The news that a body had been discovered in the Grotto cemetery had not yet leaked. Of course, he knew. How could he not with all the sudden activity and flashing lights within a stone's throw of his property line? By the end of the day, he figured, everyone would know.

"What should we do?" whispered Greta.

"Don't leave this coffee shop." He smiled at his own joke. Then he looked around furtively. "Endure and protect our son."

"Have you talked to him about what you have found?"

"No," he said tersely. "Isaac has been elusive and uncommunicative. But I will have the truth. He needs to tell me, and soon."

"I didn't see him this morning. He was gone... His truck was gone." Greta sighed, resigned.

"God will let His wishes be known. I am praying for guidance. We must be patient."

"Isaac didn't do anything sinful, did he?" Greta was fearful, her lower lip quivering.

"I like to believe not. But he needs to explain. In the meantime, while awaiting God's counsel, we need to protect our son," he reiterated.

"How can we do that?" Greta clasped her hands tighter.

"Avert suspicion. There is another person of interest. I am a witness."

"Who?"

"A person I know of and recognized. I saw him driving on Grotto Road in the morning hours last Sunday before full light. He was coming from the cemetery where the girl was found."

"Are you going to tell the police?"

Hans hesitated before answering. "That is a problem. I'm not sure that they would believe me, given our relationship, and they might think I have ulterior motives in coming forward… But yes, I was a witness. They need to take me seriously. And to your question, yes, I will tell them but in a roundabout way."

\*\*\*

For Alex Croft it was a day of highs and lows, interspersed with confusion.

First item on his list to check off was withdrawals from two different accounts and a visit to his safety deposit box totalling $10,000. After working himself into nervous exhaustion, he realized that his best option was to pay the blackmailer. Thereafter, he could only hope for the best and prepare for the worst. Although he doubted that the blackmailer would be satisfied for long, the money would buy him some time. He sorted and tied the bills with elastics, putting the neat bundles in a plastic bag. The bag was then placed in the closet until he was ready to go.

Secondly, Croft was required to go to the RCMP detachment. He didn't know what to expect or what possible other evidence they had, but Hoar assured him there probably wasn't much. A young "hot shot" criminal lawyer that the firm just hired would meet him at the appointed time.

"Listen to your attorney, say as little as possible, and stick to the story," advised Hoar. "Boyd disappeared with clients' money, which the audits will clearly show, leaving you holding the bag. Plausible enough, especially when it will be shown that Boyd stole thousands, right?"

"Yeah, there's no doubt."

"Good. Hang tight."

Still, Croft paced his living room floor nervously, resisting the urge to fortify himself with a Scotch. He was in the midst of breathing and relaxing exercises when Hoar phoned, informing him that the interview had been postponed. "It's a good sign," he said, "means they have nothing substantive to talk to you about."

Croft was elated. He could concentrate on the other matter at hand: getting the money to its destination at the appointed time. He speculated on who could have possibly been out there at the time. Hans Trovotka came to mind, and he had been known to seek payouts from gas and oil companies. Yet it boiled down to speculation, and in truth, Croft decided, it could have been anyone, although someone who recognized him!

Around four thirty, he took his duffel bag and stuffed the plastic bag containing the money into it. And after a quick peek from behind the curtains to ascertain if there were any curious neighbours, he made his way to the Jeep. Dropping the duffel bag in the floor well of the passenger seat, he drove off.

He was almost at the Jones Lake Road turnoff, making good time on a clear, sunny day, when the local radio station interrupted its regular programming to announce that a body had been discovered at the Grotto cemetery. He quickly pulled over, feeling sick. The blood drained from his face; he noted the pasty whiteness in his rear-view mirror, and his palms were suddenly sweaty. Was the jig really up?

Then came the clarification. It was a female, presumably the missing college student. He had been only vaguely aware that there was another missing person investigation. What were the odds, especially given the location!

Croft sat in his Jeep at the side of the road for a considerable time. Should he go through with the drop? Did that make sense? Not with cops all over the area? In fact, it would be quite risky — too brazen to drive to the grotto, put the package in the garbage receptacle, and drive off. The RCMP would have the area cordoned off, searching for evidence, garbage cans included! Besides, who knows what he'd run into? Surely the blackmailer would know that circumstances had changed and would contact him again to make other arrangements. *Of course he would,* Croft tried to assure himself.

It was a no-brainer. Croft put the Jeep into gear, looked carefully both ways down the highway, and pulled a U-turn heading back to the city. Once home, he would have that Scotch he promised himself and wait for the other shoe to drop.

\*\*\*

*No, no, no!* They weren't supposed to find her — not this soon. It wasn't part of the plan! Isaac was agitated as he put down his binoculars and climbed down from his observation perch, a fallen spruce, with its trunk thrusting skyward. Thick shrubbery ensured that he would not be spotted by anyone in the flashing police vehicles or those in white suits going into the quickly erected tent. He had thought he buried her deep enough. *Must have been those damn dogs,* he cursed silently. *The rain didn't stop them.*

He knew when he heard the dogs barking that something had been found and had been watching ever since. Questions flitted across his mind: How long would they be there? Would they find what they were supposed to eventually find? Was this on the news, and did Croft know? Isaac's truck, parked out of sight, had no radio, and besides, the reception was bad in the bush. If Croft heard, would he still come with the money? After all, so far Isaac had seen only one body being removed. *Guess I'll just have to wait and see,* he consoled himself.

Meanwhile, he tried to envision possible scenarios. Croft would be accused of this killing; he had made sure of that. However, it would take some time for the cops to put the pieces together — surely they would. He frowned. Meanwhile, he could extract the money because, as far as he could tell, Croft's secret still lay buried!

Hungry, tired, and cramped, Isaac monitored the ceaseless flow of people and activity. Toward 5:00 p.m. or so, it looked like they were finally winding down — at least the tent was disassembled. Good. He didn't want Croft to show up at the grotto just a quarter mile down the road with cops still swarming the area. If he showed up at all.

His thoughts were interrupted by yet another RCMP cruiser approaching the site. It stopped, and he saw two people emerge: the one in uniform he had met at the house the week before, and the other was an older, frumpy-looking woman in plain clothes he'd never seen before. They appeared to wander about and talk briefly to the two white suits packing up various pieces of equipment. It all seemed pointless. *Stupid cows.* He was too smart for them. He wished they'd leave; he wished they'd all leave and Croft would show up.

# Chapter Sixteen

Having set the stage of Canada's improbable growth as an east–west nation despite the north–south pull of geography, followed by a survey of the Indigenous peoples living on it, Myron was now ready to introduce the disruptive strangers. Who came to North America and why? It was, after all, part of a story he crafted every year in his survey courses.

There were myriad reasons, he explained, why these "aliens" came, all part and parcel of European expansion that began in the fourteenth century and continued for the next four hundred years until European "civilization" dominated the globe. Some were, if not admirable, very human-like, infused with insatiable curiosity and the desire for fame and recognition: "To know what's on the other side of the mountain, the next bend in the river or, for those Trekkies, what lay out there in the universe!" This brought a chuckle from some in the class. *Bingo! Familiar reference points make the lecture relevant.*

Of course, as with most undertakings, he explained, altruism gives way to the profit motive. European kingdoms had highly developed acquisitive and competitive instincts and attempted to get rich and become more powerful than their neighbours. "The operative word here is GREED," he averred, whirling around and writing it on the blackboard in big capital letters. "That and one other crucial ingredient." He paused for emphasis. "Religion, or rather an intolerance for religious beliefs and the conviction that a particular church — in this case, Catholic — possessed the only true faith and those who didn't adhere to it were either godless heathens or worshipped fake gods and needed to be converted."

Then a word on the arch-villain (for most revisionist historians) in this unfolding drama: Christopher Columbus. Myron reminded the class, although presumably most knew from their high school social studies, that Columbus sailed westward across the Atlantic en route to the riches of Asia. "But what did he encounter?" *Rhetorical question for poignancy.* "A whole new, as it turns out, rich world to be exploited and that would make Spain inordinately wealthy.

"Pretty soon," Myron continued, getting into his cadence, "Europe's monarchs were funding voyages in Columbus's wake, hoping to find equally large or even larger caches of gold and silver. Of relevance here was King Henry VII of England sponsoring one Giovanni Caboto (a.k.a. John Cabot), who ventured much farther north than Columbus but nevertheless thought Newfoundland and Cape Breton Island were unknown parts of Asia...

"However, most significantly, for our purposes, is Jacques Cartier's arrival bearing the flag of the fleur-de-lys. His discovery of the St. Lawrence River allowed for sailing far into the new land's interior. He was convinced that he found a passage to China and that in between lay a series of 'freshwater seas' — he heard of this from his Algonkian guides — and kingdoms that possessed enough gold to rival the Spanish windfalls in central America. Of course," Myron concluded, "it turned out to be part lie, part myth, part hope, and part self-deception..."

Myron ended on a final point to foreshadow the next lecture. "Canada's story would continue to evolve with cod off the Newfoundland coast and fur in the interior. Stay tuned." He smiled like Mr. Rogers introducing his new friends.

Perhaps not the most riveting class, but it seemed to strike a chord of interest, and he left the last twenty or so minutes for student questions and discussion.

Alas, the questions were sparse and the discussion was lethargic. Even Alexandra seemed subdued and pensive. Be that as it may, he was satisfied and would pick up the tale, next time, moving along to Samuel de Champlain!

On his way to his office, he checked his mailbox, noting that the first departmental meeting was scheduled for the following Wednesday with a long list of items on the agenda, from a discussion on class sizes to who was eligible for the choice plug-in parking spots nearest to a college building. There would be, as well, an update on the dean of arts position still to be filled. If they were about to make an appointment, Ted would probably know about it.

When he reached his office on the third level, Myron was struck by how quiet it was. No loitering students in the hallway and office doors shut tighter than a corridor of prison cells after a lockdown. No surprise that the office on his right was deserted; technically, it was assigned but to a recluse biologist who, he suspected, spent most of her time in the lab. However, most unusual was Ted's door on his left. It was rarely closed. But there it was, dark and foreboding without even daylight seeping from underneath the door. *Must have gotten hung up somewhere,* Myron thought. And here he was ready for a walk and coffee.

Instead, he filed his lecture notes away and started to scan his latest class lists, still trying to match names and faces. He was interrupted by the jarring ring of his phone. He laid the lists back down on the paper tray. It was a hopeless task anyway.

"Hello?"

"Hello, Mr. Tarasyn?"

"Yes."

"Ah, I finally tracked you down."

The voice was vaguely familiar, but he couldn't quite place it. "Who is speaking, please?"

"Hans Trovotka. We met twice, as I am sure you remember. Once at my house with your RCMP friend and more recently at the coffee shop."

"Mr. Trovotka, yes…" was all Myron could say, thrown totally off balance. Trovotka obviously went to some trouble to find him, but why?

As if he read Myron's thoughts, Trovotka said, "You are probably wondering why I have contacted you, and perhaps it is not the proper thing to do. However, I have some information that I wish to pass on."

"Oh?"

"Yes, I want to do my citizen's duty and would normally speak to the police, but as you, no doubt, know, I find the local constabulary off-putting and difficult to deal with. Given our history, I don't like them, and it appears that they don't like me. So I have telephoned you. You are not a policeman, but you are connected to one, and I wish to provide some information."

"Mr. Trovotka, I'm not sure that I can help—"

"I think you can. I thought of you when that missing female was found…"

"She has been found?" Myron was stunned; he hadn't heard.

"Ah … perhaps that isn't public knowledge. The media is not aware yet. Sorry, I know because the police discovered her body at the Grotto Road cemetery beside my property. So I know. Tragic news."

"Raglan is dead? How?"

"I don't know any details."

"I don't understand," Myron said, trying to gather his thoughts. "You phoned me to—"

"I am a potential witness."

"To what happened?" *What the hell was Trovotka saying?*

"No, no, not to what actually happened." There was a trace of impatience in Trovotka's voice. "But to a person of interest. Last Sunday, in the small hours of the morning, I was out for my usual walk along a path parallel to Grotto Road. That's when I saw a red Jeep with a man I recognized at the wheel — a realtor and land developer, I believe from Great Plains. The timeframe fits with this unfortunate soul's disappearance and … tragic end."

"What?"

"The man in the Jeep was Mr. Croft from Atop Realty."

There was a pause as Myron processed the information.

"Mr. Tarasyn?"

"You should definitely make your statement to the RCMP."

"I am making it to you," Trovotka insisted. "I explained the reasons."

"I don't think that's how the system works. You need to make a formal statement. I'm not the police!"

"True." Trovotka seemed to sigh over the telephone line. "Given my issues with the RCMP, I had hoped that you would convey what I observed."

"I will, but I'm sure that it wouldn't suffice. They'll want to speak to you. There's no way of getting around it."

"But will they believe me?"

"I can't answer that."

"It's been nice talking to you. Please relay what I have said to Corporal Osprey. It should point her in the right direction. Goodbye."

The line went dead as Myron stared at the receiver.

After a moment of digesting what he heard and gathering his scattered wits, Myron dialled the RCMP detachment number, hoping to be put through to Freta. He got the receptionist.

"May I speak to Corporal Osprey, please?" he said officiously. He knew phone calls to the detachment were recorded, and it wasn't for quality assurance.

"Who shall I say is calling?"

"Myron Tarasyn."

"Hold a moment, please."

Myron drummed his fingers on the desk as he waited. He wished he could light his pipe and indulge in a couple of calming puffs.

"She's out at the moment. Is there a message?"

Myron thought about what to say. "Tell Corporal Osprey to call at," he gave her his office phone number even though she knew it, "as soon as she can. It's important."

With that, he quickly ended the call.

*** 

"So," said LeBlanc, giving Freta a shrewd look, "maybe we should include Myron on our team?"

Freta didn't know how to take that — disapproval, sarcasm, or amusement. Reading Roberta was still a work in progress.

Freta had gotten off the phone listening wide-eyed to Myron's account of Trovotka's odd contact and story about seeing Croft driving on Grotto Road. She then explained to LeBlanc that Myron had indeed been out to Trovotka's place with her, along for the ride to see if more volunteers were needed for the search. It was a weak rationalization, and Freta didn't think LeBlanc bought it. The older RCMP detective pursed her lips and grunted something Freta didn't catch.

"Why would Trovotka phone Myron with this alleged sighting? You said they barely spoke?" LeBlanc asked after a moment's silence.

Freta was obliged to mention that after Myron had another short encounter with Hans at a coffee shop, where he discovered that Myron was not RCMP.

"This Myron of yours … he's not some sort to Clark Kent who transforms himself into a super sleuth?"

*Well, I'm no Lois Lane,* Freta thought but said nothing.

"Never mind," LeBlanc said gruffly. "Phone the Trovotka residence and tell Hans or whoever is at the other end that he needs to make an official statement and that he should come to this office by 10:00 a.m. tomorrow, or we'll come out and bring him in. I'm through chasing him while he plays games."

"Yes, ma'am," Freta said crisply.

With that, LeBlanc rolled her swivel chair backward, almost hitting the wall, got up, and marched over to Reuben's office. She knocked twice, opened the door, and stepped in, closing it firmly behind her.

Some time later, she re-emerged and plopped herself back into the seat, looking exasperated. She made eye contact with Freta, sitting two desks opposite her. "Did you get a hold of Trovotka? Or anyone else out there?"

"No, I left a message for him to come in as suggested if he didn't want us to intrude on him at home."

LeBlanc's scowl lessened, and she nodded. "If he's smart, he'll get the message. Otherwise, I am going out there, and everyone will be hauled in for questioning. They probably will be anyway, on second thought."

She paused and picked up and fiddled with a pen. "Indulge me for a moment so that I get this straight. Trovotka doesn't like cops, especially female cops, yet he wants to get this off his chest, right?"

"That's my take."

"He knows Myron is associated with you, and he tells him that he saw Croft on Grotto Road early Sunday morning about the time Raglan was in the process of disappearing and/or getting killed." LeBlanc paused and put the pen down on the desk. "Does that make sense? Perhaps more importantly, why is he telling us this? Even if Croft was out there, why step forward? Conscience or something else? I guess I don't get his motive."

"He told Myron he came forth because it was his civic duty or something to that effect."

"I'm not buying that."

"Nor is what he claims to have seen true," offered Freta. "I thought that Croft was on his way to Edmonton to catch a flight to Las Vegas."

"And possibly dump a body along the way," LeBlanc added wryly. "However, just to humour me, we better check Croft's timelines. When *did* he leave Great Plains for Edmonton, etc., etc., etc.? No, it bothers me that Trovotka volunteered this information. His civic duty, my ass! Strange, though, Croft popping up in a totally unrelated case."

"Surely the two can't be connected?"

"It would be something if the two were joined at the hip somehow. Seems unlikely, but my list of questions to Trovotka and Croft — when we get him in here — is starting to lengthen. Meanwhile, I've put a rush on that piece of torn clothing and button. Would we be so lucky as to lift a fingerprint or two? Should know by Friday."

\*\*\*

"She didn't appreciate Trovotka using me to talk to you — and the RCMP by extension, I take it?"

"I'd say no, but I barely know her, and she is hard to read. I think she was more miffed that we went to Trovotka's property on a wild goose chase while apparently he was phoning you from town."

"Well, I hope she doesn't shoot the messenger."

"For what it's worth, she thought you 'a good sort' — but that was just after our dinner, and maybe her opinion has changed."

Myron was in Freta's apartment, sharing a late-evening pizza and beer. The food and drink was Myron's contribution to a cozy night of catching up, followed by more demonstrative activities — he hoped.

"Trovotka pulled a boner," admonished Freta, reaching over and snagging a pepperoni slice from the box strategically placed on the kitchen table. "Hang-ups about cops don't cut it when we're talking potential homicide. He's got to make a formal statement. And I think he knows that. He's creating more drama than there needs to be, which begs the question, why go through this charade?"

"Trovotka the drama king. Has a ring to it," said Myron, eyeing another slice.

"Anyway, he's got no choice now if he doesn't want everyone brought into the station. Roberta is on his case big time."

"I did tell him to go to you. He has your card."

"And LeBlanc's too. She stuck one in his door and gave them out to the two adults that were there… Roberta brought up a good point that's been bugging me."

"What's that?" asked Myron, becoming attuned to Freta's sudden shift in thought.

"Why talk to anyone at all? Why the compulsion? Was it to attract attention? Admittedly, he likes being at the centre of things still… Or was it to distract us from somewhere or someone else?"

Myron shrugged and took a gulp of his pilsner. "It could be as simple as he saw Croft or thinks he did and felt obligated to report it."

"Perhaps, but I don't think so. And while attracting attention, it also puts him there, as well as Croft."

"As a potential suspect, you mean? I didn't get the idea, though, that he was thinking about himself at all."

"Umm, Roberta asked me on the way out there whether I thought he was capable of killing."

"And what'd you say?"

"That I didn't know. Anyone is capable of killing, depending on provocation and circumstances — like a fit of rage, for example. But honestly, I've never seen him get overly excited or too demonstrative, even when we searched his property. In fact, he was quite calm."

"Well, he sounded calm, almost calculating when he spoke to me on the phone."

"Roberta put Rob on verifying Croft's timelines for Saturday night and Sunday up to when he boarded his flight for Las Vegas, so we'll get an idea if it's even possible that Croft was out there. Poor Rob, she's giving him the Joe jobs — checking on Raglan's companions and friends, obtaining the paperwork for the truck searches, and now this."

"She obviously has taken you under her wing."

"I guess, riding shotgun for now."

"I must admit," said Myron. "Hearing that Raglan was dead shook me up."

"Horrible, and I don't envy Superintendent Reuben, who had to tell the parents and take them to identify the body. I can't imagine."

"Very sad for everyone. I'm sure a statement will be released to all college members in a day or so. Undoubtedly, there will be a memorial planned."

"Thanks for the pizza," said Freta, getting up from her chair. "Let's go into the living room and get more comfortable."

"Good plan!"

Freta sat and stretched on the sofa while Myron dropped into his usual spot on the love seat.

"Aside from Hans's alleged sighting of Croft, are there any other leads in the case?" asked Myron, readjusting his posture into a more accommodating position.

"The only hard evidence is a torn piece of material found at the crime scene. Maybe a long shot, but Roberta is hoping there's a print or two. Should know in a couple of days. Other than that, not much."

Myron nodded. "And no word on Boyd?'

"Nothing. He's done a Houdini, apparently."

Later in the evening when their "shop talk" ran its course, Myron readily agreed to forgo his Wednesday night smoke delight for a romantic liaison with Freta. It seemed like a fair trade-off.

"I've got to get up really early tomorrow, so no dilly-dallying in the morning," she warned.

"I'll shower at my place," he promised solemnly.

"I'm going in extra early."

"Because Roberta is a real early riser?"

"That she is. If she is going to be here for any length of time, I'm sure she'll end up taking over the detachment. Even Reuben treads lightly around her."

"What's her story?"

"Haven't the foggiest. Doesn't talk about herself, and I'm not asking. I get the feeling that she is a solitary person, on her own and set in her ways."

"What makes you say that?"

"Just a supposition and the big yellow sticker inside the lid of her briefcase."

"What'd it say?"

"After the men I've met, I prefer my cats!"

"Right."

# Chapter Seventeen

Shortly after their return from Great Plains, Hans told Greta that he was going into his sanctuary and didn't want to be disturbed.

"What if Isaac comes home?" Greta asked. "Should I—"

"I don't want to be disturbed."

Thus, he sat alone in his church, the old Trovotka bible in his hand. What even Greta couldn't fully understand was that God talked to him and often gave him a sign, a direction. The last time it happened was when God called him to come to this place in northern Alberta, a siren call somewhat like Abraham getting a new start in Canaan, he was fond of saying to his congregation. And he obeyed without reservation. Yes, he listened when the Almighty spoke and did not stray in life or faith. And it would be no different now.

He prayed and listened for almost two hours when, as if by some invisible hand, the bible fell from his grasp. Had he dozed off? He didn't think so. Startled, he looked down to see the holy book lay splayed open on the rough wooden floor, the spine and cover facing him. When he reached down from the bench and picked it up, he noted the page and verse: Genesis 22. His thumb landed on a familiar passage: *Take your son, your only son Isaac whom you love and … sacrifice him as a burnt offering…*

Hans stared at the words dumbfounded, fearful, a stab of pain in his heart. And yet he knew. There in the surrounding silence, he heard the muted voice of God. Isaac — *Ironic that I should have named him so,* he thought — had to atone. But the question remained, and Hans clung to it like a drowning man to a lifeboat: would the atonement be paid in full measure or would Hans, as was the case with Abraham, receive a reprieve?

***

**Thursday, August 22**

Isaac avoided his father and mother. Not that it was difficult. They had gone to town and were gone most of Wednesday, which allowed him to gather some supplies and go to his private place for the night. Besides, they were the least of his worries. Mother would stay silent and quietly endure while the old man could be assuaged, if not manipulated, if things went terribly wrong. *But they won't,* he reassured himself, *despite a small setback.*

His plan was a good one, except that the body was found. *Should have buried her deeper,* he chastised himself mildly, *like the first one... Never mind, the cops are none the wiser,* he told himself. He had protected himself just in case, and the plan was still in play.

And it became imperative that it remained in play! Originally, he had done what he did to simply make Raglan disappear with extracting money as an afterthought once he saw where Croft lived. *Bastard!* His back still hurt, never mind his bruised face. But the crux of the matter was he desperately wanted, nay, needed the money. He had quit his construction job three months ago — there was a stupid foreman with too many stupid rules — his remaining resources were pretty much depleted, and the pittance he was allotted by Hans for his contribution to farm chores hardly covered his gas, meals, and other sundries when he drove into town. No, forgetting about the money and going dark was not a smart option, he decided. Croft was his ticket to securing a nice lump before he went for his fall.

Time, then, to get back on track — reset the drop date. Nothing of substance had changed. Croft still had a secret to keep, and as long as the cops don't haul him in, he would pay up. He didn't know how much time Croft had, except that, from what he saw of their methods, the RCMP were not that quick!

Isaac pulled over into a grocery store parking lot and called the realty office from the same telephone kiosk as before. This time, however, he was told that Mr. Croft wouldn't be coming in. He hung up when the woman asked for his name and if there was a message she could leave.

He looked up Croft's home number from the dangling directory. He got him on the third ring.

"Same place, same time, this Saturday. Drop off the money, or I will tell."

He was about to replace the receiver when he heard an emphatic "No" from the other end.

\*\*\*

Alex Croft was still trying to get his head around the discovery of Raglan Bullock's body. At the Grotto cemetery? What did that mean? Just a strange coincidence? His heart rate shot up a few beats, and he began to sweat when the radio report hinted that she might have been buried. Buried where in the cemetery? The media stories remained sketchy, but alarm bells were going off in his confused brain.

Then came the phone call, which he expected and prepared for.

"What?" The muffled voice at the other end was surprised.

"I said no. It's too risky. Find another site closer to town, preferably in town. I can't travel too far at this time," he added in a firm tone.

There was a moment's hesitation at the other end. As if thrown off balance, the caller was thinking, trying to regroup.

Croft took the initiative. "Phone me back when you have another location."

He put the receiver down. It was a calculated gamble to change the rules of the game a bit. If he could control the where, perhaps he could discover the who. He wanted to get a sense of the person at the other end of the line. If only he could meet with him or know who he was, he could make an assessment and settle the issue once and for all. Croft shook his head, clearing the cobwebs — *and I would do what exactly?* That part he'd have to think about.

The call came an hour later.

"Same time, Saturday. At the north end of the parking lot, Saskatoon Berry Park. Go up the trail away from the pavilion. A little ways on the trail there's a sandbox — right side. It's not full. Put the money in there. Come alone, and remember, you'll be watched!"

The veneer of a thin smile crossed Croft's lips. He'd changed the narrative. It was neutral territory, which evened out the odds somewhat. Croft needed to know who was blackmailing him. The changed venue would give him the opportunity to find out.

\*\*\*

Having stated his name and that he had been "summoned" to provide a witness statement, Trovotka was escorted to a small, bare room adorned with only a table and two chairs somewhere within the bowels of the building. He was told politely by the young constable to have a seat and that someone would be with him shortly. Fifteen minutes later, an older woman — about his age, he guessed — came in. She was dressed in civilian clothes: a black, loose-fitting blouse and baggy grey pants. She had an authoritative stride and a haughty manner. Hans took an instant dislike to her, from the bottom of her baggy pants to her snarly look.

"Mr. Trovotka," she said without breaking stride. "I'm Detective LeBlanc, Major Crimes Division. Thank you for coming."

She sat down across from him, placing a closed folder on the table. It seemed from his vantage point that her snarly look had refocused to a snarly smile.

He had expected that Corporal Osprey would interview him, but apparently not. He asked but was told that she was unavailable.

"Now, Mr. Trovotka, I understand you have something to tell us pertaining to the disappearance and death of Raglan Bullock."

"I do," he said, placing his large hands on the table. And he proceeded to describe what he witnessed.

LeBlanc listened without interruption and then started asking a series of questions. "So you recognized Mr. Croft. How did you know it was him? Do you personally know him?"

Trovotka leaned back in his chair. "No, I do not personally know him, but I know who he is. He stopped by a few months ago, wondered if I was interested in selling my land. I suspected he was snooping around for one of those gas companies or a business client who had connections to them. All they care about is drilling and extraction, and if they can't lease, then they'll try and buy."

"So, that was the only time you met him?"

"Yes, but no mistake, it was definitely him."

"Okay, and you saw him at that particular time and day?" LeBlanc opened her file and gave it a cursory glance, as if to confirm his information.

"Yes," he said with an edge of testiness.

"Did you see anyone else?"

"No."

"Was anyone with you? Anyone who could corroborate what you saw?"

"No."

"Where was your son?"

"In bed, I'd imagine," he replied, although that wasn't true. "It was really early — the crack of dawn," he added.

"We'll need to speak to him."

Hans nodded but said nothing.

"But you're positive it was Mr. Croft?"

"Yes."

"Did he see you?"

"As I said, I was on a path off Grotto Road. I don't think so, and he was humming along pretty good."

"In a red Jeep?"

"Correct."

LeBlanc nodded, closed her file, and met his eyes. "You realize, of course, that by virtue of coming forth as a witness, you too were at the scene at that particular time and place, thus becoming a person of interest yourself?"

Hans smiled, unperturbed. The old bag was playing games with him. "I am already a person of interest."

"Yes, you are," she replied coldly.

"I think I like Corporal Osprey's interviews better," he said, still smiling.

"Get off on the uniform, do you?"

For the better part of an hour they sparred, and after recording and getting a signed official statement, LeBlanc told him that for now they were done but to make himself and others in his household and tenants available for further questioning. Trovotka left with a half chagrined, half bemused expression.

Freta had listened and took in the interview only a few feet away through a two-way mirror.

"You're right," LeBlanc said. "Trovotka is a cool, slippery customer who," she smiled, "would rather deal with you!"

"Where does that leave us?" Freta asked, ignoring Roberta's comment.

"He says it was Croft so … when we bring him in, we'll see what he says. Maybe he saw Trovotka in turn!"

# Chapter Eighteen

Alexandra Enfield stood naked in front of the three-quarter-length mirror attached to the bedroom door. She glanced around and sighed. To be sure, the mirror was out of place, but in truth, so was everything else in the apartment. It was shabby with age and out of date, a comedown from the luxurious condo she had inhabited in Edmonton. Of course, it had been paid for by Mr. Super Star — *the jerk,* she reaffirmed to the reflection in the mirror. He got his comeuppance — almost. Frankly, her recollection of that night and some of the other nights was hazy.

She had moved on. She had to. Her life had become increasingly frenetic and fragile as the relationship and things in general escalated out of control. The city had become a giant chessboard, and even descending into the downtown airport created a wave of anxiety. A maelstrom of darkening thoughts swirled that were not of her making, she was sure.

She gave herself a critical inspection. She had come a long way from that awkward, picked-on schoolgirl. She evolved into what her mother called a "petite rose" who caught and held wandering eyes. And why not? The person who stared back at her still possessed a youthful face and firm body with breasts that, while not overly generous, were pert enough. Ditto for the cheeks on either side of her rump. She playfully slapped the left side as if to confirm; it quivered but did not ripple.

She was out of her oppressed jungle now. The pace had slowed; she found her place and calming equilibrium. A new future awaited.

Did it matter that she couldn't explain it? He was just there (or at least the aura around him), and whatever had gone out of her suddenly rushed back in. Sweet and sour feelings now inexplicably focused on one individual — quite benign, she thought — who could be amenable or made amenable to her new life.

However, an unexpected breach appeared in her happy disposition where her troubled past threatened her recent calm. Of all the possibilities, she never thought in her wildest imagination that she'd encounter a cop who had known her in Edmonton. It was one brief encounter, but there was a spark of recognition. She would remember. Would she gossip? And did it matter?

The second problem was the other woman. Who was she? There was a definite fondness there. *This has become troublesome,* she confided to her other self in the mirror. She would need to push the acceleration button and give him a more direct hint so there'd be no misinterpretation. After the Thursday-night class, she would play her hand.

***

As was his usual routine, Myron arrived at the college early, went straight to his office, and dropped off his briefcase and outerwear. Then he made his way down to the lower level for his first jolt of java. He needed it — maybe two — before his class at nine thirty. He spotted Ted in the coffee line.

"Didn't see you yesterday," he said.

"And I didn't see you either!" Ted replied.

*Touché!* "Now that we've cleared that up… It's shaping to be a nice day. Want to go for our walk? Say around noon? It's going to be a long day with the night class."

"Sounds good. I've got my night class as well. Sheesh — three hours of it. Still have stuff to prepare." Ted shook his head.

After they procured their coffees, Ted accompanied Myron to his office without bothering to open his own. He sank heavily into the visitor's chair.

"Tragic, Raglan's death. I can't imagine," he said.

"Hard to believe. I haven't checked my mailbox but there's probably a memorial planned by Student Affairs—"

"Next Wednesday," said Ted. "The notice came this morning."

Myron nodded. Whenever tragedy struck, the college community was always there with an official event.

"Uh … any more on the case?" Ted asked hopefully.

"Not that I know of. Honestly, I'm out of the loop. It's been taken over by the RCMP Major Crimes unit from Edmonton."

For once, Ted did not press the point. The subject seemed to come to an end.

"But I have a question," Myron continued. "There's a scheduled departmental meeting for Wednesday, which, come to think of it, may be postponed because of the memorial… Anyway, on the agenda there is something about an update regarding the dean of arts position. Heard anything? Any rumours?"

"Sidney Sage, your nemesis, is not in the running."

"He's not my nemesis, and we're moving to a rapprochement since the last time he wanted to be an administrator."

"You two talking?"

"More like acknowledging each other's presence — important in departmental and committee meetings."

"Not a love-in yet, then," Ted quipped.

"No, and there's no news then. If the selection committee has chosen a dean, to date it remains a well-guarded secret."

"Well, I have some news. Yours truly is back on the Faculty Association Negotiations Committee."

"That's great and, of course, your forte."

"Thanks, I'm happy about it. Got a solid group, and our chair — actually the chair of your department, Harold Wisenburg — has decided to have a bonding session followed by a luncheon meeting to discuss our 'demands.'" Ted wiggled his two index fingers in quotation marks. "At the Saskatoon Berry Golf Course."

"Sounds good. Progress for an old Marxist philosopher like Harold, who in his younger days would never have stooped to such bourgeois methods of building comradeship."

"I don't play golf," Ted said bluntly. "That's the bonding part, right?"

"I don't either, so I can't help you with the game. But there are theories about why you should play golf. Most importantly, it's for those aspirants who desire to rise in the executive world. Just as many deals are done on the golf course as in the boardroom!"

"Good to know, but I'm not sure how that will bond us. In fact, I'll be unbonded once the team gets a load of my golf game. I just don't get hitting a small, round object with a club and walking for miles afterward looking for it!"

"Books have been written pondering the existential mysteries of the game, Ted. There's a deep, meaningful experience in bashing hard, dimpled balls off battered tees."

"Like what?"

"Not having read any of the books, I don't really know. Apparently, educated guess here, it involves some cathartic release or titillation that makes executives happy, relaxed, and prone to making deals."

"I'd rather take a mulligan!"

"And I'd rather go fishing."

"Speaking of which, did I tell you about my last and only fishing trip? It didn't work out so good. It was really about this dog, Snark—"

"I'm all ears but it'll have to wait until after class and our walk."

"Oh, right!" Ted glanced at his watch. "I've got a class coming up too."

The rest of the morning and afternoon unfolded without drama. His world history class, Ancient Near Eastern Civilizations (to be followed by The Greeks and Their Legacy and other lectures in a similar vein, topped by The Roman Empire), was a subdued affair. Myron couldn't be sure but surmised that there were students in the classroom who knew Raglan — those that came. An inordinate number of seats remained empty for so early in the semester, including, he noticed, Alexandra's. The time of students skipping classes usually didn't arrive until much later in the course. He debated taking a portion of the class to talk about the tragedy but decided that he wasn't part of the college's counsellor team and there would be opportunity for that.

After class, he met up with Ted, and they took their usual walk to the coffee shop, talking about everything and anything except Ted's fishing trip, which apparently was really about a dog. As fascinating as it might have been, Myron was thankful that the subject had skipped both their minds. He was sure that Ted would get around to telling him soon enough.

The rest of the day was a blur. He fidgeted in his office sorting files, making discussion notes, and writing student names and ID numbers in what he called his "doomsday book." He had a record of every student that sat in his class, even if he couldn't match names to faces! Finally, by late afternoon he'd had enough of his office and the college. The fridge was almost empty, so he drove to the south-side grocery store and did some shopping, then it was off to his apartment, where, after putting the items away, he had a long, leisurely pipe smoke while sitting on his balcony reading a le Carré thriller. He'd grab a burger and fries on the way to the college later. It was important, Myron decided, to have a routine. And this would be his Thursday routine, more or less.

***

The Nature of the Soviet State was the topic, and Myron dove into it energetically. "We begin with a definition of totalitarianism," he began (*always go from the general to the specific when explaining*), "a system in which all powers of state and the state itself is in the hands of a dictator. And make no mistake," he emphasized, "the Soviet Union is a totalitarian state!"

Before he could elaborate further, a keen student's hand in the first row shot up. *Damn, I can't remember his name,* Myron berated himself as he nodded to acknowledge the question. "What's the difference between the totalitarianism of a dictator and an absolute monarchy like that in eighteenth-century France?"

"Good question…" He paused to collect his thoughts. "A number of things — totalitarianism is revolutionary rather than traditional, which means it relies on coercion and terror much more so than divine right beliefs and custom to secure compliance, if not total obedience. A dictator like Stalin, for example, in contrast to, say, Louis XIV, demanded not only a monopoly over political power but also control over society as a whole, including all groups, institutions, and their activities, be it economic, social, religious, or intellectual."

"Wasn't Louis's absolute power close to your definition?" persisted the student.

"Close in some ways, but no cigar." Myron smiled at his own bad attempt at humour. "He actually had restraints of law, custom, and even duties. There are no such restraints for those in authority in a totalitarian state. Of course, where absolutism and totalitarianism converge is the tyrant or king's ability to maintain those levers of power and control."

A lively debate followed with others expressing their thoughts before Myron got into some of the characteristics of the totalitarian state, starting with the Communist Party of the Soviet Union.

Alexandra occupied her usual seat for this class, Myron noted, but as in the day classes the last couple of times (the first time she hadn't shown up earlier), she seemed reserved, if not withdrawn. In a way, he was relieved; he was becoming uncomfortable with her overt enthusiasms and unexpected appearances beyond the confines of the classroom.

After class, Myron collected his lecture notes and went up to his office. Then minutes later, he had filed the lecture into the proper cabinet, taken out the materials he would need for next day's sessions, shrugged on his coat, turned out the office light, locked his door, and headed toward the parking lot. Once through the building doors, he breathed in deeply. It was a cool but pleasant night with no wind. He was almost at his car when he felt a presence behind him. He whirled around with thoughts of a mugger or a deranged Sidney Sage stealthily descending upon him... "Alexandra!" he exclaimed. "You– you surprised me..." He paused, consciously slowing down his heart palpations.

She stopped and reached into her handbag while he gathered himself. "I know I've got my car keys here somewhere... Ah." she fished out a key ring with an oddly shaped object that Myron couldn't quite make out. Alexandra's eyes seemed to glint in the pale light of the parking lot lamp.

Myron glanced around. There wasn't a vehicle near his. This lady was giving off a strange, unsettling vibe. "Was there something in class tonight that you want to ask about?" *Keep it light and on point.*

"I need some advice," she said. Her voice had an elevated edge, or was it his imagination?

"It's late, but I have office hours tomorrow before class. If you can come then—"

"I was thinking more private than that — like your place ... or mine." Her eyes bored into his like diamond drill bits, an image he tried to shake.

"I'm not sure what you're suggesting." A frown creased his forehead.

"Oh, I think you are," Alexandra said with a sly smile.

"Alexandra," Myron involuntarily took a step back, "if you are implying what I think you're implying, it would be inappropriate and certainly unethical. Faculty–student relationships are out of bounds—"

"But happen all the time. And I won't tell."

"Alexandra, I must..." Myron's mind was still analyzing the situation, obtusely realizing that getting reeled in and compromised by a troubled woman was not on his agenda. Whatever other avoidance thoughts he had were short-circuited when Alexandra reached up her hand quickly to the back of his neck and thrust forward, forcing his mouth to hers. He felt the brief brush of her tongue tip parting his lips.

*What the hell,* he thought, jerking back, his butt hitting the driver's door.

Alexandra drew back, giving him a peculiarly solemn smile. "You'll come around." With that she turned and walked away, leaving him stunned and speechless.

# Chapter Nineteen

"Joy!" exclaimed Roberta LeBlanc. "The set of prints on the button and material found at the crime scene are useable. Our first good break." She was sitting in what was designated as the case room, just off the bullpen area were officers received information, followed up phone calls, wrote reports, and generally hung out until assigned.

Corporal Rob Rainy had arrived with three large coffees and a large box of Timbits. At the moment, he was bringing Roberta and Freta up to speed on what he had been doing as part of the "LeBlanc Team." *Designated gofer,* Freta thought and felt badly for him, but not too much so, since it was still a male-dominated profession, albeit temporarily muted by a dominant female boss. Roberta had him chasing down small loose ends of the case. Necessary perhaps, but a lot of leg work for meagre results.

"Forensics found nothing to indicate that either Kyle's or his friend's truck was used in Raglan's death — no incriminating shovels, discarded clothing, or conclusive soil samples. Her fingerprints and hair samples were inside the cabin of Kyle's truck, where we'd expect them to be, but nothing in the back or the box. And I did go over their statements again in detail. They were all wasted, they admitted, and didn't realize that Raglan was gone until late Sunday morning. Their stories are consistent, such as they remember."

Roberta nodded. "What about the missing truck keys?"

"Yeah, well… Kyle believes one of two things could've happened. Either he lost them or Raglan took them to get something from the truck or maybe to sleep in the cab because she was cold. It was getting chilly. He said they searched the campsite high and low for those keys and didn't find them. They were a little slow to realize that Raglan was gone. As I said, they didn't begin looking for her until quite late in the morning."

"Right then, after too much drinking they weren't that sharp," Roberta concluded, extracting a honey-glazed Timbit from the box with two fingers. "What about our number two person of interest? Could he have been where our number one person of interest says he was?"

Rainy took a moment to process Roberta's question and cleared his throat. "The short answer is yes. Croft's flight to Vegas didn't leave until early evening, and he didn't leave Great Plains until midmorning."

"And we know he met with Boyd around 9:00 p.m. Saturday night," Freta interjected, flipping through the interview notes. "Croft says he met with Boyd for about an hour. Huge time gap with no one to verify that he went home and slept, as he says."

"Certainly no alibi, but no motive either. We've got circumstantial evidence," Roberta said, eyeing but resisting another honey-glazed, "that he might have done in Boyd, but with no corpse, it's a missing person case with no connection to this one. It *is* possible that Boyd stole the clients' and his business partner's money and disappeared. You know," LeBlanc paused and pursed her lips, "we need to do a deeper dive into Boyd and Croft — see what they were doing before their partnership, delve into their finances, see if they had any financial or legal difficulties prior."

"I'll look into it," volunteered Rob as if in anticipation of being asked.

"Good." LeBlanc nodded. "Any other thoughts?"

"There's one possibility, but it's kinda out there," offered Freta.

"One more than we have now," said Roberta wryly. "Shoot."

"What if we assume that Croft did kill Boyd, took his body out there in his Jeep to dispose of it. He knew the area… And let's suppose that he encountered Raglan lost in the woods. She stumbles upon him with the body. To silence her, he breaks her neck and puts her in a shallow grave. He does have a black belt in karate."

"Where's Boyd's body then? Wouldn't they be dumped together?" asked Rob.

Freta shrugged. "Hard to say."

"At least it's a working theory that connects some dots to the two cases," noted Roberta, "which is more than we had a half hour ago."

"What about Trovotka and his followers?" Rob asked. "We have no way to corroborate that he saw Croft out there. Given the proximity to his place, Trovotka and/or others living on the acreage had much better opportunity. And I'm not sure that Trovotka would need a motive."

"I thought about that," said Roberta. "He's my number one person of interest — can't even call him a suspect yet. What I can't comprehend is why he came forward as a witness, placing himself in the crosshairs of our investigation. He implicates himself as much as he does Croft. Not much of this is falling into place, which means…" She sighed, giving both her young colleagues a grim grin. "We're back to those damn fingerprints. You've got Trovotka's on file here, and I believe that Croft's were taken in Edmonton after his vehicle was impounded. So, we await a match. Of course, they could both be exonerated."

"When do we reinterview Croft?" Freta asked.

"Hmm — good question. Ideally, when we know more, starting with those prints matching anyone we know…"

\*\*\*

Myron had a sleepless, troubled night. His encounter with Alexandra in the parking lot had unsettled him more than he realized. He still hadn't worked out exactly how to deal with it, hoping that maybe if he ignored what occurred, it would simply go away. No such luck. Myron found a note slipped under his office door when he arrived the next morning. It read:

*Elizabeth Apartments, Suite 237, Saturday 8 PM.*

*Holy shit!* This was getting out of control. This note ended his indecisiveness. He felt obligated to speak with a student counsellor, not only for Alexandra's sake but for his own and indeed that of the institution. He'd start a file and document the incidents to date and put that on record officially with Student Affairs. He hated to do that, since such action would have repercussions such as withdrawal from the college, but Alexandra at the very least needed to have a long, serious talk with a counsellor. He wondered if what she was doing fit the definition of harassment.

Still, he would wait 'til after the pre-Confederation Canadian history class to see if she appeared. There was a perhaps a chance to deal with this informally over a coffee and nip this obsession or fantasy — he really didn't know what to call it — in the bud.

The lecture on Samuel de Champlain went well, although students seemed less interested in his standing on the towering rock above the St. Lawrence in 1608 founding the oldest settlement in North America and establishing an enduring French presence in Canada than his marrying a twelve-year-old thirty or so years his junior. It was one of those titillating facts that came from a female student at the back of the room. For the class, it was the equivalent of a shocking Hollywood revelation.

Myron spent ten minutes discussing the norms of the period and that what occurred was just politics. Champlain had indeed signed a marriage contract with Hélène Boullé, the daughter of a very wealthy secretary with direct access to King Louis XIII. "Unseemly, yes, but it was royal court politics and a commercial deal. The marriage was not to be consummated until Hélène turned fourteen…" By the end of the lecture, Myron was pretty sure if nothing else students would remember that Champlain married a twelve-year-old!

Admittedly, Myron's mind wasn't totally focused on the subject matter, and he got further distracted going down that salacious rabbit hole. *No problem: part of the historical record.* What threw him off was Alexandra, who not only showed up but sat in her usual spot, cool and unperturbed, as if nothing had occurred. *Obsessed nymphomaniac attacks unsuspecting college prof* screamed a headline in his mind. *Unfair. Don't rush to judgement,* his inner self admonished. *There was still an opportunity to defuse and save this from further escalation…*

The class ended, and students began filing out. Myron caught Alexandra's eye. "Could you remain for a moment?"

"Of course." She smiled.

He gathered his notes and collected his thoughts while the last student exited the room.

"I got your note," he said.

"My invitation," she corrected.

"Whatever." He sighed. "I'm not coming. If you want to talk about it, we can now over a coffee in the cafeteria." *Give her one more chance before taking this matter to Student Affairs.* That was what his inner voice counselled.

"It's the other woman, isn't it?"

That stopped him mid-thought. "What?"

"That woman who you met at the restaurant with that older busybody. Not her mother, was she?"

Before Myron could formulate a response, Alexandra turned and walked out.

"Guess coffee and a chat was a bad idea," Myron muttered to himself, suddenly feeling a chill.

***

Freta phoned Myron, waited, and when the answering machine clicked on said, "I'll be working late tonight. How about going out to dinner and a movie tomorrow night? *Out of Africa* is on. It's a biggie with Meryl Streep and Robert Redford!"

She knew that Myron's taste in cinema lay elsewhere, closer to a Clint Eastwood western, but *Pale Rider* had already come and gone. The choice came down to *Out of Africa* or *Goonies* — not! She also wanted to catch him up on a number of topics, one, in particular, that she had forgotten to mention the last time they were together. "So many things happening right now … oops — got to go!" She cut her message short when Roberta came out of Reuben's office, looking flushed.

"Right, we need to get a move on," the detective announced. "A print found on that button at the crime scene has come back with a match — to Croft."

Freta and Rob looked at each other in disbelief. Despite her wild theory regarding Croft's connection to Raglan's killing, she had not seen this coming.

"We need a search warrant for Croft's home and property," Roberta declared emphatically.

# Chapter Twenty

**Saturday, 24 August**

Alex Croft rose from bed early, went to the bathroom, relieved himself, and stared into the sink mirror. Rheumy eyes, three days' worth of stubble, dishevelled-looking from the hair down. This was the look of a man quickly unravelling. Very little sleep, loss of appetite, mounting anxiety and confusion, capped by an unkempt appearance. He needed to get a grip and pull himself together.

The night with Boyd did not go well, but he was sure he would survive it, tough it out. He was strong enough mentally to do so. After all, he didn't mean for the bastard to die!

Yet he was surprised at how quickly the RCMP moved, zeroing in on him. Admittedly, he was under pressure and was careless, although given the circumstances, he had done a thorough job of cleaning and sanitizing his vehicle. And he did get rid of the shovel now lying in thick brush somewhere between Grotto Road and Great Plains. His new criminal lawyer Hoar had assigned assured him that the evidence collected was thin and circumstantial and that there were alternative explanations for the tiny specks of Boyd's blood found in his partner's office and Croft's Jeep, including that of a frame job.

All this he could handle. But the blackmail… Someone else knew where the body was buried, and now the discovery of this female in a grave (apparently) at the Grotto cemetery? What did that mean? Not a coincidence, surely? He thought about going out there and extracting Boyd from his resting place, putting him elsewhere. Aside from the logistics and the fact that it seemed impossible at the moment, he didn't think he'd have the stomach for it.

However, he had the stomach to confront the blackmailer — as soon as he figured out who he was. Taking another look at himself in the mirror, he winced. *Okay, have to become disciplined once again. Start with a shave, shit, and shower, and then a quick early-morning trip to Saskatoon Berry Park before breakfast. Call it a reconnaissance — time to take the offensive.*

Indeed, he would scout the lay of the land, so to speak. Check out the location of the sandbox. It should be easy enough to backtrack with the thick woods on either side of the trail, find a good vantage point, observe unseen, take photos, and follow the blackmailer after he took the duffel bag.

Wearing his hiking shoes, faded blue jeans, and grey sweatshirt under a green windbreaker and topped with an Expos baseball cap, Croft was about to step out the door when his driveway suddenly became a parking lot for cop cars, marked and unmarked. *Shit!*

The chime sounded, and he opened the door. There on his threshold was that older female detective with a sheaf of papers in her hand.

"We have a warrant to search your premises," she announced. "Please step aside." She waved to a coterie of cops and handed him the paperwork as she marched in.

"I'm calling my lawyer," he said.

"You do that," she answered.

***

Isaac couldn't avoid his dad, he supposed, especially since he found his private place. Thus, it was no surprise (but bad timing) when Hans materialized from behind the hut as he came down the slope.

His father got to the point. "Did you do that girl harm?"

*You mean did I kill her?* "What girl?"

"Don't play stupid with me. You know exactly who I mean."

Isaac stopped and took a moment to consider his response. *How much should I tell him? What does he know?* "Yeah, I suppose I do… No, I didn't harm her."

"Then how do you explain this?" Hans fished into his jacket pocket and brought out a set of car keys and a bracelet, the latter dangling at the end of his hand.

"Where'd you get those?" Isaac asked. *You're going to fuck this up for me, old man.*

Hans hesitated. He didn't want to admit that he'd broken into Isaac's hut and removed the bracelet. "Found the items just about where you're standing. Says Ford on the key and Raglan on the bracelet. Explain how they got here and why I shouldn't turn this over to the RCMP."

Isaac shifted his weight from the right foot to the left. *Think you're smart and me slow. I'm smarter than you!* For a moment the anger welled up and his eyes flashed. "The cops aren't our friends."

"I know that. Tell me what happened?"

"I found her."

"You found her?"

"Yeah, she was lying there." Isaac pointed vaguely to a spot where the land started to elevate into a hill. "I think she fell. Must've broken her neck. She wasn't moving."

Hans stared at him incredulously, no words forming.

"I don't want to go to prison," Isaac said, filling the silence. "They won't believe me. Even you have doubts. I can tell."

"Isaac, I—"

"So I took her away and buried her off our land — in the cemetery. I know I shouldn't have moved her. But they wouldn't believe me," he repeated. "They don't like us and would never leave us alone especially since we — you know..." *Remind him of the sabotage charges.* "Anyway, if the body was discovered here, they would find a way to blame us."

Convincing or not, Isaac knew the old man would give him the benefit of the doubt.

"Why bury her at the Grotto cemetery?"

Isaac shrugged. "It's where people are buried, and I thought that the one already there wouldn't mind." He resisted smiling at his own levity. It wouldn't have been in character.

Hans did not believe his son — not for a moment. He had found the bracelet with her name etched on the faceplate inside, after all, in the matted depression where the body had lain. Besides, God had told him otherwise; he had received an irrefutable answer.

If Isaac was convicted of the unfortunate girl's death, he would go to prison, most assuredly. And he would have a tough time of it. Whatever punishment God had in store for him, somewhere in his core, Hans still believed that Isaac was "special," a gentle soul who would not only experience the blackness of many godless, criminal souls in prison but himself be incorrigibly corrupted.

Also, there was the further consideration of his ministry dedicated to God's decree of living a simple, fundamentalist life unbridled by the state or Big Oil that he so justly fought against. This event would undoubtedly bring revulsion and suspicion on God's Light Church, already reeling with only a handful of worshippers. He desperately needed more in the congregation, not to mention local sympathizers to his cause taken aback in recent years by the sabotage of nearby sour gas wells. They supported his righteous fight (so they professed) but disapproved of his methods. *No,* he thought, *Isaac is correct in one respect: a dead young female discovered on my property would lead to disaster for me and my community.*

None of that mitigated the fact that Isaac was being deceitful. Hans knew this as sure as receiving the word from God the other day. Isaac had to tell the truth, not necessarily to the police, but to God. It was the only way to purify and save his soul. Isaac would have to confess in the Temple of God — in his church, Hans decided. After which God would pronounce judgement. There was no option.

"This isn't over," Hans said, walking past his son up the hill.

"No, it's not," Isaac muttered at the retreating back of his father. "I've got a date tonight with a whole lot of cash!"

***

It took over two hours for the search team to go through Croft's home. They concentrated mostly on the garage, seizing a shovel, spade, couple of flashlights, and a folded tarpaulin and rope on an overhanging shelf. Of particular interest was an old khaki jacket that Croft evidently used for work in the garage and outdoors. It had a sizable irregular hole around the middle where the cloth and at least two buttons were missing. It was carefully bagged. Other apparel that hung on hooks beside the khaki jacket were also bagged. This included a black hoodie, orange vest, and a pair of rubber boots underneath.

Stoned-faced, almost stoic, Croft looked on, made his phone call and, like some of his personal effects, was taken into custody. Once he arrived at the RCMP building, he sat tight and said nothing, as instructed, and awaited Stuart Findler, Hoar's rising new criminal attorney.

"Now isn't he a dandy," Roberta muttered to Freta as Findler was escorted to meet with his client.

Findler was somewhere between his late-twenties to mid-thirties, with an athletic build and erect posture, all six or so feet of him. His blond hair was longish but nicely trimmed, with no tell-tale curls at the ends, and his intense blue eyes pierced like cold, thin lasers when he focused. The eyes were, in fact, the most impressive feature; they dominated a square face made slightly incongruous by a wide forehead and narrow chin. *Those eyes are probably very effective in a courtroom setting,* thought Freta as he was led down the corridor to his client.

Findler dressed like a Bay Street lawyer: grey, fine wool suit, white shirt with a discreet blue tie. The only discordant note was the slightly scuffed Italian loafers.

After a half hour meet-and-greet consultation, they convened in the same interrogation room Croft had visited voluntarily a few days ago. The same protocols were observed, with LeBlanc informing him that the interview would be recorded and videoed, starting with the identification of those participating, the day, time, and place. Once these preliminaries were dispensed with, they got down to business. Findler could hardly contain himself.

"Why was my client's home raided?" He gave LeBlanc a cold, accusatory stare.

"Because we had probable cause and obtained a search warrant."

"Is my client being charged with a crime?"

"Not at this precise moment. But that remains to be determined, depending on the answers to some questions."

"Which my client is not obliged to answer."

"Mr. Findler, give me some credit for knowing a little law. And this isn't my first rodeo. We have enough to at the very least detain Mr. Croft for twenty-four hours and probably extend that on application to ninety-six, given the serious nature of the crime, during which time the Crown prosecutor can decide whether to lay charges. The first thing you should've asked was what is Mr. Croft being charged with? You were a little vague on that. However, I will tell you, since you are entitled to know. Mr. Croft is a suspect in the killing of Ms. Raglan Bullock. Hasn't been formally charged — yet."

"What?" Croft exploded, his face draining of colour. He turned to Findler. "I–I don't understand." His hands began trembling, and he looked, bewildered, from Findler to LeBlanc to Freta, who sat silent with her notebook, writing.

Aside from taking notes, according to LeBlanc her job was to read reactions to questions and changes in body language and mannerisms. It didn't take a profiler to conclude that Croft had not seen that coming, nor had his brash attorney. She could with unflinching certainty say the Croft was "All Shook Up." She wrote that in large letters, remembering an Elvis Presley song of the same title.

Nonplussed, LeBlanc continued, "Mr. Croft, do you know where Grotto Road and the old Catholic cemetery is?" She did not look directly at him but instead at an open folder on the table in front of her.

"Y–yes."

"Have you been there often?"

"No ... not often, just a couple of times when my business as a property assessor took me to the area."

"Specifically, were you travelling on Grotto Road early Sunday morning, on August 11 — heading west from the direction of the cemetery?"

Croft wet his lips and paused as if to think and took a furtive glance at Findler, who didn't react. He seemed as flummoxed by the questions as his client.

"I ... no. I was home at the time, in bed. I was off to Edmonton that morning, so..." he trailed off.

"Are you sure?"

"My client has answered the question." It appeared that Findler had recovered his equilibrium.

"Can anyone corroborate that you were home during this time period, say midnight to 7:00 a.m.?"

"No, my wife is away, visiting her mother in B.C."

"Right then, for the record — and you know you're being recorded — the answer is a definitive no, you weren't on Grotto Road, August 11."

"That's correct."

LeBlanc nodded and then pursed her lips contemplatively. "The thing is we have an eyewitness who swears you were there."

"Eyewitness?" Croft visibly tensed, giving a startled glance at his attorney. "Who?"

"Sorry, can't divulge that at the moment."

"Well, whoever it was, he or she was mistaken," Croft retorted in a low, gritty voice.

At this point, Findler interjected. "Look ... when I consulted with my client, we were under the impression that this was about an entirely different matter... In the light of this new accusation, I need to reconsult. I am requesting a recess—"

"Oh, you mean the missing Mr. Boyd. Undoubtedly, we'll get back to that case. But you're right, this investigation is about the death of Ms. Bullock. So, go ahead and consult. Far be it for me to deny due process. Is an hour adequate?" she asked.

Findler nodded.

"Good, I need a coffee and doughnut! Interview suspended at," she glanced at her watch, "2:15, to be resumed at 3: 15..."

"He was absolutely shocked," Freta said. "Either he is a very good actor or ... I don't know."

"It doesn't feel quite right, but the evidence is damning," Roberta said over a coffee and double-glazed chocolate doughnut courtesy of Rainy, who had been listening in on the other side of the two-way mirror. He forthwith zipped across the street to Tim Hortons.

"And there's that one very odd, inexplicable anomaly," suggested Freta, having read the forensic analysis on the piece of cloth found in Bullock's hand.

"Yeah, just finished reading that, the material being cut rather than torn … doesn't make sense. Any theories?" chimed in Rainy, looking at Freta. He had joined them in the case room.

"None, none at all," responded Freta.

"Someone in a fight for their life wouldn't suddenly pull out a pair of scissors or knife and cut a piece of the assailant's jacket," said Rainy, stating the obvious.

"Unless that's not what happened," said Roberta. "I'm letting that swim around in my brain for a bit. Of course, we still have to confirm that khaki jacket we retrieved from Croft's domicile matches the piece from the crime scene. I'll bet a whole year's supply of kitty litter that it will, though."

"Also, a small point, maybe — there are two buttons missing on that jacket. The forensics team found only one on the cut or torn clothing," Freta noted.

"Good observation. It may have fallen out somewhere or still be at the grave in the mud. The button that we have is enough, thank God. With Croft's thumb and partial index fingerprint on it should be a slam dunk, but…" Roberta trailed off.

"And why, if Croft used that jacket in the commission of this crime, particularly if the victim literally ripped it open, would he not have gotten rid of it instead of hanging it back on the hook?" asked Rainy.

"Why indeed," agreed Roberta.

*** 

They reconvened at 3:17 p.m. Croft walked in, clearly uneasy, fidgeting with his hands and casting wary glances in the direction of his attorney.

Findler, too, appeared unsettled; he focused his steely blue eyes on Freta for a brief moment before targeting LeBlanc. *Preparing for round two,* thought Freta, her pen and notebook in hand.

LeBlanc left no doubt about her line of questioning. "So, for the record, you did not know Ms. Bullock?"

"No, never met her."

"How about her parents? Ever have any dealings with them?"

"No, never."

"What about Mr. Boyd? Would he have?"

"I wouldn't know. Certainly, the firm didn't."

"The thing is — a real puzzle, actually — if what you're saying is true, how is it that we found your fingerprints on an article of clothing at the crime scene?"

"What? That's impossible." Croft swung almost fully around to his defence attorney. "I didn't kill her!"

Findler put his hand on Croft's forearm as if to reassure him.

"Please answer the question," LeBlanc pressed, her voice an even monotone.

"I don't know… I have no idea."

"No idea at all?"

"My client has answered the question," Findler interjected.

"Well, you see, Mr. Croft, it gets worse." She leaned forward across the table to where Croft was seated. "We found a piece of khaki material clutched in Ms. Bullock's hand that very much resembles the missing piece from the jacket hanging on your garage wall — identical, in fact, including the buttons. Did you know that there was a chunk missing from your jacket? Yeah, right about here." She swirled her hand around her midsection. How did that occur?"

"I–I didn't notice. It's just an old jacket that I occasionally throw on in chilly weather when I'm working in the garage or outside."

"When was the last time you put it on?"

"I can't remember — over a month ago."

"Have you confirmed that Mr. Croft's jacket is a match to the clothing sample found at the crime scene?" Findler asked, trying to reassert his presence and defend his client.

"No, but I am confident that will be the case. And, at any rate, Mr. Croft's prints were found on the material and a button at the site — we're not sure yet if it was the primary crime scene."

"I'm at a total loss to explain this," said Croft. "What motive would I have?"

"That is yet to be determined," responded LeBlanc cryptically.

"My client has no further comment to make at this time," Findler interceded.

LeBlanc pursed her lips into a placating smile and placed her hands over each other on the table. "Mr. Croft, we will be holding you in custody for the next twenty-four hours, pending further investigation and decision to lay charges."

"No, no I have business to attend to—"

"It's okay, Alex," said Findler, using his given name for the first time. "They can hold you for only so long, and if need be, I'll make application for bail."

"Oh, by the way, this business you have to tend to — it wouldn't have anything to do with the $10,000 in cash that officers found in your closet?"

"Don't answer that," Findler cautioned. "It's not a crime to keep cash on one's property. And relevance? What has it to do with … with anything?"

LeBlanc shrugged. "It was discovered as part of our search. Maybe Mr. Croft would care to shed light on its relevance."

"I wasn't made aware of this money, and I am advising my client not to answer."

LeBlanc smirked. "Seems you're not aware of a lot of things."

Freta blanched and almost winced at the low blow.

"It's okay," Croft said shakily. "I do have, from time to time, extra cash on hand for unexpected contingencies that arise."

"So, not your winnings from Vegas then?" LeBlanc asked with a sardonic smile.

***

As it turned out, *Out of Africa* came first and supper quite late. Two aspects of the movie didn't sit well with Myron: it was about two and half hours long, and, more importantly, it was boring. Freta was more favourably disposed toward the film. She didn't mind a romantic epic, albeit one that ended tragically. Both agreed that the location scenery was spectacular and that Streep and Redford "saved it."

For most of the evening they avoided talking shop, but as they mellowed over dark roasted coffee and crostata pie at Pietro's, Great Plains's fine Italian restaurant, events in their day spilled over into their conversation. In fact, for Freta, the floodgates opened.

Myron, she realized, had become a kind of confidant, someone who could reaffirm her actions that day, who listened to her observations, opinions, and out-there thoughts without too much judgement (for the most part), providing feedback and ideas that could be bounced around and reworked. And there was much to rework on this case.

She told him about the search of Croft's home, what they found, and his detention. Myron listened without comment.

"I can't tell whether Croft's lawyer is a dork or made the best of a bad situation," said Freta. "Anyway, Roberta was unrelenting and nasty. I was almost embarrassed, but I think it rattled them both." When she finished giving her impressions of Croft's interrogation, she stopped and leaned back. "You seem strangely quiet," she admonished when Myron didn't say anything.

"Just suffused with too much veal parmigiana and getting more sluggish eating this dessert pie. It does sound like you have a strong case against Croft, although I find it hard to believe that he could do such a thing, from my brief acquaintance with him. What's his motive?"

"To be ascertained, according to Roberta. My theory, crazy as it seems, was that Raglan was in the wrong place, at the wrong time — saw him getting rid of Boyd somewhere out there, and he snapped her neck and buried her in a graveyard. Maybe Boyd is similarly buried nearby. With no body, though, it's a pretty flimsy theory."

"Not to mention macabre but … plausible. Maybe worth pursuing by checking the graves in the cemetery, see if any more had been recently disturbed."

"Not a bad idea," said Freta. "And then there are the little inconsistencies that we haven't been able to explain yet."

"Ah, little things are the key. It's always the little things that bug Columbo."

Freta laughed. "Yeah, but this is real."

"Right! So, what little things?"

Freta shoved her dessert dish off to the side and leaned toward Myron. They were in a secluded booth; patrons had thinned out as the hour grew late. Still, she lowered her voice conspiratorially. "The damning evidence was the fabric and the button with Croft's prints. We found the jacket minus the missing cloth and button hanging on a hook in his garage. A slam dunk, right? But it begs the question: why didn't he get rid of it, especially if Raglan tore it? But that's the other rub: the lab report states that the fabric was not torn, but cut. Can't get my head around that one. And yet the evidence is irrefutable. We're ninety-nine percent sure that Croft's thumbprint and index fingerprint found on the button attached to the material clutched in Raglan's hand came from his jacket. And thanks to Hans, as credible or not as he may be, Croft can be placed there."

Myron again fell silent. He seemed to go off into space.

"Hello, Earth to moon man," Freta said, snapping her fingers. "What are you thinking?"

"Buttons, or more precisely a button."

"Okaaay." Freta frowned. "Care to elaborate?"

"Better I show you. We'll stop by my apartment tonight. Don't worry, I won't take advantage."

"Oh?"

"Well, only if you want me to. I do have something else of interest for you."

"I can hardly wait."

Instead of taking the elevator, they walked up the stairs to Myron's third-floor abode. "A little exercise after a heavy meal never hurts," Freta commented as they entered.

"Speak for yourself." Myron flipped the light switch and stood for a moment.

"Trying to catch your breath?" Freta asked speciously.

"What'd you mean? I'm in fine shape. I just need to remember which tweed I wore that night."

"What night?"

"The Thursday night I saw Isaac a little worse for wear in the college washroom. I mentioned it to you."

"I remember. So?"

"It was my bluish-grey weave," Myron said, moving to the closet.

Swinging open the two-piece door, he moved a couple of hangers until he had access to the one he wanted. From an outside pocket he pulled out a small clear plastic bag containing a large four-hole brown button made of undetermined material. He gave it to Freta.

"What's this?" she asked.

"It's what fell out of Isaac's pocket that night. It's a button!"

"I can see that, now that you've pointed it out," she said with mock sarcasm.

"He was in such a hurry to leave, to get away from me I guess, that he didn't notice it falling out. Anyway, I had quite forgotten about it until you brought up buttons. It may be nothing, but Columbo would think it's something."

"Nothing or everything, hmm," Freta said, inspecting it closely. "It sure looks like a match to the ones left on Croft's jacket and the one found at the gravesite. I'll have it checked out. If it is — the whole scenario changes."

"I imagine it would," Myron said. "Has Isaac been interviewed yet?"

"No. He's managed to fly under the radar thus far." Consternation clouded Freta's complexion. "You know what — tomorrow I'm meeting Roberta for breakfast at her hotel. She wants to go over some details, the loose ends that I mentioned. I think you should come with me, at least for the breakfast portion. You can explain how you came in possession of this button." She raised the bag to the hallway light, as if to reassure herself that it indeed was what it was. "I'd swear that it's an identical match, and there can't be too many of these around. Forensic analysis will give us the answer.

It shouldn't take long. The mind boggles at what this could mean. So what do you say?"

"I'm in. Breakfast sounds great. What time should I drop a floor and pick you up?"

Freta gave him a coy smile. "Since that's settled, why don't we drop a floor together to my place, and you can stay the night. Save you dropping a floor tomorrow morning."

"Sounds like a plan," he said, breaking into a smile.

# Chapter Twenty-One

Isaac waited over an hour, but Croft did not show. In his anxiety, he even took a chance, nervously skirting the trail to the sandbox and, when no one was about, lifting the lid and taking a quick look just in case he somehow missed him. "Nothing, nothing but fuckin' sand," he cursed. "And not too much of that either." What was Croft thinking, that there'd be no consequences? That he wouldn't snitch him out?

The plan had not gone wrong, he told himself. It was Croft who was messing with him. He now had two strikes against him; *three strikes and you're out.* Isaac was not inclined to give Croft a third chance. Still, he really, really wanted the money.

For a long time, Isaac sat in his truck in the pavilion parking lot. *What to do? What to do?* He was smart and would figure this out! It was almost eight; he couldn't just sit there! *Wait until nine, drive by his place, break in, and take the money — it'll be in the house, right? Sure as hell wasn't in the sandbox — if he really was going to pay me, that is…* "If I'm going to do this," he counselled himself, "I better get a ski mask or nylon stocking to cover my face. And be ready, this guy can fight!"

In the end, Isaac decided to give Croft one last chance. It seemed less risky than a break-in, and he didn't know where or even if the money was in the house. Besides, not only would he need a mask, but also a weapon. The last time he was armed only with a flashlight. He tried to hit Croft with it, but he blocked his swing, and it flew off somewhere, clanging in the corner against something.

Nevertheless, it wouldn't hurt to drive by Croft's home. Have a look. See what was what. It'd just be a quick in and out. It was now after nine, dark, and nobody would spot him or take notice if they did.

He hadn't thought out what he wanted to accomplish. When he arrived, the street was dark except for the yellowish glow of streetlamps, and Croft's home was totally dark and foreboding. Maybe he was home. Maybe not. No point in hanging around.

He knew that he should take some time and think out his next move out carefully, but he couldn't resist. He stopped at the same telephone kiosk he had used the two previous occasions and made a call. *One more chance. You're getting one more chance before an anonymous tip to the cops. The house is dark, but that doesn't mean he isn't home. It doesn't matter anyway...*

The phone rang a number of times, then a click and Croft's voice: "I'm presently unavailable. Please leave your name, number, and a brief message. I'll get back to you as soon as possible. Thanks."

"One more chance. That's it! Same place and time Monday."

Isaac drove home, thinking it sure would be nice to have some real cash in his pocket. Just to know what it felt like and whether it made a difference to the next female he met.

***

Settling in his cell for the night, Croft replayed the interview/interrogation — whatever it was called — with Detective LeBlanc. *Insufferable old bag!* Very little of it made sense, unless there was a whole lot more in play than he imagined. How did he get into double jeopardy, for example? He was being accused of killing a girl he didn't know who, apparently, had gone missing and wound up dead near or in the old cemetery. At the same time, he was being blackmailed for a crime he *had* committed. The two had to be connected, but damned if he knew how.

Moreover, how did part of his garden jacket get to the crime scene? He simply could not join the dots! It was a tangled weave, the threads of which he couldn't unravel. The one event that he attributed little significance to at the time was the attempted burglary. He found the intruder in the garage where his old jacket hung. Had the intruder torn a sample to set him up? Why? And who could it be? Not the blackmailer, surely — that would be counterproductive, trying to extort money while at the same time framing him. *No money if I'm in prison, bud!* And certainly not Hans Trovotka, whom Croft believed might have been the eyewitness. He had grappled with a younger man who made his escape in a hurry. Absolutely none of it made any sense!

*So, what are my options?* He pondered his possibilities. *Confess, tell the RCMP that I accidently killed Boyd, but I had nothing to do with that missing girl's death. It's possible I'm being blackmailed by the killer who knows where I buried Boyd's body and framed me by breaking into my garage and stealing a piece of incriminating evidence... Stop. No one would believe me. It's too garbled a story. Even I'm not sure if I believe me! No ... option two and the best option ... keep your mouth shut about Boyd in particular and see what shakes out.*

Then there was Findler, Hoar's "hot young attorney." *The jury's still out on him,* Croft decided, smiling at his inadvertent legal reference. He tried his best, but they were both blindsided by the accusation...

It wasn't until the next morning, after a restless night of attempted sleep, that Croft sat up on the bed, put his head into his hands, and formulated a way forward. He went through it again with a sharper focus: if he told the police about Boyd but that he didn't have anything to do with the young lady's death, almost certainly he wouldn't be believed and would end up being charged with a double homicide. Logical conclusion already established, say as little as possible. Meanwhile, more information was vital. And here Findler would earn at least part of the huge legal bill Hoar and Company would no doubt hand him. First, who was the eyewitness? The defence, he would assume, was entitled to know. The way Croft saw it, identifying the eyewitness equalled blackmailer and potentially murderer, even if that didn't quite add up! Secondly, it couldn't be a coincidence that this teenager was killed near or at the cemetery and apparently buried there (media reports were still sketchy). The police knew the details, and so should Findler and his defence team. Was she indeed buried, and exactly where was she buried?

Croft required information and understanding of what was being played out before he could act in any reasonable fashion. However, before any action could be undertaken on his part, Findler had to get him out on bail.

\*\*\*

Roberta LeBlanc was seated at the far end of the Great Plains Inn coffee shop reading the *Edmonton Journal* when Freta and Myron arrived.

"Got a booth for six because there will be four of us. Corporal Rainy is coming," she said without preliminary greetings. She gestured to take a seat across from her.

Freta nodded, and Myron smiled. *Nice to see you again too.*

"Coffee?"

"Love some," said Freta, reaching for the carafe sitting on the table and turning up a white cup. Myron followed suit. He wasn't going to say anything until asked specifically, he decided.

Rainy came in a few minutes later, eyed the three of them, and hesitantly slid in beside LeBlanc.

There was wariness between Myron and Rob going back to the suspicious death of the college president and Freta's reluctance to call in detectives from Major Crimes. Instead, she had conscripted him to sleuth around the campus. Myron presumed that Rob was not consulted. That the case worked out well was, for Rob, Myron knew, pure happenstance. "You got lucky," he had said over a beer after, only half joking. And here he was inserting himself into the investigation again — never mind that this time Major Crimes was involved.

They nodded pleasantries at one another.

"Okay," said Roberta, "let's order breakfast, my treat!" She smiled. "I recommend the Early Bird Special, if you're into traditional eggs, bacon, ham, or sausage with hash brown and toast, then we'll get down to business."

They all ordered the Early Bird Special.

Freta had phoned Roberta before retiring for the night, quickly briefing her about Myron's button. The RCMP detective agreed that he should give them "his report."

While waiting for the breakfast orders to be delivered, Myron related how he encountered Isaac in the college washroom Thursday night, August 15, "...fixing himself up. His face was puffy and bruised, and he appeared to have acquired a very distinct limp. The plastic bag with the button fell out of his pocket when he reached in for more tissue. It looked like he'd been in a fight, but he said that he slipped and fell in the college parking lot."

"Let's have a look at this mysterious button," said Roberta with a note of skepticism.

Freta produced a little clear bag with the button in it from her pocket. She handled the package carefully, her fingertips holding it by a corner as she set it down on the table. Roberta and Rob leaned in for a better look.

"Sure as hell looks like the button found at the gravesite," said Roberta.

"I agree," said Rob.

"I'll fast-track an analysis then. We'll know for sure soon enough. Meanwhile, let's assume that it *is* the button from Croft's jacket. How did Isaac Trovotka get it?"

They bantered around some ideas that seemed half-baked and didn't make much sense at all until breakfast came. While they ate Rob, came up with the crazy idea that maybe Isaac broke into Croft's garage and "cut out a piece of the jacket to frame Croft because he killed Raglan, buried her in the cemetery, and his father pointed to Croft to cover his son's crime or possibly his own or both."

"If that's true, why Croft?" asked Freta. "I mean why make Croft the scapegoat to cover up what they did? Did they know each other?"

"Good question. I didn't bring that up in Croft's interrogation," said Roberta. "Didn't want him to surmise Hans was the witness. Of course, his lawyer will know soon enough."

"We're still a long way from making any sense of this," Freta concluded after further discussion.

"On that we can all agree," said Roberta, sighing.

"What's our next move?" asked Rob.

Roberta thought for a moment. "Let's concentrate on the weakest link to this puzzle: Trovotka's son. Presuming Myron's button pans out, there is more than sufficient grounds to bring him in and really grill him. See what shakes out!"

"I'd like to know who beat him up," Myron finally piped in after remaining silent for most of the conversation. Although he hadn't been told to leave, he felt reluctant to fully participate in the discussion/scrum going on at the table.

"I'll be sure to ask him," said Roberta with a hint of bemusement.

# Chapter Twenty-Two

**Monday, August 26**

John A. Macdonald, Canada's first prime minister, was known as "Old Tomorrow" because he would put off difficult decisions for another day in the hopes that they would resolve themselves. Myron felt like "Old Tomorrow" when he got to his office after his post-class exchange with Alexandra. Instead of starting a file documenting his encounters with her and officially putting it on record with Student Affairs, like he promised himself, he had decided to take the weekend to think it over. But there was really nothing to think about, and here he was Monday morning sitting at his desk, having done nothing about an escalating situation. He sighed; the file wasn't going to create itself. *Better get started.*

He listed his "chance" meetings with Alexandra outside the classroom, along with the dates. Actually, once he wrote them down, they seemed innocent enough — in Saskatoon Berry Park, outside the restaurant (which could be corroborated by two RCMP officers), and, the most telling and what really precipitated Myron's concern, the college parking lot encounter. At this point an official file on record would suffice, he believed. Alexandra's odd behaviour had not led to any notable repercussions — yet.

He had just finished putting pen to paper when, by some cosmic karma, he looked up and saw Alexandra standing at his open door. "Can I speak to you?" she asked in a low, sombre voice.

Myron put his pen down, closed the file folder, and beckoned to the empty seat. "Of course."

She sat down, knees together, looking chastened. "I thought about what you said," she informed him.

He kept his face blank, not knowing what part of what he said she was referring to. *I said a number of things...*

"You are right, and I understand your concerns about student-instructor relationships." She clarified.

"Okay..." he responded slowly, not knowing where this was going.

"After some thought, I've decided to withdraw from your courses." She opened her handbag and pulled out a piece of paper. "Got this add/drop form for your initials." She laid it on the corner of his desk.

Surprised and caught totally off guard, Myron stared at the form, suddenly very concerned. Maybe he had been a little harsh in his judgement of her, interpreted intentions in exaggerated fashion. He didn't want to jeopardize her program, although his courses weren't absolutely necessary for her education degree. "Have you considered what courses would replace them?"

"Two poli scis and an introductory sociology fit into my schedule."

He nodded. The semester had only just begun, so switching courses was not a problem. And he wasn't about to discourage her, he decided. This was probably for the best both for her and him — removed awkwardness and, he had to admit, temptation. "Well, thank you for stopping by and..." he cleared his throat, "your recognition of the situation." He reached over, took the form, and initialled the appropriate spots. "Good luck in your studies." He did not know what else to say.

Alexandra took the form, folded it, and put it back into her handbag. She rose from her seat, giving him an inscrutable gaze, her eyes intense. "Well then, I better be off!"

Afterward, Myron stared blankly at the folder he had just created. He felt relieved, albeit inexplicably unsettled. Still, given what had transpired, no further action was required on his part. "*Old Tomorrow*" *was on to something after all,* he mused.

*⁎⁎⁎*

"Let's approach this as a routine matter," instructed Roberta when "Team LeBlanc" assembled in the case room Monday morning. "Since we won't know if Myron's button," she said this with a bemused smile and a quick glance at Freta, "matches the ones on Croft's jacket until later today or tomorrow morning. We'll ask Isaac Trovotka to come in voluntarily. After all, we haven't formally interviewed him, and he is on the list."

This was a different tack than Roberta had been advocating at their breakfast meeting. At that time she was ready to haul Isaac in forthwith.

"So we phone and arrange a time for him to appear?" asked Rob, preempting her thoughts.

"Yes, see what kind of reaction we get."

"He'll be reluctant," said Freta. "And Hans will run interference, possibly come with him or hire a lawyer."

"Can't do much about the lawyer — his prerogative — but Isaac is of age, right? An interview will be conducted without his father, or mother, for that matter…"

"Hans might argue Isaac's 'limited capacity,'" said Freta. "That we would take advantage of him."

"Unless there's a psychiatric report to that effect, Isaac will be treated as a 'normal' adult helping the police in their enquiries."

"Should we wait until the lab results on the button are in?" asked Rob.

"Absolutely not. Let's talk to him *tout de suite*, as we French would say it."

"I'll make the call," offered Freta. "This afternoon … say one o'clock?"

"As good a time as any," Roberta replied.

Freta crossed the corridor into the bullpen area to her desk and phoned the Trovotka residence. She came back perturbed. "Mrs. Trovotka finally picked up. Said Isaac wasn't home, she didn't know where he had gone, but she'd ask him to get in touch with us when he did come home."

"Fat chance of that! Where was Hans? I expected him to take charge and do all the talking," said Roberta.

"According to Mrs. Trovotka, he was outside on the property somewhere."

"Hmm, this is not getting us anywhere expeditiously," Roberta exclaimed. "Maybe I'm being too polite... Plan B. Let's find Isaac, get his vehicle plate number, and haul him in."

\*\*\*

Alex Croft spoke to his attorney early Sunday afternoon; he was released about an hour later, although the two events were not necessarily related. The usual proviso applied: "You're still a person of interest, so don't leave town." On his way out he was handed his personal belongings, including a duffel bag with $10,000, which had been seized and taken to the detachment for "safekeeping."

Findler promised to provide him with more details of the case against him, including the name of the witness who saw him on Grotto Road and the nature of the crime against Raglan Bullock — how and where was she buried. Meanwhile, "sit tight" was the advice. What else was he expected to do now that he was released? Carry on with his life and business as usual? Croft didn't think so.

It wasn't until early Sunday evening that he finally got around to his telephone messages. There were a number of business-related calls and one from the blackmailer.

"Son of a bitch!" he snorted as he downed his glass of Scotch. The prick had the audacity to frame him for a murder and was still expecting to get paid to remain silent! He had thought that logically the blackmailer and the murderer couldn't have been the same person, but after spending a few hours in the cell thinking about it and now listening to the message on his answering machine, he reconsidered. Who else could it be? More to the point, what kind of idiot would do that? Or was he the one who was being taken for the idiot?

"Well, we'll try this again," he said to himself. "There'll be a bag in that sandbox, and when you'll retrieve it, I'll be there observing. I will find out who you are..." First step in getting ahead of this mess: know who you're dealing with!

One potential problem: Had the RCMP staked him out? He didn't think so. Why would they? Findler thought it would bode well for his defence that the RCMP did not apply to a judge to extend his stay in custody. "It points to a weak or incomplete case," he said. In all likelihood, then, he was not under surveillance and could move freely about the city.

His plan proved amazingly simple to execute. Drop the shopping bag into the sandbox (he had jettisoned the duffel bag, since it had been handled by the police); find a suitable vintage point with a clear view and plenty of cover; get the camera focused and ready; and await the blackmailer. The idea was to take some photos and, if feasible, at least follow him to his vehicle. Once this individual was identified, he would figure out how to deal with him.

The blackmailer showed up right on time. Croft knew it was him by the nervous, gimpy walk, the swivelling of his head, and how he hesitated as he neared the sandbox. He walked by it twice before lifting the lid and taking out the shopping bag. *Now for the moment of realization*, thought Croft with a sour smile. The blackmailer looked inside the bag, and Croft registered his shocked face with satisfaction. Instead of dollar bills, all he'd find were strips of cut and bundled magazine pages and newspaper. Croft could almost read the mantra on the man's lips: "Fuck you! Fuck you!"

However, there was also a note that simply read:

*Change of Plan*
*If You Want Your Money*
*Phone Me!*

He was rewriting the rules of engagement on his terms — he hoped!

After a second rummage through the bag's contents, the blackmailer found the folded paper with the note, read it, and stuffed it in his pocket. He then unceremoniously flung the bag into bushes beside the trail. He turned, looked around, and hurriedly started to walk down the trail toward the pavilion parking lot. Croft followed, discreetly paralleling him amid the shrubs and trees on the hill above the trail.

The blackmailer, obviously agitated, brushed by an elderly couple, forcing them off the trail without acknowledgement.

"Hey!" the grey-haired man yelled but got no response. "Asshole," he wheezed.

"It's okay, dear," his partner said, taking his arm.

Croft saw his target emerging from the woods and trail, walking briskly but with a distinctive list to the pavilion parking lot, and getting into an old Chevy short-box pickup. It started with a rattle and a loud rev, dropped into reverse with a clunk, and once out of the stall, jammed into drive. A heavy foot squealed and smoked the tires out of the park grounds.

That was definitely the man he had caught in his garage. Besides the limp, he had tell-tale signs of bruising on his face. There was a familiarity about him. Croft didn't know his name, but he knew who he was: Trovotka's son. The question was what to do now?

# Chapter Twenty-Three

**Tuesday, August 27**

It turned out that Isaac Trovotka did not need to be tracked down and "hauled in." He appeared voluntarily at the detachment with his father at 9:00 a.m.

"Does he need a lawyer?" asked Hans when he saw LeBlanc ambling toward them.

"Not at this point," replied LeBlanc.

After a relatively brief but tart exchange about who would and who wouldn't be at the interview, Isaac was ushered alone into the same room where his father had his interview. LeBlanc began expeditiously, getting the preliminaries, date, time, individuals present, etc., out of the way quickly. As before, Freta took notes, conscious that Isaac kept glancing apprehensively at her while LeBlanc, with great deliberation, placed a manila folder on the table in front of her and settled in her seat directly across from him like a menacing obelisk.

"You look a little worse for wear," she said cheerfully. "What happened to your face?"

"Fell."

"Where?"

"In the bush."

"In the bush? Where in the bush?"

"Bush on our farm."

"Hmm... That's not what you told to the person you met at the college. You were there August 15 around 8:00 p.m. getting yourself cleaned up from your fall... Right?"

"I don't remember."

"Well, they certainly remember you. Right mess you were. Told them you fell in the parking lot? That refresh your memory?"

Isaac gave LeBlanc a blank stare, his grey cells working hard to formulate an answer. "I might have been there," he finally allowed with a shrug.

"I'll take that as a definite maybe." LeBlanc smiled encouragingly.

"And if I was," Isaac retorted defiantly, "so what?"

"You lost something at the college. Do you remember that, Isaac?"

"No."

"No? No that you didn't lose anything or no that you don't remember?" LeBlanc leaned closer toward him and from the folder produced a glossy photo, sliding it across. "Recognize this?"

His eyes widened in surprise. Freta made a note of it. The palms of his hands were sweating, she noticed, as he shifted his forearms from his lap to the tabletop — perhaps an involuntary reaction to the photo thrust in front of him.

"No. It's just a picture of a button."

"Oh no, Isaac," said LeBlanc in a grave tone, "not just a button, but a button in a small plastic bag that fell out of your pocket!"

"No."

"No what? That it isn't your button, that it wasn't in your pocket, or that you don't remember losing it?"

"I–I never saw that button before!"

"So ... not your button?"

"No."

"Didn't fall out of your pocket?"

"No."

"So the person that saw it fall out of your pocket when you reached for a snot rag is mistaken?"

"Yeah."

There was a prolonged pause, after which LeBlanc resumed questioning on a different tack. "Do you know Mr. Alex Croft?"

"No."

Freta noted what she thought was a tell-tale sign: Isaac blinked suddenly and more rapidly. The mention of Croft drained his face of colour, and he nervously looked away from LeBlanc to Freta. His chair squeaked as he turned.

"Never met him… Know of him?"

"No."

"Ever been to his home?"

"No."

"You don't know where he lives?"

"No."

"Odd then, because the button in the photo belongs to Mr. Croft's jacket, a brownish khaki gardening jacket that hung in his garage."

Isaac shrugged, his eyes averting LeBlanc's and briefly settling on Freta again.

"How do you suppose Mr. Croft's button ended up in your pocket?"

"Dunno. I never saw it."

"But it fell out of your pocket, Isaac," LeBlanc pressed, her tone hardened. Unexpectedly, she brought her hand down onto the metal table with elevated force.

Isaac flinched, as did Freta, less noticeably — she hoped.

"You see, Isaac, the button in the photo is part of a murder investigation. It matches the button from Mr. Croft's jacket, along with a piece of material from that same jacket. It was found at the Grotto Road cemetery, where a crime was committed. Why would you be in possession of it?"

Freta's pen hesitated. Roberta was reaching a bit, since they were still awaiting a lab report to see if indeed the button came from Croft's jacket. However, since the interview (interrogation, more like) was being recorded, she duly followed suit.

"Maybe I found it," blurted Isaac, wetting his lips.

LeBlanc pounced. "So you did have it?"

"No. I–I don't remember?"

"You don't remember that you had it or where you found it?"

"I don't know," he said, his voice strained. He was clearly stressed and flustered. *Enough to confess?* wondered Freta.

LeBlanc paused again, her brow furrowed, seemingly in deep thought. "Did you know Raglan Bullock?" The detective took out a second photo from the manila folder, one of a smiling Ms. Bullock, and shoved it toward him. "Take a good look."

Isaac gave the photo a cursory look. "No."

"Not at all? You haven't seen her around, talked to her?"

"M–maybe — in town."

"Ah, so you may have seen her. Maybe talked to her as well?"

"No, just seen her around."

"Where were you August 10 say, from eleven in the evening to early next morning.?"

"I don't remember — sleeping, probably."

"You weren't at the Grotto Road cemetery or thereabout?"

"No."

Beads of perspiration ran down Isaac's chiselled face. His eyes kept blinking rapidly, the lazy eye watering as well. Freta could smell his increasingly pungent musky odour — *the smell of fear?*

"You know, Isaac, you're sinking into the mud here — real gumbo — sinking deeper and deeper. Pretty soon it'll be over your head. It'd be better for you to come clean, unburden yourself, tell us the truth. It was an accident, right? You didn't mean to hurt her, right? Tell us what happened."

He shook his head. "I didn't do anything."

LeBlanc gave him a long stare. "Sure you did. This isn't going away."

"I want a lawyer!"

LeBlanc sighed. "Ah." *The magic words.* "Are you sure?"

"I want a lawyer!" Isaac repeated.

LeBlanc nodded, picking up the photos and placing them back in the folder. "Did your father advise you to say that if you got into trouble? You *are* in trouble, you know."

Isaac said nothing.

"Interview terminated," LeBlanc announced, gathering the folder and nodding to Freta, who closed her black notebook. She rose and left the room, followed by Freta, leaving Isaac to stew in his misery.

"That went well," said Roberta, looking at Isaac through the two-way mirror. "His world is falling apart."

Freta nodded but couldn't tell whether the detective was being sardonic or not.

"So is he the one?" asked Rob to no one in particular. He had viewed part of the questioning and now joined them.

"He did it," pronounced Roberta. "But I still don't know how the pieces fit, especially with Croft."

"Are we detaining him?" asked Freta.

"For a short time, if we wish. We still haven't got a lab report matching the buttons. So much for my rush job… And even if it's a match, it's not quite enough at this point." She sighed. "We'll let him make his phone call, or rather, talk to Hans. I'm sure he has a lawyer lined up. In the meantime, we need a search warrant for Trovotka's place. In particular, I want Isaac's room and vehicle tossed. Maybe he kept a souvenir or two from his victim."

\*\*\*

Hans knew that Isaac was nervous about the interview, which they both decided was best handled as a voluntary walk-in.

"No sense in having them come banging on our door or stopping you on the street," said Hans. "Be calm and collected." He wanted to add "you've done nothing wrong" but didn't.

Hans suspected Isaac had much to be nervous about. His son was unpredictable, and he was most certainly hiding something. He tried again to have him open up, tell him the truth, no matter how horrible, but the only concession he got was that they would talk after the interview, which Hans took to mean depending on how badly it went and what the RCMP knew.

He hoped to accompany Isaac into the interview room but was denied. The fat old cop told him that Isaac was an adult and could speak for himself. His intimation that his son was a "special adult" received a wry "so what" smile, and he wasn't going to explain exactly what he meant. He could only hope for the best, that Isaac would come out of the interrogation intact. If questions were posed to trick him, to incriminate him, which Hans believed LeBlanc aimed to do, or if he felt pressured to answer questions he didn't want to, Isaac was to stop talking and demand a lawyer. "Say 'lawyer' and shut up," Hans instructed. He phoned his own lawyer, Jessie Freisden, who had for a number of years defended him against Big Oil and the state to be ready just in case the "routine" voluntary interview went sideways. It had, and here he was outside the RCMP building, awaiting Freisden's arrival. He wished he knew what Isaac had done. The lad had to confess to God to get it off his eternal soul.

The other item that needed to be broached was Isaac's shed. "You know," he told his son, "if I found keys and the girl's bracelet around your shed, there may be more items for the police to find. You must tear it down, put everything into a pile, and burn it. Fire will destroy any other stray pieces left behind…"

"Cops don't know where my place is."

"If they search the property, they will. It's not hard to find."

"I–I don't want to burn it down."

"You can build another hut … maybe bigger, better, but this one's got to go. Take your things out and take it apart. I'll bring a can of fuel. We'll have a bonfire. It's got to be the done." *The only prudent thing to do, given what I have found.*

***

"God, it's only Tuesday, and here we are together again," Freta exclaimed as she slid into the seat across from Myron in the Great Plains RCMP detachment's most frequented Tim Hortons. It was just after 4:00 p.m. when Myron received a call from Freta inviting him for a quick coffee.

"Lucky me." He smiled, shoving a cup of brew across the table to her. "Saw you coming."

"Thanks," she said, still slightly breathless. She had walked over from the detachment. "Needed some fresh air. Can't stay too long, though — waiting for a search warrant."

"On whom and for what?"

"Trovotka's house — again! More to the point, Isaac's room."

"So you and Roberta tracked him down and interviewed him?"

"More like he walked in and got interrogated by Roberta. I took notes."

"And?"

"You're a liar, at least according to Isaac. He doesn't remember seeing the button, seeing you, or being at the college, but then he changed his mind sort of... Of course, Roberta didn't mention your name or who you are."

"Oh, I think he's figured that out by now..." Myron added a healthy dose of sugar to his coffee and stirred. "So who beat him up? Did he say?"

"Nope, said he fell but wasn't clear where, whether in the bush on his dad's property or in the college parking lot."

"Was there anything he was clear about?"

"Actually..." Freta pursed her lips and thought about it. "Very little and a whole lot. Roberta put him under stress."

"I can believe that."

"And I think he was about to crack, spill the beans, but in the nick of time he clammed up and requested a lawyer. Anyway, Roberta is convinced he's guilty of killing Raglan or at least knowing what happened to her."

"What about you?"

"His body language indicated he had plenty to hide, and by the end of the interview I was squeamish just watching him squirm and sweat. Yeah, I agree."

"Okay, so what's next?"

"As I said, he lawyered up, and we're awaiting a search warrant."

"He's still detained, though?"

"Temporarily, until we obtain the warrant and search his truck and room. Probably be released later tonight, but we'll be already out there doing our thing... Speaking of our thing — where's my doughnut?"

"If you and Team LeBlanc are burning some midnight oil, I'll buy a box of assorted doughnuts for you to take on your way back. My contribution..."

They went on to chat about Myron's day, which, he assured her, was far less exciting than hers.

"Oh," she said, as they were getting ready to leave, "with all that's been happening these last few days, I completely forgot to mention something from the other day. It's about your student — Alexandra — the one we met in front of the restaurant."

"Alexandra, yes?" Myron's ears perked up, and his face reddened. Had Freta heard some unsavoury gossip about him and Alexandra? He wouldn't doubt it, working at the college.

"Roberta did remember her from an Edmonton case." Freta proceeded to relate Alexandra's brief, unhappy affair with a hockey player and the resulting nasty consequences.

"Yikes," Myron exclaimed, shuddering inwardly and biting his tongue. Should he tell Freta of his uneasy encounters or let it slide? After all, Alexandra had dropped his classes and there had been no harm so … *no foul?*

"Yeah… That's your heads-up, and the college's too. Hopefully, it's all in the past. Whatever went on in Edmonton is a one-off and she won't 'Play Misty for Me' here."

Myron gave a nervous little smile at her reference. It was one of the first movies they had seen together, about a psychotic female stalker who was capable of anything. He thought it as a female version of Hitchcock's *Psycho* but knew it was stretching the point. Still, it creeped him out. In all of his spaghetti westerns, Clint Eastwood was less menacing than Jessica Walter in *Play Misty for Me*. "At least I don't have to worry," he said blandly. "Alexandra dropped all my courses."

# Chapter Twenty-Four

Isaac Trovotka was puzzled. It was a good plan; he was smart. So what went wrong? The police knew way too much. They were actually fingering him, not Croft, for the murder! It was the fault of that other cop or whoever he was — Corporal Osprey's friend who showed up at the farm. He was at the college that night and spied him in the washroom. What was he doing there anyway?

The bigger issue was that he lost the button he so carefully bagged. It had come loose when he cut and tore off the piece from Croft's coat. It would have been included with the other button and fabric as evidence, but he misplaced it. And now he knew where.

Isaac didn't know what to do. Confusion was setting in; he could sense the grey shrouding him like a fog. The interview had not gone well. He'd said too much, although at that moment he couldn't remember what he'd actually said. Should he confess? Tell the old man everything? Was that the way out? No, he decided he couldn't to that — not directly. He didn't quite understand why. Certainly, it had little to do with God or right and wrong. His father didn't see who he really was and that he was not about to repent and change. He liked who he was; he liked himself and his world. He wanted to stand out, create his own notoriety. Submitting to his father's holier-than-thou tenets would deny him that and submerge him further into an abyss he had tried to avoid all his adult life.

He would have his truth be known when it came time and in his own way. For now, however, there were more pressing issues. How long would the RCMP detain him? Would he be charged? What were his options? And then there was that cryptic note from Croft to call him. Should he? What good would it do? Was the money still on the table? More fog settled in the low valleys of his brain.

Finally, after a couple of hours in the cell, he hit a plateau where the mist cleared, albeit not totally. Don't say anything more and hope that old lawyer his dad always used secured his release... *And I should get back to Croft. I've got nothing to lose,* he decided. If he got the money, maybe he could make a run for it — disappear!

***

Isaac was released just after 7:00 p.m. that evening. After conferring with Hans, Freisden drove him home. "The authorities were executing a search warrant, and your father wanted to be there to defend his rights and property," the lawyer told Isaac.

By the time Isaac arrived home, the police had come and gone. Greta stood at the doorway, rubbing her hands anxiously, awaiting his return. Freisden, a lanky, wizened but gruff individual who had been practising law for over thirty-six years out of a small downtown office located over a barbershop, nodded his greetings to her. "Hans?"

"In the church."

"Thanks."

He strolled off toward the adjoining structure on the other side of the house.

On the drive home, Isaac had said very little to Freisden, whom he didn't particularly like (although he couldn't say why), and the old attorney kept whatever thoughts he had to himself. He did his job, Isaac was released, and there would be time for prolonged client–attorney conversation when and if it proved necessary.

"They searched your truck and room," said Greta as he approached the door. Isaac glanced at the forlorn silhouette of his vehicle bathed in the pale yellow light escaping the house. It sat where he had left it that morning when Hans took him into town. *At least it wasn't towed away!*

"Took nothing," continued Greta "except some sort of necklace in a plastic bag — heard one of them say it was in your drawer?"

Isaac's forehead creased in thought. There was nothing to be found, he was sure — at least as far as Raglan was concerned...

"You must be hungry," his mother said as they walked through the parlour, down the hallway into a small kitchen consisting of a dated stove and McClaren refrigerator separated by a row of high cupboards and a sink. A simple wooden table and chairs completed the basic décor.

"I'll eat later… Dad's in the church, right?" he asked as if he hadn't heard her tell Freisden.

Greta nodded. "Been there for a while. Probably be there a while longer."

"You know … maybe I will have something to eat after all…" He wanted his mother preoccupied in the kitchen while he used the phone in the parlour. It seemed an opportune time to make a private call.

***

Croft picked up on the third ring. "Yes."

"Got your message at the sandbox."

There was a two-beat pause. "Good, you called. Let's skip the introductions. You know who I am, and I know who you are."

The fact that the man at the other end of the phone claimed that he had found Isaac out didn't immediately register.

"I can't talk long—"

"Then we'll get right down to business. I can help you out of your mess, and you can help me — and get rewarded."

"I'm not in trouble—"

"So why were you in the cop shop? I have it on good authority that you are a suspect in Ms. Bullock's murder — you know, the young lady killed that you tried to frame me for." Findler had earned a small portion of the big bucks Hoar & Company were charging him when he phoned to say that there appeared another "person of interest" in Bullock's death and that he was being interviewed. Croft didn't know how or from whom Findler ferreted this news, and he didn't ask. It was meant to be a cheer-up call, but Croft felt sick. What if Isaac revealed their little secret? Evidently, he hadn't, and Croft pounced on the info as leverage.

"I–I don't know what you're talking about. And how would you know who I am?"

"Look, we don't have time for this sort of chit-chat. We must meet and figure out how to help each other out of this. I appreciate that you didn't tattle on me. I can help you."

"I–I don't know…" Isaac hesitated, unsure of how to respond. The fog was rolling onto the plateau again.

"Don't worry, I won't do anything nasty to you, but we need to meet in person, privately. It may be your only option. We can come up with a story."

"What kind of story?"

"Not over the phone! I'll bring the money. It's all yours."

"I–I don't know… I need time to think."

"Look, Isaac," Croft said with emphasis, "the RCMP are coming back to you for the murder. You're almost out of time and options. This time they'll crack you."

"I didn't do anything wrong!" Isaac insisted, raising his voice. "Y– you killed the girl, and I know where you buried the other body."

"Did you say something?" It was Greta asking from the kitchen.

"No, Mom," he called, putting his hand over the receiver.

"Isaac, you can't get out of this one. Help me and I'll help you." There was urgency in Croft's voice.

"How?"

Croft sighed. It was like he was in a continuous, repetitive discussion with a nitwit.

"Let's meet and we can see how."

A long silence ensued at the other end of the line.

"You still there, Isaac? Look, you choose the location, date, and time. But the RCMP will be knocking on your door again."

"Let me think—"

"It's really now or never."

"Okay, okay… How about Saskatoon Berry Park again?"

"Too many people, and you sure don't want to come into town, do you? Why don't we meet at the cemetery? It's quiet there now," Croft suggested.

"The cemetery?" Isaac repeated.

"But it has to be just you and me. Does your father know that you — you know…"

"I'm not saying I did anything wrong," Isaac insisted.

"Fine… But he has no suspicions? You didn't tell him anything about the girl or about the burial? Or about this?"

"N–no–no, I haven't."

"Good… Nobody can know. They wouldn't understand, including your dad — right?"

"Yeah … right?"

"So are we good? Say tomorrow night, eight o'clock. I'll bring the money."

There was another long silence. Then Isaac said, "Sure, but a small change in plan. A spot had cleared, had become fog-free on the plateau. "We'll meet at my private place."

"Private place?"

"Yeah. Drive out to the cemetery. Go to the far end and look north. There'll be a light in the woods — go toward it. I'll lead you to my private place, not far from the cemetery."

# Chapter Twenty-Five

**Wednesday, August 28**

Myron's lecture on New France and the seigneurial system was lacklustre. He wasn't fully engaged, and the students weren't either. A contributing factor, no doubt, was the memorial to Raglan in the college auditorium scheduled for noon, just after the class. Many in the room had known her and were in the throes of dealing with the trauma. Their thoughts were elsewhere. At the very least, the lecture was a diversion, he hoped, albeit a dry, irrelevant one.

The other causality was the first departmental meeting of the new academic year. Normally held over the lunch hour, it was postponed to the following week. Just as well, thought Myron; he wasn't in the mood for long-winded debates over workloads and who would sit on what committee.

The theatre was one of the institution's more visible and enduring gifts to the community. Its four-hundred-plus seating capacity, replete with plush furnishings, professional lighting, and acoustics, provided the venue for performances that ranged from popular musicals to the Royal Winnipeg Ballet and Tommy Hunter without the Rhythm Pals. It was also a place for more sombre occasions.

Myron walked in with Ted, and they snagged a couple of seats in the second tiered row along the aisle that divided the theatre into two. It appeared that most of the college had come to pay their respects.

"Did Raglan take any courses from you?" Myron asked.

"No," replied Ted. "Don't think she was in the commerce program."

"Probably not." *Not that it matters now*, thought Myron.

They both fell silent, focusing their attention on the stage, where beyond the orchestra pit were two easels with large photos of a smiling Raglan, a podium providing symmetry in between. Floral arrangements graced the photos on either side. The lights dimmed, and a tall, imposing man dressed in a dark double-breasted suit walked solemnly to the podium. Anthony Botenworth, the college's newly installed president, spoke in the mellow, modulated voice of the tragic loss suffered, to the family, to her friends, to her community, and to the college. "Raglan," he declared, "made a vibrant contribution to her fellow students and to the life of this institution. She will be profoundly missed by all…"

The dean of student affairs, Reginald Mercur, followed. What he lacked in charisma he made up in efficiency, introducing a bevy of speakers who related their remembrances of the life and times of Ms. Bullock, accompanied by a collage of images projected on a large screen in back depicting Raglan in various stages of her young life.

At the end, although too grieved to speak at length, the parents offered their thanks and appreciation for the memorial. The whole affair took fifty-five minutes, after which the lights were brightened and the people filed out, some tearful, some dazed, and others stoically off to the next class.

"So that's all there is," said Ted as they climbed the stairs to their offices.

"It would appear so," said Myron, suddenly wondering if Raglan's friends who went with her on that fateful weekend bush party were at the memorial. He didn't know them, so he couldn't be certain, but he imagined they were and was empathetic. It must have been a painful experience — loss mixed with remorse and perhaps guilt.

"I'm free 'til two," Ted said as they neared their respective offices. "Wanna walk?"

"Why not? A walk is what I need at his point," Myron said, looking at the scattered papers on his desk. "Some fresh air would do me good."

***

Isaac felt unease and mounting anxiety the moment he woke up. He had dreamt of God, a dark, towering, monolithic figure staring down at him. His father was there too, a small, shrivelled form standing off to the side, wringing his hands.

"You must confess," Hans beseeched. "You must!"

God said nothing but waited.

"You must confess to Him!" Hans was practically wailing, raising his hands to the Almighty. "If you don't, you'll lose your soul. And if you lose your soul, you will not be special!"

The dream ended abruptly when Isaac popped open his eyes, the word "special" formed on his lips. He didn't know whether he had shouted it out.

He considered the dream and what it meant. He wanted his deeds to be known, not as a confession but rather as part of his being special. He had read about other people like him. Their deeds had become known, not only known but talked and written about. They were special. They also got caught. That was the tricky part — not to get caught. *I'm smart; I fooled them all.*

After his interview, however, he was less sure. He didn't know how to extricate himself from suspicion by the RCMP. Maybe the dream was warning him: have a contingency plan to let his deeds be known in case he couldn't. Which brought him to Croft and to the forthcoming meeting. He didn't see how Croft could help him except give him the money. But then what? Use it to run from the police? Was that the only real option? Of course, Croft had to show up first, and with the money. And there was at least one other option, a "special" option to be considered. Regardless, this time he would be ready with a weapon.

The dream took hold and festered as Isaac tried to work out a plan on how to deal with Croft. He would never confess to the old man in that dinky church of his. Still, he should record the "special things" he had done so that people would know how clever he was. *Nobody will know if I don't tell them.*

He looked out his bedroom window. The van was gone, which meant that his father (and usually his mother) were probably off to Great Plains for their weekly sojourn to stock up on groceries and other household items. Hans possibly had a meeting with Freisden, although he had just conferred with him last evening. But then the old man liked to pester, go over things again and again. The point was there was no one in the house, so he wouldn't be disturbed. Here was his opportunity to ensure that he'd be talked and read about. It wasn't going to be a confessional but a statement, a listing of his special achievements.

He dressed hurriedly and had his usual bowl of crispy cereal, followed by toast and coffee. He then visited his least favourite room in the house: the parlour. He found it stifling and oppressive, even more so than the church. He couldn't articulate why exactly except that his father's presence was overpowering in both. Hans sat in the parlour every evening, in the ratty armchair with the floral pattern seat cover, reading the paper and smelling of stinky feet. His mother would be at the corner of the brown corduroy chesterfield, which had seen better days, knitting madly for no one. It irritated him, their placid righteousness and their smug superiority. He *was* special, but not in the way they thought.

He went directly to a small two-drawer table equidistant from the chair and the chesterfield, where it functioned as a coffee table. From the left drawer he pulled out some writing paper. "That should do it," he affirmed to the wall phone and its curled cord hanging between two faded pastoral scene prints.

Back in the kitchen, he grabbed a pen from a beer stein sitting on the window shelf, sat down at the eating table, and began to compose in a large looping hand "my special achievements."

It wasn't a long document, not quite two pages, but it included two rewrites and took him over an hour to do. The question was where to put it strategically so that it could be discovered if necessary but not found accidently before he wanted it to be found.

After some thought, he made up his mind. Going back to the parlour, he fished out from that same table drawer a white envelope and scribbled his name on it. Folding his epistle in two, he stuffed it in and made his way down the corridor, past the kitchen, out another door, and into the church annex. He knew exactly where to put it. The old man wouldn't have need of it until Sunday. If all went well at his clandestine meeting with Croft, he would retrieve the document and hide it in his room. If not, it would be discovered, and somehow that made him feel better. If the dream was a warning, he had heeded it.

Isaac didn't look forward to another face-to-face with Croft, but this time he was on his own turf, and he would take precautions. He still had to decide on his options…

*** 

Roberta LeBlanc was in an antsy mood, and she let her team know it. "We're going nowhere fast here. And I don't want to spend any more time in this town — no offence — than I need to, living out of a suitcase at that! My cats might disown me… So what do we really have? Boyd is still missing, with no clues as to what happened to him — dead or on a beach somewhere… We have a homicide, two suspects, and pieces of a puzzle that are so jumbled, we can't make head or tail of them. And our search of his truck and home has produced zilch! That about right?"

"What about the necklace found in his room?" asked Rob.

"No obvious identifying marks, and it will take some time to extract and process any fingerprints — speaking of which, the forensic lab report on Myron's button is still pending! What part of 'rush job' do they not get!" she exclaimed rhetorically. There was a brief silence while she collected her thoughts. "Question: Where do we go from here?" She gave a pointed look at Rob and then Freta. "Any thoughts?"

"Maybe we bring Croft in again. Take another run at him," suggested Rob.

"Ditto for Isaac," added Freta. "I think you had him on the hook for Raglan's death."

"Close but no cigar… My money is on him, and he is more breakable than Croft, who is hiding something too. They're both now 'lawyered up.'" She shook her head. "Goddamn lawyers…"

With renewed vigour, Roberta suddenly sprang up from her chair. "We simply need that lab result on the button — got to be absolutely sure. I'm going to put a fire under the forensic lab," she declared resolutely. "Right away, in fact!"

LeBlanc stared through the window of the case room across the bullpen at the superintendent's office. "I've never had an investigation turn into a dead end or become a cold case, and damned if I'm starting now. While I'm having a chat with your fearless leader and those in Edmonton, go through your notes and interview transcripts, see if we missed anything. Meanwhile, we'll need more doughnuts to keep our energy up." With that, she marched off.

\*\*\*

It was a damp, cool night with the threat of rain looming. In fact, it had drizzled for a stretch before the Jones Lake Road cut-off. A perfectly dastardly, "foul's afoot" night, thought Alex Croft as he made a right turn onto Grotto Road, slowly driving past the grotto and into the cemetery.

He had been extremely lucky, he knew. How the RCMP could uncover Raglan and not find Boyd was beyond him. But evidently that had been the case. And what possessed Isaac to bury the unfortunate female overtop, Croft couldn't even hazard a guess. It was fortuitous, though, since it camouflaged the disturbed soil from his original dig, making the RCMP none the wiser. His luck and their incompetence was the only way he could explain the chain of events. *Pays to dig deep,* he mused as he parked the Jeep under a canopy of trees and shut off the lights.

*Time to do this!* He reached into the passenger seat footwell for boots; from the back seat he grabbed a rain slicker and heavy-duty flashlight. Opening the driver's door, he took off his shoes and pulled on the boots. Before putting on his rain gear, he patted the pocket of his denim jacket. He had everything he needed, including two envelopes of cash — in case there was a reason to change his mind.

Croft thought long and hard about how to deal with Isaac, and there really wasn't any easy solution. Running through all the scenarios, only one ensured his silence. *In for a penny; in for a pound. Still...*

Flashlight slanted to the ground directly in front of him, Croft carefully made his way to the far end of the cemetery as directed along the fence line that separated the old church property from Trovotka's land. The temperature had dropped, and the rain started to fall more earnestly. He shone the light on his watch. Eight o'clock; Isaac should be out there in the woods, swinging a lantern or flashlight.

And indeed, after a few moments he saw a flickering light through the trees like a lighthouse beacon cutting through the fog. He crossed over what he presumed was the remnant of an old wire fence that divided the properties and headed toward the wavering light, keeping pace as it receded. His boots cracked twigs and assorted debris as they sank into the mixture of leaves and gooey loam. The air smelled heavy with water and spruce. Where in the hell was Isaac taking him? And what was this "private place"? Finally, Croft stood on what appeared a crest, looking down into a dark hollow, where he saw the outline of some sort of building — maybe a little bigger than a garden shed, he figured.

"Over here," he heard Isaac call. He cast his light in the direction of the voice, and there he stood beside the structure's crude door, waving him down.

Croft slid and skittered as he descended the slope into the gully but stayed upright. Isaac unfastened a rusty hinge, and the door swung open. He motioned for Croft to enter.

All was darkness and shadows, but there were no booby traps awaiting him — no cement block dropped from above, no bullet or arrow penetrated his outerwear, and no fierce Doberman pounced on him, so Croft cautiously entered a couple of feet. He saw a couple of stools and a lantern radiating an eerie pale glow in the middle. *Isaac's boardroom!* He cast his own light about quickly. Not much to see: dark and darker shades of shadows, objects hanging on the walls, and what looked like a rolled-up sleeping bag and a small gasoline can in the corner.

Isaac stepped in after him. "My private spot."

"Well, it's private enough," Croft said, keeping his distance and carefully assessing the young man. He really didn't know who he was dealing with other than this guy was a little "off" — cogent, possibly intelligent, but "off."

They sat on the stools provided facing each other.

"You brought the money?"

Croft patted the breast pocket of his jacket through the rain slicker. "Right here. Two envelopes of fifty one-hundred-dollar bills."

"Let's see."

"First, tell me, what do you plan to do once you get the money?"

"Why?"

"Well, it's rather obvious. Do you plan to take the money and make a run for it before the RCMP pick you up? Or do you just want to take my money and turn me in anyway and take your chances; perhaps you've set me up further. It's not like you can give me a receipt for it as good faith, is it?"

"I don't know what you mean?"

"Sure you do, Isaac. The options for you and me are limited and really boil down to one thing. You saw me bury a body; I can identify you as the burglar at my house who stole a piece of clothing found at a murder scene. It's not rocket science. Curious, though, why bury her overtop?"

For a long moment, Isaac sat silent, then he smiled and shrugged. "Why not? And you did soften the ground."

Croft smiled back. "Yeah, I guess I did do the spade work for you... So what do you plan to do? Are you disappearing or sticking around?"

"Haven't decided."

"Then you remain a risk to me." *Even if you ran, you'd remain a risk to me. You wouldn't go far — not on $10,000.* "On the other hand, with what I know, I guess I'm a potential risk to you, although you put yourself in the crosshairs of the RCMP, not me. I still haven't quite figured out how you managed that?"

"I want my money now," said Isaac with a definite edge creeping into his voice.

"But we haven't settled anything yet. Are we swearing a brotherly oath to each other and leaving it at that? Are you planning to run away? Or will you be getting rid of me? The problem still remains, you know."

Isaac didn't say anything but edged closer to Croft, his eyes tense and glistening in the light.

Croft was prepared, focused. No distractions. He willed his body to relax amid the mounting tension. Composed for combat. Eyes first, then the rest. As Isaac rose with the hammer suddenly in his hand, the sensei measured the movement, shifted to his feet, sidestepped the swing, breached the distance between them, and struck — *hi yee*. A direct blow, crushing Isaac's larynx. Two most effective targets in any fight: the throat and the groin.

The hammer fell and skittered off to the side as Isaac dropped to his knees with a muffled gurgle, clutching his throat. Croft quickly swung around him and applied a jujitsu sleeper hold. It didn't take long for Isaac to be totally incapacitated, if not already dead. It didn't matter at this point.

Croft moved to the gasoline can. About half full — more than enough! And it saved him going back to the Jeep to get his own more compact version of fire starter fluid. He poured the fuel on Isaac, splashed the remainder around, reached into his pocket, and produced a box of matches. He lit one and threw it on the human lump. It burst into flames; he scurried out the door.

*In for a penny; in for a pound.* Croft was pretty sure Isaac had his own version of the same plan. "I think we were on the same page," he said to the darkness as he got into his vehicle. "Sorry, bud. It was self-defence, really. You did try to kill me."

# Chapter Twenty-Six

**Thursday, August 29**

"Damn it all!" Roberta came storming out of Superintendent Reuben's office into the case room. Both Freta and Rob looked up from their paperwork.

"There's been a fire at the Trovotka place."

"What?" exclaimed Rob, his chair scraping as he twisted around toward the approaching detective.

"Along with a charred body!"

"Who?" asked Freta.

"Don't know much more. Fire chief is on the scene — an Ident team on the way. Could be a potential crime scene, so we better get out there ASAP."

"Was it their home?" asked Freta as they made their way out of the case room and through the bullpen.

"No. Some sort of shed. Someone apparently noticed the flames in the night and phoned the nearby fire brigade or whatever they're called out there."

"That'd be the volunteer fire department from High Lights," offered Rob.

"Anyway, it's a good thing it rained a bit last night, or there might have been a major bush fire. From what I gather, this fire brigade wouldn't have gotten close enough with the equipment to actually be effective. Anyway, this someone phoned Hans Trovotka to tell him there was a fire."

"Then the victim isn't Hans Trovotka?" asked Rob.

"Evidently not, but they found someone under the smouldering debris — at least one body," Roberta reaffirmed. "So I was told."

"Isaac?" Freta asked — a rhetorical question. He seemed the most likely, she thought but couldn't quite articulate why.

"Too early to tell, and speaking of which," said Roberta, "finally got the report — the button Isaac lost is a match to the button from Croft's coat found at the crime burial site. Isaac and Croft are inextricably connected somehow, and I sure hope Isaac is still around to tell us, because Croft sure as hell won't."

"I've got a bad feeling about this," said Freta.

***

Myron was having an unremarkable day, and he liked it that way. His two World History classes went well with a modicum of student interest shown in the trials and tribulations of the Roman Empire, the morning class being the livelier of the two, despite the insertion of extra jokes. (He always thought of more things to add, often humorous, when he repeated a lecture on the same day.)

Thereafter, he returned to his office and piddled about with paperwork. He'd seen Ted briefly in the morning and not at all in the afternoon. But that wasn't a surprise for a Thursday. He, too, had a night class this semester, Canadian Tax Law 303. Thus, he had been disappearing (to prepare or go home for a nap?), since he had no scheduled afternoon classes. He usually arrived shortly before six thirty, when the evening classes began. Since these classes were three hours in length, Myron didn't begrudge Ted not sticking around when he didn't have to. Myron could have gone home after his afternoon class, which ended at four, but to what end? Unless he had some pressing business or errands to attend to, he'd hunker down at his office (or sometimes hit the gym) rather than go home to his solitary and rather austere apartment. Why bother? Moreover, early dinner was readily available in the cafeteria, usually a Polish sausage or hamburger on a kaiser with all the condiments and extra ketchup packets for the fries.

Thus, he was surprised to find Ted sitting alone in the cafeteria, chomping on his plate of burger and chips.

"You're early tonight," said Myron, plopping himself and his food directly across from Ted. "What's the occasion?"

"Yeah, about an hour early... Nobody home, became too quiet. One kid's gone to band practice, the other to volleyball, and Martha has joined a new yoga studio... So here I am enjoying dinner before facing my rising crop of potential accountants."

"Well, hope the cuisine is up to your standards."

"It is. In fact, it's exactly the same as what was served for lunch!"

"Superb."

"On another topic, while I've got you here... How can you stand it?"

"Stand what?"

"This whole night class scene. It's extremely long and draining — a week's worth of work crammed down their throats in three hours — blah and ugh!"

"It's a long stretch," admitted Myron. "The way I think of it is I only have to show up once, get it over with, and it frees time during the week."

"Maybe ... but last week I said all I wanted to say before the coffee break. And I'm sure that half of it flew over their heads." Ted waved his hand skyward. "Swoosh! Canadian tax law cases seem a tough sell, even to commerce and accounting majors."

"Then give yourself a break. Tell them a story."

"About what?"

"No riveting stories about accountants, tax collectors, commerce, and finance wheelers and dealers that you can work into your lecture?"

"I'd have to think about that."

"What about your personal experience?"

"What? Doing taxes?"

Myron sighed and took a healthy bite out of his oozing burger. "Surely there's some events, amusing morsels in the financial world that could be told to enliven the night and add a little filler."

"There's my fishing trip that I mentioned the other day."

"Is it relevant? Has to be relevant in some way."

"It has a very *taxing* dog in it."

"Funny, but I'm not sure that qualifies."

Now it was Ted's turn to sigh. "Yeah…"

"But if you're keen on telling it…"

Ted took a quick peek at the large clock on the cafeteria wall. "The shortened version then!"

*No! I didn't mean to me!* Myron thought. *Too late!*

"Remember the other day I mentioned Snark?"

"The dog? Yeah, I think so." He vaguely remembered Ted threatening to tell him about his first fishing trip and a dog.

"Snark." The word came out like a staccato sneer. "He's a Jack Russell. One of those high-strung, incessant yappers who chases everything that moves, doesn't obey commands, has the attention span of a gnat, and sniffs and snorts his way everywhere. He'd piss on your shoe if you weren't looking."

"I get your drift. Snark is an annoying dog." Ted could be long-winded at times.

"Yeah… Anyway, Herman, his owner and a fellow accountant friend — 'til he moved — had no control over him. To tell the truth, Herman could be a bit out there too, for an accountant. He drove his Honda Accord like a rally car over those logging/oil rig roads to get to this lake somewhere northwest of here in the foothills. He swore that this no-name lake was used in a beer commercial — you know placid, greenish-blue water set against a mountain background where the trout gave invitations jumping out of the water and waving in anticipation of our casting our flies."

"Right."

"We parked in a little turn out and hiked in about a quarter mile or so, and there it was, just like he said. The water was aqua green, tranquil, with the occasional sound of jumping fish. Anyway, we set up a small tent on a rocky outcrop along the shoreline and got our gear ready. Later, we gathered some wood and started a fire."

"So you didn't do any actual fishing?"

"Not that night… Heated some canned stew and topped it off with a bit of brew. Then sat around and let the evening enclose us. Perfect!"

"What about Snark?"

"Oh, he disappeared on numerous romps, chasing squirrels, chipmunks, whatever... We just sat and drank until the embers finally smouldered away. He came back, his tongue hanging out, and followed us into the tent, settled in a corner, and went to sleep."

"Sounds like the ideal fishing trip — without actually fishing. That came the next day, I take it?"

"Don't rush this," Ted admonished. "I'm still developing the punch line."

Myron held up his hand. "Okay ... sorry."

"In the wee hours of the morning," Ted continued with renewed animation, "I heard a loud thump and then a 'twap' against the tent that instantly woke me."

"I bet."

"'What was that?' I whispered to Herman, who was suddenly awake too. He is a better woodsman than me, and the trip was his idea... Anyway, he didn't know and said he'd have a look-see ... unzipped the tent and peered out. It was early dawn and fairly dark, but the outline was visible: a large bear ferreting about our campsite. Herman ducked back inside and eased toward his sleeping bag. To my surprise, he produced a rifle. Popped in a shell — probably a .22, I don't know much about these things — slowly crawled out, stood and with the barrel pointed up and out over the lake, fired."

"A bit unorthodox maybe, but okay..." Myron was intrigued, despite his reluctance to listen to a proverbial fishing trip story. *So far ... no fish!*

"The boom shattered the morning peace, producing echoes in the mountains, shudders through the trees, scattering all manner of wildlife through the foliage in the process."

"I can imagine, but I sense a but."

"You sense correctly. On the bear, though, this resounding boom was less dramatic than Herman had hoped for. Instead of a hurried exit, he simply turned, got up on his hind legs, and stared."

"Uh-oh."

"Yeah. It was like our encounter with the elk — a stand-off."

"What did you do?"

"Stared back, and there were no snowballs to throw at him — or her. The good news was he made the decision to move on a little quicker than the elk."

"I guess there wasn't anything tasty in camp."

"Thank God. But after a few minutes of relief, Herman panicked and raised the alarm. 'Where's Snark? What happened to Snark?' He became a bit frantic, and we started calling and searching for him."

"Where'd he go?"

"Ah-ha. That's the point. Nowhere! Man's best friend was in the tent in exactly the same spot as he was when he settled down earlier for the night! He knew the bear was out there — how could he not? And yet he did not budge a muscle or formulate a single bark! Can you believe it?"

"A prudent dog then."

"What! No! He's a coward and a delinquent."

"I was thinking more a smart dog. Figured humans could fend for themselves, and he saved the chase for another day."

"You've taken the side of the dog and missed my point completely."

"Good adventure, though."

"So how do I integrate it into my tax course?"

Myron finished the last of his fries and wiped the corners of is mouth with a crumpled napkin. It was almost time to collect his notes and get to class. "I haven't got a clue."

***

From Myron's perspective, the night class grooved. The downfall of the Russian Tsar during World War One and the ruthlessness of Lenin and his Bolshevik comrades seemed to spark interest (morose or otherwise). His only side tour down a rabbit hole came as a result of an enquiry from a student wondering how Anastasia, Nicholas II's youngest daughter, managed to escape!

He explained that in all probability, Anastasia was executed that July day in 1918 along with the rest of the family and that her "resurrection" was highly problematic based on a woman in Berlin who dubiously claimed that she was Anastasia. "There was no real proof, but the stories continued — even a movie was made," Myron concluded. The student wouldn't quite let go of the idea that Anastasia somehow lived and, he suspected that if he took a poll, a good number would support her. Still, it enlivened the class.

Even with that aside and a longer than usual coffee break, Myron finished what he had to say about twenty minutes early. Ted's comments about the length of these sessions suddenly came home — at least for this night. He decided to let the class out early. The class had gone well, and he was in a good mood, chuckles reverberating in his head over Ted's fishing trip story featuring a smart dog.

However, as he approached his car, fiddling in his pocket for the keys, his mood dissipated, replaced by a *déjà vu* feeling.

"I'm back," she said cheerfully.

Myron froze a few feet from the Audi.

"Alexandra. What are you doing here?" *Dumb question.*

"Attending my first poli sci class, now that I'm not your student."

"Right." He relaxed a little. "We're squared away then."

"You mean that we're no longer an item?"

"Alexandra, we never were an item."

She stepped closer, her face partially hidden in the darkness, her eyes brittle bright in the available light. "I dropped your courses, you see, so that there wouldn't be this student-prof thing hanging over our relationship."

"Relationship! Alexandra I—"

"Now we're free."

There was definitely something seriously amiss with this lady, thought Myron. "I'm sorry... I don't know what gives you the impression that we somehow forged a relationship."

"We can be together now."

"What? I think not—"

"I've done what you asked."

"What I asked?"

"Removed the barrier to our relationship."

Myron made a quick scan of the parking lot. They were alone, although there were scattered vehicles about; most of the classes hadn't quite ended yet. *Guess her poli sci instructor and, coincidently, my nemesis, Sidney Sage, let the class out early too...* "It's late. Please go home. We'll talk tomorrow." *Hopefully, I can get you help for whatever delusional episode you're having — it has to be a personality disorder of some kind...* He knew that the last thing he wanted to do was engage with her at that moment in the parking lot.

"Are you trying to avoid me?"

"Alexandra — I hardly know you!" *This is crazy!*

"You will in time."

"Look ... I need to go. I am sorry. Is there someone I can call — a relative? If you're stressed, depressed ... *a complete loony bin psychopath* ... or need help in any way—"

"You *are* trying to avoid me! You shouldn't, you know... You can't."

Myron thought about going back into the college building and calling security. He didn't know whether Alexandra was a potential danger to herself or anyone else (including him), although what Freta said about her behaviour in Edmonton suddenly came to the fore. He wasn't sure how to react or what to do. Maybe letting her go on her own was not such a good idea either. "Let's go back inside."

"It's the other woman, isn't it?"

"Hey, Myron." A voice in the distance interrupted the exchange, a very distinctive, booming voice: Ted ambling toward his car a few stalls over. Both he and Alexandra turned.

"Hey, Ted," Myron called in relief. Other people emerged and spilled into the parking lot. *Thank God.*

As he swung back to refocus on Alexandra, she disappeared swiftly into the shadows, presumably to her car. He chose not to follow. He would file his previous notes on Alexandra with Student Affairs, adding this episode.

# Chapter Twenty-Seven

**Friday, August 30**

"Can't say anything for sure," said Dr. Roman Backie, the county coroner, as he got up from his prone position with a grunt. First a buried and now a burned corpse; he half expected the next one to be drowned! "Definitely ignited by an accelerant, probably gasoline — will know more after the autopsy."

"No way to tell if it was accidental, self-inflicted, or someone lit him up?" LeBlanc pressed.

"No, not at this point... Self-immolation..." Backie shook his large head and scratched his bulbous nose. "Ugh, what a way to go."

"Okay then, I'll leave you to it." LeBlanc stepped away as a couple of men in white zipped up the badly burned remains. Her nostrils reminded her that fried human flesh had a particular, quite nauseating smell. The aroma lingered, a combination of grilled pork with distinct coppery overtones.

Freta appeared beside Roberta as the white suits extracted the body bag from the rubble. She had just finished talking to Hans and Greta while Rob interviewed the remaining two families on the property. It was Roberta's suggestion that she speak to the Trovotkas, since Hans had a "history" with her and had established a relationship, however tenuous. Freta appreciated the sensitivity, if that's what it was. "You have a greater comfort level with Trovotka," she explained.

"Looks like Isaac is the only one missing," Freta said with a grimace.

Roberta nodded. "Yeah ... well, I think he's been found! Other than that, though, I don't think the site will reveal anything useful."

She gazed back at the irregular dark patches radiating from the grey-black debris, the fire's epicentre. "Hans have anything helpful to say?"

"No, not really. He was solemn and silent. No outbursts or pointing fingers. I think he was ... is in shock. He even agreed to let me take another look at Isaac's room."

"Find anything like a suicide note ... declaration of guilt ... hints of his state of mind?"

"No. It seemed undisturbed, same as when we searched it."

"So what was this structure, and why was it out here away from everything else?"

"Hans said it was Isaac's place; that he built it and often disappeared here. That's why he's certain that the body he saw discovered by the firemen is Isaac. Seems pretty broken up about it, which is natural..."

"Still wondering why he built this." Roberta glanced again at the mound of charred wood and scattered debris. "Or what he kept in it? Maybe the fire marshal can enlighten us."

"Has Rob made it back yet?" asked Freta.

"No, he's still probably taking statements from Trovotka's tenants or whatever they are. Don't think he'll uncover anything of note. Nevertheless, the T's have to be crossed and the I's dotted. We'll stop by on the way back at the Trovotka house to offer my condolences."

\*\*\*

Red-eyed, immeasurably saddened, Hans sat alone in the first pew, praying. Judgement had been rendered, he knew, and in all probability his son had taken his own life. He had to accept this just as Abraham was willing to accept the sacrifice of his own Isaac — by fire, ironically enough. Except that God spared Abraham's Isaac...

Inexplicably, he couldn't even muster the outrage he'd normally reserved for the authorities who had hassled and, no doubt, contributed to his son's dark state of mind. Hans sighed; Isaac did have something to hide and wasn't forthcoming — even to him. And therein lay the crux of the matter.

Isaac had not confessed to God, as far as he knew, and thus was in danger of never entering the Kingdom. He needed to be forthcoming to receive God's mercy.

Hans wiped a stray tear from his eye and rose, prayers done for now. It was time to console Greta. Later, he'd prepare for the funeral in his church. It would be a small group of mourners, a dozen or so.

Before leaving, he decided to go to the pulpit where the old Trovotka bible resided, tucked underneath a shelf. He wanted to find some appropriate passages about God's spirit of forgiveness, his generosity and all-consuming love. Hans realized he was still begging God to consider Isaac as special and that his soul could find a righteous path to God's grace.

*Odd*, he thought, as he reached for the heavy tome and laid it on the pulpit; he didn't remember placing sermon notes or paperwork of any kind inside the back cover, but there it was — an envelope sticking out in one corner. Pulling it out, Hans noted Isaac's scrawled handwriting on the outside. *Isaac Trovotka.*

His heart skipped a beat. What was this? Hands trembling, he stared at the handwriting for some time before returning to the pew and carefully opening the envelope and removing a folded page. Suicide note? Apology? Confession?

He read it three times; each time the contents horrified him more. He could hardly comprehend. Could it be that his son was a monster? That he really did what he claimed and moreover enjoyed it? Hans was in despair, but in the silence of that despair he had an epiphany. As horrible as his son's actions were, there was a saving grace, which literally filled him with joy. Isaac had confessed! What he had in his hand was a confession, perhaps not to him, but to the one who counted, and he had left that confession in the family bible in his church! Moreover, there was no mention of his younger sister, Hannah! Try as he might, Hans could never shake the feeling that Isaac was somehow culpable in her death. He was wrong and felt both a rush of remorse for not fully believing his son and joy. Isaac was … forgivable! Isaac *was* special; God would take him in. His soul would be saved, and he and Greta could rejoice in that!

Nevertheless, there was still earthly justice to be dispensed. Isaac's revelations would allow for that to be done. The question was how? What was the proper course of action? His son's actions could not be ignored or somehow covered up. That's not how a true confession worked, and he and Greta would have to live with that. However, there was also Isaac's eyewitness account. Hans decided to think about how he would proceed, although the answer, he believed, had already presented itself.

*\*\**

Alexandra was upset. This was not the way it was supposed to go. He was supposed to be receptive — even eager! In fact, the luminous vibes around him were stronger than when she first noticed them. In the darkness, they danced like giant fireflies, blueish-white sparks, tiny novae going off and intermingling with hers. So why the rebuff?

Perhaps her direct, frontal approach had been premature and too strong. Maybe she should have waited another month or two for him to get used to her aura. Still, it was so strong and remained so.

She had to figure it out. If his aura was pulsating out and seeking her aura, then they should have been attracted to each other — ecstatically so. How could they not be? Yet he wasn't reaching out to her, which meant that his aura was either being corrupted or blocked. That's what had happened in Edmonton, after all. He couldn't let go of the other woman whose aura interfered!

So who was this woman who short-circuited Myron's spark across the synapse? Alexandra tried to remember her name as she sat in front of her bedroom mirror, carefully rubbing in face cream before retiring for the night. *Mirror, mirror on the wall...* She gave a twisted smile at the image before her. *I'm the one who should get it all!* Her smile turned into a laugh, followed by an impish grin. *Should have been a poet, or is it poetess?*

*Think!* She was introduced to her in front of the restaurant but was caught off guard and then distracted by the older woman, a cop she had encountered under some unpleasant circumstances in

Edmonton. Frieda, was it? Or something similar! She was the aura breaker, of that Alexandra was certain. Who was she? What did she do? And what was her relationship to the older female who could say some negative, quite unjustified, things about her — *if she remembered her.* She didn't appear to.

But then it happened a while ago, Alexandra reminded herself; besides, the matter had been settled. Best forgotten, since the aura had extinguished suddenly and irrevocably. *Poof, like a pilot light going out,* she mused.

The challenge was now. For the aura to flow unimpeded, she suspected that this Frieda person had to step aside, her aura neutralized or removed. She needed to be sure. First, she needed to explain herself to Myron. *He'll understand,* she reassured herself. Secondly, observe the other woman, see the nature of the aura she gave off. Then she would know what to do.

# Chapter Twenty-Eight

The expansion of New France in general and into the Ohio Valley in particular seemed to intrigue, if not totally engross Myron's 9:00 a.m. class. Of course, he abetted this with a visual stimulus: a large, colourful map suspended over the blackboard illustrating New France's impressive thrust into the American interior.

"How could New France claim such a huge area with so small a population and hope to keep the New Englanders out?" asked a lanky teen in the front row, staring at the map. To him it seemed logically impossible.

"In the end, they couldn't," replied Myron, "but they were tenacious and quite ingenious. Beginning in 1749 an expedition of about two hundred men sent from Quebec took formal possession of the Ohio Valley."

"How? How could they do that?" This time the enquiry came from a brunette in the back row.

"Plaques," responded Myron. "A motley crew of soldiers, fur traders, and Jesuits travelled down the Ohio River as far as the Great Miami River," he pointed to their location on the map, "putting up plaques and declaring it French territory, never mind that Indigenous peoples lived there. In fact, they held conferences with the various tribes in an effort to drive away any English fur traders in the vicinity."

"So, if I get this straight," piped in a skinny fellow with a faded T-shirt featuring The Beatles, "the French put up *No Trespassing English* keep out signs?"

"That's about it, at least initially," responded Myron. "Of course, a possession claim is only meaningful nine out of ten times, if it can be enforced. Thus, in 1752, New France backed up the claim by building a series of forts through the Ohio region, the chief being Duquesne at the fork of the Ohio, Allegheny, and Monongahela rivers, present-day Pittsburgh," he added as an aside. "That naturally angered the English colonies, especially Virginia, the governor of which had plans to expand into the interior. In 1752, a certain young major of the militia, George Washington, was sent by the governor to expel these haughty French from the area."

"And what happened?" asked the lanky lad.

"First, Washington had to make an arduous six-week journey, which he did with a grand total of seven men, three of whom were native guides — and then he had to find his adversaries. He did, however, not at Duquesne but at a smaller French outpost, Fort Le Boeuf. There he delivered a letter from the Virginia governor setting out the British claim to the Ohio country and concluding with this line." Myron paused and found the quote in his notes: "'It becomes my peaceful duty to require your departure.' After which the commander of the French fort replied, 'As to the summons you sent me to retire, I do not think myself obliged to obey.' And that was the message Washington brought back to the Virginia governor about six weeks after that."

"So what happened then?" asked Beatles T-shirt. (Try as he might, Myron still couldn't remember his pupils' names.)

"Something that American history books tend to downplay," explained Myron. "Washington was sent back into the Ohio Valley, this time with about 160 men. The mission was to kick the French out of Virginia's backyard. Bottom line, he wasn't successful. The guerrilla warfare of the French and their native allies — that of sneaking up and ambushing the enemy, shooting from behind trees and rocks, compared to the European warfare of forming men into firing lines — convinced Washington and his Virginians that this was 'not a contest between civilized armies,' as he put it. In the spring of 1754, Washington and his depleted forces surrendered. Luckily for him, his enemies were more civilized than he thought, because he and his remaining men were allowed the luxury of returning home. Thus, Washington lived to fight another day!"

***

Myron opened the door to his office, feeling a bit euphoric. That was a good session, and wait until they got into the Seven Years' War! He decided to go grab another coffee and keep the high going. Dropping his lecture notes on the desk, he was about to exit when the phone rang.

"Hello." He felt a musical lilt to his voice.

"Mr. Tarasyn."

"Er ... yes."

"It's Hans Trovotka. I'd like to meet with you. I have significant information regarding Ms. Bullock's death."

That brought Myron back from his class high like a lead balloon. He was caught off guard, quickly attempting to collect his thoughts. "After our last meeting, I'd say that whatever information you have is best passed on to the police."

"Then by all means invite Corporal Osprey to come along."

That gave Myron pause. He couldn't deny it; he was intrigued. "Why not go directly to the police?"

"As I mentioned before, I try to avoid dealing with the police at all... However, I have important information that relates not only to Ms. Bullock but to two other deaths. In fact, the RCMP will not solve them without it."

Myron's attention was exponentially enhanced. *What two other deaths?* "Okay, Mr. Trovotka. Where and when would you like to meet?"

"How about three tomorrow? That coffee shop we met at last — near the college."

Myron had nothing special planned for Saturday afternoon. "See you there at three, and I will be accompanied by Corporal Osprey."

He phoned Freta shortly thereafter and by a stroke of good fortune actually got a hold of her. Often, she was quite elusive during the day.

"You're not going to believe who just phoned me," he said.

"Who?"

"Hans Trovotka."

"Oh? I am very surprised… Did he mention what happened on his commune?"

Myron hesitated: "No… I don't think so…"

"It's not public knowledge yet, but there was a fire on the property and a fatality. It's not official, but we're pretty sure it's Isaac."

"My God. How awful and how strange. He didn't mention anything about a fire or his son's death."

"So why did he phone?" Freta asked, a slight note of curiosity intermingled with impatience humming over the line.

"Says he has information on the killing of Raglan, and I quote, 'two other deaths.' Says he avoids dealing directly with the police."

"In this case, it translates into not wanting to deal with Roberta, I suspect."

"Right, but he has no objection to you. Wants a meeting."

"Okay. When?"

"Three tomorrow at Robin's Coffee."

\*\*\*

Isaac had secrets that he did not share. That much Hans always knew. He just didn't realize the extent and darkness of those secrets. Isaac was different — special — from the start. The rational, scientific part of Hans's brain suspected that his son had been damaged cognitively from birth or at an early age by the hydrogen sulphide leaks from the multiplying sour gas wells surrounding his property. He had read about how lethal $H_2S$ was, even in tiny doses — as deadly as cyanide. And how many times had he inhaled the stench of rotten eggs, its tell-tale harbinger? Indeed, he attributed the toxic emissions for their stillborn a couple of years before Isaac. And, over the years, had his cattle and sheep not experienced unusual birth deformations? In retrospect, it was not unreasonable to conclude that Isaac may have been affected in some insidious way.

However, Hans's spiritual mind balanced science with faith. God knew his own, and Hans accepted that God made Isaac the way he was because He had a purpose for Isaac that only He, and not an earthly mortal, could divine.

Yet doubts filtered through occasionally and flared like a nagging toothache, as they did now while he sat alone in his church. Who was his son really? What made him act the way he did? But most of all why — why did he kill, and why did God allow it? Hans sighed, knowing that he simply did not understand. In fact, the totality of Isaac eluded his grasp entirely.

Freisden had told him about a button and a piece of clothing from Croft's jacket found at the crime scene that the RCMP suspected was planted by Isaac. If that were true, how did Isaac obtain the items? Did he meet Croft? Did they know each other? Did Croft have anything to do with his son's death?

The last thought popped in unannounced and unsolicited, jarring Hans. He hadn't thought that there was any foul play involved in Isaac's tragic passing. How could there be? It was an accident that he helped to create by suggesting to Isaac that he burn down his shed: "You have to do it," he'd emphasized. "The RCMP will snoop around, and you don't want anything found in there…" He had even supplied the can of gasoline.

The possibility that Croft had somehow harmed Isaac seemed remote, far-fetched. Still, Hans needed to ease his mind. And as he continued to pray, in the silence he heard a quiet voice imploring him to seek the truth. He had heard this voice many times before, and rarely had it steered him wrong. A riddle: What did "seeking the truth" mean? And where to look? The thought, when it finally took root, seemed counterintuitive given the fact that he had to give Isaac's confession to the police (to bear witness if nothing less) and that Croft would have to answer for his own crime. Nevertheless, Hans decided that he should go and speak to Croft — perhaps (he hoped) before the police did — to ascertain what he knew about Isaac and his demise.

\*\*\*

"Yes?" Alex Croft opened the door to face a haggard face with a green Co-op baseball cap and a bushy beard. "Can I help you?" Croft gave a quick glance around to see if anyone else was with him. The man in front of him did not look like a Jehovah's Witness canvasser.

"I hope so," said the man in a sombre, authoritative voice. "I'm Hans Trovotka."

It took a moment for the name and its significance to register.

"Mr. Trovotka… What can I do for you this afternoon?" It was actually early evening.

"Did you know my son, Isaac?" Trovotka asked calmly.

Croft frowned and pinched his lips, appraising the man before him. *Certainly doesn't beat around the bush! Keep cool; he probably knows nothing.* "No … sorry, I don't."

"Police say he came into possession of some of your personal items. How would he have done that?" Trovotka had a penetrating stare, an unrelenting focus. Croft tried to match but couldn't maintain the other's intensity.

"Well, Mr. Trovotka, I know no one named Isaac and have no idea how your son acquired some articles of mine. You have to ask him that."

"Isaac died in a fire. Would you know anything about that?" Trovotka's words wavered ever so slightly.

"My condolences … and no, I don't. Why would I?"

Trovotka started to say something and then decided not to. He studied Croft's face intently. Finally, as if groping for an answer, he simply said, "He's in God's domain now."

"I'm sure he is … Mr. Trovotka. I didn't know your son, so why are you here? What is it that you want?"

"To understand — to ask you why the RCMP believe that you and Isaac are connected."

"Rest assured we're not," Croft reaffirmed, trying to keep his voice even. "The RCMP don't always get things right, do they?"

"I saw you out there early that morning, you know." Trovotka declared this with an undercurrent of suspicion.

Croft rubbed his chin. "Ah … you are the witness mentioned."

"Yes. I am that witness."

"Well, you were — are — mistaken. I wasn't there, wherever there is, exactly?"

"Grotto Road. And yes, you were. Both Isaac and I saw you. Isaac observed you burying a body."

Colour drained from Croft's face, but he kept his voice steady. "I can only repeat. You and your son are mistaken. As for burying a body — that's absurd!"

"We shall see, won't we?" Trovotka gave Croft a thin smile.

"What do you mean?" Croft couldn't help it; his austere, stone-faced reserve was folding onto itself.

"Before Isaac died, he made … his peace with God."

"Well, good for him." The words slipped out of Croft's mouth before he could contain the sardonic tone.

"You may mock it, but he did confess his sins before the Lord and will be rewarded by His mercy. He saw you bury a body."

"Rubbish, I did no such thing."

"That's what he wrote down, and we'll know soon enough!" Trovotka stated emphatically.

"And why is that?"

"I will be turning over Isaac's last words — his written statement — to the RCMP. No doubt, they'll go the Grotto cemetery and check. They'll verify the truth of his words, I believe. Isaac was quite specific as to the location of the burial."

"Leave my property," Croft ordered, his face grim.

"Gladly, with the answer to one more question. Did you kill my son?"

"No." Even to Croft's ears it was a flat and unconvincing denial. "Now leave my property."

Trovotka nodded in some sort of sad realization and started to walk down the drive toward a brown Ford van parked farther down the cul-de-sac.

"Wait!"

Trovotka stopped and turned. Croft stepped off his porch and took a couple of strides toward him, his eyes suddenly wide and scanning nervously for nosy neighbours and other potential witnesses. "Frankly, I would hate for the police to be involved," he said in a quiet, deliberately measured voice. "Is there some way to make this go away — make it so that you don't visit the RCMP? You've had trouble with them before, and I know that you don't like them much."

"Mr. Croft, are you trying to bribe me?"

Croft took a moment before responding, trying to gauge how far he could go with a nonconformist, fringe personality that he knew very little about. "I just don't want the added bother of dealing with the police — bad for me and the business. You can understand that. And while I'm innocent of any wrongdoing, either to your son or anyone else, I'm willing to suitably compensate for your suspicions if you keep to yourself what you think you know."

"I see…" Trovotka said solemnly, his eyebrows furrowing.

"Give me a figure. We can work something out."

Trovotka slowly shook his head. "I think not. The die has been cast. The good Lord has given me direction. And we both know what you have done."

Croft took a step toward the older man and stopped, seemingly to decide better of whatever he had in mind. A bribe wasn't going to work. Nothing was going to change his mind — not this zealot.

Croft stared at Trovotka's receding back before he turned, went back inside, and closed the door. He parted the bay window curtains in time to see Trovotka slowly climb into his vehicle and drive away.

"Fuck!" he muttered. This changed everything. Was what Trovotka said true? Were the cops really going back to the cemetery? And if they were, when and how long would it take them? Most importantly, what were his options?

First things first. He looked up Findler's home number and dialled. The lawyer sounded a bit put off that his client should disturb him, but all calls were billable. He reassured him that he had not heard of any further developments in the case since the last time they had talked and that he'd update him if he did when they met later in the week. Somehow, that was not reassuring.

The question was should he just sit, wait, and grit it out, see what developed and what could conceivably stick to him, or should he make his exit now? If RCMP were at the cemetery and digging up

Boyd, then the game was up. It simply wouldn't bode well for him. And he always knew he'd have to disappear. It was simply a question of timing.

Finances, however, wouldn't be a problem — at least for a while. Boyd initially siphoned off clients' investments into an offshore account, but a good portion of that had been redirected into Croft's own numbered accounts. Boyd had been rather careless in leaving his nefarious transactions in his office desk! The point was that by the time the auditors figured out that Boyd did not have as much of the misappropriated funds in his accounts as could be reasonably expected, Croft would be gone.

That was the original plan: have Boyd confess, absolve his shocked partner, and be left holding the bag. No one was supposed to die in the original plan, let alone two! Boyd would be tried for embezzlement (and he deserved it), and Croft would be the honest innocent until the auditors finally got a handle on the accounts and started asking questions. By the time that occurred, he would have made arrangements to disappear.

This scenario had to be readjusted, more specifically his time for departure. He poured himself a Scotch — just one for the road, so to speak — while he contemplated his sudden travel plans. Ostensibly, he'd go for a drive and not come back. Ten thousand in cash would facilitate his immediate needs, but he realized it all depended on the efficiency of the RCMP. Hopefully, it would take them some time to find and process what they discovered before calling on him. Nevertheless, he was surprised by how quickly they had tracked him down in Las Vegas. It was an anomaly they wouldn't likely be able to repeat — he hoped.

Gulping the last of his drink, he strolled to his closet and took out a couple of suitcases and his duffel bag. Time to pack! The business was a bust and not worth lamenting over, but the executive home was a different matter. Undoubtedly, his wayward wife would only be too happy to fully claim it once he was gone. Alas, it couldn't be helped.

# Chapter Twenty-Nine

**Saturday, August 31**

Freta arrived at the arranged coffee shop at ten minutes to three. Myron was already seated at a corner table away from the flow of regulars. Her coffee was one of two steaming mugs on the table evidently set aside; presumably, the other was for Hans. He came in a minute or two after the hour, wearing a green Co-op baseball cap and sporting sunglasses, which he didn't take off until he reached them. His shoulders were slumped, his eyes red, and his beard impossibly tangled. He looked like a man who had a troubled sleep to match his troubled mind.

Myron offered his condolences, and Freta enquired about Greta, and the pleasantries were over.

"This is difficult for me," he said, acknowledging with a nod the coffee mug Myron slid over to him, "but there's no way around it… Not for a man of God." He reached into his thick, checkered work shirt and produced a long, white envelope with *Isaac Trovotka* written on it. "It's in there," he said quietly. Freta and Myron scanned the document before them, looking shocked.

Finally, Freta broke the silence. "You are willing to make this public?" It was more a statement of incredulity than a question. If a member of her family had committed such egregious crimes, she wondered how she would react. Would she so readily facilitate public exposure and all that went with that?

Trovotka thought about this for a moment, staring at his large hands around the coffee mug. "It can't be hidden," he said slowly. "Not if my son is to be saved. I am acknowledging his sins. He can't do that himself now. It is part of his repentance and salvation. It cannot be kept a secret. And … justice must be served," he added.

*** 

At 4:15 p.m., the reassembled LeBlanc team huddled in the case room, going over the new information Freta brought in less than ten minutes before.

They were scrutinizing Isaac's confession and charting their next course of action. Roberta carefully read the document for a third time:

*I write this to let everyone know. I did two of them, Lucy and Raglan, and nobody figured it out. Lucy was easy. Nobody knew about her, so no questions were asked and nobody came looking — nothing.*

*I am not fibbing. I buried her in the cemetery. You can find her in the grave beside the one where I buried Raglan.*

*I did them because I'm special and they were sluts who didn't like me. I didn't really want to do it, but I had to show them.*

*The cops are really stupid. They dug up Raglan but missed the other body below her that Alex Croft put in. He must've spent half the night digging. He did the work. So I put her overtop.*

*Later, I came back and made sure that if Raglan was found, Croft would be blamed. That was smart. And I've been smart not to get caught.*

*I'm going to be famous.*

There was no date or signature.

"Hardly a sorrowful confession," Roberta snorted. "More like a narcissistic statement of 'look at me: I did it. You can't catch me. I need to tell someone.'"

"True, but as far as Hans is concerned, it saves his son from the eternal flames of Hell," noted Freta. "For Hans this is a confession of Isaac's sins to God, sincere or not. That's why he came forward."

"To Myron ... and you," she pursed her lips sourly.

Freta said nothing.

"Well, he's taking a very liberal interpretation of his son's confession, but I suppose it's understandable," Roberta conceded.

"Regardless, it's a bombshell!" exclaimed Rob.

"Bombshell all right," agreed Roberta, "if it's genuine."

"Hans assured us that it is. He swears that it's his son's handwriting," said Freta.

Roberta nodded. "He's no literary genius. Nevertheless, what he has written is simple and direct enough. And … he's not wrong as far as the public and media are concerned, if what he says is true about us missing another body underneath a body!"

"Can that really happen?" asked Rob.

"Probably has, although I can't think of an example at the moment," replied Roberta. "Obviously we have to go back and dig a little deeper to find out. Theodore…" She flipped open a file. "…Polanski's grave and do the same for the grave on either side, starting with…" She consulted the file again. "…Marie Polanski, Theodore's wife, presumably. Let's see if this Lucy is residing above her! Speaking of which, let's see if there's a Lucy who has gone missing in … I'd say the last five years in this area, and if not, expand the search to the rest of the province, B.C., and Saskatchewan as well."

"On it," said Rob.

"What about Croft?" asked Freta. "He's implicated."

"A moot point until we actually find bodies. Once we have a body or two," she said wryly, "then we go after Croft. For now, it's hush-hush. Don't want this leaking out."

"And Hans?" asked Rob. "What if he talks?"

"Oh, I imagine he'll keep it under wraps for as long as he can," replied Roberta with a small, dour smile. "Would you broadcast that your son was a serial killer in the making?"

The point was well taken normally, but Freta wasn't so sure. Hans had spilled the beans, as it were, to her and Myron. He operated on different motives and principles. However, she kept her own counsel.

"Well then," continued Roberta, "let's get the paperwork started so that the Ident unit can start digging again."

\*\*\*

"Alexandra!" Alexandra seemed to materialize out of nowhere just as Myron inserted the key and turned the knob of his apartment door. He fumbled with and almost dropped his keychain as the door swung open. *This can't be good. I'm being stalked!*

Alexandra looked pale and drawn, appearing to have lost some of her carefully groomed presence. Her hair was more askew than he had noticed before, matched by imperfectly applied rouge on her lips. "Can I come in?" she asked in a small, quiet voice.

It was early evening, and he had just come from his usual burger-and-fries dinner with a stop at the smoke shop along the way. Freta was working late, and he anticipated being on his own, looking forward to a quiet smoke and a large dollop of mindless TV. A potentially mad as a hatter woman was not on the agenda.

"I don't think that's such a good idea," he replied, surprised and unnerved at the same time.

"I don't blame you. I'd like to apologize for my behaviour earlier and talk," she said in a steady voice that managed to be both contrite and ominous.

Myron hesitated between *what harm would it do* and *don't let her in!* He glanced down the empty hallway. There was no one to witness this encounter.

"Promise, I won't make a scene or upset your neighbours. And don't worry, I don't have a Saturday night special in my pocket. You can frisk me if you like." She smiled coyly, raising her hands.

He ignored her double entendre and would take her word for it, since he wasn't about to pat her down. Besides, from what Freta had told him, Alexandra was into knife fights, not shoot-outs! *Don't be flippant,* he reminded himself. This was serious; evidently Alexandra had some fixation, and it was best to de-escalate before the situation really got out of hand. *Let her in* or *keep her out?* "Okay, you can come in — to talk."

He stepped aside and allowed her entry, closing but not locking the door. In the few purposeful strides to his sparse living room, he berated himself for not acting on his instincts and reporting Alexandra's obsessive behaviour to Student Affairs. From stalking to conduct bordering on criminal insanity wasn't that long a stretch, it occurred to him. He was sure there was a complicated backstory to Alexandra's actions that he would eventually unearth. However, he wasn't keen on exploring it at that moment. "The place could use some décor," he said, a bit flustered and embarrassed by the shabby state of his apartment.

Alexandra didn't seem to notice but moved closer to him, invading his personal space. He stepped back.

"Sorry," she said. "Didn't mean to crowd."

"Please, have a seat." He gestured at a recently purchased love seat while he took the rather forlorn green sofa opposite. She followed his lead and sat down. "You said you wanted to talk?"

"Yes … first to apologize. I was too forward with you. Came on too strong. Especially since I've only known you scarcely a week. Quite unlike me. A bit embarrassing. I was … too bold." She spoke in short, breathless sentences, giving him a demure smile when she finished.

Myron cleared his throat, not sure how to respond. "Well, no harm done. In a way I'm flattered." *Don't say that! It'll encourage her!* "However—"

"I know," she interjected, "I was inappropriate. Didn't respect student–professor boundaries. I get that."

Myron nodded. "As I said, no harm done, and we can move on."

"But you weren't chosen randomly," she said earnestly, leaning forward. "That's what I want to explain."

"Oh?" Myron shifted uncomfortably in his seat. "There's really no need to—"

"But there is," she insisted, "because if I don't, you won't understand."

"All right…" It sounded like she seriously wanted to unburden herself. "Can I make you a coffee or tea while we talk?" He deliberately excluded mention of alcoholic beverages.

"No, thank you." She loosened her grey topcoat and settled back.

"Okay then…" Nervous tension beset him, and he was tempted to pull out his favourite Brigham, light up, and let the aromatic tobacco invade his senses, calm his mind. Notwithstanding the image of serenely puffing on his pipe à la Freud, he wasn't a particularly good listener. *Was Freud?*

"It's your aura," she stated bluntly.

Myron frowned. "My aura?" Of the clichéd list of psychological disorders — *childhood and/or adolescent trauma, daddy/mommy issues, a frontal lobotomy gone wrong* — this one had him drawing a blank.

"Yes. It's hard to explain."

*I bet.* "Try me," he said with assurance, mustering as much Freudian empathy as he dared.

"It's like I envision what I think in radiating light and colours. I often *see* my thoughts manifested…" she raised her hands upward, "as a glow, an aura that's getting stronger and focused on you!"

The revelation caused another uncomfortable shift in Myron's posture. *Lucky me!* He didn't know how to respond. *A glow with colours? An aura?* All he could think of was luminous light, a dictionary definition. *Is there such a condition — medical or otherwise?* "An aura? What kind of aura?" he asked to fill in the sudden silence.

"Yours is awesome!" she enthused. "The right kind for me."

*Not a helpful answer.* "How do you know that it's right …right for you?"

"Because it aligns with mine."

*What aligns? Some cosmic force? The Earth, moon, and sun? The hands on a clock?* After a prolonged pause, during which no further elaboration came, he pressed on. "So … this aura. What is it? And how does it align? I'm not quite understanding."

"It's hard to describe."

Alexandra seemed calmer, Myron thought, not as edgy. *Keep her talking.* "Give it a shot."

"It's a bluish-white light radiating about you, mostly from around your head. It was there the first time I saw you. I've thought about you every day since, you know — delicious thoughts, the kind that want to kiss you all over. We're immersed in the aura as we sit. I can see it."

*Whoa, too much info.* Myron felt the blood rushing to his head. He was sure he'd turned crimson.

Her erratic behaviour was a manifestation of this phenomenon, he reasoned. Most certainly he wasn't her first fixation, given what happened to the fellow in Edmonton that Freta mentioned. "You've experienced this aura before?"

"It appears and disappears," she admitted. "Yours is particularly strong. Makes me want to wrap around you and—"

"Did you have a similar experience in Edmonton?" Not a very subtle question, but it popped hastily into his head before she could gush on with her fantasy. "You were recognized by the detective you met the other day," he elaborated. "She remembered you from an incident in Edmonton." It was perhaps an overly sensitive, even risky topic to raise, he realized, but it redirected the conversion to a firmer reality — he hoped.

Alexandra tensed, narrowed her eyes, and fidgeted with her hands. He half expected her to be curious as to how he knew the detective and about Freta as well. Instead, she shook her head, as if disappointed. "Too bad ... she saw me only once, and we didn't speak. I didn't think she'd remember ... but it doesn't matter." She sighed. "Water under the bridge."

"What happened, if you don't mind me asking?"

"His aura got corrupted."

Myron detected a trace of bitterness mixed with regret. A fragile topic: he had to tread carefully. "You mean his ... aura didn't align with yours?"

"Oh, no!" Alexandra sat up more erectly. "We aligned perfectly. The flow between was corrupted, unpurified because he didn't reject the other woman."

There was that phrase again. She'd said it in their parking lot encounter. Her rival, the one who stood in the way. Still, Myron wondered how it played out in her mind, considering that she attacked the object of her presumed affection *(aura mate?)* and not "the other woman."

"Sorry, just to clarify... The other person got in the way. Is that what you're saying?"

"Yes."

"And you had an altercation with him as a result?"

"No, my aura did! I really don't remember that part."

Mentally, Myron did a double-take. *I'm not getting this straight, or am I missing something?* "He was…" *choose your words carefully* "… accosted because he didn't stop seeing her?"

"He was … deceitful," Alexandra confirmed, offering no further insight.

Myron nodded as if he understood. Clearly, there was a cognitive disorder at work that he couldn't begin to fathom. Thus far, however, Alexandra had chosen to talk, but he wasn't in a position to continue the conversation, at least in any meaningful way, for much longer. She needed professional help, and from his perspective, that began with a college counsellor who could direct her to the proper mental wellness services. It was time to close their discussion as amicably as possible and usher her out of his apartment.

"Well, Alexandra." He gave her a smile, "I'm glad we were able to talk — to clarify a few things." He put his hands on his knees, ready to rise. "I think you should meet with a college counsellor next. Come by my office on Monday and we can arrange an appointment and—"

"You're not getting it!" Her voice suddenly rose and her tone became harsh, agitated, and insistent. "I just explained to you. Our auras align. They're glowing around us. We match! You must find me attractive."

Taken totally aback, Myron opened and closed his mouth, aghast and floundering to form a reply. "Alexandra," he tried to keep his voice neutral and even keeled, "I'm flattered … by your attention and thank you for your candour, but I can't help you. I can't allow—"

"It's about us!" she shouted.

"Alexandra, there is no *us.*"

"I thought that if I explained, you'd see. Be on my side."

"Your side?"

"That you'd reject the other woman."

"Other woman?" Stunned, he repeated the phrase, sounding like an echo chamber.

"The one I saw you with. That's the problem — isn't it?"

"I'm committed to a relationship," he declared honestly. He considered telling her that Freta was a police officer and that charges could be laid if she persisted in what amounted to harassment. However, he bit his tongue. He relationship with Freta wasn't the issue, and furthermore, it might trigger an unpredictable reaction, sending his former student off the deep end — if she wasn't there already.

"Tell her it's over. You don't want to see her again."

"What! Alexandra, I can't do that." Myron tried to keep his growing unease and anger in check as Alexandra's voice took a shrill tone.

"She needs to know," she snarled. "It'll be your fault if you don't. She can't be allowed to interfere. She'll spoil everything."

Myron rose from the sofa. This had gone far enough. *I need to extricate myself from this! Get her the hell out of the apartment.* "Sorry, Alexandra, I can't do that, and you must leave now." His throat constricted; his mouth felt dry. *I've put myself in a weird, compromising situation. She needs to leave or this won't end well.* He sensed her mounting fury.

Alexandra rose from the love seat, her eyes black orbs as inviting as Medusa's stare. Myron's thoughts went askew. His body tingled, a chill running down his spine. A long silence followed. He braced for some sort of psychotic break with nasty repercussions. Yet a reprieve followed (or perhaps he was simply in the eye of a catatonic event). For Myron, time stopped even as the second hand on the radio clock ticked on. She seemed to relent. With a twisted smile she announced, "Well, I've said what I came to say. I tried." With a last disdainful look around his apartment, she made her exit out the door and down the hall without a glance backward.

Myron closed and locked his door in one uninterrupted motion. With a sigh of relief, he extracted from the inner pocket of his tweed jacket a battered Brigham, followed by a full pouch of Sail tobacco. He'd have a smoke, reflect, and talk to Freta about his encounter with Alexandra. The talk could wait until the next day, though; he was suddenly quite tired. First thing Monday morning, he promised himself, no more Old Tomorrow. He would submit his report on Alexandra (with the latest update) to the college counselling office for whatever action they deemed necessary.

# Chapter Thirty

**Sunday, September 1**

Hans Trovotka's Sunday service was a dress rehearsal for Isaac's funeral; the remains had yet to be released. As usual, the congregation was small: Greta, the two families, and their multiple siblings who lived on his land, and a few of the friendlier neighbours. It was a sombre service and, for Trovotka, who could preach on at length, relatively short.

He concentrated on the messages contained in three psalms beginning with Psalm 16 and the affirmation of belief in the Lord, from whom the faithful will never waver. "For thee do I put my trust," he quoted from the appropriate passage. "We will always set our Lord," he averred, raising his hands in exaltation, "above everyone and everything else, and from this we will not be moved. This is the solemn compact we have with God, for 'thou will not leave my soul in hell.'"

Next came Psalm 23. He debated quoting from it because it was so iconic and used in frivolous ways by unbelievers. Yet the message was still germane to him, to Isaac, to his earthly life and beyond. "Fear no evil," for God was with Isaac — especially now in death. That thought resonated and sustained Hans as he read.

Finally, and most significantly, came the delivery of Psalm 32. Its verses jumped out at him. "Misfortune is the result of sins one committed," he admonished. "Oh, how very true. However," he emphasized, "also blessed is he whose transgression is forgiven, whose sin is covered." *Isaac acknowledged his sins. He confessed his transgressions unto the Lord, and* "thou forgavest the iniquity of his sins."

"Many sorrows befall to those who do wicked acts," he paraphrased. "But he who trusteth in the Lord shall find that mercy compasses him about."

Hans did not reveal the nature of Isaac's transgressions. They'd know soon enough, and he and God's Light Church would deal with the fallout then. For now, it mattered that the passage was clear, unequivocal. Isaac was in the presence of the Lord, that He was the shepherd of his son's soul, and that whatever Isaac did, forgiveness was at hand.

Long after the congregation had dispersed, Hans remained in his church, his sanctuary. He needed to find a path to come to terms with Isaac, with himself, and indeed with God's will. He was certain that Isaac had not died accidently but that Croft was responsible. He had no proof, no logical explanation, just a resolute, unshakable feeling after meeting with him. What should he do about it? He had no confidence in the authorities or the justice system. They had thwarted him at every turn for most of his life. God would let him know, he believed, and send a clear signal. He was his counsel on the matter, and only from Him would he take direction.

In the afternoon, Hans decided to walk along his property line adjacent to the cemetery. He wondered when the police would arrive, cordon off the area, and start digging. He was surprised that there was no one there yet. Had they not taken Isaac's confession seriously?

He returned to his sanctuary, sat in the front pew, and prayed, the old family bible in hand. How long would it take the RCMP to arrest Croft, if not for the killing of Isaac, then the other murder he committed? What if he left town? What if he got away?

For the next hour, he wrestled with two conflicting decrees: "Never take your own revenge but leave room for the wrath of God…" (Psalm 58: 10–11) and "… take a life for a life, eye for an eye, tooth for a tooth…" (Exodus 21: 23–24).

By nature, Hans was not one to readily turn the other cheek. With the Almighty's blessing, he had demonstrated that with his fight against Big Oil. The question to be answered was would God permit him the same latitude in the case of Croft? He was not sure. Thus, he prayed for retribution, and then he prayed that he would be God's instrument of that retribution. He wasn't seeking revenge, he assured himself, but retribution — recompense, as it were — although he wasn't exactly sure what the difference was. Many relevant scripture passages and prayers later, Hans was muddled. Nevertheless, he would proceed while he awaited God's answer.

The air was cool and crisp as he walked with resolve to one of the numerous sheds behind the barn. (He'd have to do all the chores now, he realized sourly as he passed by the structure). Inside, he noisily strained to move a heavy workbench that he and Isaac had shoved against the north wall. Once it was sufficiently out of the way, he took a crowbar off one of the shelves and pried up a couple of rough boards. Thereafter, with a grunt, he got on his hands and knees and fished around in the dark, dank hole beneath for the heavy-duty garbage bag containing the materials he sought, the materials the RCMP had failed to find when they searched the property. There was less than a kilogram left, not much really, but enough to do the job. He set the garbage bag on the bench and carefully took out what was inside. He'd need to retrieve and assemble the various accessories, which included a nine-volt battery, a timer, an electrical switch, and lots of tape.

He worked slowly and with God's grace got it right. He hadn't put together such a device in quite a while; indeed, he thought that after the RCMP's raid he was finished with the stressful and risky business. Once he had the "package" ready, he found a cardboard box, carefully positioned his handiwork inside, and gingerly carried it out to Isaac's forlorn pickup, opening the passenger door, tilting the split bench seat, and placing it in behind. It was a nice, snug fit.

"Greta," he said, finally coming into the house for supper, "I'll be going to town tomorrow."

She nodded, looking at him with a mixture of sadness and trepidation. "Shall I come?"

"No, not this time. There is something I need to do alone. We'll go together another day."

He let his announcement lie there. She knew better than to ask.

***

"Whew, talk about 'Play Misty for Me'!" exclaimed Freta. "What were you thinking letting her in?"

"I guess I wasn't — not clearly, anyway..." Myron took off his glasses and rubbed the bruises where his pinching nose pads rested.

They sat at a back table enjoying breakfast at Barney's Café, a palatable greasy spoon on the main street of Great Plains not far from the cop shop.

"Not a great move to let her into your apartment," reiterated Freta.

"Probably not," agreed Myron with his newly discovered 20/20 hindsight. "Tomorrow, first thing, I'll go to the Student Affairs office, hand in my report, and let them deal with her. She needs help."

"I'd say."

"The good news is that no irreversible harm was done. She may even salvage her academic year."

"Not if she persists in stalking and harassment!"

"Well, I think the cat will be out of the bag tomorrow, and she'll be on the college's intervention radar."

"And ours," Freta said wryly. Drinking the last of her coffee. She glanced at her watch. "I better go. Roberta is chomping at the bit."

"When will you get results?" Myron asked, scooping up the bill to pay at the till.

"That's the problem, Roberta wants the Ident team at the gravesite like yesterday." Freta spread her hands. "Not that easy. According to Roberta, eyebrows were raised at RCMP headquarters. Questions like 'What do you mean a body was missed?' And 'How do we explain this to the media?' She thinks the higher-ups are worried about public perceptions."

"I can see that."

"Anyway, they'll probably be out there tomorrow, depending on the paperwork and how quickly the team can be brought together again and get set up. Even if we do find Boyd's body, though, there's still the formal process of identification, autopsy to determine how he died, and whatever other evidence there is to be found and analyzed."

"Then there's the reference to another body in Isaac's epistle," said Myron, thinking out loud.

"Yeah, that too. The answer to your question is nothing's happening for a while. Roberta just wants the LeBlanc team to be ready."

"The LeBlanc team, eh?"

"Yup, that's what we are."

***

After Trovotka's visit, Croft was ready to run and get as far away as possible. It was a de facto warning, a heads-up, that the ignorant preacher gave him. Yet here he was, still debating, still inert. He'd heard no further news, and it didn't seem likely that the cops would come banging on his door immediately. But he couldn't be sure ... of anything. His mind raced. And even if they unearthed Boyd's body, they had to link it to him in some concrete fashion — didn't they? The Trovotkas were eyewitnesses, but Isaac was dead, and whatever incriminations the weirdo wrote Croft would emphatically deny. And as for Hans Trovotka — who would believe him?

The real question was had he left any hard evidence behind that would tie him directly to the transport and burial of his business partner? In truth, he couldn't remember. The night seemed a blur now. Of course, they did have minute samples of Boyd's blood found in his office and vehicle but, his lawyer assured him, it was not enough to charge, let alone bring to trial and convict. That would most certainly change with the discovery of Boyd's body. His argument that the swindler had left town and was living on a beach somewhere would instantly evaporate. Perhaps he had prevaricated long enough and should just get out of Dodge!

# Chapter Thirty-One

**Monday, September 2**

As was his routine, RCMP Constable Brad Chirychuk stopped at the Tim Hortons on the outskirts of town. It was just after six in the evening, time for his usual, a large double-double. It had been a calm night on patrol, with no major traffic accident or nasty domestic dispute eruption (the worst kind of call in his book, especially if it was violent). He hoped that it stayed that way for the rest of his shift. The burly officer had just made it to the door when an enormous bang, complete with a flash of light and smoke, assaulted his ears and eyes.

"What the—" His double-double slipped from his grasp, fell, and splattered over his regulation shoes and pants. "Shit."

An old pickup parallel parked in a lonely corner of the lot gave up the ghost in spectacular fashion. The passenger side door hung limp on its hinges, the windows blown out. Fortunately, no fire followed, just black smoke dissipating into the early evening sky. Since the truck hadn't been parked near other vehicles, it looked like the damage was limited to the old beater.

As he hustled out the door, Constable Chirychuk spoke rapidly into his radio. There had been some sort of explosion, he informed the dispatcher, giving the location. Fire and rescue and possibly paramedics were needed — *just in case,* he thought. While the few stunned customers inside looked out, trying to comprehend, he slowed and more cautiously approached the crippled vehicle. There was no one in it, as far as he could tell; however, a large man with a beard to match was painfully rising from the pavement a few yards away.

"Are you hurt?" asked the policeman.

The man didn't answer right away, obviously shaken. After a moment, he straightened. "No, I don't think so." He then took a couple of steps and with his left hand picked up a green ball cap, placing it on his head with a grimace. Chirychuk noticed that he gingerly grabbed his right wrist afterward.

As he got closer, Chirychuk's posture stiffened. He recognized the man: Hans Trovotka, the fellow they suspected of sabotaging gas wells. Chirychuk had been one of the officers who participated in the search of Trovotka's property.

***

Getting personnel to the cemetery took longer than LeBlanc would have liked. Equipment and people had to be assembled and transported — again. She appreciated the logistics and resources involved; still, she couldn't shake the idea that a degree of skepticism and paperwork drag from headquarters in Edmonton was equally to blame. Superintendent Reuben disagreed. "The Ident team will be on site and properly set up by this afternoon," he curtly told her, "which is pretty expeditious, I think."

LeBlanc grunted a begrudging acknowledgement and with a sour face turned to her own paperwork. She thought of driving out there with her team, but to what end? They had to let the forensic crowd do their thing. For now, it was back to the investigative files to see if they had missed anything and figuring out what to follow up. There was still so much forensic evidence to come in. She wondered about Croft. She had put off interviewing him a second time, but if what Isaac had written was true, then he emerged, if not consolidated, his spot as the main suspect in Boyd's demise. How the Boyd-Croft-Bullock-Trovotka foursome related to each other remained a mystery. She instinctively believed they were inextricably connected, but she just couldn't wrap her head around the puzzle. LeBlanc did not like this kind of inscrutable mystery. It led to loose ends and pitfalls.

As the afternoon dragged into early evening, LeBlanc, still pondering how to proceed with Croft, was jolted out of the doldrums by a report of a truck explosion, one legally registered to Isaac Trovotka. Hans Trovotka was driving.

"When did this happen?" LeBlanc asked the dispatcher on duty, who was standing at the entrance of the case room.

"About an hour or so ago," said the petite, efficient civilian who occupied the position.

"Was anyone hurt?"

"No, not seriously," she amended, looking at the notepad in her hand. "Mr. Trovotka was the only casualty — a sprained or broken wrist. Apparently, he was out of the vehicle walking toward the coffee shop when it blew up."

"Literally blew up?" LeBlanc rose from her chair and arced her arms outward.

"Appears so, according to…" She checked her notepad again. "Constable Chirychuk."

"Any obvious cause determined by the constable?"

"Didn't say."

LeBlanc nodded. They wouldn't know until the vehicle was towed in and forensically inspected.

"Given that he recognized Mr. Trovotka, Constable Chirychuk thought it best to detain him."

"Good," the detective interjected. "Are they on their way over?"

"No. Mr. Trovotka has been taken to the hospital to get checked out. He'll be there for a while, if emergency wait times are any indication."

LeBlanc thought for a moment. "That's fine. Thank you. I'll go over there now."

It was getting on in the evening. Rob had gone home earlier, and Freta was preparing to do so as well. It hadn't been a particularly fruitful day, but at least the forensic unit was finally sent and ready to begin their excavations. As the dispatcher made her way back to the front of the building, LeBlanc grabbed her coat and followed straight to Freta's cubicle, peering around the partition. "You're coming with me."

"Where?" asked Freta, in the midst of shrugging into her jacket.

"To the hospital. It seems that Hans has had a mishap. His truck — or, more precisely, his late son's truck — which he was apparently driving, blew up."

"What?" Freta shoved her swivel chair snug against the desk.

"He's okay… Let's go find out what this is all about," Roberta said grimly. "Machine malfunction? Someone trying to do ol' Hans in? Or was he unsafely carrying explosives?" The last question was asked with a smirk.

\*\*\*

As it turned out, Hans was not about to cooperate. He sat in the emergency room holding his limp wrist, stoic and sullen. LeBlanc had a few words with Constable Chirychuk, after which he gave a brief nod and departed. Freta tacitly understood that other than a perfunctory greeting, her role on this occasion was to remain silent and take notes.

"Where were you heading when this unfortunate incident occurred?" LeBlanc asked.

"To town for supplies."

"Rather a late hour to be coming in, isn't it?"

Trovotka shrugged. "Got a late start. Had to finish up the chores now that my son is gone," he replied pointedly.

LeBlanc let that pass. "Tell us what happened," she said. They had moved to a small nook off the waiting room, away from curious eyes and sharpened ears.

"I don't know."

"I understand the truck exploded," LeBlanc pressed.

"It would appear so," he said, sounding reedy and hollow, his gaze focused on the pillar beside which the detective and Freta stood. He wasn't engaging.

"Trucks don't normally explode on their own," LeBlanc stated flatly, her expression deadpan.

"No," he agreed.

"Were you hauling explosives of any kind?"

"No."

"It's your son's truck?"

"Yes, it was."

"Did he, on occasion, carry any volatile materials?"

"Not that I am aware of."

"Do you know of anyone who would want to do you harm by placing an incendiary device in or near the vehicle?"

"You mean like a bomb?" Trovotka curled his lips into a faint smile, knowing exactly what she meant.

"Yes, like a bomb."

"Big Oil and the RCMP maybe." The lip curl brightened into a small, laconic smile as if to say *I can play this silly question and answer game for as long as you want.*

LeBlanc gave him a long glare. "Well…" she finally relented, "you've given your statement to the constable. Evidently, there's not much more you care to add. We'll keep in touch to let you know how the investigation is going." Then, in an obvious reference to Isaac's confession, she said, "Thank you for providing the information that you did a couple of days ago."

"What are you doing about it?" he asked with an edge to his voice.

"Conducting a thorough follow-up and investigation. Again, my condolences for your loss. Take care of your wrist."

With that LeBlanc turned and walked out of the emergency entrance, Freta following. "Arsehole," she muttered, getting into the car. "Bet you dollars to doughnuts there'll be traces of potassium nitrate when they examine that truck!"

"What do you suppose he was up to?" asked Freta.

"That is the question, isn't it? I suspect we'll never know."

\*\*\*

A chastened Trovotka watched the two female cops go. They hadn't chastened him; his own actions did and no doubt would cost him some grief. God had delivered his judgement. *Never take your own revenge but leave room for the wrath of God.* He had overstepped, misinterpreted (wilfully disregarded?) his prayers for retribution. This was not like the struggle against Big Oil and the state, where he became the Almighty's instrument to smite the evildoers. No, this was of a different order, closer to the realm of Heaven and Earth, His domain, requiring His intercession, not that of a mere mortal who, although given free will, was flawed in his understanding. He got it wrong; he took a misstep in thought and action.

It was fortunate that God was merciful and did not take him for his presumption. As soon as he got home and to his sanctuary, he'd pray for forgiveness and let divine and earthly justice take their course, although he had little confidence in the latter.

Meanwhile, he was stuck in the hospital (hospitals he did not like much) waiting to get his wrist X-rayed. He didn't think it was broken, but it hurt like hell! From a public phone, he called Greta to tell her that he had a minor accident and that she might have to do added chores. Then he dialled Freisden, his lawyer. He needed a ride home.

# Chapter Thirty-Two

**Tuesday, September 3**

Alex Croft was on a knife's edge, his clarity of thought made sodden by Bushmills Irish whiskey and fitful sleep. His mental disposition did not improve when he put the phone down. At the other end, Findler casually informed him that, although there was nothing particularly new to discuss, he heard that the RCMP Ident unit was going back to the gravesite where Ms. Bullock had been discovered.

"When was that?" Croft asked, trying to keep the anxiety out of his voice.

"Can't say, really. In fact, I can't confirm it without actually driving out there, but that's the scuttlebutt from my source… Nothing to worry about, right? Just don't want to be blindsided," he added.

Croft knew that attorney-client privilege protected him, but there was no way he would tell Findler that, depending where exactly the RCMP was digging, they might find Boyd. Full disclosure was not an option. Nor, he suspected, would his defence counsel be happy if he did. He imagined knowing your client was guilty as charged only served to complicate matters.

"No, not that I'm aware of."

"Good. As you are probably aware, Isaac Trovotka, the lead suspect in Ms. Bullock's death, has died in a fire. Tragic, but it could bode well for your case, depending on what evidence the police have on him or come up with. The only issue for us is how he got hold of your clothing and why?"

"As I explained, I was out of the country for almost a week. He could have broken into the garage, I suppose… As for why, he would want to frame me — I have no idea. Could have just been random."

"Hmm…" Croft could almost hear Findler's mind ticking in thought, trying to puzzle it out, a riddle that could not be readily explained.

"Never met him; he's a total stranger." And technically that was true; Croft didn't know of him until later. Now he had to stay consistent. He couldn't admit to the home invasion or an altercation with a burglar. It would substantiate a link to Isaac and raise other questions.

"Well, any speculation aside, it might be a moot point if they conclude that he was the person responsible for her death," Findler reassured Croft. "Maybe that's why they're out there again. Although I can't imagine how they could have missed anything significant the first time. I'll let you know of any further developments."

A trip out of town was way overdue, Croft realized when he put the phone down. His lawyer, of course, had missed the point: it wasn't Ms. Bullock but Boyd, or rather his corpse turning up, that Croft was worried about. He should've hightailed it right after Trovotka's visit. He packed his bags but inexplicably stayed and debated with himself between shots of whiskey on the couch. He hadn't been thinking clearly…

Where to? Two choices now presented themselves: either motor to B.C. and in due course head south across the border or west to Vancouver and beyond. Or drive to Edmonton and grab a last-minute flight to any number of destinations, depending on what was available. Unfortunately, he'd have to use his own passport. He hadn't initiated the complicated business of acquiring a false one. He'd thought he had plenty of time for such an eventuality.

Should he simply go now or slip away in the evening? Did it matter? It did if the RCMP forensic team was already out at the gravesite, digging away! He glanced at his watch — after lunch already. *Best be gone.* He had hung around too long as it was, and his lawyer's call confirmed it. *Edmonton it is.* He'd figure out where to from there en route.

*Travel light.* One suitcase (already packed) and a duffel bag containing a good chunk of his $10,000 bundle. That should get him to almost any place in the world. Once in Edmonton, he'd simply leave the Jeep in a car park and walk away. He felt better, more in control, now that he had made his decision. "Take your shot," he reasoned. If caught, he could always say that he became stressed and panicked and … ran. Sounded lame, even to him.

He had parked the Jeep in the garage the night before (again anticipating a departure that never materialized). Without further reflection, he proceeded to the vehicle, loaded up, and, with one last look around, hit the wall remote, got in, and started the engine, suddenly impatient as the large double door made its noisy ascent.

With a clank, the door came to a jarring stop, and he put the Jeep in reverse. A brown Crown Vic appeared in his rear-view mirror. He didn't recognize the person behind the wheel, but he did see LeBlanc sitting on the passenger side. Another blue and white RCMP cruiser pulled in behind.

"Fuck!" He turned off his motor and exited the Jeep.

"Going on a trip?" LeBlanc asked, smiling like a Cheshire cat as she got out and approached him.

"Just a short errand."

"Well… I come bearing news. We've found Mr. Boyd!" Her smile grew wider. "And guess what? He didn't go all that far after all. Certainly not to some sunny beach. But you knew that, didn't you?"

"I don't know what you're talking about."

"Oh?" Her eyebrows shot up.

"I wish to speak to my lawyer."

***

"Thanks to Isaac's confession, Roberta thinks we got him!" Freta exclaimed that evening to Myron as they shared a pepperoni deluxe at the kitchen table in her apartment.

"Did he resist?" asked Myron, pulling a slice out of the box, the cheesy entrails resisting in spindly stretches.

"I wasn't there, but apparently not. Roberta thought that he was about to flee, though. He had a packed suitcase and a duffel bag full of cash, among other things."

"Did he say anything?"

"You mean like confess? No. In fact, he clamped up. Now that we have a body, though … well, it's a game-changer and improves the case against him expediently."

"Okay, so Boyd is found dead and buried. Cause of death?"

"Don't know yet; awaiting an autopsy report."

"So, nothing obvious like a karate blow to the throat?"

"Your point?" Freta asked, a hint of annoyance creeping into her voice.

"Technically, you don't know that he was murdered." He shrugged. "Just being facetious."

"Certainly, a crime was committed. To begin with, Boyd didn't bury himself."

"Good point," Myron conceded. "Just wondered."

"We'll know the cause of death soon enough, tomorrow or the next day. But there's other evidence that the Ident team unearthed — literally — that's got Roberta hopeful."

"Like?"

"Like a tarpaulin covering Boyd, which is being analyzed for fingerprints. Anyway, Roberta believes that there's enough to charge Croft in Boyd's death."

"So, Roberta's satisfied that she's nailed her man?" Myron asked, chewing a piece of pizza and taking a sip from a pop can.

"She's far from satisfied — still lots of loose ends dangling out there. But unless something dramatic presents itself, like Boyd's resurrection, by the end of the week, there will be enough to lay charges. Of course, it's up to the Crown prosecutor… Anyway, she thinks this is the last week for her here. Sees no point in hanging around for things to shake out. It could take weeks to dot the I's and cross the T's."

Myron nodded. "You sad to see her go? I got the feeling she could be a bit of a curmudgeon."

"Yeah, actually, I am," Freta admitted, "curmudgeon or not. She's been good to me — better than she is to Rob — and it was a good experience working with a detective from the Major Crimes unit."

She paused, put down her remaining crust of pizza, and looked directly at him. "She made me an offer of sorts."

"Oh?"

"Encouraged me to apply to the Major Crimes Division. She thinks I have potential."

"You most certainly do!" agreed Myron.

"Offered to write me a letter of recommendation and be a mentor, said there could never be enough female detectives in Major Crimes."

"Well then, opportunity knocks. You said you wanted to be a detective. Are you going to take her up on the offer?"

"I'll seriously think about it. It's a big step — courses to take, exams to pass, and probably a move to Edmonton. And there are other considerations."

"I can appreciate that," said Myron, taking another swig of cola. *Like you and me and how this would affect our relationship, particularly if you move away?*

"It's a bit unsettling, and I know I can just as well get posted elsewhere in my current position. Still, I'm feeling pretty secure here... Plenty of time to think about it, figure out what's best." She gave him a meaningful look.

"True, it can be discussed at a later date," he said, suddenly remembering John A's "Old Tomorrow" nickname. "Meanwhile, let's forward the pizza box to the living room and see what's on the boob tube."

"Great, we can watch *Love Boat*. I think it's on tonight."

"I can hardly wait."

***

Next morning, Myron ushered himself expeditiously out of Freta's apartment. No time for dalliance, since the LeBlanc team began their day about an hour and a half earlier than his.

Still, he too had a full day ahead, not extracting confessions, scouring over forensic reports, and/or chasing various leads, but delivering a couple of lectures, talking with some students, and attending at least one long and tedious academic council meeting.

Committees were in full flower, both departmental and college-wide, and he sat on his fair share, as did many of his colleagues. He also wanted to follow up on another important matter.

At the beginning of the week, he had spoken to Reginald Mercur, the registrar and head of student affairs, giving him a heads-up about his disturbed student, along with his report. Alexandra Enfield needed an intervention before her issues escalated out of hand. "I'm worried about her state of mind," he explained without elaborating on her "aura" vision. Mercur listened and nodded gravely, reassuring Myron that protocols were in place for such incidents and that Ms. Enfield would be contacted by a counsellor.

Although a bit stiff and formal, Myron knew that Reginald was efficient and would get counsellors on it. Mental health ranked almost as high as financial issues when it came to student stress and could not be ignored by the institution. Nevertheless, it had been two days since he talked to Mercur, and he hadn't heard any news. Nor did his growing anxiety abate when he called Student Affairs for an update. The counsellor assigned was having trouble reaching Ms. Enfield but promised to inform him as soon as she did.

Around two o'clock, Myron's phone rang just as he opened his office door. He had finished his Canadian history class caffeine filled and more than a little revved. Maybe it was the counsellor, he hoped, picking up on the third ring, slightly out of breath from the trek up the stairs. "Hello."

"How's your day going?" asked Freta.

"Good… Thanks for the pizza. I enjoyed last night, by the way. How's it with you?" She didn't usually call during work hours just to talk.

"Lots of developments, which," she lowered her voice conspiratorially, "I shouldn't be talking to you about?"

"Like?"

"Croft will be charged with manslaughter, indignity to a human body, and other related charges."

"So, he did confess?"

"No, not at all. It was like talking to a fence post, to quote Roberta. But enough solid evidence was found, including his fingerprints on the tarpaulin I mentioned, to go ahead. Oh, and the Ident guys did find another body where Isaac indicated, beside Polanski's grave — actually in Marie Polanski's plot. They're trying to identify who. No ID on the body — pretty decomposed."

"Then Lucy was real."

"I'm afraid so. And that's about all we know thus far… Anyway, Roberta has decided to go back to Edmonton Saturday morning. She has a court appearance next week and some other cases to tie up."

"The investigations here have concluded then?"

"No, the files are open, and we're still gathering evidence. But unless something significant emerges, officially it looks like all the boxes are being ticked off."

"Okay, let's see if I got this straight. Isaac killed Raglan and Lucy, then he dies by misadventure."

"Unless otherwise determined."

"And Croft does Boyd in. How *did* he die? Has that been established yet?"

"My, you are inquisitive. Coroner's report suggests a heart attack, but there's signs of an altercation and him being restrained as contributing factors — that's why it's manslaughter, subject to an upgrade."

"Last question: have you figured out the connection between the two cases, other than Isaac witnessing Croft getting rid of Boyd?"

"Ah … and that's why it's not wrapped up as neatly as Roberta would like. At this point, it is what it is… Anyway, the reason I called you, though, was not to provide an update but to ask if you'd come to Roberta's goodbye dinner Friday night. She invited Rob and me and suggested you come as well. After all, you gave 'input,' her words, into the LeBlanc team's investigation. I presume you're available." Freta sounded vaguely bemused over the line. "Seven at the Great Plains Inn."

"I'm a member of the LeBlanc team?"

"Honorary member, one night only."

"Right. She paying?"

"I'm sure it'll come from her expense account."

"Count me in then."

"Good, come by the apartment about six thirty."

# Chapter Thirty-Three

**Thursday, September 5**

"The more idealistic utopian Bolsheviks believed that a new social order would emerge," Myron expounded to his evening class students, many of whom had large take-out coffees resting beside their notebooks. They were anticipating a long session.

"After all," he flexed his rhetorical voice, "hadn't the revolution inaugurated a radically new society freed from bourgeois norms and obligations? Weren't they building a state where the conflict of the individual and the collective was being harmonized?

"Of course, this wasn't the view of Lenin and his 'orthodox' communist followers," Myron continued, feeling he was on a bit of a roll. "Consequently, the tenets of communist morality and ethics were debated in the early years of Bolshevik rule while the larger political forces played out."

The students seated before him had looks of bewilderment intermixed with skepticism and growing boredom. What was this prof nattering on about?

Myron homed in and framed his topic. Nothing like a specific subject rather than abstract notions to get the class focused, he decided. "One interesting aspect of the new code of ethics being debated was the living relationships between men and women in the new communist state, especially the institution of marriage. The question stems from the writings of Engels, in particular, who maintained that men derived their moral ideas from practical relations on which their class position was based, depending on the economic stage society had reached. So, relationships between the sexes were fundamentally one of economic oppression of the female by the male in the institution of marriage."

A few heads raised, someone snickered, and suddenly everyone's eyes seemed less droopy. *Good, interest has been sparked!* He leaned over the lectern and adjusted his glasses.

"What Engels, and Marx as well, meant was that man is the bourgeois, the woman is the proletariat. Man appropriates and enslaves woman as his means of production of legitimate heirs to whom his private property would be transmitted. In order for this not to happen in the new proletarian society, the economic foundations of monogamy such as marriage had to disappear."

He paused and let that sink in. "Engels and Marx believed that marriage was the simple consequences of economic supremacy and thus had to be dissolved."

"Were Marx and Engels married?" asked a petite blonde at the end of the second row whom Myron recognized as Janet. (He was starting to place names to an increasing number of faces, albeit slowly.)

"Good question." Which he hadn't anticipated and racked his brain to answer. "As I recall, Marx was married and presumably happily so, since he sired six children and lived as a typical mid-Victorian master of the household, although financially strapped and counting on support from Engels, his wealthy collaborator."

"So, Marx never practiced what he preached." Janet made it more a statement than a question.

"You're right!" As far as Myron knew. "Karl Marx did not practice what he wrote, but Engels did — sort of. He lived with an Irish woman, whose name escapes me, for over twenty years, until she died in the early 1860s. They never married formally."

"Still, he had a pretty monogamous relationship?" Janet persisted.

"As far as is known."

Before Myron could elaborate, another female from the back row asked, "If marriage is dissolved, what replaces it then?"

"Another good question. Essentially, nothing..." Myron paused to formulate his thoughts. "Other than individual attraction: love and sex, according to Engels. Relations between the sexes, if I understand his writings on the subject correctly, would be based on nothing more than mutual consent, much like his own relationship, I would guess. And if affections faded and/or were supplanted by a new love, well…" He shrugged. "So be it. According to Engels, such an attitude would benefit both parties as well as society."

"Sounds a bit flakey, out there, to me," interjected Jonathan, who had participated previously in a number of lively discussions when the mood hit him. "Wouldn't it be destabilizing to the family and create social anarchy? Besides, how is that an improvement over the whole bourgeois man dominance over the female proletariat thing?"

"You've got a point, and in fact, it was impractical and did not contribute to the stability of the new communist society, but for utopians, it represented a blueprint of how things should be, the argument being that in this new society the means of production would be transferred into common ownership, that the family unit would cease to be relevant, and that the care and education of children would become a public affair, a societal responsibility. The old economic, social, and moral problems would become non-issues, just like religion, which Engel described as the opium of the people."

"Still doesn't make a lot of sense," Jonathan griped.

"Theoretically, abstractly, it did for Marx, Engels, and their followers, though," Myron insisted, "perhaps in a skewed sort of way. Certainly, Engels believed in individual relationships without the intercession of the state or God. He thought this new freedom of what he called 'sex-love' within communist society would be beneficial and do away with all sorts of unhealthy exploitation."

"Like what?" Jonathan wasn't convinced.

Myron smiled. Jonathan had given him the perfect segue. "Like prostitution! If sex was liberated, so to speak, then, according to Engels, prostitution would wither away and die."

There was a laugh, and someone remarked on the veracity of such a thesis. "Really?"

"So wrote Engels." Myron chuckled. "And I agree, neither Marx or Engels were particularly insightful when it came to human nature and the thesis that everything in life was class- and economics-driven — well, if not off the mark, it certainly needed refinement. Still, the utopians in the Bolshevik Party took these ideas to heart. It really hooked them… Who's heard of Alexandra Kollontai?"

Blank faces stared at him.

"Right. She was a high-ranking Bolshevik — rare in itself because of her gender — who epitomized the new communist morality, at least as envisioned by the utopians. Kollontai rejected 'standard morality,'" he put air brackets around the term, "and believed it was irrational," he flipped a page of his notes to find the paraphrased quote, "to waste the moral forces of the struggling collective on the sideline of love and courtship that did not serve directly the cause of the revolution. She wrote a couple of novels, *Red Love* and *Free Love*, in which she espoused her attitude toward socialist sex. For her, it was part of emancipation of women, a sexual revolution against bourgeois moral standards."

"You mean like the sex sharing, flower power hippies in the sixties?" piped in Jonathan to more snickers from the class.

"Hmm … a bit more profound, I'd say." Myron wasn't sure if the comparison was valid other than both could be construed as revolutionary (or counterrevolutionary) movements against the prevailing norm. Challenge to the status quo was certainly part of the rhetoric; however, from there any similarities became fuzzy in his mind. "Kollontai's heroines," he continued, finding his spot in the lecture notes, "were those who protested against the universal servitude of women in family and society and who were liberated from the moral fetters that threatened inner freedom and independence."

There was a rustle in the room as more students wanted to join in the discussion. Myron waited for the class to be quiet. He didn't want to veer off totally about sex in the Bolshevik state. "This attitude," he continued, raising his voice slightly, "applied not only to the institution of marriage and relationship of the sexes, but also to more mundane social behaviours, silly things like abolishing handshaking because it was an invention of the bourgeois designed to spread disease among workers and peasants. Same for the wearing of neckties — careerism of the worst kind."

This brought elevated chortles.

"So, what happened?" asked Janet. "None of it worked out, right?"

"True. Lenin, for example, was not as free-thinking as Kollontai, and in his purely Machiavellian mindset, he systematically subordinated questions of individual freedoms and the emerging socialist morality of the utopians to the practical maintenance of power. Finally, Stalin completely snuffed out these ideas in 1936 with the proclamation of a new constitution that strengthened the traditional family and emphasized the 'bourgeois' sense of morality for those living in a socialist society. Soviet men and woman had to readjust to a morality based on obedience and social conformity. Utopian ideas died on the hard rocks of 'socialist realism.' Nevertheless, they had their moment in the early and mid-1920s..."

At the end of class, Myron was surrounded by lingering students who wanted to discuss and debate a variety of ideas advocated by Kollontai and her communist colleagues. Overall, a successful session that his pupils related to, thought Myron, giving them a perspective — historical or otherwise.

***

Tired but pleased, Myron finally made his way upstairs to his office. After his performance, he was looking forward to dropping off his notes, going home, and having a long, unadultered smoke. He noted how quiet it suddenly got as the classes dispersed. The distinct conversations on the first floor, often heard intermingled with a constant general din, had gone. The concourse below had emptied the last of its jabbering humanity, allowing for the faint, vibrating cacophony of the building's mechanical soul to take over. Somewhere from the bowels of buried boiler rooms, the edifice was getting on with the business of self sustaining, its steady droning somehow reassuring.

He came to his office door and fished out his keys, his exhausted mind absorbed by splintered thoughts about nothing in particular. It was at that moment that Alexandra appeared, seemingly out of nowhere. There was no aura or any other form of illumination, just the gleam in his peripheral vision of a long, slender object — *a knife?* — slicing through the air. He might have received the pointed end somewhere between the neck and shoulders if not for a sharp, alarmed cry that caused a flinch and a violent, evasive movement out of harm's way.

"Watch out!" Ted bellowed in his authoritative voice, a voice that cut through any doubts or hesitation.

The pointed end of the long, slender letter opener (as it turned out) hit the cork bulletin board on his door, splicing through his office hours schedule. And she wasn't quite done. Having failed to deliver a quick, decisive blow, she took one more stab at it as Myron staggered sideways, trying to regain his balance. This time she managed to penetrate the right sleeve of his tweed sports jacket, ripping it open but fortuitously avoiding his arm.

The only form of communication was a solitary scream, "Bastard!" as she took her second swing. Myron was too stunned to formulate a proper reply.

Indeed, it all seemed to happen in slow motion, which would have continued had not Ted's heavy steps and gyrating bulk broken the spell. With her weapon enmeshed firmly in the folds of Myron's garment, she stopped and as if coming out of a trance, blinked in surprise, and hurried away down the corridor to the nearest stairs.

"Are you all right?" Ted asked, wide-eyed and panting from his unexpected exercise to prevent a murder.

Myron nodded, glancing around for his scattered lecture notes. "I owe you a beer."

"Who *was* that?"

"A student."

"What? Didn't like her grade?"

"Touché, Ted, touché."

"Shouldn't we go after her?" Ted was warily scanning the corridor.

"No … no point. I'll call the cops while you get a hold of campus security."

***

The following morning, even as Myron was settling into his office chair to enjoy his coffee and review his lecture notes, Ted marched in and plopped down on the only empty seat available. He didn't seem any worse for wear after their harrowing encounter with Alexandra. They had waited at the college for quite some time to give their statements, a perfunctory one to a young campus security guard who nodded and took notes diligently, and a more detailed one to Freta, who arrived with a very young constable in tow.

Myron had phoned Freta at her apartment, explaining his near brush with mortality. After rummaging around scattered papers on his desk, he found Alexandra's address that she had shoved under his door a few days before. Freta then put out an alert on Alexandra and told him to stay in his office; she'd be there shortly. "Better take your jacket," she told Myron after he and Ted described what had occurred. "Evidence."

"Right." He handed over his damaged tweed jacket (alas, one of his favourites), complete with the embedded letter opener in its lining.

"So," Ted exclaimed after he had comfortably settled himself in. "Did your lady cop get her?"

"Yes, Alexandra was picked up without incident at her apartment late last night. She's being held at the remand centre pending a psychiatric evaluation. That's all I know."

"God, you get all the excitement." Ted shook his head. It was hard to tell if he was empathetic to Myron's near demise or envious.

"Not the kind of excitement I would crave," Myron answered, feeling subdued and not overly talkative. But he owed Ted — big-time. So, tell me, what's the story? Why did she attack you?"

"I can't tell you much. Obviously a distraught student who lost her way."

"She's in your class?"

"*Was* in my class," Myron corrected. "She left ... with issues."

"I'll say. It was like as scene from *Psycho* last night. Did she mistake you for someone else?"

"I was her target," Myron answered truthfully. "She has difficulty in distinguishing what is real from what she imagines and a rather strong, if not unshakable, belief that what she imagines is true."

"You mean she's delusional."

"More like she's suffered some sort of psychotic break."

"How did she act in class?"

Myron could sense Ted's increasing need to know, his always curious mind intrigued. He was a witness, after all, and was entitled to an explanation.

"Quite normal, actually — for the short time she attended my classes."

Ted nodded. "I read somewhere that psychos can behave normally, continue to function and socialize, not show any odd behaviour until it's triggered by some event, object, or person. Then, they hear voices that tell them what to do — and it's usually bad stuff!"

"She didn't hear voices; she just saw those around her differently." Despite himself, Myron couldn't help but fill in some gaps for Ted. "I was the object of her obsession. She saw this aura," he waved his hand vaguely around his face, "that set her off."

"Aura, eh?" Ted leaned forward.

"Hard to explain."

"She wasn't one of those erotomaniacs, was she?"

"A what?"

"Erotomaniac. I read about them in a magazine — someone who is in love with another who isn't aware that that is the case. Unrequited love and all that?"

"That's probably part of it, but I don't really know. Probably nobody does for sure. The mystery of the human brain."

"You mean a chemical imbalance in the neurotransmitters. I read about that too."

"As good an explanation as any. Whatever it is. She saw this light, this aura that attracted her to me."

"No shit!"

"I kid you not."

"Something like that elk on Sulphur Mountain."

"Exactly."

\*\*\*

Midafternoon, Freta phoned to see how Myron was feeling, given the traumatic events of the night before and to let him know that if he was not up to Roberta's farewell dinner, she'd understand.

"Not a problem," he reassured her.

"Great! A couple of things, though… Keep the conversation light and avoid police talk."

"Police talk?"

"Anything about the investigation. You're not supposed to know half the things I've told you. Talk about the college, the weather, your predictions for the Edmonton Oilers. There'll be only the four of us. Superintendent Reuben had to beg off because of a prior engagement."

"Just the LeBlanc team then."

"Yes — plus one."

"What if she talks about the cases?"

"She won't."

"Or she's not interested in college affairs or follows sports."

"Improvise! You're good at that."

The get-together proved anticlimactic, much to Myron's relief. Although LeBlanc was indeed not overly enthralled by what he did at the college or any aspect of sport, she turned out to be less of a sourpuss than he had thought. Mostly as a listener, while Freta and Roberta chatted with the occasional input from Rob, he learned that the detective lived on the south side of Edmonton near Southgate Plaza; that she had three cats named Curly, Larry, and Moe (one of whom was a female — she didn't volunteer which); and that they missed her terribly.

"How do you know?" he asked. "Cats are so inscrutable." At least what he knew of them.

She gave him a chagrined look and pursed her lips. "Because they disappear into their various secret hideouts when my cat sitter comes in to feed and check on them."

"Oh." He didn't understand at all.

"It's the trauma. I'll see them tomorrow."

He also discovered that she enjoyed sweets (no surprise, given the doughnuts, she consumed — this info courtesy of Freta) and hoppy beer. Curiously, there was no mention of a significant other, and Myron wasn't about to pry.

The only item that came close to police talk was when she acknowledged his encounter with Alexandra. "Heard you had a close call last night," she stated casually, digging into her prime rib.

"Yes … still recovering from the shock a bit."

"Don't know how much Freta told you about your student, but if it's any consolation, you weren't the only one. Hopefully, you will be the last. She definitely will be going into treatment."

*Good to know.*

After that, he and Rob had a restrained and polite conversation on a variety of topics from the Oilers to the development of the oil sands. Rob hadn't exactly been a fan of Myron's involvement in police business, but he was civil enough.

Also, it seemed that Rob was in LeBlanc's good graces more than Freta had let on. It became apparent that the old detective had extended the same offer of recommendation and support to Rob as Freta if he decided to apply to Major Crimes. "Think about my offer," she told them both with a wry smile.

The night ended with pleasantries all around and a toast to a job well done.

*Amen.* Myron was exhausted and just wanted to go to his abode, have a languid smoke, and sleep, in that order.

# Epilogue

**Five Weeks Later**

"Alex is still maintaining his innocence, I take it?" Myron was popping a stray olive into his mouth. He and Freta were having dinner at Pietro's, their favourite Italian restaurant in Great Plains. But then there were only three others to pick from.

The bizarre homicides had made a news splash, not only locally and provincially but nationally as well, putting Great Plains on the map, and not in a particularly complimentary way. The story had all the elements of high drama: fraud, intrigue, double-cross, and ultimately murder, not to mention a touch of the macabre with bodies buried over bodies in a cemetery.

"It appears so," said Freta as she cut her veal parmigiana into smaller portions. "I won't take any bets on his chances once this goes to trial."

"The pieces have finally fallen into place?"

"There are a few aspects that frankly are still baffling," Freta admitted. "Mostly, Isaac's link to Croft; but without him talking, we can only speculate."

"Couldn't the defence use this to its advantage?" asked Myron, having gotten hooked watching Perry Mason in dramatic courtroom action.

"They can try, but the case against Croft is strong." She put down her knife and fork and started to enumerate points on her fingers. "The obvious: Boyd is dead and did not abscond with the money, as Croft claimed. He was the last to see him alive. Not too far of a stretch, given what we know, to conclude that there was an altercation and your black-belt friend prevailed. The evidence to support this is hard to refute."

"Alex was never a friend, exactly," Myron interjected.

Freta carried on, "Boyd died of a cardiac arrest, which, according to the autopsy report, was induced by a physical attack and the use of restraints that elevated the stress. The evidence is quite convincing, albeit circumstantial. But there's more. Something that hasn't been released to the public."

"Oh?"

"It appears that Croft was a crook, no less so that Boyd."

"What do you mean?"

"Now, I don't know the details, but it seems that when Croft uncovered Boyd's fraudulent activities, instead of alerting the authorities, he helped himself. He redirected a large portion of the ill-gained funds into offshore accounts."

"What?" Myron coughed as the Sauvignon Blanc went down harsher than expected.

"That's what the forensic auditors are saying. Basically, he took the money Boyd stole and put it into his own pocket, all the while trying to make Boyd confess to fraud and duping his hapless business partner. That's the scenario the Crown prosecutor is working on, anyway."

"Could he have gotten away with it?" Myron asked, setting down his wine glass. "That's incredibly audacious."

"I'm not that well versed in how these things are done. I guess he thought so. And apparently, he was sneaky and clever in his transactions but not skilled enough to hide what he had done. The auditors were able to 'follow the money,' as they say."

"Let me get this straight. If Croft had pulled it off, Boyd would have been found guilty of embezzlement while at the same time discovering that his embezzled funds had disappeared?"

"That's about the size of it. If he lived, that is. And who would have believed him? It turns out he was convicted of fraud in the past and was on the radar of everyone from the provincial realty board to the province's attorney general."

"While Croft appears above board."

"Actually, no, not exactly. Croft, too, has a dodgy past in Vancouver. He was cited for unsavoury, ethically challenged practices as a stockbroker. Got reprimanded and paid a fine but was never convicted. He allegedly misappropriated some funds, but apparently it was deemed a 'misunderstanding,'" Freta framed the word with her fingers, "and with restitution, the charges were dropped, as was the review of his broker's licence."

"So, unlike Boyd, he didn't show up in any criminal records?"

"Right. Rob found this out through some judicious digging into his background."

"Okay, Alex was setting up Boyd. That wouldn't constitute a reason to kill him, though."

"No. He wanted him very much alive to confess to his crime. Evidently, things just got out of hand — that's what the prosecutor will argue."

"On the other hand," Myron speculated, "Alex would have a good chance of getting away with it if the body was never found."

"At least until the auditors figured it out," said Freta, reaching for her wine glass.

"There's that," Myron acknowledged.

"My third point, though," Freta got back to her finger counting, "and really damning is the tarpaulin left in the grave with his prints on it. Stupid thing to do, really."

"Can't think of everything, I suppose," said Myron. "Guess Boyd wasn't supposed to be found."

"And he wouldn't have been if it wasn't for the disappearance and murder of Raglan, courtesy of Isaac."

"I'm a little hazy on how he fits in with Croft, other than burying Raglan overtop of Boyd."

"Yeah, that last part is a very sore point with the Ident team."

"Okay, but that goes back to my earlier point. If Alex had Perry Mason, the argument would be that Isaac not only killed Raglan and planted stolen evidence on her implicating Croft but also killed Boyd. All the defence has to do is create reasonable doubt, right?"

"Doesn't hold water. Boyd died of a heart attack, not a broken neck. There is no motive."

"That we know of," interjected Myron. "Besides, did he need a motive? Little of what he did made sense."

"There's that, but I think we could make more sense of his actions if we knew for certain what went down. You're right, though. In the courtroom, the defence will muddy the waters — as if they aren't muddy enough — and propose some theory that blames Isaac for Boyd's death. And dead men can't defend themselves."

"Then there's Hans. Didn't you tell me that he saw Croft on the Grotto Road early that morning? Substantiates Isaac's statement about seeing Croft burying a body."

"Doesn't strengthen the case too much. Can be discredited as an eccentric, notorious, and unreliable witness with a grudge."

"You mean that interview he gave a while back?"

"Accused Croft of killing his son! Didn't go over well, for obvious reasons. Letters to the newspaper lamented that if Croft did, good riddance and too bad he didn't do it sooner! Hans Trovotka has gone silent, a recluse almost. Not much sympathy in the community after what Isaac did — not that there was much to begin with. By the way, there's absolutely no indication that Isaac's death was anything but an accident."

"And his truck being blown up?"

"Ongoing investigation that probably will lead nowhere."

"Getting back to Isaac… Is it too far-fetched to suggest that he may have set out to blackmail Alex, given what he saw?"

"It's plausible. There was that $10,000 in cash in Croft's house when we searched it. Still, boils down to speculation. The prosecutor can't link any of the money to some sort of payout, especially since it hadn't been paid out!"

"What I can't comprehend is how Isaac got a hold of a piece of Croft's jacket, and why plant it on Raglan's body? Makes no logical sense to me," said Myron.

Freta shrugged. "He marched to a different beat, that's for sure."

"So, I guess we'll never know how Isaac fits into the Croft-Boyd case?"

"Not unless Croft talks. Roberta suspects that silence is his ace in the hole in terms of the trial. If we can't connect all the dots…" she trailed off. "All we have are educated guesses. Nevertheless, the case against Croft killing Boyd is convincing. As for Isaac, he was a budding serial killer with a macabre sense of humour when it came to getting rid of bodies."

"What about his other victim?" asked Myron, digesting what Freta had said.

"Lucy Blanchette. A sad case, really. Originally from Prince George, a runaway who wasn't reported missing for quite some time."

"When did she die?"

"Can't determine precisely but has been buried for over two years. Got as far as Great Plains; a couple of individuals remember seeing her, but that's it. We don't know when or under what circumstances she encountered Isaac, but he killed her. We can speculate about the details, but there's no denying the autopsy report. Her neck was broken in much the same manner as Raglan's and her body buried in Marie Polanski's grave."

"Being clever from his perspective, I suppose. She wasn't discovered for two years, and no one was looking, right?"

"That's about it." Freta sighed. "Just another missing girl. Leaves a troubled home, disappears without a trace, briefly surfaces here, and gets murdered by a predator. The only tangible item she left behind was that necklace found in Isaac's room."

"Almost the perfect crime, and if he hadn't mentioned her in his confession, no one would have been the wiser. Hopefully there aren't others he didn't mention."

"Believe me, we've checked and double-checked," Freta said, a pained expression creasing her forehead. "The RCMP haven't come out of this unscathed. We're the Keystone Kops who missed a second body in a grave. Jokes are circulating, like 'getting one out of two ain't bad.' The internal memos are flying over this one, I'm sure. There's a lot of egg to wash off. Meanwhile, this case has petered out to a conclusion, somewhere between a bang and a whimper. It's up to the courts now."

"What about Croft's embezzlement of Boyd's stolen money?"

"That will be handled separately, but we're many, many months away from an actual trial."

"So, there we are!"

"Aren't we just... Oh, screw it! It is what it is, and justice, in whatever form, will take its course," Freta exclaimed, draining the last of her Pinot Noir.

"Speaking of which — time to go home?"

"Yeah, thanks for dinner. Let's have dessert at my place." There was suddenly a mischievous gleam in her eyes. "You remember those flashy red briefs I got you a while back?"

"I do."

"Still got them?"

"Yep, keep them in a special place for special occasions. Want me to stop by my apartment and put them on?"

"Splendid idea."

"On one condition."

"Oh?"

"That you resurrect your lacy black bra with the fancy frill around the edges. And don't forget the accessories, the red garter and sheer black stockings."

"Done."

"We can discuss your prowess as the great detective, Ms. Holmes."

"And you as my favourite dick, Mr. Watson."

# Acknowledgements

First and foremost, I am grateful to my wife, Diane, who encouraged me and cheerfully put up with my writing hibernations, and to my wonderful daughters, Alisha and Halyna, all of whom initially vetted the manuscript and provided insightful critiques.

I also want to thank Allister Thompson and Amanda Feeney for their careful copy edits/comments. A huge kudos to Melissa Novak for a great cover illustration and Jonathan Relph for the cover design. Finally, my appreciation to Cheryl Hawley and Greg Ioannou of Iguana Books for their support.

Any errors of commission and/or omission are entirely mine.

www.ingramcontent.com/pod-product-compliance
Lightning Source LLC
Chambersburg PA
CBHW031052020726

47495CB00007B/1838